Betrayal
Will Stone In Vietnam

by Brad Kennedy

Plain View Press
P. O. 42255
Austin, TX 78704

plainviewpress.net
sb@plainviewpress.net
1-512-441-2452

Betrayal: Will Stone In Vietnam is a work of fiction. Any likeness of its characters and events to real people or situations, past or present, is purely coincidental and certainly unintentional, except for references to well-recognized historic personages and circumstances. Portions of this work have been previously released under the title *Heroes or Something*.

This story contains offensive language, including racial epithets that are an intrinsic part of a storyline that lays bare the relationship between racism and war. It seemed necessary to leave the language alone and to change, instead, our way of thinking about war and race.

Contents

Part Three: Heroes Or Something

To my parents with respect,
To my wife, Barbara, whose patience never fails,
To Greg, Starr, John, Sierra and Gianna, my hopes for the future,
To all those who suffered as a result of this war,
To the Vietnamese people, who have always deserved better. . .

Part One:
A Soldier's Call

Chapter 1
Learning To Kill

Two Bullets Marked "Campbell"

Will muscled himself into the seat next to Campbell on a bus bound for Andrews Air Force Base. From there, they would take the cross-country flight to San Francisco. It was one year to the day since Will's induction into the US Army in the summer of '65 at the age of twenty. The days leading up to his induction had been all he thought about—until Campbell.

"Lighten up, buddy," Campbell said. "I'm not going anywhere. Where am I going to run?"

O

The buzz around the platoon had been about Campbell's capture. Will had been one of the first men back from leave as the unit formed up three hours earlier. Not that he was early. Will was barely on time. The Army did not much mind the infraction as long as the others were not too late, as long as they made the bus. The Army had bigger things to worry about that night, like shipping out a thousand troopers, including this flight risk Campbell.

"Campbell's back," Specialist Fifth Class Montana told Will, nodding to their right. "They brought him back yesterday." Will spotted Campbell seated on a wood and concrete bench. He sat with his hands between his legs, obscuring the manacles holding him to the first slat of the bench. Campbell stared bleakly between his legs. Montana went on, "Somebody's gonna have to guard him, once we get going."

Will barely knew Campbell. *Why did he do it? How could he face himself if he made it? And now the humiliation of a desertion charge. Takes balls to buck the Army like that. But you can't hide from your conscience. Did he run with courage or out of fear?*

"Gonna drop the charges against him, I hear, so long as he gets on that ship for Nam," Montana drawled.

Will glanced back at Montana. *Just like the Army. This guy's been AWOL for two months, probably trying to beat it across the border, and he's gonna get treated the same as the rest of us.*

"Probably they'll have to issue live ammo to whoever guards him," continued Montana. "Bastard might run again."

Will nodded. *Don't wish him harm. I guess where we're headed is going to be bad enough. But how can there be discipline without reprisals? For a US like me or Campbell, the reward of rank is meaningless. There are only reprisals.*

"Heard if you shoot one of our own, like if you're guarding Campbell and you kill him, you get transferred to another unit," whispered Montana. "Cause of the possible hard feelings, you know. Might not even go to Nam."

Will searched Montana's face for any hint of satisfaction from the situation. Montana had been busted from staff sergeant back to private for slugging an MP before working his way back up to E-5, the same pay grade as a buck sergeant. All that had so conditioned Montana's animal cunning that he sensed what Will was looking for.

Montana carried fifteen pounds more lean muscle and was half a head taller than the five-foot-seven-inch, hundred-fifty-pound Will. Rarely did Montana confront bigger men, but he had a menacing way of slouching when he confronted smaller ones. Defying Will's scrutiny with his own steely glare, Montana dipped his knees and hunched his upper back just enough to lower himself to Will's eye level. *Montana wants the job. He might even take pleasure in killing Campbell. He'd like boasting the first kill, even if it were one of us. He'd like it better if it got him out of this boat ride and into some cushy assignment in Europe. I had him pegged all along, and he knows it.*

"Gotta go," said Montana, clapping Will on the back and hanging on to his shoulder. Abandoning his drawl for a moment, Montana squinted at Will and grinned, "You'd want the job, wouldn't you?" Then he moved on without waiting for a reply.

Will watched the returning soldiers in their civvies filing past the gate to the troop area, past the handcuffed Campbell. Many stopped next to Campbell's bench long enough for a farewell embrace with their sweethearts or parents. Campbell largely went unnoticed. Despite all the talk, he was not so important to anyone—except to Will.

"You been drinking today, Stone?"

"No, sir," Will said.

"Didn't think you had," said Lieutenant Brown, the How Battery Executive Officer. "See the armorer and draw out your M-14. Here are two live rounds. Stick them in a magazine. Lock, but don't load. You're guarding Campbell. Understand, Stone?"

"Yessir," answered Will.

"Stick to him like glue. Don't let him take a piss without you. We don't want to lose him again. Is that clear, Stone?"

"Yessir."

"If he runs, aim low!"

O

"I said where am I going to run?" Campbell asked. "We're on a fuckin' bus."

Will glared back. "I have no quarrel with you," he answered, "but I'm your guard, not your buddy."

Campbell smirked and poked Will with his elbow.

"So don't take off on me," Will said, patting the M-14 between his legs.

Campbell's face flushed, and he leaned toward Will until their faces were no more than a foot apart. The large pores on Campbell's nose and the pockmarks on his cheeks momentarily distracted Will. He noticed the bead of sweat on Campbell's upper lip and the throbbing vein on the top of his forehead where his hairline had receded. He wondered what Campbell noticed about him.

Campbell might have zeroed in on Will's dark-haired cowlick if Will had not been wearing his regulation-issue, olive drab baseball cap. Campbell might have noticed the dimple that often appeared on Will's left cheek when he smiled, but Will harbored no cheer now. Campbell, though, should have recognized from the set of Will's square jaw and his stiff neck on broad shoulders, or from the penetrating, tight-lipped stare he now managed through those icy blue eyes, that Will meant business.

"Back off," Will said. "It could be a long night. You better get some sleep."

"You better not," Campbell said. "I have friends on this bus, you know." He laughed and turned away from Will.

Will studied Campbell for several moments before leaning his own head back against the seat. Once more, Will brooded over the events of a year ago, the events that led to his induction.

Josh's Choice

"What exactly is going on here?" a voice called from the foot of the porch stairs. The glare of two flashlight beams spotlighted Will with Jen in his arms on the porch. They eased themselves apart, squinting to make out the two men in uniform climbing the stairs behind the rising light beams. Josh, Will's roommate and long-time mentor, was sidestepping away from them.

Will had arrived at his rooming house only minutes earlier. Baffled by the commotion, Will had waved for Josh, who was a World War II vet to come to the porch. Josh told him that Mr. Lyons, Jen's father and their landlord, was banging on the stair-side of the basement door and in other ways creating an awful racket. Then, Jen had burst forth in tears and, before Will knew it, run into his arms.

The sheriff tracked Josh's movements with his light beam, while his deputy kept his light on Will and Jen. "Well, what we got here, boy?" asked the sheriff. "Where you think you going? You on the wrong side of the tracks for this time of night, ain't yeh, boy?" The sheriff stood at the top of the stairs one foot in front of the other, leaning forward like he was looking into a dark hole rather than at a man's face. His leg muscles bulged his trousers and his sinewy fingers and forearms tightened around his flashlight and his nightstick. The moonlight glistened on his sweaty scalp through his crew cut.

"Well, sir, you see—" Josh said as the sheriff's deputy stationed himself at the top of the stairs behind the sheriff.

"You, quiet over there, boy," the sheriff drawled, straightening himself erect and relaxing some. "When I want to hear from you, I'll let you know. Don't you worry 'bout that."

Josh looked the sheriff in the eye and nodded.

Will recognized the sheriff's deputy as having graduated from his high school two years ahead of him, although he did not know him. *Played right tackle the year the football team was undefeated. A real bruiser, goes along with the group more than he should, gets carried away.*

"Now you pay attention, little lady," the sheriff continued, shining his flashlight in Jen's face, "you may learn something valuable here tonight that may save you from learning something the hard way when you're older."

"How about we turn the porch light on, sir?" Will said.

The sheriff redirected his beam at Will's face. "When I want the porch light on, I'll see that it's on. I don't need any help from the likes of you to do my thinking for me." Turning to Jen, he added, "Go ahead and turn on the overhead light out here, young lady."

Jen complied, looking first to the sheriff before easing her way back to Will's side.

"That's better," the sheriff continued, taking a careful look at each before his scrutiny returned to Jen. "How old are you, miss?"

"Sixteen next month."

"That's nice," the sheriff said, turning to Will, "and are you fifteen, too, mister?"

Will shook his head.

"For the record, how old are you?" the sheriff asked.

"Twenty," Will said.

"Interesting, twenty and fifteen," the sheriff said. "That could be something, you know. Let me tell you something, mister. You been protected. You been protected in this town for years. I know you know why—your father's partners are big here. What you may not know is all that's over now, as of tonight. You understand? From now on, you gonna be treated just like any other wise-ass in this town. You got that straight, mister?"

The deputy was looking over Jenny until the banging in the basement resumed. The light above the side porch next door came on. The sheriff looked over as the neighbors next door came out on the side porch and waved to him. The sheriff smiled at Will. "They're the ones who called about all the ruckus here. I was ready to turn in for the night till they called. You can bet that call pleased my missus. Now what the hell is that banging, Stone?"

"Old Man Lyons, I guess, must be locked in the basement," Will said.

"You guess, huh," the sheriff said, staring at Will before turning to Jen. "Is that your pap in the basement?"

Jen nodded.

"Well, why don't you go open the door for him, little lady, and bring him here?"

While she did that, the chief eyed Josh's face once more and then gazed at Will. "I know you just had some sort of confrontation with your old man down in the center of town—at this time of night. Are you now telling me this young lady's pap locked hisself in the basement by some kind of accident? Think good before you answer, mister. This is your chance to get off on the right foot with me."

"Hey, Sheriff," Josh said, "isn't it me you really want? There's no point in badgering the kid."

The chief winced, turned slowly to Josh and once more sized him up. A smirk crossed his face as he said, "You was being so nice and polite I almost forgot about you." Then he glanced back at the deputy and said, "Hey, rookie—oops, sorry—Denton, go down to the squad car and fetch from the trunk that black hood with the drawstring around the opening—the one we use for moving prisoners still uncooperative after they's cuffed.

"I hope we won't need it," he continued, grinning at Josh, "but we better be ready. It's in a cardboard box."

"What does the box say, Sheriff?" Denton asked. "Hood?"

"Hood? Nah, too easy, something like 'Head Restraint.' Best you tote that shotgun in the trunk back here, too."

Jenny burst through the screen door. Her father followed tentatively. She positioned herself next to Will, and her father stopped in the doorway with the screen door half open.

"You're still drivin' over-the-road," the sheriff said. "You been drinking, Lyons?"

"Just a little since I got home. Got in about two hours ago."

"What you banging on down in the cellar this time of night?"

"What'd they tell you?" Old Man Lyons asked, nodding at Josh and Will.

"Nothing, and I wouldn't have believed them if they did. Now what the hell's going on?"

Lyons stepped into the light a couple of paces and glanced at Jen. "She gotta be here?"

The sheriff gave a nod. "I'll say when she stays and when she goes. Where's your missus, anyway? What in hell is going on here?"

"Last I could tell, Sheriff, the missus was inside throwing up," Old Man Lyons said. "Look, maybe we all just had a little too much to drink."

"Takes more than a little to lock yourself in the cellar, don't it?" the sheriff asked.

"I didn't lock myself in no cellar. Somebody did that for me—from the upstairs side. Don't know who. Coulda been my missus. It's been done before."

"So you saying, Lyons, you all were getting along all right, 'cept maybe you were getting too loud cause of the drinking. That it?"

"Well, yeah, Sheriff," Lyons said, looking at Jen, " 'cept there was one thing—"

"Young lady," the sheriff said, "go see if you can fetch your momma. But you be careful not to rush her none. You hear me?" Jen re-entered the house. The sheriff looked at Old Man Lyons and said, "Go ahead."

"We was getting along OK, like you said, Sheriff. These guys are OK. I didn't even know Stone was here till I come out here with you—"

"Didn't know he was out here on the porch with your daughter?" the sheriff said.

"What? She was right there in the next room asleep the whole time. Like I said, we was knockin' back a few and getting' along just fine. But—"

"But what, man?" said the sheriff.

"But there was this moment. I'm not sure when or for how long, when—maybe it was the drink—I just got the feeling that that buck over there," Lyons said looking at Josh, "was feeling just a little too cozy toward my missus."

The sheriff leaned close to Old Man Lyons's ear and said, "You ever see or hear anything?"

"No, Sheriff. It was just this feeling come over me. I sensed something, you know, not right."

"Where's your wife, man? Get your wife out here, but don't you say nothing to her. Let me do the talking."

Once Old Man Lyons went in the house, the sheriff smiled and said to Josh, "You got your teat in a wringer here, boy?"

"Hello?" Mrs. Lyons called as she made her way onto the porch.

"Come on out here, Mrs. Lyons," the sheriff said, stepping forward to hold the door for her. "We're trying to straighten out a situation that never should have occurred.

"Now, Mrs. Lyons, the first thing you need to know is that we're here to help you, to defend you, to protect your reputation, if you will, as a lady. You got nothing to worry 'bout, so long as you can help us work things back to the way they supposed to be. Now, there are a lot of people talking 'bout you and that fellow over there, Josh. You know him, don't you?"

"Yes."

"What they're saying isn't nice, Mrs. Lyons. It's not something you would want said about you if you had a choice. Some are saying they've seen you—actually seen you—in a position with this *boy* that no respectable white woman would ever put herself in. Now Mrs. Lyons, I ask you, knowing you are going to give me the right answer, you are a respectable woman, aren't you?"

"I feel awfully weak, Sheriff," she said. "I was sick inside just a few minutes ago. I need to go back inside now."

"Just a minute, Mrs. Lyons. I asked you, you are a respectable woman, aren't you?"

"Yes, I try to be."

"You either are or you ain't. Now which is it, Mrs. Lyons?"

"Yes, I am."

"Am what."

"You know none of this is true!" Josh shouted.

"You keep your trap closed, boy," the sheriff said. He strode three paces closer to Josh and brandished his nightstick before Josh's eyes, "Or you'll be tasting this here nightstick for a long time.

"Now, Mrs. Lyons, you either are or you ain't. Now say it. Which are you? Let me hear you say it."

"I am. I am respectable. I need to go in, Sheriff."

"Of course, of course, of course, you're respectable. We know that, Mrs. Lyons. That's why we are here now—to defend your honor. And of course you can go inside after one more question. This can be as easy as you want to make it. Now, Mrs. Lyons, being you are a good and respectable white woman, it goes without saying that if some people did see you in a position with this colored boy that no respectable woman would put herself in, it can only mean that colored forced you somehow into that position, isn't that so?"

"Let me go inside."

"Answer the question first."

"Yes, yes, yes."

"You know what I want to hear. Say it, Mrs. Lyons—"

"Just how low will you go, Captain?" Josh called out.

"You had your warning, boy," the sheriff shouted, bearing down on Mrs. Lyons. "Now—"

"Never you mind her, Sheriff. You didn't answer my question," Josh said.

"He's been drinking, sir," Will said, tugging on the sheriff's sleeve.

"Quiet, you," the sheriff said, wrenching his arm free.

"Don't you worry 'bout that, Will," Josh said. "This man has me real sober."

"I have to go in—" Mrs. Lyons said.

"You go in, Mrs. Lyons," Josh raised his voice. "The sheriff here has his hands full. He just don't know it yet."

"Well, well, well, boy," the sheriff said, turning toward Josh. "You asked for it, and you gonna get it." Staring and nodding at Josh, the sheriff crouched and swallowed hard, then sprang forward, poking his forefinger into Josh's chest and shouting, "Kneel, boy!" As he did, he glanced back at Denton and shouted, "Hood!"

In that moment Josh clamped his left hand around the sheriff's forefinger. He bent it back so hard and fast that the sheriff was on his knees with tears in his eyes. "How quick the tables can turn," Josh said, holding fast to the sheriff's bent finger and leaning so his face was hardly a foot above the sheriff's. "Now tell your man to stand down."

"Do what he says, Dent."

"Sheriff," Josh said, "everyone here knows that stuff you were peddlin' never happened, but you couldn't let it go, could you? You had to try and make somethin' of nothin'. Now that we understand the problem, you ready to find a solution?"

"Yes!"

Jenny opened the screen door and stepped onto the porch, catching her breath with her hand when she saw what was happening. As soon as she stepped out of the way alongside Will, her father reappeared in the doorway and gulped.

"Now, Sheriff," Josh said, "you can have your finger in one piece because I will let it go, provided you can let go of this whole incident here tonight. Well?"

"Ooooh! Yes."

"Rookie," Josh called, "is the sheriff here a respectable white man? He hasn't shown me much honor. Can he be trusted to keep a deal?"

The deputy froze. "For God's sake, answer the man," the sheriff cried.

"Yes, he can," Denton called back.

"OK, then here's the deal, Sheriff. I let go of your finger, I walk out of here right now, you never see me again, and this whole incident never happened. Nothing happened here tonight, Sheriff. You got it?"

"All right," the Sheriff yelled. "Anything!"

"And what about you, rookie?" Josh called out. "Can you keep a deal? Even if the sheriff orders you to break it?"

"Yes!" shouted Denton.

"Yes, what?" Josh said, grinning and shaking his head.

"Yes, sir," Denton shouted.

"Thank you," Josh said softly, looking across the porch at Denton. Then he turned his attention to Will and whispered. "I gotta enjoy this 'cause I could be payin' for it the rest of my life. Now, Will, listen up! It's time we parted ways. We had our time and it was good. I'm sorry I couldn't have been stronger for you this past year. I dumped a lot of stuff your way, but this one's on me. You stay out of this one, son, you hear? There's gonna be hell to pay, and there's no point the two of us payin' the same bill."

Josh glanced at the sheriff and then Denton, before continuing. "These guys will never keep any deal, but what can I do? I gotta give 'em the chance, right? I may not spout the verses or sing the songs, but I am a Christian.

"Denton, get that hood restraint on the sheriff here now," Josh said, increasing the pressure on the sheriff's finger. "You tie that cord just as tight around his neck as you was going to around mine." The sheriff squirmed but submitted to the restraint because Josh maintained just enough pressure on the sheriff's finger to break his will.

"Now, Will, when I spoke up, that was for Mrs. Lyons—to spare her this grief, which maybe I brought on her. But I spoke up for me, too. I'll play their game only to the point where it would change who I am. What you do is who you are. Remember that, Will. You do what's right and you can walk tall. I won't kneel to be brought down. Kneel only to pray."

Josh looked around at the others. "Everyone, no surprises," he called out. "I be letting go of his finger and walking out of here for good. Will, goodbye. Jen, goodbye. Say goodbye to your families and thank them for allowing me close to them. It's time now."

Josh gave the sheriff's finger a little twist before pushing the sheriff away with it as he let go. The sheriff dropped to the floor and writhed in pain before starting to free himself from the head restraint. During that time, Josh strode to the other side of the porch, eyeballed Denton, and stepped past him and down the stairs. He was twenty feet down the walk when the sheriff, still on the floor, called to Denton, "Where is he? Stop him."

"What?" Denton said.

"Stop him, goddammit," the sheriff yelled as he fought to his knees, still working on the knot in the drawstring around his neck. "You can't let'im bag me like a coon an' jus' walk away."

Denton snapped the shotgun to his shoulder as Will cried out "No!" But the deputy fired away. Josh flew face forward to the ground halfway down the front sidewalk.

Will recoiled from the blast, grabbed Jenny and turned her away from Josh, burying her face momentarily in his arms. Raising his hands to her shoulders, he looked directly into her eyes. "Jen, go inside to the phone," he said. "Dial Operator and tell her we need an ambulance here. Tell her it's 'cause a cop's been shot. OK?"

"I'll do it," she said.

Once he let her go, Will bounded toward the stairs but the sheriff, finally free of the hood, intercepted him. "Whoa, Stone," he said, catching him with an iron grip around the chest. Will saw Josh struggling to his knees. Once Will stopped resisting, the sheriff eased his grip. Nobody moved or spoke. Lights came on in the houses nearby and families emerged on their front porches. All eyes were upon the fallen man as slowly he got to his feet in a stooped posture. The back of his shirt splattered with blood, he twisted and turned to straighten himself as he hobbled sideways as much as forward. Josh teetered, looked around, then wobbled ahead. His stride lengthened and his chest swelled with each step.

"Dent," the sheriff said, tightening his grip around Will, who resisted. The deputy caught the sheriff's nod, shouted "Halt," returned the shotgun to his shoulder, and fired once more. Josh again flew face forward. The neighbors gasped and watched Josh struggle to reach his knees again. This time his efforts were futile, though he kept struggling until he collapsed.

Will shook himself loose of the sheriff's grip and headed down the stairs to where Josh lay. The sheriff glanced about at the neighbors and called out, "You all saw it. Everybody saw it. That nigger resisted arrest, assaulted an officer, and started to run when Denton called 'Halt!' Anybody here see it different?"

Will was the first to reach Josh. Moments later, the sheriff paused there but, seeing no sign of life from Josh, passed them by in his rush to the next door neighbors' side porch. Denton hung over the porch railing, puking.

Will knelt and leaned forward so he could speak in his friend's ear. "Josh, can you hear me, Josh? Are you dead?"

"Feel like it," Josh answered, opening an eye and moving only his lips. "They watching me?"

"Not now," Will said, straightening up enough to look around. "How do you feel?"

"Breathing funny. No feelin' below my waist. Other than that, just plain vanilla lousy," Josh said. He wheezed a few seconds before continuing. "Will, I'm a man an' nobody is gonna force me to be anything less. Walk tall, Will. Walk tall. You remember that, son."

A middle-aged man in robe and pajamas hustled across the street. "Has someone called for an ambulance?" he yelled.

"Now that's nice of you to worry, but I'll take care of that," answered the sheriff, returning from next door. "That's what we got radios for. I'm just gonna see if somehow I can make this boy more comfortable first."

"I'm a doctor. You get that ambulance. I'll do what I can for him here." The man glanced over his shoulder. "My wife's right behind me with my bag."

Will looked up and saw Jen wink at him. She bent toward him. "Mom made the call," she whispered.

"Will, I told you something important just before," Josh added, sweating profusely now. "It's time you got on with the rest of your life. Best leave me be, Will."

An ambulance ground to a halt in front of the growing commotion. The driver cranked down his window. "Is this where the cop was shot?" he called.

"Yes!" Will shouted without hesitation.

"What do you mean, a cop shot?" the sheriff said as he strode toward Will.

"Somebody must have thought you were down, Sheriff," Will said, still kneeling.

"Jesus Christ!" the sheriff said, shaking his head. "Don't you think of pulling out of here till I'm through with you, Mister Stone.

"You want to talk to me, you call my old man's attorney," Will said. "You know who he is."

"Ha! Yes, I do," the sheriff said with a smirk. "He's the one that told me I shouldn't protect you."

"Yeah, well, not protecting us and shooting us in the back aren't the same thing," Will answered. "I'll be following that ambulance to the hospital."

"That boy is my prisoner—what's left of him."

"That man is my hero—what's left of him."

"All right, get out of here," the sheriff said and walked away.

Jenny squatted to say goodbye to Josh. The ambulance squad slipped a blanket under him to lift him onto a litter. While they loaded Josh into the ambulance, Will hugged Jenny and they said their goodbye. "Tell your mom, I'll be back tomorrow for our stuff, OK? The world is a dangerous place, Jen, unless you have someone protecting you. That's what your mom and dad are trying to do when they make their rules. It's best you listen."

When the ambulance pulled out, Will was behind it in his rat of a roadster. He sat in the hospital waiting room for two hours, replaying in detail what had happened to Josh. Finally, an intern sat next to him. "Mr. Wyatt will be out of surgery shortly. He appears to be in stable condition. It may be some time, though, before we know whether he'll use his legs again. Not much point in waiting. He won't be awake for hours and, besides, we'll need permission from someone in authority for you to see him. He's a prisoner."

O

Campbell stirred in his seat, causing Will to return his attention to the present.

Campbell shows no remorse, no shame. What if he runs? Say at the airport he gets his chance and makes a break for it. Would I waste him? I'd run after him, tackle him. I could run till he wore down. But what if I let my guard down and he got the jump on me? What if he kicked me in the nuts and I started after him but was gonna lose him? Say I yelled Halt! but he kept going and was going to turn a corner to who knows where. Say it was clear behind him so I didn't have to worry about a stray round. Say it was take the shot or lose him. Say I dropped to one knee and raised the barrel and got him in my sights and could squeeze off a round. Would I just tear off his leg, or maybe miss and blow him away? Is that my duty? This guy's a deserter I'm ordered to guard. Montana says if I shoot him, I might even get shipped to Europe. Could see Sarah while she's studying in Paris; miss this whole thing.

Will saw the drill in his mind—kneeling, aiming, firing, the muzzle flash, the ear-piercing crack, the recoil, and the sight of Campbell flying forward for a face-down landing with a piece of his right hip blowing out sideways. *Where the hell are the cuffs? Why didn't they just give me the cuffs, so I didn't have to worry about him running. No warning shot! I didn't have time. Did I shoot him to get out of going to Nam? Maybe I'm not so different from Campbell. At least he didn't shoot anybody to get out of this thing. Shooting him would be a heavy load to carry the rest of my life, especially if I didn't go to Nam. How's it different from them shooting Josh?*

It was dark and quiet on the bus. Most troopers were lost in fond reflection upon their fourteen-day leave, unwilling to give in to the quiet despair of the few who already had looked ahead to the year's tour of duty in Vietnam. One by one, though, each would yield to the irresistible fascination of the unknown. Trained to ignore discomfort and accept hardship, each still fell sway to one inescapable fear: *Will I be back?* The doors closed, the engine started, and for them time stood still, at least as it was ordinarily counted. Days, weeks, years no longer mattered. They would suffer them without reckoning—if only the tour of duty would stop short of forever, if only the Estimated Termination of Service were this side of eternity.

Not even Will could take heart in the adventure ahead. *It comes down to getting back or not, though we don't have much control over that.* He stopped short of thinking, *Nothing else much matters.* A lot mattered to Will. The past year had reshaped his understanding and expectations, but it also left his purposes intact even as he continued to think things through.

"Why?" Will called aloud, surprising himself as much as Campbell.

"What?" said Campbell, waking up. "Why what?

"Why'd ya take off?" Will asked.

"Why not?"

Will waited, but Campbell held back. "Were you trying to make it across the Canadian border?" Will asked.

"Hell, no," Campbell said. "Stone, get this straight. I don't give a crap! Got it? I just went back to living my own life. I don't care about your Army and what it wants. I was having a good time on leave so I figured I'd take a little longer. What can they do to me? Send me to Vietnam? Can they make me run away and throw my whole life away? I'm not that scared of them, Stone. I'm only here because I gotta be. You're my guard, but I'm not afraid of you or the whole damn Army. You know what we always say. 'They can work me long, but they can't work me hard.' Now you tell me why you're so gung ho. You were drafted. You should feel the same way I do."

"Look, I was ordered to guard you," said Will.

"Of course you were," said Campbell, "and I bet it breaks your heart. But you're still gung ho. If anyone of these NCOs says boo, you jump. They trained you better than they could the rest of us."

"It's not training," responded Will. "It's a sense of duty. I believe in what our country stands for, and I'm determined not to let it down."

Campbell faced Will directly and whispered, "Well, Stone, then this country has shown you something it hasn't shown me."

Will kept still, as he tried to make out Campbell's meaning. "I thought I was supposed to catch some *zzzz's*," Campbell said.

"Yeah, sorry," said Will. *Why the hell did I get into that with him?* He leaned his head back again and tried once more to put the past year in perspective. *I'm not ready to start giving speeches urging men to their graves, but this is the right thing to do. If you believe that you gotta do this, you don't talk about it. It's a private commitment you nurse inside you until, when the time comes, you do it. Truth only exists in action and sacrifice. Each risk is a new test of will. It's a private commitment between you and...who? Between you and who you would be, and those you would honor.*

Honor? Will had only to think of his father, Sam, killed in the Phillipines with the Seabees in World War II. What Will knew of his natural father came largely from the glowing tributes of Harry, his uncle who adopted him and who himself had been wounded defending an Aleutian airstrip under Japanese attack. Then there was one of Will's trusty scout leaders, Bill Corbett, who stormed the beaches of Normandy in order to battle on to Berlin. And, of course, there was Josh, who'd been a much decorated squad sergeant in a segregated cavalry unit in the battle for France. Will knew about honor.

A Trojan Horse

Will gazed at Campbell snoozing next to him as the bus pulled into the airport. Alarm shot through Will's every faculty. He had to be ready in case Campbell found a chance to bolt. He had to be ready for anything. Most on the bus were fast asleep. Four or five rows back, however, an ongoing conversation continued. The soldiers involved deliberately raised their voices.

"He's no different than we are, I tell you," said one voice. "I've talked to him. He's an ordinary guy, not some devil with horns. He just wasn't in any hurry to get his ass shipped to Vietnam. Who is?"

"So why they gotta guard him with live ammo, anyway? He's going," another said. "He said he was. That's good enough for me."

"Fuckin' Stone is gung ho enough to use his '14 on him. Somebody's got to talk to that boy."

Will could not place the voices. He could not even keep straight when one voice stopped and another started. *Can't let these guys stop me from doing what I gotta do.*

"A lot of what Campbell says makes sense," the conversation continued. "Stone ought to just talk to him."

"Campbell, Campbell." Will poked him. "Better wake up. We're at the airport."

Campbell blew out a short breath and shook his head. "So what?" he mumbled.

"Wake up, will ya?"

Campbell straightened up, looked around, and smiled. "All right, sweetheart, but how come everyone else is still sleeping?"

"What did you mean when you said this country hadn't shown you anything?"

Campbell scratched under his right arm. "Huh?"

"I want to know what makes you so sour on everything," Will said.

"Stone, goddammit, I'm not sour on life. It's death I abhor, and the Green Machine is the grim reaper," Campbell said. "I'll let you in on something. My father was killed in Korea. He was an FO, a forward observer, got it, like they wanted me to be and like you'll probably wind up being. The army, your sacred country, didn't do shit for us—not for my mother, not for me, not for my little brothers. I was a twelve-year-old kid then. My mother has been working herself ragged ever since to keep us all going. I was just getting to the point where I could start helping."

"So you deserted? I mean, how's that helping?" Will said.

"C'mon, Stone," Campbell said. "My father wasn't any lifer. He was some guy who got ripped away from his family to fight in some war in which he had no stake or care. He was an English professor. You hear me, Stone? I said my father taught English lit at a college. He really was a great guy. He cared about people. He cared about me and my mother. One day he got the letter to show up. He wasn't a romantic like you. He had no choice, more like the rest of us. So he went and that was that. Now you tell me, Stone, you think my mother wasn't glad to have me around that extra time, before we put out? I mean, do you think I didn't know they were going to catch up to me there? Gimme a break, will ya?

"This may surprise you, Stone, but my mother is an Italian immigrant. That's right. My father met her when he was studying in Europe. She's a classy lady, but once we lost my father, everybody saw her as just another wop with a language problem. If you can imagine what it meant to her that my father was an English professor, then you can understand what my following in his footsteps meant, too. I'm not doing it just for that. You couldn't. My father passed along the love of it, and it's just my bent. I'm not apologizing for it, not in any way. But here I am a Ph.D. candidate, and you can see what's happening."

"You're what?" Will asked.

"I have my Master's Degree, and I am working at Pasadena in a doctoral program. I'm part of the English department, Stone."

"What do you teach, Campbell?"

"Freshman Comp, what else? The point is I have this sense of foreboding. I see happening to me what happened to my father. And for what? That's what I'd like to know. For what? Just because some politician doesn't know how to get out of a box?"

This guy's trying to con me, and I'm falling for it. I've got to think clearly. I can't let him get away on me. I've got to do what I've got to do. Yet there's something to what he says if it's true he was right there in his hometown. But how do I know that? I can't just take his word for it, but I can't discount it either. It all comes down to if he runs or not, and that's up to him, not me. If he goes, then this is all bullshit and whatever happens is on his head. If he doesn't, then I'm not hurting him by reserving judgment. Either way, whatever he says is irrelevant to my actions, so there's no harm in listening. It may count toward my future opinion of him, but that's all. For tonight, it still comes down to if he runs or not.

"For what, Stone?" Campbell said. "Don't have an answer for me, huh? Why are we in Vietnam? I somehow thought you might be the man to have an answer ready."

"Why don't you lay off, Campbell?"

"Should I go back to sleep?"

Will bit his tongue. *I deserved that.*

"Actually, Stone," Campbell said, "having watched you for a time, I'm prepared to make some concessions. You're not as bad as you might seem. If someone must guard me with live ammo, you're probably the best of those they'd consider."

Will pursed his lips and blew a long, silent whistle.

"I'm dead serious," said Campbell. "Let's hope it won't come to that."

"It's up to you," said Will.

"You don't quit, do you?" said Campbell. "However, besides being, shall we say, relentless, you have several other qualities that are underrated around here. You are moderately intelligent, responsible to a fault, logical, and most importantly, remarkably open-minded—all qualities any man should want in his son, or, I guess for that matter, in his keeper if he must have one. But by themselves, these qualities are not enough. You also must be knowledgeable, and that can be a life's work before you're entitled to an informed opinion on some matters.

"This Vietnam thing probably falls in this last category. Nonetheless, the urgency of the subject to us accords us the right to some shortcuts in forming our opinions, but, of course, only at the expense of the quality of those opinions. It may be true, as is commonly said in these circles, that opinions are like assholes in that we all have them, but they don't all smell quite as sweet."

Will thought before responding, "I accept what you say about the need for our opinions to account for the facts as well as to be, say, logically consistent. However, in the matter of these smells, I must defer to your far greater experience."

"*Witty*, I left out *witty*," Campbell laughed aloud. "Stone, have you studied Philosophy?"

"The basics," Will said.

"Now in Philosophy, we encounter arguments all the time that are exceedingly difficult to disprove but near impossible to believe. How do we deal with those arguments, Stone?"

"Go back to the base assumption, sir," Will answered. "There's always an unsubstantiated assumption on which the whole argument rests."

"Now Stone, please tell me upon what prime assumption you base your argument that duty calls you to Vietnam."

"You're a regular, fuckin' Trojan horse, aren't you, Campbell?"

"From Pasadena, I told you," Campbell whispered politely. "Now may we continue, Mr. Stone?"

"*Specialist Fourth Class* to you, Private," Will answered. "We're stopping now. We gotta get ready."

Campbell twisted at the waist and faced Will directly. "We're sitting on a rainy airstrip in the middle of the night, and there are no planes out there yet. There's no reason to rush out there. Now let's cut through the bullshit, *Mr.* Stone. Having gotten this far in this conversation, it's clear you're governed by reason, not authority. And that means you're no more dependable a soldier than I am. You are just of a different opinion—right now. Your first assumption, please."

"I have none."

"That's unacceptable, Stone," said Campbell. "You know damn well there is always an underlying assumption, and you are too analytical a thinker not to know what yours is."

"I don't want to get into this now."

"You gave me the right to ask my question when you engaged me in this conversation," Campbell went on. "Now we both are obliged to see where it leads, not as adversaries where one is victor and the other vanquished, but together where whatever truth we uncover is celebrated as our common prize. We are either seekers of truth, or we are not. It is this rational faculty that sets man apart from the rest of nature. Now, you have put your faith in the rules of reason when others have placed theirs elsewhere. You must step down a level if you would have it otherwise. Mind you, I never said you were humble."

"You really are going to make an issue of this even if I just want to beg off?" asked Will.

"If I don't, you will, Stone, someday," Campbell responded. "If you live long enough."

"Look, it's not that I don't trust myself," Will said. "OK, give me a second. This is just between you and me. I'm here because it would be unjust to let others do the fighting and dying for me, assuming it was my turn to go."

Campbell leaned back away from Will and rubbed his chin. Will looked at him anxiously.

"I'm not going to laugh at you, Stone. This could be, as we said before, dead serious, and your nobility has not gone unnoticed. Yes, there's a sort of *noblesse oblige* about it. Now, you tell me, Stone, make believe you're looking at someone else for a while, tell me, what is your first assumption, your first assumption?"

Oh, damn, I can't believe I didn't think this through. "I didn't qualify that this was a just war," said Will. "I just assumed that someone should be fighting it."

Campbell gave Will a hint of a nod before offering, "Stone, theologians debate just wars. Diplomats at best claim their necessity. Is our fight necessary?"

"The President says so," Will said.

"Isn't that the same one who said he would not send American boys to fight a war that ought to be fought by Asian boys?" Campbell asked. He bobbed up out of his seat past Will and into the aisle.

Will dropped his brow in his hand for a moment's respite before quickly rising. "Wait up, Campbell," Will called in a whisper. "Wait up."

Campbell whispered back to him, "Just stretching, Stone. We all can use a good stretch now and then, can't we?"

Chapter 2

Troop Transport To Vietnam

Aboard In San Francisco Bay

Soldiers everywhere crowded the deck of the troop ship, now three days at sea with twenty to go. They sprawled anywhere they could to snooze in the life-giving sea air. They lined the ship's rails, gazing at the ocean's movements, conversing with anyone who would listen about what they left behind and what might lie ahead. They read dime-store novels with covers typically featuring a sultry blonde in a tight, red satin gown that wrapped from front to back. They read over and over the letters from home they received before setting sail and wrote multiple replies they could not mail until reaching port. They sat on deck in tight little circles playing poker for nickels and dimes. When playing for their paychecks or shooting craps, they huddled in corners by the stairwells. The more days at sea, the fewer games there were of this sort, as the stakes fell prey to the same hands.

Only a little more than half of the twelve hundred officers and men on board could rest on deck at any one time. The others remained below, either working at various duties or awaiting their turn in the open air. Together, they represented the first of the three squadrons in the armored cavalry regiment shipping over. Dressing them all in green jungle fatigues and combat boots did not obscure that each was his own man. One had only to look past the uniform to see as many differences as similarities. Each had his own story, his own hopes and dreams. Out of this individuality was born a preciousness, a common and equal claim to life each staked for himself. Yet they knew, they all could feel down to the marrow in their bones, that this claim was not necessarily recognized by the US Army and that it was surely contested by the enemy they were journeying to meet.

Beneath the Golden Gate

At first, Will was grateful to set foot aboard ship, because it meant he no longer had to guard Campbell. But a sense of foreboding accompanied him up the gangway early that first morning, a gnawing suspicion he was prone to seasickness. Later that evening, it gave him an additional concern as he jammed the side rail with the rest of the troops grumbling about having spent the entire day docked in San Francisco harbor, when they might never get another chance to see the city by the bay.

Early the following morning, Will readied his nerves for the voyage. Long ago, he had concluded boredom to be the Army's greatest hardship to date, so he was amused to catch himself habitually repeating one of Josh's old litanies, "All things pass in time." Notwithstanding his misgivings, Will welcomed the word that buzzed aboard the ship just after breakfast: "We set sail at 0600."

That was fine as far as his nerves were concerned, but not his stomach. "0600 hours" quickly became "0700" and then "45 minutes more." The ship cast off at 10:30 a.m. when Will was down below in the chow line with the rest of his platoon. The enlisted men's mess was two levels below deck and in constant service. The chow line was a permanent fixture on board, as it snaked its way through the labyrinth of tiny corridors on that level. Will had intended to skip lunch in deference to his anxiety, but he stood in line for an hour before the ship set sail. When he entered the mess hall not to eat seemed an awful waste.

"Gotta admit, don't feel half bad," Will said to the shopworn corporal in front of him, as they neared the serving area. The corporal could have passed for a military version of Friar Tuck.

"Take it from me," the corporal replied, leaning his head toward Will to such an extent that he featured his horseshoe hairline, "I spent thirteen years at sea—got my time-in-grade in the Navy—before coming over to the Army. Listen, everyone wants to go it on an empty stomach. That's the worst thing. The thing to do is to fill your stomach up. The heavier the better, that's it."

Will studied the evident conviction with which the corporal made his point. His ample girth suggested he practiced what he preached. *All right, I might as well eat.*

"More. Give him more," the corporal directed the mess steward dishing out spaghetti and meatballs. "He's worried about his stomach, you know."

The burly steward's biceps flexed with each perfunctory attempt at shaking the pasta stuck to his serving spoon onto Will's tray. Finally, he nodded for Will to continue in line.

Will followed the corporal past as many as thirty tables on either side of him, each twelve feet long and fastened to the mess hall floor with black iron pipe and flange, before they found empty seats. "We're just sailing around the bay," said the corporal, pointing to the porthole at the end of the table. "Now eat up."

Will did not know the others at the table, but he noted they seemed content to be eating. He looked out through the occasional sea spray slapping against the porthole to the shoreline rising and falling with the roll of the ship. *Doesn't seem too bad. Maybe I'll be glad later to have gotten something under my belt.*

"That's it, pack it away," said the corporal, waving his fork skyward with a meatball stuck on it. "You want to eat as much as you can, you know."

Will forced himself to eat even as he kept one eye on the porthole. Finally, someone called out, "We're headed out to sea." Will glanced to the porthole for a momentary view before the backs of soldiers' heads blocked it. *You can feel it already. The seas are getting rougher. Maybe it's not going to bother me. Maybe this is all in my head, after all.*

"Eat," the corporal said. "Pack it away."

Will raised his fork to his mouth. Not sure I feel right, but gotta keep eating.

The ship rolled to starboard and Will's tray slid away till he caught it with his arm at full extension. He drew it toward him, but now the spaghetti appeared like worms wiggling in the bowl. He looked about at the others, who calmly continued their meal. The corporal smiled. Will meekly returned his smile and re-focused on the bowl.

"I gotta get topside," he said. "Need some air."

"Good idea," the corporal said, looking after him. In a panic, Will rushed out the mess room door and fought his way against the long line waiting to enter. The heads of the tallest troopers brushed against the low ceilings, making the corridors seem longer and more oppressive. I'm gonna be sick. He rushed past a stairwell door before halting at the next corridor intersection and backtracking to it. This has gotta be it. I don't care where it comes out, so long as it's on deck.

After bolting up the two flights of stairs, Will burst forth amidships into the fresh sea air. He steadied himself against the door jamb as the ship rocked. When he stepped away from it, he shifted his weight back and forth with the ship's movement. He glanced from side to side before realizing they were moving fast upon the Golden Gate. Involuntarily, he put his hand to his mouth. *I can feel it coming on, goddammit.* When he started to work his way through the thinning crowd to the side rail, the corporal from the mess hall came upon him.

"Turn around, face into the wind," the corporal said, guiding Will with a hand on his shoulder to the very center of the foredeck. "Now take a deep breath. Go on. Take a deep breath. Face into the wind."

Will looked up in amazement they were already directly beneath the rust-colored span shimmering in the sun. *Gotta get to the side rail.*

"Take a deep breath of this wind," shouted the corporal, as a tremendous air current from the sea almost bowled them over.

Determined to give himself every chance, Will turned square to the bow and took a mighty gulp of the salty sea air before he instantly convulsed and was barely able to turn his head before letting loose what seemed like a whole sea itself from his stomach. The flow caught itself on the wind and blew straight away sternward, parting soldiers in its wake as far as Will could see until he fell to his knees and retched up the very last of the offensive worms that drove him from the mess table.

The soldiers nearby laughed and smiled at Will's plight, but Will was oblivious to them. Several worried they might be next, but accepted that inevitability as a small part of their collective curse. All made sure to stay clear of downwind from anyone turning green.

After two or three minutes, Will found the strength to pull up his hangdog head. The corporal was gone, and the bulk of Will's mess was gone with the wind. A couple of patches of messy spaghetti noodles was all that lay in front of him. He was grateful for that much. Nobody seemed to be paying much attention to him.

Will pushed off with his arms and set back on his heels. He fought for his senses and was aware of the relief in his stomach, but his dizziness and headache were unabated. His brain felt like a milk shake, agitated and in suspension. It took all his energy to get his eyes to focus and his foamy mind to act with some purpose.

The rail of the bridge was lined with officers overlooking the enlisted men on the main deck. Will figured it would be easier to bring the bridge into focus, because it was about the farthest point he could see that rose and fell with the ship, making it seem relatively still. Under normal circumstances, he might recognize the somber faces along the rail, but pressure within his head still surged with each roll of the ship.

"Bastards," he said aloud, surprising even himself. It was the first time since he entered the Army he had even thought of uttering an epithet against an officer. Of course, there had been times he felt frustrated or disappointed or antagonized, but generally he accepted the need for leadership and tried to take a broad view when he felt aggrieved. Even in his weakened state, Will sensed he may just have crossed some private Rubicon of his own.

What irked him was not so much how the officer corps led, but whether they were going to at all. Clearly, this was not going to be smooth sailing ahead, literally and figuratively, and any consideration, any gesture of mutual respect or concern was in order. But ever since setting foot on board, Will had perceived only contempt from the officers and the senior noncommissioned officers, who were billeted with the officers.

Will had heard stories about the officers' mess hall, where steak and turkey were served with red or white wine on linen with place-setting service. At one point, he had thought it might be worth being roped into KP there, just to see for himself. One of the guys who told Will said the meal alone would be worth the fourteen-hour kitchen detail.

Bastards. He pronounced the word silently as he glared up at the bridge rail again, defying any who would challenge his stare. One by one he sought out those with whom he had direct contact in the squadron's howitzer battery.

He scanned each person along the rail from left to right, looking for some familiar face to confront, to no avail. By the time Will's glare reached the extreme right side, he was losing heart. Yet there stood a lone captain who seemed another sort entirely. His captain's bars glistened on his open collar, as the wind tousled the hair beneath the rim of his cap. His broad smile seemed a natural part of his countenance. Blond and blue-eyed, tall and trim with delicately chiseled facial features, he was perfectly cast for the part.

What a phony! Will bore down mercilessly on the unwitting captain, holding the stare with all the ferocity he could muster. Defying his own weakness as much as his victim's authority, he strained every faculty at his command. The captain started to look Will's way, and Will reached back even further to every indignity he had ever suffered for the fire to challenge this one last pretense at superiority and legitimacy.

Will caught the captain's glance and locked on it with all his fury, when at once the captain raised his right arm and casually waved and continued glancing about the teeming deck below. *He waved. The bastard waved. I can't be sure it was to me, but it doesn't make any difference. He paid his respect to somebody out here. With a simple wave, he acknowledged that we count.*

Will gazed upon the captain, now leaning on the rail with his elbows, until Will was prodded from the side. Will turned and looked. "Thank the Lord for small favors," he said to the corporal, who had returned with a pail and wet rags.

"Better wipe that up before they put you on detail cleaning the whole ship tonight when the rest of these landlubbers go belly up. Now that you spilled your guts, you'd be a good risk for something like that."

"Who is that?" asked Will, pointing to the bridge rail, as he took the bucket from the corporal. "Who is that captain on the far right?"

"Captain Mike? That's Captain Michaels. Runs the motor pool. Said to be fair and knows what he's about. Most like him. Why?"

"Just wondering," said Will. "Thanks for the pail. I appreciate it."

"That's OK, soldier," responded the shopworn corporal.

Someday I'm gonna speak to him, just for the hell of it. Someday I'll find an excuse to drop in on Captain Mike.

Will would not have so long to wait for this encounter.

○

After 1:00 p.m., Will's group rotated deep below into the hull. They reported to their respective cabins, in Will's case a large chamber made smaller by the presence of some eighty other men. These others comprised more than half of the artillery battery to which Will belonged.

A constant state of dusk ruled below, cast in surreal shadows. During daylight hours, illumination in the semi-lit chamber came in part from three portholes on the starboard side, but mostly from a ten-foot grid pattern of undersized, bare bulbs inside wire cages mounted to the ceiling.

Will's head surged with each roll of the ship. It was all he could do to make it past the ten-by-twenty open floor area obstructed by seated and reclined soldiers in order to reach the rows of hammocks stretched out four high.

"Sit in for me, Stone. Gotta hit the head," Jenkins said, accosting Will with a poker hand at the end of his lanky reach.

"You don't want me, man, not now," Will said.

Jenkins smiled weakly. "I was sick, too, man. Go ahead."

Will made it to his hammock. He knelt on the floor and checked to make sure the padlock was still on his duffel bag. All six bags under the bottom hammock seemed in order. Two had no locks, but that was how they started out. Will reached in and stretched out his hammock sideways. *It'll be a neat trick to get in this thing with this guy above me.*

It seemed to make sense to pick the lowest hammock when he staked his claim. It was nearest his duffel, and he would not have to climb over other people to get in. Of course, the consequence was that others climbed over him trying to get a footing to reach the upper hammocks. Stacked four high, they were slung less than two feet above one another. Depending on the weight and size of each occupant, the clearance between the person above and the one beneath could be as little as eight inches. In fact, this was the case with Will and the trooper above him.

Will squirmed into the sack, jostling the guy above him in the process. *Goddammit, I don't think this guy above me has washed his ass in his entire life. I must not smell so sweet right now, but this guy is ripe. Better try and forget it, just ignore it. But who is this guy? I never saw him before. Everybody here's from the battery but him. How come I get stuck with him above me? Just forget it. It'll pass.*

"Did you fart?" the guy above said.

Will ignored him.

"You heard me down there. Did you fart?"

"No, go back to sleep, mister," Will said.

"Well, you smell like shit then," the guy said.

Just what I need now, some asshole above me. Will gauged the man's size by the displacement of his hammock and figured he was bulky but not huge.

"You heard me say you smell like shit, didn't you?" the guy above said.

"It's in your pants," said Will to a smattering of snickers from surrounding hammocks. Will did not count on the audience. *This guy's got to react or lose face, but let the first guy walk on you and everybody'll try it.*

The man rolled over in his hammock and struck down at Will, who was expecting it and dodged the fist. Again, the man struck downwards, this time grazing Will's arm as his hammock swung toward the blow with the roll of the ship. Will lifted his knee into the underside of the hammock above with just enough force to let the guy in it know he was vulnerable.

"Fuck you," the guy above said.

Will ignored him, but waited vigilantly for another attack. Will feigned sleep, keeping both fists clenched and one eye cracked to any movement from above. He monitored the guy's breathing for close to forty-five minutes before accepting the guy was truly asleep.

During that time, Will craved the relief that only sleep could offer from the ocean's relentless pounding inside his head. But he dared not yield to its temptation. Instead, he forced his mind to go over once more Josh's shooting. *Did I do enough that night? Did I do too much that afternoon with Harry? How could I have done less? When the sheriff said I'd long been protected but no more, he meant by my old man's partners. Harry never would have allowed anything like this, but his partners—I don't know.*

Will studied the movements of the hammock above him. *That guy still smells like shit.* Then Will rolled on his side long enough to draw his knees up one at a time and unlace his combat boots. As he did, his mind once more returned to the day Josh was shot. He was not alone in that. Back home, over a late supper at that very moment, his adoptive parents were reflecting on that day, too.

"That day, could I have foreseen even twelve hours earlier any of what would happen?" Harry said.

"I remember you were singing Will's praises to me over lunch that day," Margaret said.

"He was back, Maggie! That was all that mattered to me then," he said, waving half his sandwich in the air. "If not for good, it could have been a start. I thought it was a start."

Harry and Margaret were looking back on their lunch at home that fateful day, before they knew things were going awry. That day, Harry had been crowing not just that Will was back operating earth-moving equipment for him. Harry had been desperate to find someone, anyone, to complete a dangerous backfill operation for him. Margaret was never privy to the financial straits of his building business, so she could never have understood how urgent it was that this job be completed immediately.

"He's back in the fold," Harry had said, pausing to savor the twinkle he had spied in Margaret's eye as he had patted her hand. Then he had withdrawn his hand and fallen quiet, gazing at an empty chair. The smile had faded from his face. She had nodded and leaned closer.

"What is it?" she had asked finally. "It's Josh. You're back on Josh again."

"Goddammit, Maggie," Harry had countered, "I hate when you do that. What are you, a mind reader? Listen, none of those bastards would do it for me, this backfill. Called it a chute to hell, the way it's dished in toward the foundation with all the surface rock on it. Hell, my ass. Will'll show 'em. Something good is going to happen. I can feel it in my bones, old girl."

"Maybe Will shouldn't be doing it either."

"Ha, that's all you know, Maggie. About your own son, I mean. Josh always said Will was a goddamned Indian on a machine, and that's what I was just thinking about now. Ah, the hell with Josh, too. I don't need him. I'm done with Josh. He's nothing but trouble. I got my Will back."

Will's return had meant more to Harry than the mending of torn family ties. It would be the fulfillment of his life's dream and work. Harry Stone had built his development business with the sweat on his swarthy back and cash equity from not-so-silent partners. As much as he had envied their cut, he also had acknowledged that the moneymen contributed necessary expertise. Harry's long-standing hope was raising his sons to plug that gap in professionalism.

His oldest someday would provide legal expertise. At much the same time, his next son would be ready with a degree in banking and finance.

Soon thereafter, with his youngest son, Will, as his strong right arm in the field, Harry would make the break so the family could retain the sixty percent of the profits paid to the partners out of each house-sale closing. This would get Harry even and a promising new start. The older boys had been right on schedule. Will had been astray.

"Maybe, dear," Margaret had said, waiting first to catch Harry's eye before proceeding, "now is a good time to bring about some sort of reconciliation with Josh."

"Forget Josh," he had cut her off.

"You listen to me, Harry," she had said. "Will is not just a business asset, he's our son. He's a good boy. But he's been away from us three full years, since the day he graduated high school at seventeen, because of this trouble between you and Josh."

"Now you listen to me, Mag," Harry had said, "I know all about Will and Josh, and you don't know the half of it. It was no good. That's all there is to it.

"I was liberal when that skinny rooster Josh Wyatt came to me for a job," Harry had said. "I gave him his shot, even though he was colored. And don't think I didn't hear about it from my partners and all their well-heeled friends, not to mention the subcontractors. Do you think they appreciated me bringing in a colored to work alongside them? Ha! They think I did it to get a better price. That kept them on their toes, though, and for a long time. Better than thirteen years."

"Josh has been gone near four now," Margaret had said, "and things have been going downhill with Will ever since. Do you really think you're going to put your little scheme together with Will without first somehow coming to terms with Josh?"

Harry had jumped up, looming his six-foot-one-inch frame over her. "He had a drinking problem, goddammit."

"He had a drinking problem for as long as we knew him," Margaret had said, tapping the back of Harry's chair until he slid back into it. "How many times did you tell me it did not affect his performance on the job? You know that Josh taught Will everything that he knows about your greasy iron. And more than once, we've both heard Will say that it was Josh who taught him to be a man. What'd he mean by that, anyway?"

"Who knows, Mag?" Harry had said. "Will never tells the whole story till he's ready."

"The fact is," Margaret had said, "that Josh filled some sort of void in Will's life that we couldn't."

The two had fallen silent. Only the clinking of their spoons inside their soup bowls had competed with the sound of the breeze blowing through the side window. When they had lifted their eyes toward one another, Harry reached across and hid Margaret's hand in his. She had smiled faintly. They had known each shared the same thought, the same sorrow, the same recollection of Sam.

O

Sam had been Margaret's older brother, but over the years he had become just as dear to Harry. Sam had been a young civil engineer for a construction company in Forsburg when Margaret had introduced Harry to him in 1936. Sam had found Harry work with his company at a time when men were like dogs and jobs like bones. At the time, Harry had been twenty and a high school dropout supporting his mother and siblings still in school.

Sam had guided Harry through the company ranks for the next several years and tutored Harry in field surveying, site grading, utility installation and foundation construction. The training represented no small step in Harry's development, for it had instilled in him the habits of rational thought and planning. Harry had never been sure whether Sam did all this for him or for Margaret, but he had never doubted that the two of them had turned his life around when it had seemed most hopeless.

By the time the company landed its Aleut contract, Harry and Margaret were happily married with two young boys. With war imminent, the US government contracted with Sam and Harry's company for the construction and maintenance of several airstrips on the Aleutian Islands to bolster American strike capability against Japan. Sam was designated to head the project, and Harry was to be his right-hand man.

The work went smoothly, but it was still the first quarter of 1944 by the time construction had been completed on the last airstrip. That's when Sam had received a fateful directive from the company:

> Board Stone on outgoing flight for reassignment to Seabee combat support group as advisor or go yourself if, and only if, you judge Stone unequal to the task. Prefer you lie low maintaining strips there.

The company should have known Sam would never put Harry's neck in a noose in order to save his own. So Sam had gone himself notwithstanding his every confidence in Harry's abilities. Nonetheless, without Sam to set things right, the company had placed a black mark by Harry's name, and he had been called up by the Army with the next levy. He had continued to do the same work after induction, but he had been paid less.

Ten months later, Harry had received Margaret's letter informing him of Sam's death in the Pacific. Over and over, Harry had read her opening paragraph, trying to deny its message. Each time, he would stuff the letter in his chest pocket and try to forget it. That night he had spent the long hours of darkness trying to discern what legacy Sam had left behind. The following morning, when he actually finished reading Margaret's letter, he had known.

Margaret had received word of Sam's death from the War Department at her father's home on a Monday. Early the next morning, a nurse had appeared at their door, newborn in arms, to see her father, Dr. George Wilson. When the nurse left without the baby, George had explained, "She says it's Sam's child, that her new beau won't have it, and that she will have to give it up unless we take it in."

"Is it a boy or a girl?" Margaret had asked.

"A boy," George had said with evident pride. "Name's Will, just Will. Can you imagine, 'Will Wilson'?"

Harry, too, had been as captivated by this news as he was shattered by Sam's death. "It was meant to be," he had written back. "I take it as my sacred obligation to raise Sam's baby. Can you imagine, 'Will Stone'?"

◯

Margaret had slipped her long slender fingers from Harry's grip and patted his hand. "Harry, please don't take this the wrong way," she had said. "I think that Will feels toward Josh some of what you felt toward Sam. Does that make sense to you?"

Harry had nodded three times and smiled.

"Somehow," Margaret had continued, "we've got to make some gesture to Josh. I don't think it means that you have to take him back."

"You're a good soldier, old girl," he had said. "I love you—even though you drive me nuts trying to read my mind. I wasn't even thinking of Josh. Listen, I told Will I'd be back on the job as soon as we were done eating lunch, so I better get rolling."

"Of course," she had said, pushing her chair away from the table and rising. "Harry, dear, lay off this *Old Girl* stuff, please."

"I'm sorry, darling, of course. I've just got to straighten out one or two things with the kid. Then, maybe you and I can put our heads together on this Josh thing."

"Keep me abreast of these things, Harry," Margaret had said. "It's better when we talk like this."

"Hey," Harry had responded, "I ain't doing so bad by us, am I?"

Back on the troop ship, Will was ready to take his chances sleeping. Before falling asleep, though, his mind took up a new concern. *I hope these guys above me don't get seasick.*

The Great Captain Mike

They did get seasick, but not before they cleared the sleeping area. When Will awoke about 8:30 p.m., it seemed like the whole sea was sick and the ship was caught in the convulsions. The ship rose and fell fore and aft, as it surmounted tumultuous waves. At the same time it twisted side to side, tossed about by the storm's fury.

The cabin lights dimmed and the portholes momentarily shone like headlights, before a mighty thunderclap told the story. Will fought for his feet and pulled on his jungle boots. *It's like fireworks out there.* While he laced his boots, he monitored his own condition. *Head still aches, got this surging, but stomach seems OK. Can't be sure, though. Better get up on deck and see what's going on, play it safe. My luck, the goddammed ship could be sinking and no one would tell us.*

Will careened off the row of hammocks to his right, before he regained his sense of the ship's rhythm. He stumbled past the ten-by-twenty common area, now lifeless except for an occasional groan. The soldiers there lay listlessly, some staring through eyes glazed with a ghoulish hue.

Outside the cabin door, Will was confused by the furor. Soldiers scrambled around the stair tower and to and from the bathroom down the passageway. They rushed to the bathroom with both hands over their mouths, their green skin made pale only by their darker uniforms. Laundered from the inside out, they returned stiff and gaunt in jerky motions.

Determined to make it up on deck, Will reached the line at the stairway. There were a half dozen men in front of him. He caught a glimpse of the bath area while he waited for the line to move ahead. Men were retching everywhere within—over the sink basins, toilets, urinal troughs, and, as far as Will could see, on the way to the shower stalls.

Will shared a knowing glance with the guy behind him in line, before they were both repulsed and pushed on the guy in front of Will to get moving. "What's the holdup?" the guy behind Will called out.

"Someone's trying to come down," a voice answered.

"Well, goddammit, we gotta get up," shouted the guy behind Will to no avail.

Finally, some overweight trooper with a paper bag over his mouth emerged from the stairwell, after struggling his way down against the flow. "What's going on up there?" demanded the guy behind Will.

The soldier looked down the passageway both ways and then bolted for the bathroom.

The stairs were pitched more like a ladder, but with wider treads than ladder rungs. Will was at the bottom of a continuous file climbing upwards, when suddenly the line swerved to avoid a seasick spray from someone near the top. It just missed Will, instead splattering on the floor next to him, but a part of it must have hit the guy in front of him. "Fuckin' cocksucker," the guy in front yelled, as he tried to avenge himself by climbing over the men in front of him.

Will grimaced and continued up, being careful where he grabbed the handrail in case it was hit with the spray. When he reached the next level up, the next stair tier was impassable. The rush down from the top deck far exceeded the demand from the lower levels to get topside.

"What the hell's going on?" someone shouted.

"They must be sending them down from the deck, afraid the storm will wash them over," another said. "They're all wet. It must be washing over the sides."

Soon the storm would be classified a typhoon. Then the ocean would indeed wash the ship's deck. For now, these soldiers decided for themselves they had had enough topside when the rain picked up and soaked them through. Their descent was sufficient to back up the normal traffic flows. The press of flesh was aggravated by temperatures ten degrees higher than on the deck just beneath.

All the way back to the next corridor intersection, men collected against the passageway walls ready to enter the stair tower, many with paper bags to their faces. Will glanced down the corridor in the opposite direction and saw the bathroom there was even more soiled than its counterpart below. The ship lurched less predictably now. Will felt queasy. *I gotta find another way up on deck.* He headed down the corridor away from the bathroom, counter to the oncoming line for the stair tower.

No sooner had he turned the corner than he was shocked to see the line stretched all the way to the next intersection and probably beyond. As Will walked along the corridor, it seemed like one in three he passed were using paper bags. Evident in the eyes of the other two was the same glaze of wary anticipation through which he himself peered ahead to the next corner.

A lanky trooper near the next intersection shuffled his way forward, every now and then tugging a GI laundry bag after him. When he was not yanking on the laundry bag, he dipped into it to pass out brown paper bags to each man along the way. The whole time he used one of his hands to cover his own face with a brown bag. Every so often the man would wince and turn away from the oncoming line to retch and then pull his face from the bag for a gasp of fresh air. Will watched him trade in his own bag for a new one each time he passed a trash drum, and then carry on, until he turned the corner. *How noble, this wretched soul!*

Will's survival instinct preempted any lengthy consideration of this circumstance, prompting him instead to pick up the pace as he passed by the lanky trooper. Noble was one thing, wretched quite another. *I'm wretched enough without getting snagged on this one. That's always my luck. Now's as good a time as any to start making my own luck, because I'm sure gonna need some.*

Will's haste was his own undoing. He rushed around the corner so quickly he could hardly have been anticipated. Just as he was about to scoot by this noble soul, out went his sinewy arm across the passageway, bag in hand. Will ran right into it. He was distracted trying to steal a look at the fellow, but unsuccessfully, because the guy was turned partially away from Will, retching in his bag. Will stopped short and froze in the face of the challenge. *I really can't just push my way through, when this guy's doing this. You gotta draw the line somewhere.*

Will glanced to his left at the guy, whose face was still in the bag. Immediately shifting his weight, Will leaned back off the guy's arm, which just as quickly started to wave for someone to take the bag. *That's it, Will. Just take the bag and get going.* But before he could do so, the next soldier in line on Will's right reached out and grabbed the bag, saying, "Thank you, sir."

The word *sir* set off an alarm throughout Will's body. Never had he entertained the possibility that this woeful soul was a commissioned officer. That any officer would allow himself to be caught in such a circumstance, let alone subject himself to it, was unimaginable. Will looked again to his left as the man withdrew the bag from his face slowly. He now faced Will squarely and stood erect, except for his stoop in deference to the low ceilings. Will spotted silver captain's bars on the man's collar, as the bag was still coming down from his face. *Holy shit, railroad tracks! How in hell did I miss them, goddammit?*

Will waited expectantly for the face to take shape once apart from the brown bag. First it was the eyes, then the nose and mouth, finally the chin and neck. The two men focused on one another through the blur of glazed eyes. "Captain Mike?" Will asked.

"Uh, yes, Michaels," he responded.

Will marveled at the contrast between his recollection of the jaunty, smiling captain waving from the bridge and this rain-soaked, washed-out, puking figure in front of him. *He was the only one who waved. The only one who would give any acknowledgment, the only one with enough strength to share some with us. He waved. I didn't wave to him first. I scowled at him, the way they do at us. But he waved to us to pay us proper respect. He didn't return a salute. He saluted. He was the only one who did. Now, he is the only one here.*

Will took a closer look at Captain Michaels, who was still trying to make out Will. *I know that look. This guy's got it bad, as bad as I had it before. I don't know how he's doing this. I don't think I could have done this at lunch. Man, I just had to collapse.*

"Do I know you, soldier?" Captain Michaels asked.

Will made sure he looked the captain in the eye before answering, "You shouldn't be expected to remember, sir." Will fought back the urge to ask what he was doing there. In the end, he would not dare and, anyway, he knew the answer.

He needs help. He deserves help. Get away, fool. Quit while you're ahead. Don't play the sap. This guy can quit whenever he's had enough, and go back to his linen tablecloths and private stateroom with orderly service to provide for his every whim. You won't be able to turn it on and off like him. You'll get your ass on a detail you'll still be working on when he's slipping between silk sheets after a nice, hot freshwater shower. Get topside, Will.

It's his bloody nose, Bozo. You got yours yesterday when they put you on KP for eighteen hours, and you'll get it another three or four times before this trip is over. That was one thing when we were docked. It'll be another now that we're at sea, the way you've been feeling. Don't forget that those officers were out touring San Francisco while you were scrubbing pots and pans. You can't start jumping in every time someone's playing the donkey. Where's it gonna stop? We're going to war, man. Wake up, before you don't one of these days.

"Do you want a bag?" Captain Michaels asked.

Will reached out and took one and stuck it in his trouser pocket. Then he glanced around at the line of soldiers facing the captain.

Will turned back to the captain a final time. *He's the only one here, and that's cause he's the only one who would come. He wasn't sent. He just came because he knew we were hurting and it was right. There was no leadership here until he came. The others would rather pretend that somehow they're above all this up wherever they are. Get out, Will! It's his bloody nose. If Captain Mike used your selfish illogic, he'd be up in his stateroom. But who can deny that we are better off that he is here? What it comes down to is, I owe him a return salute.*

Will heaved a sigh of relief to have made his mind up in favor of his heart. "Can I help you, sir?" he asked.

"That would be great," the captain replied, perking up. "You up to it?"

Will nodded before stating quietly, "Yes, sir."

Cause To Kill

Up on deck the following day, Will interrupted his reverie about Josh to watch Layton squint into the sun. In front of Layton was Lamont, grinning from ear to ear and walking the deck along the ship's rail with uncharacteristic animation beside Artsy, the FO section chief. Like everyone else that day, the two buck sergeants wore only their tee shirts. Lamont, who usually seemed uncertain of himself and wary of everyone else, appeared relaxed. He was unaware that Layton tracked his every step and peered after him long after he was out of view.

Intrigued, Will slid across the empty hatch cover surface to where Layton sat. Layton glanced Will's way before peering back toward Lamont's last sighting and shielding his brow with both hands. Once satisfied Lamont had not reappeared during the moment's distraction, Layton spoke to Will out of the nearest side of his mouth, all the while maintaining his lookout for the sergeant. "I'd love to catch that guy like that without his stripes on."

"What's with you guys?" asked Will, who marveled how perfectly suited the two were to go at one another. Will never could grasp how Lamont could stand his life as an NCO if he truly were as afraid of all the men as he seemed. If Layton had to clash with authority, Lamont was the perfect mark. Layton would never have stood much chance against any other NCO because he was so small. For the same reason, though, Layton was a likely target for Lamont's displaced frustration.

In fact, it was Sergeant Lamont's job to name troopers from Headquarters Platoon, particularly from the Commo Section, for many unpleasant assignments. "Lamont, give me three men for KP," the first sergeant would yell back in the stateside training camp, "and two to clean the shit house. And I need four men for guard duty tonight and one to pull CQ." In itself, this was not enough to damn Lamont with the platoon. After all, it was not his fault that this is how all armies work. Nonetheless, the way he responded certainly scored two strikes against him with the men.

First, if the top sergeant or Sergeant First Class Grovel bellowed for more, Lamont was ready to comply without any regard for his men. He never spoke up and said, "Sergeant, my men are tired. They were out on guard duty last night. Besides, my men have pulled KP every day this month. How come Firing Battery isn't pulling its fair share?" He simply turned tail and went about his dirty work.

Second, and probably more to the point, Lamont had no more regard for common fairness in assigning these details than he did in accepting them from higher up. It was not a conscious perversity governing his manner but rather some inherent weakness of character. The men in the platoon sensed Lamont was afraid of them. So whenever he attempted to assign them to work details, they either dodged him or laid some excuse on him about why they could not comply. Lamont knew he was getting the runaround, but he was intimidated enough to let them get away with it at least half the time. In these instances, he could not come back empty-handed, so the fall guys were Layton and Martini, who was just as short as Layton but lacked his bulk. The only real difference between the two was that Martini did not know enough to get angry at Lamont rather than at the Army.

"What's with us?" Layton responded deliberately without turning his attention from where he had lost sight of Lamont. "I'll tell you what's with us. I'm gettin' fucked over by the guy. That's what's with us. And that cuts both ways. Wait'll we get in the field with live ammo."

"Think what you're saying, Layton," Will responded. "You're talking about killing one of us."

"He's not one of us. He's a lifer," Layton said, "and he's got it comin'."

"Look, Layton," said Will, "I don't know how much of this is real and how much is bullshit, but either way, it's not something you go around talking about."

"I don't really care, Stone," Layton answered. "I don't really care who knows it. I'll tell Lamont. In fact, that's a good idea. I'll tell Lamont. Why not? The fuck'll piss his pants." Layton paused for Will to respond, but Will said nothing. "That's the way it is, Stone, when you want to kill someone. That's the way it is. You don't care who knows it. You don't care what they do to you afterwards. You just want the fuck dead, and you want him to know ahead of time that it's coming. You want him to squirm, but I don't care really about him squirming. I just want him dead. It's like stepping on a bug in your house. You just want it dead. You don't make a big deal about it. You just do it. You don't feel anything."

Will stayed silent. He had gotten more than he bargained for. He tried to recall what signs of this animus he had missed before. Otherwise nondescript, Layton seemed slovenly in that he took no pride in his appearance. His uniform was always somehow out of sorts. It might be a shirttail sticking out, or his belt buckle an inch-and-a-half off-center, or one trouser bloused noticeably longer than the other, or his bangs showing over his forehead beneath the bill of his baseball cap. Everyone always took it for the limits of Layton's ability. Now Will wondered if there weren't a method to his madness, some subversive attempt to maintain his individuality.

Will knew it was a constant sore point between Lamont and Layton that Layton always looked like he needed a shave. One time Lamont made him shave right in front of him, and when Layton was finished, he still looked like he needed a shave. Now Will wondered if Layton duped not only Lamont but also the rest of the platoon that was watching by shaving without a blade in his razor.

For the most part, Layton was not one to catch the eye. He was almost always quiet, even lethargic. When he spoke, it was in the softest, most measured manner, and his eyes would move in a slow, controlled way. His eyelids seemed always to be half-closed, as though he was ready to drop off to sleep, but he had a ready grin for any gripe about the Army.

Since Will stretched himself ramrod straight to make the most of his five feet seven inches, he was surprised to note how Layton always stooped his shoulders and slouched his five-feet, four-inch frame to seem smaller. Will did not work much with Layton, because he was in Survey and Layton in Commo, but sometimes they were on general details together. Layton's work was adequate. *Slow and steady. He isn't out to take advantage of the guys he's working with, but he isn't about to give anything away to the Army either.*

Will had found Layton to be friendly but his conversation held limited interest, at least until after hours at the enlisted men's club. Layton liked to tip a few every night before turning in, and generally he loosened up then. Ultimately, it was the smaller men who gravitated to him. He and Martini and a couple of small, muscular troopers from the firing battery were like brothers.

"You know, Layton," Will resumed, as Swindell and Shard from the FO Section slid across the hatch cover to join them, "Lamont named you to that latrine detail yesterday only after I told him Campbell couldn't make it. I mean he picked Campbell first."

"Yeah," interrupted Shard sarcastically, "how the hell did you get Campbell, Campbell of all people, to help you clean the shitters all night long?"

Will turned to respond to Shard. Swindell and he were grinning as if they were in a toothpaste advertisement. They had been together since they were drafted in Philadelphia. Both dropped out of college, Swindell for lack of tuition and Shard for love of parties. Layton interrupted Will's thought.

"Stone, I know you didn't fuck me. Lamont did," Layton said. "You were just trying to see Campbell didn't get fucked over. But Lamont had to pick me. The mealymouthed bastard had to pick me. That cocksucker knew I had KP the day before. He put me on that, too."

"You know why Lamont's a lifer?" asked Shard. "He told me once. The only job he ever had in the real world was selling candy apples at some two-bit, traveling carnival."

"You know what NCO really stands for, don't you?" Swindell asked Shard.

"No Chance Outside," Shard replied. "They never can make it."

"Look at Lamont," said Swindell, stroking his chin to hide his grin as he leaned between Layton and Will. "He looks like a squirrel, doesn't he? Look at his face twitchin' around."

"He's back. He's coming back," Layton whispered urgently. "There he is. I'm gonna kill that bastard as soon as we get to the field."

"Layton," Will interrupted, reaching for Layton's forearm.

"All right, Layton," Swindell cheered at the same time. "Blow'im away."

"Hey, get your candy apples here," Shard called out with his hands cupped in front of his face, just as Lamont passed before them.

"Lay off, Stone," said Layton, shaking off Will's restraint. "I mean, think about it. I have. I have thought about this a lot. I mean, why shouldn't I kill Lamont? He's a lifer who's dickin' me over. We're going into this nightmare where everybody's killing everybody else. How do I know this fuck isn't gonna try to get me first? He must have some reason for dickin' me over left and right. What it comes down to, Stone, is that I got a helluva lot more reason to kill Lamont than I do to kill some little guy in his own backyard who never did me no wrong, some guy in someplace I never heard of ten months ago but takes twenty-three days to get to on this slave ship. But that's all right, huh? Kill him, huh?"

"You can kill him 'cause we know he's gonna try and kill us," Will said.

"What would you do if all of a sudden this slant-eyed guy dropped out of the sky in your backyard all hot to trot with his friends and without an invitation?" asked Layton.

"You got your invitation, Shark?" called out Swindell.

"Nah, let's crash it," Shard responded.

Layton grinned, "It's gonna be one helluva party."

On the Side Of the Angels

The rhythmic lapping of the calm sea against the sides of the troop ship, anchored since midday, belied the restiveness of the soldiers on board. It was their twenty-third day aboard, and the glimpse of what they took to be Saigon brought them face-to-face with destiny. The larger buildings near the shoreline were barely visible and the mountains in the distance were backlit by the setting sun. It was an exotic view, yet for most any natural restlessness to set foot on land was overcome by a heightened sense of mortality.

After they dropped anchor, word quickly spread they would go ashore the next morning. Another ship anchored behind them and the one in front advanced, adding to their sense they would know this land soon enough. Now was the time to savor what might be life's last precious drop.

Will was the exception. If others were content to sit, he was ready to participate. Gazing across the ship's rail, he could hardly contain himself as the sky darkened. Faraway gunfire occasionally punctuated his fears and fascination. He watched the illumination rounds fired by shore gun batteries over the eastern strandline. *Is the situation so bad they have to land us in a hot zone? Can this really be the mouth of the Saigon River? Is Saigon really a deep-water port?*

Underlying these questions was another more pervasive set. *Where will all this lead? What horrors are headed my way? Is this my destiny? Is this my end?* Will wanted to act to snap this tension, but there was nothing to do but wait.

Yet what Will was not worried about was just as significant as what concerned him. First, he never doubted he would stand true and withstand the test of fire. Will knew somehow he would make himself stand fast and face his maker if he must. He wondered only from where he would find the strength.

Second, Will never doubted that he was doing the right thing and that, given the chance, he would do it over again. By this time, though, a gnawing suspicion beset him about why it was right. It was not so much that the war was justified, but rather it was right he served so he could pass along his observations if he made it home. For now, Will could only look to the night for his answers.

The next morning the men were back on deck. Campbell spotted Will again at the ship's rail and worked his way next to him. "A penny for your thoughts, Stone," he said.

"I didn't see you there," responded Will. "Were you there long, I mean, when I came up to the rail?"

"No, you were here first. That's why I stopped. So tell me, now that you've been peering out there so long, what do you see?"

"You know, the whole trip, everyone's been hounding me how I got you to help clean those latrines that first night."

"Yeah, they badger me about that, too. Fact is, I did it cause you had no right to ask. I mean, the Army couldn't order me to do it. But for once, I don't know, no one was making me do it, and there was no moral objection, and it was right that someone do it, and, well, let's just say maybe the company wasn't so bad, so, I guess, it was as good a time as any to do my part."

"Is that how I should answer them?" Will asked.

"Are they still asking?"

"Now and then."

"Can't we tell them you blackmailed me?" Campbell smirked. "Stone, you'd be making a grave mistake if you think you can rope me into any of your volunteer missions on shore. I haven't yet figured out why you do it. Maybe for the adventure, but please don't count on me bailing you out because it ain't gonna happen."

"So I'm on notice," Will responded. "Thank you. Now, may I ask you something?"

Campbell looked intently at Will and then to either side, before nodding.

"That time on the bus when you asked if our fight was just or necessary—" Will paused when Campbell groaned. "This is just part of the same conver—"

"I know you have the right to bring this up, Stone," Campbell said. "I was just hoping to avoid it, that's all."

"I'm just trying to get it straight," Will said. "How can you dispute that this is about stopping the spread of communism?"

"I didn't say anything, Stone."

"We're just picking up where the French left off," said Will.

"The French!" bellowed a sinewy black medic standing next to Campbell. "The French did nothing for these people. They bled the Vietnamese dry for a hundred years." The medic rushed between Campbell and Will and shouted. "How can you compare us to the French, for God's sake? Why should the French rule these people? Damn the French. Don't people have a right to be free?"

"Of course they do," answered Will, looking into a glare reflected from the medic's dark wire-framed glasses.

"You bet your ass they do." He leaned toward Will before storming away.

Campbell made no secret of his amusement.

"But we're fighting the same enemy the French fought," Will said.

"Exactly," said Campbell, "and I got the feeling you were about to suggest ours was a fight for freedom."

"Well, yes."

"Stone, let me leave you with this thought," said Campbell. "Sometimes it's hard to tell who is on the side of the angels."

"What he said about the French is a gross oversimplification," protested Will, holding open a book for Campbell to inspect.

"Of course," said Campbell, "but there was enough truth in what he said that you couldn't refute him so easily." Campbell paused a moment and fanned the pages of Will's book. "Stone, you've been carrying this red book with you everywhere you've gone for twenty-three days now. I've watched you, and you're only on page 122. So you've read something about the French in this Mr. Fall's *Two Vietnams*, but you're ready to embark on what may be your last voyage and you haven't read a lick about what he has to say about us there, or here, I should say. That's inexcusable.

"I've watched you, Stone. You start to read, you doze off. You snap to, and you start over again. I'll give you credit for trying. Listen, when you get back to the States, get a hold of Mortimer Adler's *How to Read a Book*. I'll bet you I can tell you more about this book just from flipping through it than you can after twenty-three days with it. You're doing something wrong. You got your mind on idle when it should be at full throttle. Let me go, man. I gotta check out my gear for tomorrow."

"Yeah, sure, see ya," said Will. He turned back to the side rail. *Yeah, sure. Mortimer Adler.*

"Got more than you bargained for with that medic?" asked Deddson, who had been leaning over the rail to Will's left. Deddson was a wiry five feet seven, so he could look directly into Will's inquiring gaze. Will had not had much contact with Deddson, but had observed him to be quiet, thoughtful and steady.

"So it seems," Will said, laughing. "We have a semantic disagreement about the word *free*. Does it mean independent, or should it mean protected, you know, rights, an open society, liberty?"

Deddson casually redirected his gaze to the harbor and Will remonstrated himself. *Semantics. Now you're going to truck up semantics for discussion here in the Army. When in hell are you ever going to learn?*

"I'm not sure either definition applies here," Deddson replied, "but what I am sure of is that it shouldn't have anything to do with me."

Deddson was a picture of relaxation, leaning against the side rail as he surveyed the shoreline beyond the harbor. He seemed neither to want nor need a response. As far as he was concerned, his word was final.

Will looked him over, not sure he had heard him right. Deddson was jut-jawed and clear-eyed, exhibiting none of the tension Will felt about what lay ahead. His tone revealed frustration for having been put upon, but no hint he would let the imposition spoil his day. At that moment Will knew Deddson would do what he had to, that he could be depended upon, and Will felt profound respect for him.

Deddson never complained, shirked, or disappointed. He neither reveled in his off-hours, nor found satisfaction in his work. He was simply doing hard time, and he was doing it with grace.

"What about our duty to our country?" asked Will.

"Stone," said Deddson evenly, "when men of good will, men like yourself, can't figure out which side is freedom's friend, then you have no duty. These politicians have no right to drag guys like us into something like this. They haven't done their duty, and they are abusing the trust you and the American people have placed in them."

"That's all?"

"Isn't that enough?" said Deddson.

"Are you saying you have no duty to our country? That we don't need an army that leaves these decisions to our leaders?"

"I mean exactly what I said," said Deddson. "Nothing more, nothing less. Do we need an unquestioning army? I don't know. Ask someone else. Do we have the right to make citizens into soldiers? Not if it's me. Not without first answering questions about a clear and present danger. Questions that in this instance have not at all been addressed, let alone answered, by our government. Hell, Stone, you've been running around mumbling the right questions, but I haven't heard our government give the right answers, and I've been listening real hard."

"What are you going to do about it?"

"Try to stay alive," answered Deddson.

"What about when you get back?"

"If I get back, I'll crawl under some rock where they won't find me again."

"How many of the others feel this way?" asked Will.

"I speak only for myself, Stone," Deddson responded, "but we're all caught in the same trap, and I suppose we all know it. You're the only one I know who's really gung ho, including the officers. I do hear a Lieutenant Ranksaw in I Troop is gung ho, too. But he's a West Pointer, so he's got an excuse."

Will looked over Deddson's shoulder out to sea. *This is ridiculous. I'm not gung ho. I'm just trying to do what's right. I'm simply not sure what that is just now, so I'm giving our government the benefit of the doubt. Jesus Christ, it was only yesterday that again they showed us that film "Why Vietnam"? It's the third time they showed it, but I can hardly remember what it was about.*

Let's see. There's a global struggle between freedom and communism that's being fought in a thousand places. This struggle stuff is no bull. The history of the first half of this century is all about the collapse of civilization into global war because good men sat on their hands while demagogic dictators built up enough power to contest the very existence of democracy. The precious lesson from all this, paid for in the blood of our fathers, is that you can't appease tyrants. You have to stand up to them wherever they rear their ugly swords. The essence of the Cold War is taking such a stand, containing the Red menace.

These tyrants, whether Hitler, Mao, or Stalin and his successors, would have us believe this really is about choosing a valid and preferable way of life to our democratic, free enterprise system. The historical facts are that Hitler murdered some six million civilians in his concentration camps and Stalin forcibly imposed policies on his own people resulting in the death of tens of millions of Russians. This is apart from the carnage of World War II and the suffering caused by the post-war communist invasion of Eastern Europe. This is not about choice. It is about coercion.

Vietnam has now flared up into one of the hot spots of containment. We can't let our position erode by conceding Nam, or it will be one country after another that we'll lose, eventually upsetting the balance of power. And the Vietnamese people deserve better than that. They want our help throwing off the yoke of oppression.

The Cong come into their villages, mostly at night. They grab the young men and force them to join at gunpoint. Those who resist are executed, as are the government officials. Their heads are paraded around on sticks. Captured Americans are given much the same treatment, first paraded around and then executed. It's for keeps with these bastards.

It all makes sense to me when I think about it this way, but Campbell and Deddson and the others don't seem to buy it. "Is the war just or necessary?" Campbell asks. "Is there a clear and present danger to us?" Deddson questions. "Do the Viets really want us here?" Layton demands to know. Implicit in the President's campaign statement is the question, "Whose fight is this, anyway?" These are the questions, I gotta answer, and soon.

Later that day, as he climbed down the flimsy rope ladder slung over the side of the ship, Will still had these questions firmly in mind, at least until he descended into the amphibious landing craft rocking in the sea below. *Wow, it's just like in all those World War II movies I've seen.*

Part Two:
In-Country

Chapter 3
Life By Different Rules

First Night

"Holy shit! What a fuckin' day, and now on we go into the night," said Shard, ostensibly to Swindell, but really to anyone who would listen. Not that anyone in the Survey and Commo sections, collapsed on the ground alongside Shard, needed to be reminded how long and hot and tiresome the day had been.

"I can't believe how long it took us to make it here to Long Binh. This is MACV Headquarters, you know," answered Swindell loud enough for the others to hear. "I mean, we didn't do anything except travel. Here, look, it's only an inch on this goddamned map, about 25 miles, tops."

"Of course it seemed longer. We didn't land in Saigon, for crissake. It was Vung Tau," Campbell said, "and the map's in klicks, kilometers, not miles. About 25 klicks."

"Right, klicks," said Swindell. "That's less. And we spent the whole day, first in that goddamned landing craft."

"I was so sure I was going to be sick in that thing," interrupted Shard.

"Me, too." Swindell raised his voice, continuing, "But it was duck soup. Didn't bother me a bit."

"Don't think it bothered anybody from what I could see," Campbell said. "But then there was the waiting on the beach for the trucks to pick us up for the airport."

"You got stuck on the detail loading all the gear on the trucks, didn't you?" Shard asked Swindell.

"Fuck the Army," Swindell said, shrugging his shoulders. "Hey, it was better than just standing there waiting. What the hell did they make us stand for, huh? It must have been two hours waiting before I was put on the detail. Why the hell couldn't we sit down, anyway?"

"Cause it's the Army," said Campbell.

"Quit your bitchin', will ya?" shouted Montana.

"Yeah, this sucks enough without listening to someone bitch about it all the time," Layton called out.

"Shut up, Layton!" yelled Montana.

"Jus' backin' you up, Sarge," Layton replied.

"Shut up, Layton!" yelled Montana.

"Did they make you stand the whole time I was on that detail?" asked Swindell.

"Zack told us to take a break right after you left," answered Shard, "but then 'bout a half hour later Top comes along and bawls him out and gets us all on our feet again. Soon as he leaves, though, Zack tells us to crash but be ready to snap to, and he stations a lookout for Top, Grovel, or any of the officers. I guess maybe he's not such a bad guy, after all."

"All things are relative," said Campbell.

"He was too tired to stand up himself," Montana said. "He doesn't care about you guys."

Sean O'Rourke, an impetuous but good-natured Irish immigrant, leaned toward Deddson and whispered, "Then why didn't Zack just leave Lamont in charge and go off and hide out with the other senior NCOs?"

"What'd you say, O'Rourke?" demanded Montana, jumping to his feet and standing over O'Rourke with both fists clenched. "Say it to my face."

O'Rourke remained reclined on his side, propped up by an elbow on the ground, facing Deddson. "I dinna say anything about you," O'Rourke said calmly.

"Don't give me that crap," said Montana. "What did you say?"

"I dinna say anything to you," O'Rourke said. "It was something between me and Deddson."

Will looked on with keen interest. *O'Rourke knows he's got trouble cause Montana's got rank, but Montana has got to be wondering what the hell he bit off here. Look at O'Rourke's bulk, for God's sake. He's all muscle and it's clear he's got the heart to see this through.*

"What'd he say, Deddson?" Montana shouted.

"Leave me out of this, will ya?" answered Deddson.

"What'd he say, Deddson?" Montana said through gritted teeth.

"We all need showers," said Deddson.

"Don't try to change the subject, Deddson. I asked what he said?"

"That's what he said," Will said.

"Shut up, Stone," Montana ordered. "You keep out of this."

"That's what he said," Will responded.

"What?" demanded Montana, turning his full attention to Will now. "What did he say?"

"That we all need showers. That we have to find some way to take showers."

"Bullshit!" Montana yelled. "Then how come he didn't just tell me that."

"He did," responded Will. "Deddson did just tell you that."

Montana shot a glance back at Deddson and O'Rourke, while Will resumed, "So maybe you could scout around and see what you can find out about us getting showers tonight."

"Yeah, Montana," Campbell piped in, "how about it? Can you use your pull to work showers into the program here?"

Montana looked around at the expectant faces. He grabbed Will by the shoulders and slouched in order to put his face right in Will's. "Listen, Stone," he said under his breath, "you don't tell me what to do. I tell you."

"Montana, they're not going to listen if you send any of us," Will whispered. "You're our best shot at maybe, maybe getting it done."

Montana looked around one more time. All eyes were upon him. "All right," he said, raising his voice, "I'll give it a shot." No one said anything. "I'll see what I can do about showers."

The others looked at him silently, before Will finally spoke up, "Thanks."

Montana turned and strode in the direction of the battery headquarters. When he was a few strides from the group, several of them cackled. Montana hesitated before picking up his pace.

"You're on his shit list, Stone," Deddson said.

"What an asshole," someone said to a murmur of agreement.

"I'm gonna kill Lamont," said Layton.

"I didn't think you had it in you, Stone," said Shard.

Will looked after Montana. *No damage done. He's been after my ass anyway since the day I joined the Cav.*

O'Rourke arose and stepped over to Will and said to him with the utmost gravity, "I said nothing about showers, and it's none of his business what I did say. I'm not afraid to deal with him." Failing to provoke a response, he finally broke into a smile and feigned a punch at Will's shoulder. "Thanks," he said.

"You'd think they could've had these tents set up for us by another unit," said Swindell, "rather than making us do them in the dark."

"This is the Army, Swindell," said Campbell. "What I want to know is why they kept us standing so long. You'd think they wouldn't have exhausted us so, given they didn't really know what was in store for us."

"Setting up the tents was a bitch," said Shard. "I'm ready for bed. The hell with a shower."

"What d'ya say we sneak into Bien Hoa and find some pussy?" asked Swindell.

"That was quick," said Deddson, pointing toward the oncoming Montana.

"What about it?" the group called out to him.

Montana gave no answer until he was on top of them. "All right, on your feet," he said. Once they rose, he waited for their complete attention before shouting, "We've got to fill sandbags till they tell us to stop. It'll be two hours at least. And no goddamned bitchin'!

"Stone," he continued, "you and White Man are on a little cleanup detail in the morning. Report to Headquarters, Headquarters Troop 0530 hours."

Will was a sweaty mess by the time he laid his bedroll on his cot. Although it was late and he was dead tired, Will's mind returned to Josh's shooting and how events earlier that day had led to it. Josh had shown up in the afternoon at the construction site where Will was working that day, but Will now began to focus on what had happened that morning.

The Color Of Skin—Part 1

"You're doing great, kid. Keep it up," Graves called to Will on the dozer. Graves climbed back onto the floor deck on the foundation and took his place on one side of the shield he had made of twelve-foot 2 X 6's and plywood. Johnny manned the 2 X 6 handle on the other side. The rocks Will was pushing towards the back of the foundation were too big and coming from too high not to deflect them before they hit the foundation wall. It was difficult and dangerous work. Accomplishing it smoothly helped ease some of the tensions created when Graves, Harry's foreman, had offhandedly referred to Josh as "Nigger Josh."

When coffee arrived, Graves drew a finger across his throat to signal Will to shut down the machine. Will slid down the slope where he had started the backfill and made his way along the bottom of the footing to where Graves had lowered a ladder for him to climb up to the floor deck atop the foundation. Johnny sprawled out on the plywood floor deck. Graves sat on his toolbox with his head in the *Daily News*. Will took his coffee and stretched out on the floor, propping himself up on one side with an elbow. Graves put down his paper and began the conversation.

"Like I said, kid, you did great. Let me tell you, if I was the one on that machine when you was hopping around down near the edge of that drop, I would've just parked that momma and called somebody to come pick it up. You got guts, kid. I'll give you that."

Will nodded.

"Those goddamned niggerheads was really throwing you around."

"Do you have to call them that?" Will asked.

"That's what they are, kid. Everyone knows those rocks are nigger-heads. I mean, what do you want to call them?" His question was for Will but he glanced at Johnny.

"Good question," responded Will. "I don't know what I'd call them, but not that."

Graves rubbed the nape of his neck three or four times while stretching and then asked, "Uh, why not, kid?"

"I figure there's something sacred in all men that gives them their worth," Will said. "You disrespect that worth in others and you deny it in yourself."

"Sounds like a wet dream, kid," Graves said.

"Man, didn't that mean anything to you?" Will said.

"We're talking about rocks, booby," Graves said. "If I want preachin', I go to mass."

"Will," Johnny said, "what about you dropping out of school? You quit or what?"

Will bit his lip.

"What's the matter, boy?" Graves asked. "Cat got your tongue?"

"You quit school, Will?" Johnny asked.

"Not exactly."

The two eyed Will patiently. Finally Graves asked, "Well?"

"Go screw," Will responded,

"You flunk out?" Johnny asked.

"I heared he got some girl in trouble and her old man—" Graves said.

"Harry cut me off a couple of years ago, in '63," interrupted Will, "when I told him I was going to the March on Washington."

"You went to the civil rights rally in D.C.?" Johnny said.

"No, actually. I never went," Will said. "I missed the bus."

"You missed the bus," echoed Graves. "Your old man cut off your tuition for going but you never went. What do you mean you missed the bus?"

"It was more than just that, but that's what it boiled down to. I missed the bus," said Will.

"You got your head up your ass, kid," said Graves.

"Look," said Will, "I just couldn't be sure I was doing the right thing. I had to make that choice by myself when the group pulled out. So, you see, that's all it took to turn me back."

"I don't give a goddamn about your bus, kid," Graves said. "You missed a bus. Big fuckin' deal. But you ain't going to school on account of your old man thinks you made that bus."

"Yeah, what about that, Will?" added Johnny.

"Why don't we just let it go?" Will said.

"That ain't likely," said Graves.

"Go on, Will," said Johnny. "We want to hear it straight."

"When I heard King speak from Washington, I knew it was history in the making. Negroes were claiming their rightful place in society. But even more than that, the people of this country—colored, white, whatever—were rising as one to rid themselves of an injustice. Imagine, a country that rights its own wrongs. This is my America, what I pledge allegiance to, what I'll fight to defend."

"You got up quite a head of steam there, kid," said Graves, "but who the hell are you? I mean, kid, what kind of person? Your old man thinks you was down there with those niggers and you wasn't. How you think he's going to feel when he finds this out and you still ain't going to school? And that's the shame of it, you still ain't going to school, though I'll be damned if I can tell if it's made you smarter or dumber."

"Don't you understand?" asked Will. "America needed me, and I missed the bus."

"America can get along just fine without Will Stone, yessir," said Graves. "It's a big place. Go back to school, babe."

"Why didn't I go to D.C.?" said Will, "I was afraid, Graves. Not of you or Harry, but of doing the wrong thing by going to D.C. Well, I was wrong, all right, but wrong for not going. I should have stood up and been counted. And I'll pay any price there still is for taking that stand. Not paying that price goes against everything I believe. This shit's coming to a head. We're gonna have to deal with this, and if Harry doesn't like it, too bad."

"You trying to piss off your old man," asked Graves. "That why you live with Nigger Josh?"

"His name's just Josh, Graves. Josh and I worked together and we're friends, so I'm helping him. Who knows, Graves? Maybe you and I will find ourselves in the same boat some day."

"How come you and Josh are so tight?" Johnny asked.

Will looked up. *Gotta keep my big mouth shut.* He shook his head and began, "I was sixteen and screwin' around on a rubber-tired backhoe when I wasn't supposed to. This was when Josh still worked for Harry. I could run the machine OK, but I still slid it next to an open test pit, maybe twenty feet deep. I was on the uphill side of the pit where the grade was so steep I couldn't get traction on the topsoil. No matter what I tried, I kept heading for that hole. I was scared shitless.

"Finally, I spotted Josh watching me," Will went on. "I was sure he'd come running, take over the controls and get me out of there.

"But he didn't till I called him, and then he kept me on the machine without even saying a word. He pointed for me to cross the open pit with the machine. That pit had to be five feet across. I was scared out of my gourd, but I did it because he expected me to. He signaled me through each movement of the rear boom and bucket, step by step. Would've been easier for him to have done it himself.

"When I finally made it across, Josh was already headed back up the street in his pickup. I caught up with him in front of another house being built, and he just grunted for help with some railroad ties. It took us until just past 4 o'clock to bucket-load all those ties up behind that house.

"I expected him to see some sort of triumph in my crossing the pit," Will said. "At least, his not talking about it spared me an ass-kicking. Behind the house, Josh shut off my machine. He pulled out a cold beer from his cooler and held it out for me to take. Josh always had a couple of cold beers at quitting time, but he never offered me one.

"When I reached out to take it, he wrapped my fingers around the cool brew, smiled and gave me a pat on the back. I knew I had passed some test. But what?

"I figure Josh kept me on that machine because it was my problem. I created it, so I had to fix it. You can't ask another man to risk his neck in your place. We all have the same right to life. Josh never said a word, but he expected me to clean up my own mess," Will said. "When it's your turn in the barrel, it's your turn. You're not a man if you don't take it. I don't know what you are—a child or a weasel or a rat. All I know is you're not what a man's supposed to be. Not by my lights anyway."

"So, is that it, kid?" Graves said. "Is that why we can't call them rocks niggerheads? Because this dumb colored man fooled you into risking your neck when he could've bailed you out a hundred different ways without either of you taking that chance?"

"What?" Will said. "When I said there was something of worth that all men of any color have within them, something we deny only at our own risk, what do you think it was?"

"Your dime, kid," Graves responded.

Will stood up, shaking his head. He glanced at Graves once, gritted his teeth, and started to walk away.

"Well?" Graves shouted. Will ignored him and kept walking. "Well?" Graves shouted even louder. "My answer?"

"Well, you're an asshole," Will yelled. "That's your answer."

"What'd you say?" Graves stormed after Will.

Will turned and faced him. "I said you're an asshole."

"I'm an asshole. You get that?" Graves shouted, looking around at Johnny. "You lay this whole sermon on us, kid, about something this and something that. Then you ask me what this something is like I'm supposed to know. Then, when I ask you what the hell it is and you can't tell me, suddenly I'm the asshole?"

"It's our humanity, you sonofabitch," Will shouted back, "the spark of divinity that separates us from the rest of the animal kingdom, and you can't snuff it out in others without making it flicker in yourself."

Graves grinned. "You're bent, kid, b-e-n-t, bent. You belong either in a pulpit or up on that machine. Which is it gonna be?" When Will's jaw dropped, Graves strode across the floor deck, picked up his half of the shield and hollered, "Johnny, get your *humanity* over here."

Will made his way back down the ladder and up the earthen bank to the crawler. *I deserved every word of that. The less said the better. Jesus, when will I learn?*

Will spent the rest of the morning pushing boulders with the dozer blade down at the men below. Graves's every muscle was tested to the limit with each impact to the shield, yet he took every blow with a laugh or a smile. In the middle of it, he said to Johnny, "Perfect day, huh, kid?"

Naked Came the Strangers

Will had no trouble rising after his 4:45 a.m. wake-up call. He was anxious to get a look at his surroundings in daylight. Soon he stood on a line of six soldiers, each on one detail or another and waiting to fill their steel helmets with shaving water. While waiting, Will's eyes roamed the battery area for a water trailer, in order to know where to get refills.

Don't see any trailer nearby. Carrying these jerricans here must have been a real arm-stretcher.

Will was washing his upper body outside his tent when Whiteman grabbed him by the arm. "Stone," he whispered, "Horton told me there's a place we can shower, just the other side of I Troop, over there. The officers did last night."

Will looked at his watch. "We can make it," he said, grabbing his towel. "C'mon."

"We gotta get Franklin," Whiteman grinned. "He's on the detail, too. He's in the tent yet. I think he went back to sleep."

"Jesus," Will said, "just grab your towel. Leave the rest of your shit here. We don't have a lot of time."

Will signaled for Whiteman to lead the way. The two hurried into the tent to Franklin's bedside. The one luxury they did enjoy the previous night, despite the disorganization of their arrival, was their steel cots.

Franklin was making the most of his when Whiteman and Will arrived. Without hesitation, Whiteman reached his strong arm under Franklin's torso and lifted him to a seated position.

"What?" Franklin complained, as soon as his eyes opened.

"We're on detail, so we gotta go," Will answered. "Snap to. If we boogie, we got a shot at catchin' a shower."

"What detail?" Franklin said.

"C'mon, don't fuck us outta a shower," Will answered.

"Shower sounds good to me," said Franklin, as he bounced to his feet and bent over his duffel bag, seeking a towel.

Will watched Franklin drop to his knees to invade his duffel under his bunk. *Jesus, he must've gone right to bed last night without even trying to wash his face.* Franklin nodded to Will, as he withdrew his towel.

"Let's go," said Will.

The three hurried out of the tent with Whiteman in the lead and Will bringing up the rear. Once they appeared in the open, Whiteman hesitated, which gave Will another chance to check his watch. "Five of," Will said, as he signaled the way to the left. "We gotta hurry."

As soon as they crossed the I Troop area, which was two rows of eight tents each fronting on a center street, they saw the shower structure against the backdrop of the rising sun. It was a wood floor system propped up on cinder blocks with two bare wood frame walls on opposite sides carrying pontoon-like containers of water overhead. The whole structure was approximately six-by-twelve feet. They could see right away that the showers were not in use. No one said a word, but Will figured all harbored the same worry. *Any water left?*

Whiteman reached from outside and turned the faucet handle until water gurgled down through the half-inch copper supply line and cascaded from the regulation chrome shower head. Will nudged Whiteman with his elbow and pointed at the lettering on the sky-blue tanks overhead.

"Dow Chemical Company," Whiteman read.

Franklin looked up solemnly. "Napalm."

"It's now or never, gentlemen," Will said.

Whiteman and Will pulled off their boots and socks, and Franklin kicked off his flip-flops. They stepped out of their trousers and shorts and secured their stuff in a dry spot.

"What's that?" Franklin questioned, pointing further east.

Will looked and answered tentatively, "Coolies."

Whiteman turned on the water again, this time stepping into the stream. "It's cold," he laughed. "It feels like ice water. It feels so good to be cold after being so hot for so long yesterday."

"You know the drill," Will said, "just enough water to lather up, then just enough to rinse off."

"We'll see who's looking," grinned Whiteman. "Hey, look where these guys are now." He pointed at the coolies who had advanced on the dirt trail to a position only twenty feet away. "They're not just guys."

Will took his first careful look at the long-suffering Vietnamese. Even though the rising sun lent barely enough light to make their jet-black hair glisten in the wisp of a breeze, their dark eyes shone back with interest. The Viets were mostly lean and bony with delicately sculptured, bronze faces. Will was surprised they were mostly as tall as he was.

Old and young alike were animated with an enthusiasm for life. Their chatter was enlivened by laughter that revealed the elders to have dreadfully darkened teeth, stained by years of chewing betel nut leaves as a stimulant. There were no young men, but the young women and the few children tagging along, by way of contrast, boasted bright smiles. The young women moved with a grace that was apparently worn away from their elders by years of travail and toil. Accordingly, the young appeared elegant in their simplicity. Their elders just appeared simple.

The coolies were on their way to work at various menial positions within the MACV headquarters compound. They had paused to wait for a woman relieving her bladder. Like most, she wore the silky, black, loose-fitting, pajama-like garb characteristic of the Vietnamese peasant. She had simply hiked up her baggy pant leg all the way to her crotch and pulled it aside, so that when she squatted along the side of the trail she would not soil herself. Her cone-shaped, straw coolie hat hung on her back by a cord slung under her chin.

Whiteman blushed with shame for having overseen her procedure, even as he realized he was just as much a subject of their fascination. Born to a Minnesota dairy-farming family and bred for eighteen years on their Protestant ethic, Whiteman was a virtual bodybuilding poster boy. What fascinated the peasants, though, was the stark contrast between Whiteman's sun-crisp face and arms, and the rest of his lily-white body. Long ago, life on the farm had inclined him to accept his body as one more natural wonder, just as he was apt to accept the peasant women's need to squat as natural. Nonetheless, the singsong banter and giggling of the coolies made him self-conscious when they pointed at him.

"Didi mau!" Whiteman shouted with great authority, repeating his sole recollection from the one-hour indoctrination with Vietnamese language and culture given all of the troopers aboard ship. The coolies were startled by his vigor and jumped a step back before resuming their chatter. "Didn't they understand me?" Whiteman demanded of Franklin.

The streets of Pittsburgh tempered Franklin with a deep-seated cynicism. He knew he had a scraggly body compared to Whiteman or even to Will. He also was sure he appeared all the more incongruous because his head was oversized. At one point, he had thought his body was just underdeveloped, and that bodybuilding would bring his skull and frame into proper proportion. A couple of weeks of weight training had convinced him he might likely appear more wiry as a result, but it would take a Herculean effort for him to bulk up that much. He grabbed his crotch with one hand and, extending his other toward the amused coolies, shouted out nonsense: "Chong yong, mama san!"

Will, too, was embarrassed by their attention, but quickly waxed philosophical. *In Rome, do as the Romans do. They must be dependable if they let them inside this compound, but how do you know one of them isn't gonna pop you or pitch a grenade? Helluva way to go, this'd be. But we don't know any such thing about them, so Franklin is outta order to insult them like that.*

"Didi, didi," Whiteman repeated forcefully. "Didi mau!" Again, the coolies retreated at his command, and this time they turned away from the shower area and resumed their trek down the trail.

"Where are your weapons, men?" a voice called out to the three in the shower. Will, Whiteman and Franklin spun around at the sound of authority. Catching a glimpse of captain's bars, Will instinctively clicked his heels together but gratefully restrained his forearm just as it started to snap off a crisp salute. Instead, he reached up and shut off the water. The others looked to Will to respond because he was a Specialist 4 and they were just Privates First Class.

"We haven't been issued weapons yet, sir. We just got here yesterday," Will answered.

"Oh, you're with the Cav, huh?" the captain asked.

"Yessir," the three responded in unison.

"Well, you should be aware, men," the captain resumed, "that you carry your weapon here at all times with at least one extra magazine of live ammo. That's all the time, men. I don't care whether you're going to the shower, the mess, or the latrine. At all times. Well, your officers will tell you. You never know when you might need it, and please don't use all our water." He pointed to his steel helmet to remind them of that requirement, too, before going about his business.

"Where's his weapon?" Whiteman muttered.

"He's got a sidearm," whispered Will.

"This is my gun," said Franklin, grabbing his crotch, "just for fun."

Will looked after the captain. *I wonder if he was warning us about those coolies.*

"We better make time," said Whiteman.

In the Dumps

The first hint of what was in store for them this day came after they reported to the squadron headquarters clerk for instructions. "Report to DiMaio at that deuce-and-a-half over there at 0600. He's the driver. He'll show you what to do. He does it every day," said the clerk. "Headquarters mess is already open, and it looks like you have a half hour to chow down. Better eat light, though."

Will, Whiteman, and Franklin glanced at one another. "Why light?" Franklin asked once they left the clerk.

When they arrived at 6:00 a.m., DiMaio instructed them, "Hop in the back. We're going for a little ride."

The men moved around the back while DiMaio climbed into the cab and took the wheel. "Uh-oh," observed Whiteman, "this is a five-ton."

"It's a lot higher than a deuce-and-a-half. That's for sure," said Will.

The truck roared down the oil-soaked dirt road past block after block of company-sized unit areas, just like I Troop's or their own, How Battery's. The company streets down the center were for foot traffic only. Vehicular traffic traveled around the outside, between units. Units were ganged together, so that most company areas were accessible from a single side by vehicle.

Just when Will had thought he had seen it all, the collector road would angle slightly, more or less parallel to Provincial Highway 316, and continue on indefinitely past as many unit areas as before, and then some. Finally, the open-backed cargo truck ground to a halt at the furthest extreme of the entire MACV compound. When they heard DiMaio open his door, Whiteman, Will, and Franklin hopped off the back of the truck. "Why couldn't it have been a deuce-and-a-half?" grunted Franklin as he let fly.

"As you cherries can see," DiMaio began, "this is a mess hall."

Will's mind shifted into high gear chasing the purpose of this insult. He grasped its implication of naiveté, but he thought it a reach from a rear-area support soldier. Will looked DiMaio over carefully for any sign of war wounds or front-line service.

DiMaio was a match for Will in height, only he carried a good ten pounds more mass around with him. On the surface Will could detect no sign of DiMaio's having seen combat. He wondered about DiMaio's tendency to withdraw so quickly after giving an instruction. *I can't figure this guy right off the bat.*

"Matter of fact," DiMaio continued, "every time I stop, it will be in front of a mess hall. Don't think I'm gonna get out from behind the wheel every time we stop. I'm just the driver, so don't expect me to help with your job. I gotta do this every day. You guys will probably get away with this just once."

DiMaio paused to sense if they would heed his instructions. "So here's what you gotta do," he continued smugly after taking a few steps into the mess area. "See this here can and these two next to it. They're filled with grease from the drippings from the grills. You have to load these up on the back of the truck. Not the shiny aluminum garbage cans, mind you, just these old ash cans full of this congealed grease. Well, it's mostly congealed, maybe not on the top sometimes."

Will stared at the heavy galvanized steel ash cans and mentally weighed them compared to the bright shiny aluminum ones when empty. But he could not begin to imagine how much the heavier cans could weigh when full of grease. "I don't know if we can lift them," he confided to Whiteman and Franklin, once DiMaio headed back to the truck.

"Still warm," Franklin observed, running the palm of his hand around the outside of the top of one of the cans.

"Jesus," said Will.

"Well, there's one for each of us," Whiteman laughed.

"I wonder what we do once we've got these guys loaded up," muttered Franklin.

"C'mon, let's go," yelled DiMaio on his way back to the truck.

The three nodded to one another and moved awkwardly toward the first can, trying to figure out how to go about the task. Will latched onto the handle of the least full ash can, though it was still full to within four inches of the brim. He tried tilting the can enough to roll it on its bottom edge, but he could not get enough angle on it without the grease starting to run over the low side. "Gotta keep these babies level," Will said.

Next, he tugged on the handle, lifting somewhat in order to free the lead edge from friction as he dragged the can. So heavy was it, however, that the rear bottom edge plowed up a furrow. "Pull on this with me," Will said to Franklin, who was closest to him.

Franklin stuck in his right hand, so Will switched to his left. Whiteman watched with as much amusement as concern as the two strained on the handle like dray horses harnessed side by side.

"Hey, pick it up," a bald-headed black cook called out from the nearby mess tent. "Don't screw up our walk."

Jesus Christ, thought Will, catching a sympathetic glance from Franklin.

"Wait," called Whiteman, as he lumbered to the other side of the can. Reaching down first with his right hand, he tested his strength against the load. Then, he added his left hand and straddled his arms and the handle. "OK, you lift and pull nice and easy," he continued, "and I'll hold this end level with you."

In this way, the three managed to reach the edge of the road with each of the three cans. Will and Franklin competed for handle space upfront, and Whiteman walked on his heels in back, holding up his end of the bargain. "Back the truck up, will ya!" called out Franklin. "That's twenty feet we don't need to carry this motherfucker."

While Whiteman was agreeing, Will was watching DiMaio in the passenger-side mirror. When he spotted DiMiao's dismissive gesture, he said, "Maybe he needs a little encouragement. Hold up."

Whiteman eased his weight onto the brim of the can and watched Will stalk around the driver's side of the truck. When Will was out of sight, Whiteman exchanged a puzzled look with Franklin, who was mopping his brow with a kerchief. "0650, and I'm already sweating like a pig," said Franklin.

Will caught DiMaio off-guard when he jumped up on the doorstep and shouted in the window, "Back it up, sport."

"Now, listen, you," DiMaio said, but Will cut him off.

"We got a job to do, you and us," Will hissed, "and we're gonna get it done. Better it's the easy way, cause the hard way is we drag you outta here and stick your head in one of these cans."

DiMaio's face flushed crimson and he started to bluster gibberish. Then, all at once, he seemed to relax and said, "You guys ain't so bad, I guess." Then, he threw the gearshift into reverse and added, "OK."

"Thanks," said Will. "You're a good guy. Just stop the rig at each mess hall."

DiMaio smiled and nodded. Will jumped off as he felt the truck lurch backward.

"He didn't hear you," Will said to Franklin upon rejoining them. "OK, gotta do it."

Whiteman dragged the first can behind the center of the back of the truck. On the harder road surface, the back edge slid rather than plowed. Will and Franklin set the chains on each side to hold the tailgate in the level position. When they were ready, the three took an anxious look at the can.

"Ya gotta get it up to me," Whiteman said, using the top of the can to climb up on the tailgate.

Will and Franklin looked at Whiteman's imposing figure peering down on them.

"Oh, shit," Will gasped, "let's do it."

Will dropped his shoulder and his knee alongside the ash can with his back almost against it, requiring him to twist his neck hard to the right to keep one eye in contact with Franklin. Franklin had assumed the more conventional position used by Whiteman before, straddling his legs on both sides of the handle of the can. Franklin took one look at Will, as they both fought with their handles for the best grip possible. Will thought, *There's no way he's going to let me out-lift him and spill this slop on him. Gotta keep up with him.*

The two looked across the can at one another. Will bobbed his head rhythmically, once he established eye contact, and said, "On *three*, one, two, three."

As Will bobbed his head back the third time, his utterance of the third count was truncated not by the force he threw into the lift, but by the resistance of the load. *Oh, no*, he thought, when it felt like the can had not even moved, but then he saw it was two inches off the ground and he commanded his arms to redouble the effort. The can kept rising ever so slowly. The two seconds it took for the can to rise to one foot off the ground was a battle of wills, but not against one another. It was each man against himself. Every fiber of strength had to be lent to the lifting. The focus could not be disrupted, nor the strength misapplied.

Will wavered in his resolve. *How much higher can I lift this? Just lift. What if these handles give out? Just lift. What if Franklin can't complete the lift? Just lift.* Then, sensing Franklin may be weakened by the same doubts, Will grunted aloud, "Just lift!"

At that moment, something wonderful happened. Whiteman, who had lowered himself by spreading his legs wide and bending at the knees and waist was able to reach down well below the tailgate and catch his fingertips under the top rim of the can. "Just keep lifting," he said, as Will and Franklin felt the load lighten by at least a third.

Now the load rose at the rate Will initially had anticipated, so that a moment later the two on the ground were able to lodge a knee under the bottom of the can. This and pinning it against the tailgate with their bodies enabled them to reposition their hands. Whiteman took the handles, and Will and Franklin dropped their grip to the bottom of the can.

"Ready, halfway now," said Whiteman. "Let's go!" The three snapped at the command and brought the bottom of the can up to the height of Will's waist where they again pinned it against the gate. Will and Franklin exchanged a knowing glance and in unison dipped their knees so they could lift it the rest of the way with their legs and shoulders.

As they slid the bottom of the ash can securely onto the tailgate and then onto the truck itself, the men on the ground breathed a sigh of relief. "Well, we know we can do it," said Will.

"Yeah, but how many times?" Franklin said.

Whiteman glanced at Franklin and smiled.

Will sighed. "I guess as many times as we have to." That would prove to be about thirty times by lunch. They were pleased to find out that three loads of grease per company-sized unit was the exception, not the rule. So the exertion of lifting was interspersed with more travel time. Moreover, the rhythm they developed with increasing experience more than offset the mounting toll of fatigue.

Nonetheless, by lunch, the men were disinclined to eat. "Here's the way it works," said DiMaio. "You don't have to eat if you don't want to, of course. And you still get your half hour. But, see, I get off when the run is done. I don't have to do anything else today. Should be the same for you. So, if you're not gonna eat, I'll just grab some grub in the mess and eat in the cab. I got a date downtown tonight, as soon as I get off."

"Downtown," asked Franklin, "where's that?"

"Bien Hoa, man," DiMaio responded. "Where else?"

"See if you can grab us some apples," Will requested.

"We better refill this water can," Whiteman called after DiMaio.

"I got it under control," DiMaio called back. "I'll stop at the next water trailer."

The men sat quietly at the back of the truck behind the grease cans. After a minute, Will said, "I don't care either way whether we hang out for ten minutes or a full half hour. You guys can decide. But don't think for a minute that if we rush back to the battery we'll have nothing to do. The odds are we'll be filling sandbags till dark."

Franklin and Whiteman looked at one another. "Fuckin' Army," Franklin muttered.

"Why the hell do they have all these sandbags around everything, anyway?" Whiteman asked.

"Mortars," Will answered.

Whiteman nodded his understanding, but in a moment asked, "OK, but why at night? What is this? Why do they have to work us day and night? I mean, I can do it. I'm not saying it's hard. But why? What's wrong with some time off?"

"They want their sandbags," said Will. "What commander wants to swing because his troops were killed without them."

"Like they're really going to save us," Franklin said.

"It's gotta better our odds," said Will. "Besides, it's a part of training. Toughen us up, you know. Instills discipline."

"Fuck discipline," Franklin said. "We'll do what we gotta do when the time comes. Until then, give us a break." Will said nothing more. Neither did Whiteman. So, Franklin continued, "Why can't they give us a break? Don't they realize any of us could be dead at any time. Why won't they let us enjoy the little time we have? Answer me that, Stone."

Will looked to Franklin. *This guy's been hanging out too much with Shard and Swindell.* "You know, Franklin, I don't even know your first name," Will said.

Franklin looked at Will and caught his eye. "Rick," he said after a pause.

"Rick, I'm not the Army. I'm a guy like you and White Man," said Will. "But you ask me why the Army doesn't give you a Last Supper. My guess is they're still bent on keeping you alive, even though you may have given yourself up for dead. And, they figure, the better you carry out orders, the better your chances."

"You guys ready?" DiMaio called, as he approached.

"What'd ya think?" Will asked Franklin.

"I don't know," Franklin answered in a low voice. "Maybe you're right, though there's a lot who'd say you're gung ho."

"We ready to roll?" Will asked, raising his voice.

"Yeah, let's go," Whiteman said.

"What about you, Rick?" Will asked gently.

"Let's rock 'em and roll 'em," Franklin spoke out. "I can use a change of scenery."

"Head 'em up, move 'em out," Will called to DiMaio.

DiMaio pulled the truck forward a block to a water station, where the men filled the water cans. "Better put up that gate," DiMaio called to the back of the truck.

Will and Whiteman complied, while Franklin continued topping off the jerricans. "I still say they're overdoing it," said Franklin. "I don't buy that they're running us this way to train and save us. I think they don't give two shits about us. They just want to be able to say that why they did this was to train us and save us. This whole thing is just a half-ass attempt to cover their own asses."

Whiteman agreed. "They are overdoing things just a little bit. You know, Stone."

"Who?" Will said, looking at Franklin. "I don't even know who or what you're talking about."

"The whole shtick here, man," said Franklin. "The Army, man, from top to bottom."

"You mean our battery officers, too?" questioned Will.

"And the NCOs!" added Franklin.

"We've been in-country only a day-and-a-half," said Will.

"Not just here, but in the States, too, and on that sardine can," Franklin continued. "You saw how we were treated."

Will could not say anything. All he could think of was the contrast between Captain Michaels and the rest of the officers and senior NCOs.

"You guys ready?" DiMaio interrupted.

"Go!" Franklin called out, once he handed the nozzle of the water hose to the station attendant. "Someday, if I'm lucky, my grandkids will ask me what I did in the war."

The truck lurched forward and DiMaio swung it around to backtrack their steps until he came to the main entrance from Provincial Highway 316. Will and Whiteman hung on to the side rails and each propped a foot against the grease cans nearest them. Franklin sat on the jerricans backed up against the tailgate with his legs stretched forward so the soles of his boots held the two center cans of grease from sliding.

"Well, Franklin," said Whiteman, "I guess you could tell your grandkids that you were a hydraulic lift on the back of a garbage truck."

"See, that's what I mean," Franklin said. "OK, maybe we don't have that type of equipment. But you know, you both know goddamned well that there's more than three gun bunnies sitting on their asses right now over in firing battery that could make this detail a helluva lot more tolerable. One of them could be lifting with each of us. Think about it."

Will said nothing. The truck lurched each time DiMaio changed gears. "Breeze feels good now that we're moving," Will said.

"Well, what about it, Stone?" Franklin pressed. "You think it makes any sense to have three men do what six men should?"

"I guess not," said Will, "but I don't say I know how to run an army."

"You don't figure it's good training?" asked Franklin.

"No," Will replied quietly, but his utterance was drowned out by the moving truck. Just the same, his resigned demeanor told the story.

"Not gonna save us, huh?" asked Franklin.

"It's their army," said Will.

"It's our lives they're fuckin' 'round with, and they ain't doin' such a great job," concluded Franklin.

"You married?" Will asked. "I mean, you got kids? Ya know, you mentioned grandkids and all."

"A wife, sort of. No kids," Franklin muttered.

"How old are you, Rick?" Will asked.

"Gonna be twenty soon," Franklin answered.

"White man," Will asked, "how old are you?"

"Just turned nineteen a month or so ago," Whiteman answered. "And you?"

"Pushing twenty-two," Will answered.

"You're an old man, compared to most of us," said Whiteman. "I don't mean the lifers."

"A lot of the guys are still eighteen," said Franklin. "Some enlisted at seventeen so they could get a specialized trade that would keep them outta here, for all the good it did them."

"A lot of 'em are US," Whiteman said.

Will glanced back and forth from one to the other. *Most of these guys are fresh out of high school. Never had a job or been to college. Never been anywhere but their hometowns. I gotta look after these guys if I can and help keep them alive. I shouldn't have asked.*

The truck ground to a halt as DiMaio downshifted on approaching the crossroads at the main entrance. "I'm short!" he screamed out his window to no one in particular.

The men in the back of the truck eyeballed one another and smiled. "How short?" Franklin called back.

"Nine 'n a wake-up," DiMaio's voice trailed off as the truck lurched forward in advance of its left turn to the highway.

"Can't wait till I have only ten days left in this motherfucker," said Franklin.

Whiteman nodded his head. "Wouldn't mind that myself."

Will shook his head a moment. *Too much to hope for. I can't allow my mind to think of such a thing. I'm here forever. I'm here till I die. It's just a question of when, and I suppose it doesn't make much difference.*

The crew pulled out straight across the highway and onto an unimproved trail, recognizable only by the ruts left in the dirt cartway from repeated heavy truck traffic. When they changed directions, Will noted the sky darkening severely to the southwest. "Looks like it's gonna blow," Whiteman said.

Will nodded. "Monsoon season," he said. He was tired of talking. He wanted to survey the country outside the American military compound. An apparent wasteland was not what he had expected.

Ahead were piles of smoldering garbage. Open flames licked around the edges of the piles. As soon as the truck was a short way off the highway, the men's eyes burned from the smog. Now and then oncoming tandem-axle dump trucks passed them, having exited from an area filled with earthen piles intended for use as primary landfill cover. Will peered around the piles to the level shelf beyond to see how deep the garbage was piled before it was covered. By now he had concluded that the road they were riding on was built on landfill all the way back to the highway.

"Hey, ya remember that little speech that captain gave us at the shower this morning?" asked Franklin. "Well, here we are outside the base with no weapons."

"Does DiMaio have a weapon?" Whiteman asked Will.

"He's got a grease gun," said Will, referring to a .45 caliber submachine gun. A hundred feet away in the haze, groups of Viets milled about fresh piles of garbage. As the truck edged closer to the embankment, there were more open flames, in some cases revealing the burning of whole garbage piles dumped below the road grade. Mostly, though, they signaled the combustion of escaping methane gas. Though the smoke became more and more dense, Will could still make out vermin darting in and around the nearest piles.

"We're headed for hell," Will said, as the truck wended down a final grade to where other five-tons were dumping. "I wonder how DiMaio knows where to go. There's no one supervising this, and it seems they keep switching where they dump."

Franklin, who was fashioning a bandanna from his handkerchief as the truck bounced them around said, "Maybe he's made a pact with the devil. Maybe he is the devil."

"Maybe you just know these things when you're ten days short," Whiteman said.

DiMaio swung their truck to the right fifty feet past a garbage truck dumping general food waste. He backed up to the edge of the level shelf. Will and the others looked over the gate at the smoldering fires below. Without fresh fuel to feed them, the open flames typically rose no more than eighteen inches above the base of the existing smoldering piles. The fleeting methane flames rose no more than three inches above the surfaces from which they emerged.

It took Will a moment to recollect where he had seen flames like the fleeting methane before. *They flit around like static lightning, like on the silver ball of one of those generators they used to bring out in high school physics, Van de Graaff generators.*

DiMaio interrupted Will's train of thought. He climbed from the cab along the side of the truck until he was past the grease cans and into the back of the truck bed with the others. His submachine gun was slung on his shoulder. Will looked in the direction of DiMaio's gaze. There were Viet peasants behind the garbage truck to their left, both on the truck's level and on the lower earthen shelf to which it backed up. As peasants foraged for edible scraps, they had to climb the fresh garbage pile to elude the flames around its edges. Their scramble kicked down loose matter that fed the flames that then lapped up at their heels.

Will was dumbstruck as he watched through the surreal ether. Whiteman and Franklin were equally affected. "OK," yelled DiMaio, "let's get this shit outta here. Lower the gate."

Will, Whiteman and Franklin could hardly take their eyes off the other truck. Finally, Will said, "C'mon." He nudged Franklin's elbow and pointed to the far side of the tailgate. Will gestured to Whiteman to get ready with him to slide the cans to the gate. As soon as the gate was set level, Will turned to DiMaio. "Now what?"

"Pour it over," DiMaio ordered, "and make sure you don't splatter the truck."

Will glared at him.

"Unless you want to clean it," DiMaio added.

"What's this for?" Will asked, fingering the shoulder strap of DiMaio's grease gun.

"Maybe you'll see."

Will and Whiteman slid the ash can to within six inches of the edge of the gate. Just as they readied to pour, they realized that they were too close to the edge. They would never be able to handle the weight once they tilted the can out far enough to pour. This second thought spared them from letting the can fall and retrieving it later from the grease and fire.

They slid the can back another twelve inches. When Will nodded, they tilted it quickly so the grease would fall and not run back the underside of the can. The grease splattered down ten feet below the level of the tailgate. The flames roared up three to four feet in places.

Will and Whiteman had to lean into the hot greasy smoke as they lowered the can more on its side to a level position. Even as they strained against the weight of the load, they heard an oncoming commotion. Half the Viets who had clamored at the back of the other truck now approached. The lead one was no more than twenty feet away.

"Jesus Christ," Will said, "they're in bare feet." The Vietnamese flitted their way to beneath Will's truck to avoid contact with the unpredictable flames. Will could not tell if their singsong shouting signified purpose or was a painful response to burnt feet.

Still they stayed there, hopping from one foot to the next and waving for Will and Whiteman to continue pouring. Will nodded to Whiteman and the two dropped the can on the edge of the gate and picked up the bottom of the can to drain the dregs. As globs of grease, mostly the consistency of wallpaper paste, rushed downward, the Viets lunged closer, sticking their cupped hands, or in some cases tin cans, into the onrush to capture what they could.

Suddenly, there were hands right at the flow as it left the ash can. The Viets who had stayed at the road level around the other truck now rushed to Will. For one moment, as Will leaned down holding the can, he looked into the desperate glare of a pre-teen boy. The boy's eyes seared Will's heart.

As soon as the peasants caught some of the grease, they brought their hands to their mouths and ingested it. Will and Whiteman looked at one another across the can and swallowed hard to hold down their own stomachs. At Will's nod, they pulled the empty can back.

"Didi mau, didi mau," DiMaio shouted, waving his grease gun at the nearest peasants up at road level. "Get away from here."

Will tried to catch his breath and slow his pulse. His legs were unsteady. *Maybe from holding that position too long. Maybe from not eating.* The Viets were old people, women and children, just like the coolies at the shower area, except not as prosperous. Yet, unlike the coolies, these Viets looked back at him not with curiosity but with sullen resentment.

"Only twenty-nine more cans to go," said Franklin.

"You keep bringing them forward," Will said.

Whiteman and Will latched onto the next can. They repeated the last procedure, but this time not so far out, so there would be less strain. Again, when they were finished, DiMaio brandished his submachine gun, and yelled, "Didi mau! Didi mau!" His effort was directed mostly at the peasants closest to the truck.

"Only the worst hunger could make this sauce seem hearty," said Will. Suddenly, he had an idea. "Whiteman, where are those apples our friend DiMaio here brought us from the mess hall?"

Whiteman looked to Franklin, who held up a brown paper bag. Will reached into the bag and withdrew his apple. He flipped it straight up in the air once about eighteen inches and caught it with the same hand on its way back down. A bold smile lit up his face.

"Hey," Will shouted to the Vietnamese, once again flipping the apple up in the air and catching it. "Hey!" Will tossed the apple toward a dwarf-like girl on the outskirts of the group.

The girl reached out with both arms, but before the apple reached her, a wily, gray-haired man hopped in front of her to intercept it. A dark-toothed matron caused him to fumble the apple, however, by her own attempt to make the catch. This sent several peasants, young and old, diving and scrambling on the ground for the apple. Every so often, a dash of methane gas would flame beneath them, causing shrieks and cries even louder than the prevailing mayhem. Finally, the pre-teen boy, who earlier had seared Will with his stare, scrambled to his feet and ran away from the group with the apple firmly in hand and mouth.

"Whew!" said Will to Franklin and Whiteman. "Too bad we only have two more."

"Yeah," agreed Whiteman.

"Go ahead," said Franklin, "pitch 'em mine."

"Yeah," said Whiteman, "me, too."

DiMaio nudged Will with his elbow and gestured with his weapon to look to the southwest. It was raining like blazes only five hundred feet away. Will marveled at being able to see the line where on one side it was dry, but on the other teeming rain.

Quickly, he flipped the second apple, this time to the crowd to the left of the truck. Again, a frenzied scramble ensued. Once everyone was rushing to his left, he again signaled to the dwarf-like girl to his right. As she held out her arms, Will underhanded a rainbow pitch right on target to her, but again a few stronger ones, having held back from the scramble to Will's left, lunged for her prize.

Will looked on as half the peasants wrestled on the ground fighting for one apple or the other. Rain splattered his face, but he was no more deterred from the sight than were the peasants from wresting for the prize.

The next thing Will knew tracer bullets were flying by his head. DiMaio had opened fire right between the peasants scrambling on the ground to the left and those standing watching directly behind the truck. Alarm shot through Will. His knees buckled momentarily. *What is it? What's happening? An attack? Snipers? Sappers?*

DiMaio interrupted his fire long enough to wheel his gun barrel to the right and send a burst of tracers past the dwarf-like waif, who remained frozen in place even as those around her fell to the ground. For a moment, she and Will locked gazes and it was as if he, too, was paralyzed by her terror. Then she hopped as a flame singed her bare foot, breaking their eye contact.

Will spun and forced the barrel of DiMaio's gun skyward, just as DiMaio was grunting, "Got him."

The gun barrel burnt the palm of Will's hand, and he let it go as quickly as he had grabbed it. "Don't never do that, you understand?" DiMaio snapped, before quickly resuming his glee. "I got him. Did you see that? I got him."

Will was confused, but the peasants were on their feet shouting and rushing to the garbage pile behind the dwarf-like girl. DiMaio glowed with anticipation. Finally, two men dragged a dead body from behind the garbage pile.

"A warthog," DiMaio announced. "They'll eat good tonight."

Will exchanged solemn stares with Franklin and Whiteman, before looking DiMaio up and down. *Is this what we are to become?* DiMaio let himself off the side of the truck and continued down the slope to the shelf below. He rushed in and among the peasants to attend his victim. The peasants made way for him.

"What's a warthog?" Franklin asked.

"Type of wild pig," Whiteman answered. "Thought they were only in Africa."

"Probably are," said Will.

DiMaio knelt over the critter. He set his machine gun down next to it and drew his hunting knife. Taking no precautions for his own safety, he threw himself into butchering the pig.

"How does he know who he can go among and who he can't?" Whiteman asked.

"Probably doesn't," said Will.

"Rick, why don't you slip down there and see if you can't take charge of that grease gun before someone besides DiMaio does?" Will said. "White Man and I will keep off-loading this slop."

"Deal," Franklin said.

○

By 4:00 p.m., having not just emptied this load but repeated the whole process once, Will, Franklin and Whiteman trekked back to How Battery with new resignation. Wet with repeated dousings of rain and saturated with sweat, their clinging fatigues resisted every step. The residue of grease slop caked mostly on their trousers gave off an unseemly perfume. They could tolerate one another only because they could not escape themselves.

"Wonder what they'll have in store for us when we get back?" Franklin wondered aloud, after a long silence. Without breaking stride, Will and Whiteman looked first at one another and then to Franklin, who returned their gaze with equal resolve. He nodded and finally uttered, "Guess it doesn't make any difference."

In a bit Franklin said, "Wonder what we'll have to eat."

Will and Whiteman again swapped glances before turning to Franklin, who nodded and said, "Whatever it is, I guess it'll be a whole lot better than these folks'll have."

The three paused at the edge of the battery area. "Here we go," said Whiteman.

Will was content to let the others step ahead of him. As soon as they reached the battery street, Montana and Lamont shouted, competing for their attention.

"Over here, over here, you dummies," Montana called. "You guys gotta fill sandbags, too. What'd ya think you're better 'n us, or something?"

The three returnees grinned and headed toward the waiting shovels.

Things Not To Write Home

"Mail Call!" Horton called out.

Will resisted showing interest. *I don't give a shit about mail. It's from a different world, a world I'll never see again, a world with no place for me. So what am I doing here with these saps? Look at Martino offering up his best imitation of prayer, like that'll get him a letter. Look at Franklin, sick over whether his new wife has quit her vows. Look at these other guys writing replies to letters they've yet to receive.*

"O'Rourke!" Horton called out, waving the first of some forty air mail envelopes. "Deddson!"

Look at Deddson. At least he's got some dignity. He folds up his letter and tucks it away to be read in privacy, not like some of these guys who tear open the envelopes as if their lives depended on the contents. Some do it right in front of your face, even though they know half of us will go away empty-handed, empty-hearted. What do I care if I get a letter? Shit, it's one less to answer if I don't, one less complaint to put up with, one less duty to discharge. Someone might send word of Josh, though.

What am I gonna say to them, anyway? Would I tell them I was stirring shit from 7:30 a.m. to just before dinner at 5:00 p.m.? Tell them that beneath our latrine seats are fifty-five gallon drums cut off to a third height, and that every day one of us has to clean 'em out and burn the shit up? Do I write how hard it is to get the shit to catch fire when it's covered with piss, no matter how much diesel fuel you flood it with? Or that we always have to start it burning with paper or wood and that sometimes we gotta float some gasoline on top? Or how about the smell when the shit burns and how we've got to stir it so the diesel doesn't just burn off the top? Do they really want to know about that or what it does to a guy who has to do it every day? Would they want to know I was assigned this detail for pissing in the breeze? Will's mind raced back several weeks to his first few days in-country.

In and outside the latrine, nearly fifty soldiers with serious bladder pressure lined up. They had been kept overtime in a cultural awareness class. Most shifted their weight from one leg to the other, nudging guys in front of them and calling out for those ahead to speed it up. If the two funnels were in use when they made it inside, they scarcely missed a beat marching to the plywood deck where two rows of four toilet seats backed up to one another. As soon as one guy lifted a seat, others rushed to double up at the holes. Once inside the latrine, guys unable to wait dispensed with even attempting to hit a hole. The plywood deck and floor soaked up urine like a sponge. The only order was down the far end, where some cook with the runs from his Monday anti-malarial pill closed the toilet seat next to him and swung out at anyone attempting to get near him.

No sooner did Will glimpse what was going on inside the latrine building than he made off for one of the few clumps of trees left in the MACV headquarters, which happened to be in the battery area. Relief had never felt so fine—until he heard the unmistakable boom of Corporal Woodman's voice.

"Pissin' in the breeze, uh? Yuh pissin' in the breeze, Stone? Well, now I got yo ass but good."

Will concentrated on finishing his business without response.

"You hear me?" Woodman yelled.

"I hear ya, I hear ya," Will answered. "I'm just finishing up here. Be right with you."

"Don't yuh give me none of yo smart ass, white college boy lip," Woodman ordered. "Yuh come with me an' see Sergeant Grovel up in the orderly room."

Will fell in step alongside Woodman, who stood six foot three and weighed 220 pounds, all of it muscle. *The guy looks like a Greek god, except he's pitch black. He was ahead of me in the line for the latrine. He knows what this was about. He didn't have to see me. I don't know why, but he's got it in for me.*

"What yuh got here, uh?" yelled Corporal Grouse, coming out of his tent as Woodman marched Will up the battery street.

"Pissin' in the breeze," Woodman called back with a smile.

"Well, good, yuh fix his smart ass, yuh hear," said Grouse, who looked like a replica of Woodman, only scaled down to normal size. "Ahm sick of his highfalutin talk."

So would I write home that that's how I caught latrine detail? But not before Sergeant Grovel made an example of me. Grovel liked that he could get his thumb on me, but he also sensed the situation was a colored/white thing, and, being a Southerner, he didn't like that.

The first sergeant was somewhere else, so Sergeant First Class Grovel was in charge. Before Woodman arrived with Will, news of what was going on at the latrine had reached the headquarters tent, and Sergeant First Class Grovel had been stewing about what to do about it. After hearing from Woodman and Will, he called for a battery-wide formation in front of the latrine. It was about 2:30 p.m., and most of the men had yet to eat lunch due to the culture class.

Do I write them about how Grovel stood me up in front of the formation, and said I been pissing all over the place? Do they really want to know that he had Woodman march the entire formation single file through the latrine? Or that Grovel dismissed all the others for lunch and, when he had me alone, told me it was my job to figure out how to clean up the shitter then and there, but I'd have regular latrine detail the next day, too? What kind of a letter would that make?

"O'Rourke!"

Horton's voice brought Will back to the moment. *O'Rourke got another letter. Good for him.*

"Jenkins," Horton called out, "and Layton."

Layton. How about that? That afternoon at the latrine, Layton had bailed out Will. Seeking a way to transport water to the latrine, Will found himself by the stream where Layton was flirting with one of the young Viet girls. The Viets squatted in the muddy red waters and beat GI uniforms with smooth rocks against the sandy bottom of one sudsy pool after another. A woman at the last pool passed them along to women on the other bank for dipping and rinsing. From the first, Layton had gotten buddy-buddy with Binh, the interpreter. The object of Layton's attention in the stream was Binh's sister.

When he noticed Will's approach, Layton laughed and pointed to a long row of two-and-a-half-gallon, galvanized pails lining the near side of the stream. "Socks," he called aloud. "They stink so bad you just gotta soak them. They got one pail for each laundry bag they're working on. That way, they can keep them straight."

"What are you doing here?" Will asked. "You on detail?"

"Nah, I just got lost here," Layton responded, before signaling to his left. "I wanted to hang around with Bai. Bai, come here."

A young peasant girl approached, her eyes cast downward until Layton reached out, lifted her chin and said, "Bai, this Stone, and vice versa. He's my friend, Bai."

Before long, Layton had twenty coolies toting water in the sock buckets to the latrine. It took them several trips.

"Thanks, Layton," Will said.

"Thank them," Layton replied, nodding his head toward the coolies. They smiled, enough to reveal the telltale betel-nut stains on their teeth, and bowed.

"Martini!" Horton called out. "Martini!"

"I'm here. I'm coming," called back the diminutive immigrant.

"Shard!" Horton yelled. "Shard!"

"He's back at our tent," Swindell said. "I'll take it for him."

Will watched Swindell saunter up for the letter, as if he had not a care in the world. Will knew, though, that the nineteen-year-old college dropout cared very much about staying in this world of which he had seen so little.

Wonder what he and Shark tell the folks back home when they write. Surely, not about our first trip to Bien Hoa.

O

It was Will's first trip to Bien Hoa, although Campbell, Shard and Swindell had sneaked into the town their first night in-country. Some ten days later, however, the four of them were surprised to receive four-hour passes. Since Campbell, Shard and Swindell headed for Bien Hoa, Will tagged along.

By this time, their unit had been issued M-16's with seven magazines of live ammunition. They carried the rifles everywhere they went in the base camp, just as the captain at the shower hooch on the other side of I Troop had said that first morning. In a few days it had seemed normal to see naked men headed for the shower with rifles slung from their shoulders. So when they got to the gate to Provincial Highway 316 that night, the sentry took them by surprise when he said, "If you're going to Bien Hoa, no rifles, no weapons."

"Why?" Will asked.

"Too much fighting among friendlies. It was getting too bloody with everyone armed to the teeth. The MP's will arrest your ass if they catch you with a weapon."

"You're kidding us," Will said. "What about the VC?"

"It's pretty safe this close to Saigon," the guard answered.

"How do we get to Bien Hoa?" Will asked.

"You can go outside the gate and catch a lorry, these little trucks or jitney buses the gooks run back and forth in," the sentry responded, "or you can wait here for one of our vehicles headed that way."

"Let's take the lorry," said Shard. "You know, make sure we get out of here."

"You're forgetting something, Shark," Will said. "What about our weapons?"

"Shit," Shard responded.

"Can we leave our weapons with you?" Swindell asked the sentry.

"Can't do that," he answered. "You're supposed to check them with your company armorer."

"Do we have an armorer in the battery?" Shard asked Swindell.

"I gotta take care of this deuce-and-a-half coming in," the guard said, moving toward the other side of the five-by-five guard post.

"I'm on my way to Bien Hoa," shouted the driver, "but I'm leaving the truck here for the night. I'll park it in the lot over there." He pointed straight ahead. "Just got laundry and a few gooks."

The sentry nodded as the driver revved the engine, engaged it in low, and pulled ahead past the four-way intersection into the parking area to the right.

"Let's go," Campbell said. Nudging Swindell and Shard, he nodded in the direction of the truck coming to a halt. Will strode after them.

"What do you want to go to town for?" the driver asked Campbell.

"Pussy," Shard spat back.

"Shit, no need to go all the way to Bien Hoa just for pussy, gents," said the driver. "We got some fine poon right here." Hopping to the ground, the driver made his way to the back of the truck. "Mama-san, Mama-san," he called out.

The faces of several older women appeared above the tailgate. A woman, in her early twenties, emerged from behind them. "Mama-san, GI's here want short time," the driver said. "How much for short time?"

The oldest woman glanced back at the youngest, who retreated nervously behind her, and responded, "For you, short time seven hundred P," the older one said.

The driver turned to Campbell. "Seven hundred piastres is a very good price. You'll never do as well in town."

"Where?" Campbell asked.

"Right in the back of the truck. It's all laundry bags back there. If you're in, pony up."

"Will you show us the way into Bien Hoa afterwards?" Swindell asked.

"Sure, no problem, man," said the driver.

"OK, I'll do it," said Swindell.

"Whoa, no you don't," Campbell said. "I go first. I'm standing here with my money out."

"Well, I'm next," Swindell said.

"Then me," said Shard, flashing his money as Campbell climbed over the top of the gate.

"What about you?" the driver asked Will.

"No thanks," Will answered.

"Why not?" questioned Shard.

"Not my style." Will said.

"What do you mean?" Shard asked.

"If we were back home," Will answered, "we would have no trouble agreeing that the lady must say *Yes*, that she can't be forced. Here, I figure, she has little choice. Her circumstances are such that she's forced to do it. I'm not going to exploit her."

"You're full of shit, Stone," Swindell said. "If she didn't need the money, maybe she wouldn't do it, I agree. But she decided—not us—that she'd rather have the money, and you would take that choice away from her."

"She gets to choose about her, and I get to choose about me," Will said.

"Stone, we could get wasted anytime. It'd be a shame to go without having tasted life's sweet wine."

"Life's sweet wine?" Will shrugged his shoulders.

"He's hopeless," Swindell said to Shard.

"What about our rifles?" Will asked the driver. "What can we do with them when we go into Bien Hoa?"

"Hide them under the laundry bags in the back of the truck."

"Sure they'll be safe?" Will asked.

"We do it all the time," said the driver.

"Are there weapons back there right now?" Will asked.

"Yeah."

"With the Viet women back there?" asked Will. "How do we know they're not VC?"

"We know."

"It can't get any deeper," Will said, "than the shit we'll be in if we lose these weapons."

"They'll be OK." The driver laughed.

"Let's pitch them up to Campbell," Swindell said.

Will shook his head. "I don't know," he said.

"Campbell," Swindell yelled.

Campbell's muffled voice sounded from the back of the truck. "I'm busy, not now," he said.

"Take the rifles, Campbell," Swindell said.

"Goddamn you guys. I'm trying to crack off a piece."

"I'm next," Swindell said, clambering up the tailgate. "Pass me up the rifles, soon as I make it."

Will checked his safety and backed out his magazine to make sure the chamber was empty. He toyed with the idea of keeping the magazine but finally snapped it back into the M-16. Then he passed it, stock first, to Swindell's outstretched hand.

"Some nasty stuff going on up here, man," Swindell said. "Big time." Will and Shard glanced at one another. Shard started the climb up the tailgate, and Will moved in front of the truck to wait. *Don't suppose what's going on back there is right, but it's not so wrong that I should interfere.*

The Brothel

The truck driver kept his promise to get the four safely to Bien Hoa, and then bugged out. None of the signs on the shops or billboards were in English, although a few were in French. The commercial district was first and foremost for the Viets. Still, GI's were everywhere amid the rattle and clatter of the street traffic. They walked among throngs of pedestrians and loiterers. It was a free-for-all in which pedicabs, scooters and rickshaws fended for themselves, nudging their way through foot traffic by sounding their horns. Everywhere were signs and lights for the barrooms and sidewalk cafes that lined both sides of the street. Viet women and GI's hung out second- and third-story windows and balconies. MP's were strategically stationed throughout.

The four troopers fought their way through the thick crowd as street merchants accosted them to hawk watches, jewelry, cameras, and electronic gadgetry. A lot of the merchandise looked like it was right off the shelf at the PX. Five or six pre-teen street urchins tugged on Will's left arm. "GI, you want short time?" they yelled. "Hey, GI, you want short time? C'mon, uh, this way. Maybe you want long time. You want short time?"

"Christ, I just about ripped my arm out of its socket pulling my wrist loose from those little peckers," Will called after the others. *A lot of good these guys did me. Where the hell did they go? There's Shark. Better beat it after them.*

"Where you headed, Campbell?" Will called, once he closed the distance between them.

"Whorehouse," Campbell shouted back. "This guy'll show us the best whorehouse in town. He's an ARVN soldier, so he's supposed to be OK."

Will hustled to catch up. *Voracious appetite, these guys, but what else are we going to do? Might as well check out the scene, at least.*

The front door led them through the masonry facade on a wood-frame, three-story building. Inside was a tiny lobby with a stairway. At the top of the stairs, flimsy partitions separated small chambers on either side of a narrow, dimly lit hallway. After a word with the dragon lady, the ARVN soldier slipped away. She waved each of the four through a different, beaded-cord doorway.

"The ARVN was right," Shard said to Swindell. "No waiting lines."

"Let's do it," Swindell said.

"Duty calls." Campbell laughed. "What about you, Stone?"

"I got a headache," Will said and curtsied.

Campbell cast a hasty glance up and down the hall. "Then keep a lookout for us, huh, Stone?"

Will watched them disappear into the chambers until the dragon lady nudged him toward one. The candle-lit room piqued Will's curiosity. *It's bigger than most people's bathrooms back home, but the walls are like paper. I can see the glow of the candle in the room next door.*

Suddenly Will realized his would-be consort already lay on her side on a small cot built into the back wall of the chamber. She beckoned him with a finger. Will stepped backward and waved her off. She slid her red sequined skirt up her thigh, high enough to reveal a black garter at the top of her dark stockings. The garter matched her long, straight hair. She smiled—her bright white teeth glistening in the flickering light, her almond-shaped eyes sparkling with anticipation. She thumbed her chest and said, "Mi Jayn."

Me Tarzan, Will thought, but he held his tongue.

She popped out her chewing gum and stuck it to the bottom of the bed rail. *She's beautiful, but she's no older than Jenny. Jenny'd be seventeen.* Will lifted his hands in protest. She sprang to her feet and flung her arms around his neck. Will squirmed, gave in to her embrace for a moment, and then pulled her arms off him. She let out a high-pitched wail.

Edging backwards, Will bumped first into the door arch and then into the mama-san, the dragon lady. He peeled off a thousand piastres and passed it to Mi Jayn, as he turned to get by the dragon lady. The payment seemed to ease Mi Jayn's pain and embarrassment.

"OK? OK?" the dragon lady demanded of each of them.

Will nodded and answered, "OK, OK."

Mi Jayn sighed. "OK," she said. The dragon lady nodded and withdrew through the beaded-cord doorway. Mi Jayn looked to Will and said, "No OK." Once again, she beckoned him.

Will kissed two fingers and placed them on her forehead, shaking his head in disbelief. As he backed to the doorway, he smiled and bowed his head. He continued through the beaded cords backwards, unable to see for sure but flattering himself into thinking that maybe she wiped a tear from one eye. Mi Jayn fingered the thousand piastres.

As Will backed into the narrow hall, a middle-aged Viet man ran toward him. "Go, go, GI, go now. Here now come." The Viet man held up his palms so Will could see he had no weapon. "MP come now. Must go. MP come."

So what? Will thought. *I didn't do anything so bad.*

The dragon lady reappeared. "Back here, you hibe back here, come," she said in husky tones. "You orp limit here. MP put you in stockade. Then you no come back here. You come now."

"Hey, you guys," Will called to the others. "We're off-limits."

"Yeah, we know," said Campbell.

"The MP's are coming," Will told them.

The three of them responded in unison. "Oh, shit!"

Campbell was the first to appear. He held his field trousers and boots in one hand. "Who's the gook?" he demanded.

"Our best hope," Will answered, as the others appeared, pulling up their pants and running in unlaced boots at the same time. "Let's make tracks."

The Viet man realized they were ready to move and led them up a dark staircase and out a doorway. There was enough moonlight for them to tell they were outside on a third-story fire escape in a narrow alley. "Shh," the Viet directed.

Candles lit some of the windows of an adjacent building, but most were dark. Tonal Oriental music came from a lower-level flat. It was the only sound until someone emptied a pail of waste water from a window. There was a groan from below, most likely from someone who'd been splattered, someone else waiting in the alley till the MP's left.

A match struck and a cigarette glowed in the dark. *What an easy target that makes. What an easy target we'd all make if the VC sprayed the alley with automatic weapons from the rooftop.*

"Wonder if the MP's will come back here?" whispered Shard.

"Wonder how long we'll be stuck here waiting for them," Swindell said.

"We should be looking for a lorry back pretty soon," said Campbell. "What time is it, Stone?"

Will raised his wrist closer to his face to read the luminescent dial, but there was no glow. He slid his right hand across his left wrist. "Shit," he answered. "My watch is gone." He remembered the street urchins.

"The slicky boys," Campbell said.

"My grandfather gave it to me."

"We better be out of here pretty soon."

"Yeah," Will grumbled, as he rubbed his wrist.

Gotta Have a Code

Will glanced at Horton, who was still passing out mail. *I guess the other guys are no more apt to write home about this stuff than I am. Let's see, how would it go? 'Dear Gramps, I lost the watch you gave me on my way to a whorehouse.' What would I tell them? About filling all these sandbags? Don't want them to think I'm bitching.*

I could tell them how I went to squadron personnel yesterday to see if I could get a military intelligence assignment, to see if they needed my French or if they wanted to switch me to a line troop. I dealt with the same guys at squadron that I did when I put in with the Cav. They reminded me they made me a standing offer to reassign me to Personnel. They remembered I was a battalion clerk in the States. These were US's, like me, and they supposedly could get their officers to sign off on the necessary paperwork. Guess Mom and Harry wouldn't be too happy to know I turned them down. Sounds good—sitting in an air-conditioned trailer with the big brass. But it's one thing to switch to something more dangerous like a line troop, and another to transfer to something safe like squadron headquarters. That'd be running out on these other guys. If one of them got knocked off, I'd always wonder if it should have been me.

"Stone!" Horton called out.

Will jumped to his feet and looked around for the most certain route front and center through the crowd of anxious soldiers.

"Thanks," Will said, as he slipped his finger under the flap to peel open the envelope. It was from Jenny.

"Stone!" Horton said again.

Quickly Will tucked Jenny's envelope in his right chest pocket and reached for the next. *From Harry and Margaret,* he concluded, tucking it away, too. Someone grabbed his leg below the knee.

"Hey, Stone," Jenkins said.

"Hey, Jenkins," Will responded. Grouse and Woodman were seated next to Jenkins.

"We're gonna come see you later," Grouse said.

Will ignored him, looked at Jenkins and tapped his pocket. "Gotta go read these."

"Yeah, me too," Jenkins said.

On the way back to his billet, Will noticed Franklin sitting alone on a sandbag and dragging on a cigarette. A letter was on the ground in front of him. He was tracing an outline in the dust with his pointing finger.

Will headed over and grabbed a sandbag from a nearby pile. He dropped it off his shoulder next to Franklin. A dust cloud emerged on impact. "Mind if I join you?" Will asked.

"Ah, fuck it," Franklin responded before waving his arm and hand in hospitality across the waiting sandbag.

"Who'd you hear from?" Will asked.

"My mom."

"That's good. Nothing like a mother, I guess."

"So it seems," said Franklin. "Old Mom says she hasn't heard from my wife in two weeks. Neither have I."

"Well, this is the first mail I've received," Will said. "I guess it's having trouble catching up to us. Your mom's pretty good, is she?"

"Yeah, she's OK."

"That's good," said Will. "We all have something to be thankful for."

"She's a lawyer," Franklin said. "Went to law school before she got married to my pop, but then she had my brother and me, so she stayed home to raise us."

"So she never practiced?" Will asked.

"Just in the last couple of years after my father died, now that us kids are out of the house."

"What'd your father do?" asked Will.

"Worked in one of the steel mills," Franklin answered. "I guess I take after him 'cause I sure don't have her brains. Wish I did. Yep. Wish I did."

"I bet she's right proud of you."

"Could be," Franklin answered, "but it don't figure my wife is. She goes to the local college. Lot a ruckus going on there, I hear, about this war and all. Some making us out to be the bad guys."

"I can't say I got much of this stuff figured out myself," Will said. "I got more questions than answers. That's what Campbell says, anyway."

"Campbell, yeah, I guess he's got brains," Franklin responded. "But does he use them?"

"Meaning?"

"You know what I mean," Franklin answered. "He knows a lot of stuff and all, but it's like separate from his life. He doesn't make it a part of his life. He's a lot better at picking at other people's faults than his own. On the other hand, Stone, some would say you think too much, but I'd say you're coming into your own. You think and you act, but you always think first. I've watched you, Will. I'm trying to learn from you because I respect you. Maybe it took me and the rest of the guys a while to warm up to you because you're different, but you're different in a good way. You're square. I mean like fair. You don't ask for any quarter and you don't give any. It's a good way to be. Everything's so fucked up here that it's good to see someone trying to live right. I feel better just watching you. And it isn't just you, it's Deddson, too, and O'Rourke and there's others."

"The hard part is knowing what's right to do," said Will.

"Maybe, but at least you're looking for it," Franklin said. "But who are you kidding? It ain't so easy to live it, even once you see it. You pay a price."

"What do you say we head back to the tent?" Will asked.

"Yeah, I reckon."

"Mrs. Franklin has every reason to be proud," Will said as they got to their feet.

"Maybe," Franklin answered. "I am trying harder now, and I feel better about myself. I spent too much time listening to Campbell and trying to be like Shard and Swindell."

"You gotta live with yourself," Will said. "That means you gotta like yourself, and if someone else does, too, that's great. If they don't, that's too bad. But when you like yourself, your needs change. You're sort of self-sustaining. You don't need someone else's approval so much. And when you enjoy someone else's company, it's based on respect for one another."

"My wife seems short on that for me."

"Maybe she doesn't know you the way you are tonight," Will replied. "How well do you know her?"

"She's got a great bod," Franklin said. "Quite a catch for an ugly dude like me."

"You gotta like yourself," Will said. "Once you like yourself, then the rest falls in place. Some things work and some don't, but those that don't somehow aren't so important so long as your self-respect is intact."

"What does that mean in terms of my wife?"

"It's not for me to say," said Will.

"Will, I could use a hand," Franklin said. "This is coming down pretty hard on me. This once spell it out for me, huh?"

Will blew out a long, deep breath. "If you do like yourself, but she doesn't, then you don't like the same things. So what kind of relationship would that be?"

"Well, OK," Franklin said. "I guess there's something to that, but what about opposites attracting?"

"You gotta respect the same things."

"So if I like me, why wouldn't she?" Franklin asked.

"People are different, my friend," Will replied. "You know that. We all follow all sorts of false trails looking for the right path. The point is—"

"The point is that if I'm satisfied with me, she should be, too, or she's not all she's cracked up to be," Franklin interrupted. "So maybe it's not such a great loss."

"Keeping all that within proper limits," Will said, "I'd say that's pretty good, Rick. I'd say you got a good handle on the thing now."

"I feel a lot better about the whole thing now," Franklin said. "If I can just hang on to it and keep it straight in my mind. You married, Will? How come you can tell me so much about all this? "

"I've looked into my heart."

Smash-Mouth Football

Will fully reclined on his bunk before pulling the two letters from his chest pocket. He examined the envelopes. *Making us out to be the bad guys?*

A familiar voice broke in from the far end of the tent. "All right, you guys. Who's playing football?"

Dressed only in athletic shorts and combat boots, Corporal Woodman stood at the entrance, flexing his muscles as he flipped a football from hand to hand. Grouse squeezed his way far enough in to see past Woodman. Jenkins and Royce, the head of the mess section, also entered. It had the look of a challenge from the blacks of Firing Battery to Headquarters Platoon, which was lily white, except for Camper.

Montana sprang to his feet. He was properly cautious of the towering Woodman. By the same token, he considered himself the de facto leader of Headquarters Platoon.

As he approached Woodman, Montana held out his hands for the ball. Woodman backed away from his path and flipped it to him. Woodman was farsighted enough to anticipate Montana being promoted to Staff Sergeant E6 at any time, which would clearly outrank him, even if he, too, were promoted to Sergeant at the same time. In that case, it would not pay to have Montana as an enemy.

"Who's playing football?" Montana shouted. "What about you, Martini?"

Martini, fresh from a shower, in only his underpants, froze when Montana singled him out. His back was toward Montana as he knelt over his footlocker and craned his neck halfway around to answer. "I gotta write letters. I just got my mail."

"You talking tackle or touch?" Franklin called out.

Montana turned inquiringly to Woodman.

"Tackle," Woodman boomed.

A groan permeated the platoon tent, followed by a chorus of catcalls. "Screw that." "Fuck it." "Up yours."

Montana began to anger. "What about you, O'Rourke?" he called.

"Wha' was Firing Battery doing while we were filling sandbags all day, huh?" O'Rourke responded. "How come they got so much energy now?"

"Franklin?" Montana asked.

"I don't need a beating," Franklin responded.

Will looked on from the far end of the tent. He was now seated upright on his bunk, lacing up his boots. *Wouldn't do for these colored guys to think all us whites are too afraid to mix it up with them. I don't blame anyone for not wanting to get into it. I don't either, but somebody better.*

Woodman's gaze scoured the tent from front to back, until it fixed on Will. Grouse focused on Will, too, and nudged Woodman with his elbow. "I'll play," Will said.

"I'm glad to see somebody in this platoon's got some balls," said Montana. "Who else'll play besides Stone and me?" No one answered. "Nobody? Might've figured. Let's go, Stone."

Woodman grinned as Will arose. "How come you're playing?" asked Whiteman from the next bunk.

"For love of the game," said Will.

On his way to the playing field, Will consoled himself that at least the sides could not be Headquarters Platoon versus Firing Battery. Also, he took comfort when he saw two or three white members of Firing Battery had been waiting outside the Headquarters tent for them to come out. *So it's not such a racial thing. It could be, though, that this is somehow directed at me.*

Will lagged back until he was next to Jenkins. "What did you mean at mail call that you guys would be coming to see me?" Will asked.

"Here we are," answered Jenkins.

"Yeah, but why?" Will persisted.

"Football? I don't know." Jenkins resumed. "Gotta do something, don't we?"

"We never played football before. Whose idea was this, Jenkins?"

"Grouse's, I guess," Jenkins answered. "Something Grouse cooked up with Woodman."

By the time the sides were picked, the coin tossed, and positions assigned, the only thing important to Will was that Woodman and Grouse were both on the opposing team. *Guess if I were fielding the team, given my size and speed, I might have put myself someplace other than the line. Well, here we go.*

Grouse took the first snap in a shotgun formation and pitched out to Woodman in motion to his right. Will braced for Woodman's charging mass of muscle and bone. Instinct and training as a high school wrestler enabled Will to slip under Woodman's onrushing elbows and set his right shoulder against Woodman's driving thigh. Will felt a dull thud, but no sharp pain. The impact slowed Woodman momentarily, allowing Will to reach across the big guy's waist and grab his hip while swinging out of his way to the opposite side. The corporal's next thrust yanked Will onto the back of his legs, enabling Will to hook his right leg around Woodman's ankles, crashing the big guy, face forward, to the ground.

Woodman bounced up kicking and swinging his elbows, but Will already had rolled clear of him. As Woodman returned to the huddle, he glared at Will. So did Grouse. Will thought, *What did I ever do to these guys?*

The next play was a repeat of the last. Again Woodman bore down on Will, this time making a point of charging knees high. But high-kicking forced Woodman more upright, making him less balanced.

Again, Will stood his ground, but at the last moment he sidestepped Woodman and clothes-lined his neck. Immediately, Will let his weight go dead like an anchor and Woodman's legs ran out from under his torso. Flat on his back, Woodman flung Will's arm off his neck and sat up. He pointed to Will and said, "Watch it." Again, Grouse glared at Will.

On the next play Grouse faked the pitchout and passed incompletely. Just the same, Woodman kept coming for Will. When Will saw Woodman did not have the ball, he stepped aside to give Woodman the running lane. But Woodman quickly adjusted course to head for Will. Without the ball, Woodman bore down on Will with arms outstretched to prevent his escape. With no place to go and about to be run over, Will relied on the age-old wrestler's trick featured in old cowboy movies. At the moment of impact, Will rolled backwards as he grabbed Woodman's arms and lifted his foot to Woodman's stomach to propel the big guy on and over him during the roll. Woodman's own momentum sent him flying.

Confused, Will sat up. He brushed red clay from his face and hair. A hand reached down to help him and he grasped for it. A strong arm pulled him up. On the way up, Will saw a fuzzy black face with giant white teeth on the other end of the arm. Once upright, Will realized it was Woodman, smiling, then clapping him on the back, then hugging him around the shoulder.

"You all right?" Woodman asked.

"Yeah," Will said weakly. He watched the corporal retreat once more to his huddle.

The next play was the opposite of the first two. Woodman took Grouse's pitchout, only this time charging to his left and bursting through for a touchdown. "Now that's better," Woodman called out. "I'm not messing with this boy any mo'," he continued, as he pointed at Will. "He plays too rough. As for you," Woodman said, turning to Grouse, "fight your own wars."

Will looked down at the red dust powdering his body. *Just fucking lucky.*

Nightfall hastened the end of the game. "We'll have to do this every night," several members of Firing Battery agreed, while limping back to the battery area.

Will did his best not to limp. *Every night? I'll have to check my dance card. Nope, they have me down for sandbags the rest of the week. Sorry 'bout that.*

What's a Brother

By the time they reached the battery area, the limping athletes had fallen quiet. Suddenly Royce yelled, "What's that? Something's going on behind Headquarters Platoon's tent. Lotta brothers there. Better check it out, man."

On their way, they intercepted Horton, who was sneaking to battery headquarters. "What's happening, brother?" Grouse demanded, fingering the front of Horton's collar.

"Trouble, man," Horton whispered, glancing around. "I'm headed for Top."

Woodman had been stretching his neck to see what the commotion was, but now he also turned to Horton. "Hold up there, little man," Woodman directed. "This looks like something we brothers should be handling ourselves."

"The first sergeant would—" Horton protested, before Woodman knelt in front of the diminutive clerk and gently interrupted.

"What exactly happened?" Woodman asked. "Do you know, Horton?"

"Bandle was mouthing off before," Horton said. He tried to whisper, but his naturally hoarse voice excitedly jumped a couple of octaves until he seemed to plead with Woodman to accept his account and let him go on with his duties. "Bandle definitely had too much to drink, turned nasty, and called one of the brothers a *nigger*."

"The magic word!" Royce said, brandishing the hunting knife that he sheathed on his rifle sling.

"The *N*-word," Jenkins said as he glanced to Woodman and Grouse and Will, too. "We can handle this, Horton," he continued. "Let's get over there."

Behind Headquarters Platoon's tent was a group of some twenty soldiers. Eight or nine, banded together on one side, were black. An equal number on the other side were white, with more whites looking on from the end of the tent. In the middle stood O'Rourke with his burly arms widespread to keep Bandle and Hampton from mixing it up. O'Rourke was red in the face with excitement.

Hampton, a light-skinned black from Philadelphia, was in his early twenties. He stood a full six feet and gave the impression of being overweight, although he was not. He just carried closer to his waist more of the bulk that would normally be found around the shoulders of a gun bunny who had been humping 155mm ammunition for the past two years. Those who knew him regarded him as someone to be reckoned with. "You better clean up your mouth before I do it for you," Hampton said to Bandle.

At one hundred seventy pounds, Bandle was no slouch for a nineteen-year-old, but he would be no match for Hampton in the best of circumstances. Now too much beer would affect his balance and reactions, just as it already had his judgment. A full-blooded Cherokee, he was defensive about his ancestry. "Fuck you," Bandle responded, "I ain't taking nothing back."

"Fer crissake, will yer just shut up, Bandle," O'Rourke said, before turning to Hampton. "Fer crissake, man, yer can see he's drunk as a skunk. Why can yer not just walk away from it?"

"No way, man," someone from the black contingent yelled out.

"Make him eat his own shit, Hampton," called another.

"We're not taking this shit anymore," cried out a third.

The returnees from the football game swelled the black ranks in numbers and enthusiasm. The white soldiers stood by sullenly, reinforced only by Montana and Will, who stood apart from them. They took Bandle for one of their own and felt they could not abandon him, but they resented his putting them in this position. Their misgivings increased as they watched the black ranks swell. One white soldier fidgeted with a pocket knife.

Montana elbowed Will and nodded for him to follow. With Will on his heels, Montana strode to O'Rourke's side. "Should have come to play ball with us, O'Rourke," Montana said under his breath. "It would have been more restful. You were going to get some rest, as I remember."

"All right, everybody," Montana suddenly called out, throwing both hands open over his head and turning slowly in a three-quarter circle, like a boxer at center ring. The crowd hushed and he continued. "All right, it's over. Private First Class Bandle was wrong, he knows it, and he's just apologized. Isn't that right, Bandle?"

"Bull—" Bandle started to shout, before Montana's right fist cut off the final syllable. Bandle fell backward but was caught by the group behind him. Blood gushed from his nose. Montana rushed over him, poised on his toes, his eyes bulging, his left arm cocked ready to unleash a hook. Will stepped past him, extending a handkerchief toward Bandle's face.

"Fuck you, Stone," Bandle cried and batted away Will's offer. "You hate me 'cause I'm Indian. I hate your guts, too."

"Get him outta here!" Montana yelled. "Get him into the tent, god-dammit." Three men from the white contingent dragged him back into the tent, as Bandle continued to yell.

Will called after him, "Bandle, hey, you're here, I'm here, we're all the same, we're all here, we're all brothers."

Montana turned toward the black contingent to take its pulse. "Brothers-in-arms, at least," he said. "We're all soldiers. We just did *our* duty and cleaned up *our* own mess. Now it's time we all go about minding our own business. What do you say, Royce?"

Suddenly Royce perked up at the chance offered him by his fellow Specialist Fifth Class to assert some authority. Not to be outdone, Woodman and Grouse were quick to join in.

"OK," Royce called out.

"Move out, men," Woodman shouted.

"Let's go, men," Grouse yelled. "Back to your tents."

Approaching Will, Hampton spoke up. "Stone, my man, you cool. C'mere, c'mere, will you? Over by the light! I want to show you some-thing."

Hampton palmed a photo he had just pulled from his wallet and baited Will with it, leading him to the light coming from the back of Headquarters Platoon's tent. Woodman and Grouse were curious enough to tag along. Headed that way anyway, Montana and O'Rourke followed.

Satisfied they were all in position, Hampton held out the photo for Will to see and asked, "What do you see here, Stone?"

Will studied the picture a few seconds before Hampton interrupted him. "That's my family and that's my mother, man," he said. "So what do you see?"

"Looks like a nice family," Will answered.

"It's one of your own. Look at her, my mother. Don't you know one of your own when you see one?"

Will stared once more at the picture. *What's he driving at? Of course I see it.*

"Don't you see, Stone?" Hampton said. "My own mother is just as white as yours, and I'm telling you, you can never be my brother. You can never be one of the brothers. Got it? Maybe you're a nice guy, but you can never be one of the brothers."

Will looked up from the photo and gazed at Hampton, who leaned closer to him and said with a smirk, "Now give me my picture."

Will passed back the photo. Grouse smiled. Woodman averted Will's gaze stolidly.

"Later, buddy," Hampton said to Will, clapping him on the back before retreating with Woodman and Grouse in tow.

"Well, Stone," Montana asked, "which was more fun, the football game or the post-game show?"

"Yer dinna have to hit him," O'Rourke suddenly burst forth, brushing his way past Montana.

"You watch your ass, O'Rourke, or you'll be next," Montana yelled.

Bad News From Home

Will sighed in relief when he made it back to the tent. Franklin called out to him. "Take a seat for a moment, Will."

Shard and Swindell were on the next bunk talking with Campbell. *Never realized Campbell's hair was so thin on top. Shard and Swindell look like kids compared to him. Funny relationship.*

Will turned to sizing up Franklin. "Man, Rick. You look like I feel."

"That obvious?"

"God, do I need a shower," Will added.

"Got KP tomorrow," Franklin said. "Me, not you, me. Tomorrow, and the next day and the next day, and the ones after that."

"What are you saying?"

"Permanent KP," Franklin said. "Lamont says I wasn't moving fast enough around here. 'Moping around,' he said. Well, if he had to worry, like me. Well, Jesus Christ."

"Rough break, Rick, no doubt about it," Will said. "When did you hear this?"

"One of the cooks told me in the shower. Royce told me. Can you imagine that? Lamont didn't even have the guts to tell me."

"Maybe it's not so," Will said.

"Say it ain't so, Joe." Campbell intruded without seeming to pay Will and Franklin any heed.

"Listen, Rick," Will said in a hushed voice, "maybe it won't be so bad. Once you're there every day, you get to know the cooks and what's expected of you. Then it's just a job, like you were one of the cooks. I've seen it stateside. When a guy's with them all the time, he's one of them. They don't harass him like when you're there for one day at a time."

"So I'm supposed to hang out in the mess while you guys risk your necks?" Franklin asked.

"Surprised Lamont didn't take the job himself," Shard commented.

"See, it has its virtues," Will said.

"Yeah?" Franklin asked. "Well, how am I supposed to like myself when I'm a permanent KP?"

"Rick, you know this," Will responded. "It's not so much what you do, but the way you do it, that says who you are. This could be a good chance to work on that."

"Yeah, well, I'm not sure I get it," Franklin said. "Exactly how do you work on it? How do you like yourself? What has to happen?"

Will stroked his chin. "You have to believe in something, a code, and then be true to it. We are what we hold true."

Franklin stared at the floor. "What code do you believe in, Will?"

"I guess truth, justice and the American way."

"Up, up and away?" Shard said.

"Look up on the ridge pole," harkened Swindell. "It's a bird, it's a plane, it's Super-Stone."

"I better get showered," Will said. "Anyone know whether there's any water left at our showers?"

As Will rose to leave, Campbell caught his arm. "Truth, justice and the American way are not necessarily all one and the same."

Will headed for his bunk at the far end of the tent.

"Thanks, Stone," Franklin called after him.

O

Back from K Troop, where he found a shower with water, Will settled down with Jenny's letter. First, he retrieved his flashlight from his foot-locker, having already draped his army blanket over his mosquito netting to observe proper sound and light discipline. Confined within this setup, Will turned on the light and opened her letter, which read:

> Dear Will,
> Words cannot tell you how much we all miss you. Well, especially me but Mom talks about you, too. Of course she's usually complaining about one thing or the other. Last night, it was something about throwing the rugs out your window. And Pap, well, actually Josh kind of left a bad taste in his mouth, and you kind of got lumped in with it.
> Really, Will, you are a hero to me, being over there and all that. I don't care what the other kids say about you guys. A lot of us still think that we are right. You got to stop the commies somewhere. So to hell with all these people parading up and down the streets saying we don't belong there.
> Really, darling, I think of you all the time. Don't put me down for calling you that, cause that's how I feel. I told all the girls at the pep rally last night that I would just die if you did. They all felt so

sorry for me having you snatched away from me. We had the greatest time at Sip 'n' Sup afterwards. You should have been there. I'm the only one with a boyfriend at war.

Will, I'm going to follow in your footsteps. I feel you sort of showed me the light. You know, to want to learn just for the sake of understanding things. So I'm studying French, and I figure on doing my junior year abroad, like you wanted to, if I can get a scholarship to college. Of course, all those Frenchmen just waiting for me has a little something to do with it. Just kidding, Will, ha ha, but I do have some very cute boys in my French class, so you better get back here soon.

Don't worry, everyone knows you're my boyfriend, so no one's going to try anything with me.

I turned 17 a month ago. I don't blame you for forgetting my birthday, but I wish you could keep my age straight. I'm not a little girl anymore, so don't think of me as one. OK? I'm 17, not 16, soldier, so I'll be of age when you get back, so hurry up.

Luv ya,

XXXX OOOOO XXXXX
Jen

A lot going on in her head. Very young. Needs someone to keep an eye out for her. Not an easy one to answer, that's for sure. Should I answer this one first and then read the next? Yeah, that's the only way it'll get done. Pretty beat now already. Gotta read both. I'll have to answer both tomorrow. Sure, can't just scribble anything to Jen.

Will examined the similarities and differences between Jen's envelope and Margaret's. He fingered Margaret's, trying to reconnect to a world that seemed so foreign. *I never wanted to cause you any hurt, Mom.* Horton shook Will's mosquito netting and whispered to him.

"Stone," Horton hissed, "are you awake?"

"What's up, man?" Will answered. "You running CQ?"

"Yeah, listen, Will, you're taking most of Survey Section with you to the new base camp just south of Xuan Loc. It's just jungle now, they say. So you have to stake out all the roads and major facilities."

"What do you mean, me? I mean, me taking Survey. What about Montana?" Will asked.

"He's going back to the world," Horton answered. "His old man is dying. Some sort of Air Force brass."

"Right," Will mumbled, as Horton moved on silently. *Rough break for Montana.*

He fingered the envelope from Harry and Margaret. *If it could happen to Montana's dad, it could happen to Harry or Margaret.* That thought returned him to the world back home and focused him sharply on their letter. He ripped open the envelope:

> Dear Will,
>
> How have you been, son? Your dad and I worry about you. You are our pride and joy.
>
> We were slow coming to it, but you showed us the way. We just weren't quick to recognize our country was at war. It just sort of crept up on us. So, of course, you were right to answer the call.
>
> I wish we didn't have to, but we must stop these communists from taking over everything. Our way of life is at stake. So, we are proud of you not only for doing it, but for seeing it as your duty.
>
> We live in fear for your safety, though, Will. We hang on every broadcast for word of your cavalry unit. So, we won't really know joy till we have you home with us, once again.
>
> We received the letters that you wrote on board the troop ship and mailed from the Philippines. I'm glad the trip gave you a chance to rest. I was worried you might get sick and be cramped below deck. See, this'll all work out for the best. We just all need to have faith. Don't you lose heart, Will. You are in our prayers.
>
> Harry is writing you, too. I know you prefer to call him that, although it bothers him when you do. I wish you two didn't always so disagree. Anyway, he said he'll stick his letter in the envelope before it is sealed. I don't think I'm going to get to see it, so I can only surmise what he wants to say to you that must be kept private from me.
>
> I was hoping not to bring this up, but apparently Harry will, so if you read mine first, please listen to me. Promise me that, will you, son?
>
> Harry and your granddad have had the most serious disagreement, and it's over this damn war, Will. Honestly, they hardly speak to one another anymore. Gramps has decided, I don't know why, that we shouldn't be in Vietnam. I guess he means it's some sort of mistake. He doesn't make any sense to me or to Harry. So, please don't let it upset you.
>
> Anyway, Harry, of course, is 100% behind you and all our boys over there. And he's given your grandfather 'what for' for not getting behind the President.

Will, President Johnson looks so tired, because of his heart-ache for all you boys overseas. His responsibilities weigh heavy on him and it shows. Harry and I were not in favor of him, as you know, last election, but he's our only president now, so we're behind him. Differences over foreign policy stop at the nation's shores, Harry says.

Will, it's awful. I mean, you know, Harry yelling at Gramps for not supporting the troops under fire, and Gramps saying it's wrong. We can't see it, why it's wrong. Harry won't even let him say anything on the subject. Just cuts him off and says it's treasonous.

Will, I don't know if Gramp's written to you on the subject. I've asked him not to, so you wouldn't be upset, but he's taking this matter to extremes. Really, Will dearest, you must know how much my father has meant to me all these years, but I've never seen him like this.

Oh, he's not like Harry, yelling and trying to drown you out, but Gramps'll never let the matter drop. He's very patient. He lets you have your say, but then he won't agree with you. He insists on stating his differences. We just cut him off. We don't want to hear it.

Harry's very much involved with the American Legion now. The idea of Gramps marching in the streets with this college crowd just drives Harry insane. I don't know why he would do it. I can't believe it's my own father, but it is. He's always going into Forsburg for meetings to organize protests against the war efforts.

I can imagine how upsetting this must be to you, Will, honey, that's why if you had to know, I wanted to be sure you knew that the rest of us are truly behind you. And you can count on our support to never waver.

God bless you, Will, and love,

Mom

What the hell did he say, goddammit. Jesus, she spent all that time apologizing for him, and she never said exactly what Gramp's objection was. I don't think they know. Did they ever just listen? Did they consider he might be right? We're not dealing with some wacko here; this is Gramps. Let me see what Harry says.

Will stuck his finger back in the open envelope and pulled out a single sheet of lightweight, nearly transparent paper.

Dear Will,

For several years now, you have made my firing Josh a thorn in our relationship. You have acted like I had no care or concern for the man, after the thirteen years he worked for me. That's not true, and you should understand why.

The truth is, I did it for you. That's right, I fired Josh to protect you, not to hurt him. Josh had a drinking problem. I could accept that, so long as it didn't interfere with his work on the job. Generally speaking, it didn't. He had his package after we quit. But I certainly wasn't going to allow him to be a bad influence on you.

One day, you were about sixteen at the time, I'm sure you'll remember if you think back to just before Josh was fired, you two were supposed to be working on the second of the Hillside Avenue lots. Josh picked up a load of used railroad ties to be brought in the backyard, and then you two were to start the tie wall.

Well, I got there at four o'clock, a half hour before quitting time, and there the two of you were, sitting on the ties in the backyard, each with a bottle of beer in your hand and no notion whatsoever of starting construction on that wall that day.

That's when I realized that Josh's bad habit could ruin you, and when I resolved that he was through. I never told him or you why, because I didn't want an argument. It was my decision, my right as an employer and my duty as a father, and that's all there is to it.

I'm telling you now, because you should be man enough to understand and respect my decision. I made it so that you would not be corrupted, although it may have backfired because you used it as an excuse to distance yourself from me and to pal around with Josh.

I'm not sure how much harm that may actually have done to you, because the fact of the matter is your mom and I are very proud of you. No man has better reason to be proud of his son. You haven't disappointed me, and if Josh deserves some credit for that then I'll owe him that.

This is going to be hard, Will, but you'll have to accept that last week we received word that Josh had finally succumbed to complications from his wounds. I didn't tell your mom but I paid for his burial arrangements and sent something to his wife, although they had been separated for years. I know this comes hard, son, but from what I could tell Josh never stood a chance of much of a recovery from being shot. Your grandfather paid him regular visits in the hospital, but held out little hope for him. He said Josh did take comfort in the visits and always spoke well of you.

Your father,

Harry

Will fell back in bed and wiped his eyes. *Josh is dead. He's dead. Could I have done something more for him? Was I ever doing him any good with his drinking? Did this have to happen because of the way he was living? Would it have happened if Harry hadn't cut him loose? Harry had no right to fire him without cause. See, you don't know, Harry, you don't know. That's the thing, you always think you know, but you never listen, never consider that you might not have all the facts. That day on Hillside, you son of a bitch, Josh saved my life and made me into a man at the same time. He wouldn't bail me out, even though he could've waltzed that machine out of there himself. But, no, Harry, no, you couldn't even ask what the hell was going on between us. You couldn't even tell us what was under your skin. No, you just had to do it your way. Everything's your way. Will you open up your mind? None of us is always right. We can always be wrong.*

Will tried not to think of the letters, the day's events, the past, the present, or the future anymore. It all hurt too much, so he shut his eyes and heart to it. Finally, just before he fell asleep, he suddenly sat up, startled. *What do I believe in? Yes, of course, that is the first and last question, always.*

Chapter 5

Shooting Stars

The Listening Post

Will and Whiteman were unwanted reminders of a bleak prospect. Nobody wanted to be sent with them on the listening post, the LP, and nobody wanted to replace them if they failed to come back.

As usual, Whiteman was ready first and standing by while Will got his things together. Campbell, Swindell and Shard sat behind the track vehicle watching Will rummage around inside on his hands and knees. They avoided Whiteman's every attempt at eye contact. In a few minutes, Will and Whiteman would be gone and things would go back to normal for the three of them.

Will sniffed the chalky sweat stains on the outside of his flak jacket. *Smells better.* He had scrubbed its inside with a bar of Dial soap and water a half hour earlier. Still dripping wet, it felt heavier to him when he swung it on now. He slapped his chest pockets, confirming each contained two M-16 magazines. A corner of one jutted through a weeks-old tear in the left pocket.

Temperatures had begun to fall, though it was still a hundred degrees in the early-evening shade. Will grabbed two fragmentation grenades and jammed the handles in the chest-high webbing of his jacket. As he did, the wet back of the jacket soaked through his jungle fatigues. *Feels good.* He grabbed his webbed ammunition belt, opened the ammo pouch and made sure there were three magazines inside, one jammed sideways. The belt was designed to accept two M-14 magazines, which were wider and slightly thicker than those for M-16's, so a third one fit angled sideways. He swung the belt around his back and twisted the ends to interlock them securely around his waist.

Out of habit, Will ran his finger part way down the barrel of his M-16, which he had cleaned before he washed himself. No oil came off when he wiped his finger on his pant leg. He turned to Whiteman. "Got your shit together?"

Whiteman smiled but made no reply. His closely cropped blond hair and fair complexion allowed the sun to render his head a perpetual pink. At his feet was a poncho bound up together with an entrenching tool, a folding shovel. Will grabbed more hand grenades and pitched two to Whiteman, who jammed the handles of the grenades in the sides of his ammo pouch. Will did the same with his. Automatically Will patted the bottom of his canteen to check it was full. Then he slung over his shoulder a canvas bandoleer filled with M-79 grenades and shotgun shells and trip flares. Finally, he hooked a roll of trip wire on his canteen, grabbed the field radio with his left hand, his rifle with his right, and looked to Whiteman.

"Want me to carry the radio?" Whiteman offered.

"I got it," Will replied, stuffing it in an olive drab cloth case and shouldering the strap, too. "Maybe you can do the digging, though."

"Said radio," Whiteman murmured with a smirk. "You know where they want us?"

"Yeah," Will said. He nodded toward the other side of the laager.

"Good night, ladies," said Whiteman, grinning as he took a final look at the other three, who stared at the ground.

Campbell grunted. Shard and Swindell remained silent.

"Good night, gents," Will said, as Whiteman and he headed across the encampment.

The laager was made up of a line troop and a howitzer battery, both company-sized elements of an armored cavalry squadron. Armored track vehicles, stationed less than a hundred feet apart, guarded the perimeter. These vehicles included two M-48A tanks on loan to K Troop and two 155mm self-propelled howitzers. Most of the perimeter, however, was made up of ACAVs, or armored cavalry assault vehicles. An ACAV was an M-113A armored personnel carrier with armor plate gun shields added to protect the three machine gun positions. For a temporary defensive position, this perimeter could render devastating firepower and offer exceptional shelter.

Consequently, most of the troopers on or within the perimeter were happy to be where they were, rather than outside the perimeter manning some LP. Inside were not only the rest of How Battery's howitzers, deployed in the proper firing pattern, but also the headquarters elements of both K Troop and How Battery, including their support trucks. That night some one hundred thirty men would enjoy relative safety within the perimeter. But for Will and Whiteman, manning the LP had become a kind of ritual.

The two checked in with the nearest perimeter post where they would exit and presumably reenter the following morning. A guard from that ACAV walked them through the fields of fire so they would avoid any trip wires, and then opened the concertina wire for them to pass through. Once they were in the clear, the guard re-fastened the coiled barbed wire and returned to his post. It was dusk as Will and Whiteman cleared the perimeter, just as planned.

Once outside the perimeter, Will handed off the radio to Whiteman and took the point position. Will walked straight out from the perimeter close to eighty meters into an open area with elephant grass growing in spots. He turned and nodded to Whiteman, who was trailing by ten paces, before hunching over and darting sideways for the protective cover of a patch of tall grasses. Will squatted just inside the edge of the grasses till Whiteman caught up.

Whiteman started to off-load the radio. "Wait," Will said, "let's move through the grass toward those trees in case Charlie saw us jump in here. When it gets really dark, we'll move somewhere between those two trees. That's where we're supposed to be."

Slowly Will led the way through the tall grass in a duck walk, with Whiteman waddling in tow like his mate. Both were careful to keep their beaks below the grass line. By the edge of the tall grass closest to the two trees, Will peeled off his steel helmet and sat on it like he was hatching an egg. Whiteman followed suit.

They looked about without need for words. The two had made the trip to an LP for eight weeks, starting on their first night of field operations in-country. The Listening Post was not to engage the enemy, as would an ambush patrol, but rather to detect the enemy and communicate an early warning to the perimeter. In that circumstance, Will and Whiteman ideally would remain undetected, and the perimeter would deal with the enemy presence.

No one had discussed what would happen if Will and Whiteman were detected. If they did their job correctly, the enemy would have to stumble upon them in the dark to find them. If the two were found, given the cover of darkness and fire support from the perimeter, they would have a decent chance of holding out until a rescue column from the perimeter reached them.

O

That first night of operations in the field, when Sergeant Zack came around just before dark and announced he needed two men for an LP, all of Headquarters Platoon winced. Will foresaw the next few moments of his life in slow motion. Though detached and disapproving of what he was about to do, he was unable to stop himself. "I'll go," he said.

"So will I," added Whiteman.

Will jerked his head toward Whiteman. *What'd he do that for? What the hell did I do that for?*

Zack was glad he did not have to order volunteers. At the same time, he did not want Whiteman and Will carrying the platoon. When earlier that night Zack had ordered two other troopers to string the concertina wire, they whimpered until first Will and then Whiteman had volunteered to do it instead. Will and Whiteman had just finished when Zack returned about manning the LP.

No one spoke a word after the duo volunteered for the LP. Maybe the others felt they had just dodged a bullet, but Will recognized that Whiteman and he may just have stepped in front of one. *I just can't sit here while some other guy walks out there and maybe comes back, maybe doesn't. Not unless I've taken the chance, too.*

"Why'd you do that?" Will asked Whiteman.

Whiteman grinned. "So I'd have a chance to ask you that question."

"C'mon," Will countered. "Why the hell'd you volunteer for this? It isn't like stringing barbed wire in front of our perimeter outpost."

"You're different somehow from the rest, Stone," Whiteman responded. "I want to find out if you're better."

"What the hell are you talking about?" Will rejoined. "We're gonna be parking our asses out there where we can't even see right now. Now's not the time for bullshit. What's the matter with you?"

"You're going, so I'm going," Whiteman answered. "When we were stringing that concertina, you said something about not having to give in to fatigue, about it largely being a mental thing. Well, my father used to talk to me that way on the farm, only he died when I was twelve. Grew up the rest of the way with his brother. Unc never said too much like that. So I want to see what you can tell me I might have missed. Stuff maybe I might not dope out myself."

"Only thing I can tell you right now," Will said, "is to keep your head down. Let's get our shit together. Sargie's waiting to take us through the perimeter."

"Lead the way," Whiteman said. "It'll be good to get away from these crybabies."

"Some of these guys are only eighteen and nineteen," Will said.

"So am I," Whiteman responded. "So how come you volunteered us?"

Will looked at him. "I hope this doesn't disappoint you, but maybe I was too scared to just sit there waiting to see if Zack was going to pick me. Look, I wanted to face this. It's easier to face it than to try to avoid it."

"Easier to get blown away, too," Whiteman said.

"Yeah, well, you have to come to terms with that. You have to have a reason for taking the chance. Anyway, I couldn't stand the suspense. This way, if it happens, it happens. That's all, folks."

"What's your reason?"

"Gotta live with myself," Will said.

Whiteman nodded. "If I stick with you, I *will* find out how your mind works. Besides, it was getting pretty damn boring with the battery all the time. When my time is up here, I'll go back to the farm. I got to bring back something more to remember about all this than just detailing for Survey Section."

"It might get us killed," Will said emphatically, before adding with a smile, "but we both know that between the potheads and the juicers on the perimeter, somebody's gonna miss Charlie one of these nights when he comes calling. We could be just as well off outside the laager where he's not looking for us."

After a few nights, it was accepted that Whiteman and Will were going out on the LP. The others were spared, unless more than one LP was needed on a given night.

O

So having their ass in the grass was old hat for Will and Whiteman. Ordinarily, they would have enjoyed the rest that waiting for darkness would afford. They might have enjoyed one another's quiet company, free from the intrusion of arbitrary authority and confident in the security of their own self-discipline. Whiteman could sense, however, that Will was still mulling over the day's events, and he waited patiently to see what Will would make of them.

Finally, Will said, "You know, White Man, we've spent so many days racing helter-skelter in these tracks, and this morning seemed the first time we were doing anything that made sense. We race up the highway through the villages, then someone gets a call from Big Three, and we race back the other way. Heaven help any man, woman or child who gets in our way. They'd get no more mercy than that pig that wandered under our tracks yesterday."

"You see that woman wail?" Whiteman interrupted. "I barely felt him when we went over him. That was two-hundred pounds of pork, you know."

"I mean," Will continued, "we get stuck in rice paddies, knock over gravestones, trespass in temples, and invade villages—but to what end? Can you tell me? What does it mean? What are we doing? Then, this morning, finally, for the first time, something made sense. It was consistent with our stated purpose of helping the Vietnamese."

"The Medcap?" Whiteman asked. "What does that mean, anyway? Where do they get these names from?"

"I think I remember that it's short for Medical Civil Action Program," Will said.

"Oomph," Whiteman grunted, before fingering the soft grass stalks. "Nice stuff." Will knew Whiteman was grateful not to be foraging through razor-sharp elephant grass.

"I know this was K Troop's third time back here, their third week of the Medcap," Will said. "But, well, it was our first week with them on this, and it felt good to bring medical treatment to this village. Didn't you feel good about it, White Man?"

Whiteman hesitated before responding. "OK," he said.

"So we come to the edge of the village and maybe the people don't welcome us, but at least they're not hostile because they know we're just there to help them," Will said. "We've been there before. We escort the doctor and a couple of medics into the hooch, and the people line up with their infirmed.

"Pretty good duty at this point, huh? I mean, we got them there without incident. The people are being taken care of. We only have to get the medical people safely back, and then we've done something that we can understand. Something that not only made sense, but something that was good. But then what happened?"

"Whoosh, whoosh, whoosh," Whiteman intoned, rotating his index finger toward the ground to simulate a helicopter rotor.

"The Air Cav swoops in from the north," Will muttered.

"And we get orders over the net to seal off the village from the south," Whiteman said.

"The next thing you know our mission of mercy has been converted into a cordon op," Will said.

"Yeah, I guess whoever doped this one out was pretty slick," Whiteman said. "You can't say this one didn't make any sense."

"I guess not, White Man. It was logically planned, but shortsighted, perhaps."

"Meaning?" Whiteman asked.

"White Man, did you see those two little boys with their mother? They were right next to us in line. Did you see them when we started our engines up? Did you see them hide behind her, the terror in all their eyes, all of them in line as we took off to move into position? That little girl with the bad arm was no more than twelve. Did you ask Doc how many patients he had after the alert?"

Whiteman let his head fall to his chest, and shook it slowly. "No," he said quietly, fidgeting with a grass stalk.

"What's that mother gonna tell those two boys later?" Will asked. "What're they gonna believe when they're old enough to tote a weapon?"

"We took some prisoners," Whiteman said.

"Two grizzled old men," Will answered. "No fighting-aged men. No weapons. No rice stores. No young women. Just two worn-out farmers detained for questioning for God only knows why."

"The interpreter must know what he's doing," Whiteman said.

"I'm sure he does," Will said, "but do we?

"Huh?"

"Look, White Man, I don't know what the guy was doing. But that's the point. None of us do. The guy knows he's here to finger the VC. If he doesn't nab anybody, after a while, we're gonna suspect him. So he knows he's gotta finger somebody, even if they're gonna release the guy as soon as he gets to an interrogation center. So just because this guy put the mark on those detainees doesn't mean this op was such a great success." Whiteman turned away in frustration. "Better do a commo check," Will said.

Whiteman swung the radio in front of Will, who picked up the telephone-type handset and said, "Seven, this is Lima Peter One, commo check, over."

"This is Seven. Read you Lima Charlie, Lima Peter One, over," the battery operations center advised, indicating in phonetic code that they had heard Will loud and clear.

"Roger, out," Will acknowledged before breaking off the communication. "It's time," he said, rising to a crouch.

Whiteman and Will moved to the edge of the grass and visually surveyed the terrain as well as the dusk would allow. They wanted to wind up somewhere between the two large trees, which would give the laager perimeter a sense of their direction. From a safe distance, they also wanted to overlook any traveled byways in order to maximize the chance of detecting the enemy and minimize the chance of being detected.

"It really bothered you?" Whiteman asked Will.

"I don't know what I thought," Will said. "I guess it bothered me at first, but now that I've thought about it, I don't know what to feel. Other than it's a pity. On the scale of things, it's not exactly the horrors of war."

"You made your point, though," said Whiteman. "You want me to do the digging?"

"You look so clean," Will responded.

"Shut up!"

"Cover me while I move to the right of that tree," Will said. "When I'm in position to cover you, make your way to the high side of that gully, so we can see in the gully and over the bank, but so we won't get our tootsies wet if a monsoon moves in."

"You got it," Whiteman responded.

"I'll be over to help you dig as soon as I'm sure no one's sitting out there waiting to blow your ass away."

On many another night, Will had thought nothing of rising from the tall grasses and quietly walking to his position near the tree. But now he took into account that they were parked on the northern edge of the hamlet that they had cordoned off and searched today. *There might be retaliation, so why not take advantage of the visual screening offered by the shorter grasses between here and the tree?* These shorter grasses were still sixteen to twenty inches high, enough to hide Will if he chose to crawl into position.

Will pulled out his recon compass from his collar. He wore it on a shoelace hanging around his shirt collar, but tucked it inside his fatigue jacket, so it did not bounce around. He shot a bearing on the direction to the tree. He could crawl through the grass without having to expose his head until he was in his covered position by the tree. He started crawling while Whiteman looked on. At first, Whiteman saw the grass tops disappear under Will's traverse, but then he could not be sure where Will was. Will's determination to crawl was reinforced by his respect for the enemy. *If Charlie is coming by here, this is the way he'll come—on his belly. He'll come all the way in through these grasses without ever being seen. If he can do it, so can I.*

Will paused to check his compass reading and noticed he was headed downhill and that as the elevation fell, the soil was getting wetter. *If Charlie's coming in through this grass, this is where I should set the trip flares. Better get to the tree, so White Man can get started. I'll set the flares on my way over to him.*

After shooting another bearing with the compass, Will forged ahead. As the ground fell and became wetter, the grass became taller, allowing Will to scamper ahead on all fours like a monkey and avoid dragging himself through wet soil. *Must be near the trees. Gotta surface and see where I am.* Will eased his head up above the grass line for a look. *Twenty feet. I missed it by only twenty feet. Hallelujah. Now, where the hell is Whiteman? No sign of him.*

Will stood and walked to the tree, so Whiteman would see him. He carried his helmet and his M-16 in his hand so his silhouette would be less identifiable to others. He reconnoitered around the tree and then sat on his helmet about five feet on Whiteman's side of the tree. *No sign of him still. What the hell's Whiteman doing? Taking a dump? All this sexy, hi-tech stuff you're always hearing about and we got no way to communicate with one another, not even a red flashlight.* Will waited, looking intently for any sign of movement from Whiteman's direction. *There he is at the bottom of the gully. He must have broken through the edge of the grass as soon as I showed my head.*

Will slipped down onto his side, put on his helmet, and slid to where he had a clearer line of sight to Whiteman's path. Whiteman walked slowly, but upright. Every now and then, the moonlight would break through the clouds overhead and reflect off his blond hair. *Funny, nobody's ever been issued camouflage grease sticks.*

Will continued to scan around his position and Whiteman's. He searched for any sign of movement, any noise, any light. With one eye, he observed and approved Whiteman's site selection for their foxhole at the military crest of the gentle rise overlooking the gully. Some weeds growing around a felled tree trunk next to them would allow them visibility but obscure their position from any distance. Will sighted from his own position to the laager. Their foxhole would be right in line with Will's tree, as seen from the closest point of the perimeter. Clearly they were still within range of crew-served automatic weapons fire support from the perimeter.

Christ, will you look at White Man dig? Better get my butt over there and give him a hand before he has a heart attack. Everything looks hunky-dory from here, no movement along any of the avenues of approach. Holy shit, what's that? In the distance a file of soldiers approached. Will tried to identify them. *It's got to be an ambush patrol from our encampment. If they stay on that course, they'll give away our position. They ought to know better, for crissake. I gotta get over there.*

Will took one last look at the oncoming patrol and then panned the open area back to the perimeter. He headed off deliberately for Whiteman's foxhole.

When Will approached, Whiteman had just finished digging their foxhole to a depth of about twenty-four inches, and he was spreading his poncho as a ground cloth. Though he had removed his flak jacket before digging, his fatigue jacket was soaked with sweat and clung to his powerful torso. Whiteman turned to face Will as he stepped into the foxhole. Whiteman's face was even ruddier than usual, and what little light there was glistened on the beads of sweat on his face.

Will pointed with his M-16 toward the oncoming silhouettes. "Looks like a dozen," he whispered.

Whiteman first had to swing on his flak jacket. "Are they ours?" he asked as Will and he dropped to their knees and lowered themselves close to ground level.

"Anything goes here, White Man. You know that, but that's my best guess."

"Are they VC, I mean?"

"Could be NVA, but probably not," Will said. "They're regulars. Probably friendlies. Probably ours. We'll know soon enough unless they change course, which it looks like they're starting to do."

Will reached for the radio handset. "One broke off from the group and is headed this way," Will continued.

"He's shorter than the rest," Whiteman confirmed, "but broader than any gook I ever seen."

The two waited in readiness, as the lone figure, seemingly uncertain of his destination, stumbled toward them. Finally, Whiteman announced, "It's Zack. I'm sure of it."

Will grabbed him by the sleeve. "First confirm he's American," Will said.

"That's Zack," Whiteman said. "Probably got half a bag on. Should I go get him?"

"See if he keeps heading this way first," Will said, scrutinizing the silhouette to satisfy himself that it was indeed American. Before long, Will made out the shape of the steel pot, the flak jacket and M-16. "Yes, it's Zack, all right. Let him keep coming this way by himself, as long as he does," Will said. "We'll go get him only if we have to."

In two long minutes Zack was almost upon them, stumbling and looking harder for his footing than he was for the LP. Will nodded to Whiteman, and threw a stone just to Zack's left. Zack spun around. Then Will tossed one to the right of Zack.

Zack fell to the ground, his rifle to his shoulder, his head twitching. Whiteman smirked at Will.

"Bring him in," Will whispered.

Whiteman started to rise before Will grabbed his arm again and cautioned, "He may fire on you."

Whiteman nodded and eased himself back down. He whistled the first bars of a popular beer jingle, "Schaefer is the one beer to have...."

"You know," Whiteman whispered to Will, "that Lena Horne is really something."

"Yes, she is," Will said, maintaining his focus in Zack's direction. "Do it again."

Whiteman again whistled the famous bars, this time attempting more of Miss Horne's stylized inflection. Will and Whiteman grinned at one another when Zack rose to his feet and headed their way. He started to wander off course just once in his approach, but Whiteman brought him back by making a clicking sound with his mouth, like he was calling a horse.

When Zack was on top of them, he started to ask, "What're—"

At once Whiteman and Will were upon him and pulled him into the foxhole.

"Pretty scary out there, was it?" Whiteman asked.

Zack looked him in the eye before answering, "You sonofabitches were playing with me. Jesus Christ."

With Zack seated between them, Whiteman and Will leaned forward and smiled at one another. Zack resumed, "What are you sonofabitches doing out here?"

"We were just talking about Lena Horne, that's all," Will said.

"She's no spring chicken, you know," Zack said. "Been around since the thirties."

"Best reason I ever heard of for integration," Whiteman said.

Will turned around in the foxhole, so his back was to the laager. He looked from left to right, seeking trouble. Finally, he said, "I thought Schaefer was local to the Northeast. Didn't think you guys in Minnesota would ever have heard of it."

"We've all seen Lena Horne do that bit at least once," Whiteman said, "and once you've seen it, you don't forget it."

Zack burped. They all fell quiet.

Whispers In the Dark

"What are you doing out here, Sarge?" Will asked after a long spell, keeping his focus ahead of him.

"I'm going to spend the night with you guys tonight," Zack explained. "I decided I couldn't send you or any of the others out here anymore unless I'd done it at least once myself."

"Oomph," Whiteman said.

"Brought a little something with me," Zack said, pulling out a bottle of beer from each of the cargo pockets of his jungle fatigues.

Will took a long look at him. "Not out here," he said, "not for us."

"Don't be such a boy scout," Zack said.

Will and Whiteman continued studying the terrain in front of them and said nothing. "You're right," Zack said, placing the bottles on their side along the rim of the foxhole.

The three sat silently, maintaining the vigil. Finally Will said, "Why don't you grab some shut-eye, White Man? We'll take the first watch."

Whiteman nodded and adjusted the ground cloth so it would ride up the edge of the hole where he would lean his head. He settled back. Will's sense of duty heightened. Their survival rested solely on his shoulders. Zack could not be counted on. He did not know the drill and, anyway, he was impaired.

"What's that?" Zack suddenly rasped. "Out there. Shh! It's a light. Someone's coming. Nobody's supposed to be coming. We're supposed to shoot on sight."

Will looked hard where Zack pointed and finally spotted a light. "That wasn't there a few minutes ago," Zack continued.

"No. I don't think it was."

"Maybe we better pop it," Zack said. "That light makes an easy target."

"It's awfully far away," Will said. "Let's hold our horses."

"What do you figure it is?"

Will sighed. "I don't know, Sarge. We'll keep an eye on it."

"It's moving," Zack said. "I say let's shoot while we have a good shot. They may turn that light off when they get closer."

"They're awfully far away, Sarge. No telling how far without knowing how bright that light is."

"It's bright enough," Zack said. "It's got to be an enemy patrol scouting us out."

"Maybe there's a hooch out there and the guy's lit a candle," Will said.

"It's a flashlight," Zack said. "I can tell."

"Sarge, we can't tell what it is, who it is, or how far it is," Will said. "We gotta wait it out."

"We ought to shoot while we got the shot."

"It may not even be in range," Will said, "but if we shoot, we'll be giving away our position."

"Oh, man," Zack said. "OK, we'll keep our powder dry a while."

"What are you really doing out here?" Will asked.

Zack looked him in the eye, but before responding broke wind. "I, uh, what a fart," he said.

Will was thinking the same thing, but said nothing.

"What do you do in a situation like this, Stone, when you have to fart?"

Will looked at Zack. *I can't believe the army has shipped me to the other side of the world, and sent me in the dark of night into hostile territory with the scantiest of training, under the care and tutelage of this most senior NCO, who now seeks my advice on proper farting technique.*

"Well?" Zack asked.

"Leak it," Will said. "Now what are you really doing out here?"

Zack chuckled but said nothing further. Will looked across his fields of fire for any sign of trouble. He focused his concentration as much on hearing as looking for danger. In time he felt he had himself in a zone where he could maintain his heightened alert while thinking about other things. He started to feel thirsty, and he glanced at his canteen, slung from his ammo belt, which lay against the earthen side of the foxhole. The earth caught his attention and he compared it to the rocky soils he had pushed around on Harry's construction site the day Josh was shot. Thinking about taking a drink made him remember the lunch break that day.

The Color Of Skin—Part 2

By the time the workers on the construction site broke for a late lunch, the strain of the difficult and dangerous work had waxed their tension over racial matters into a grudging respect for one another. Will sat on a rock by the tractor where the backfill was highest between the foundation and the shelf he was cutting for the backyard. Johnny stood on the floor deck talking with the plumbers and electricians. Graves beckoned to Will from the foundation, "Come on over here, kid."

Will slid down the side of the bank and latched onto Graves's outstretched hand. Graves pulled him atop the floor deck. "Ain't you got a lunch, kid?"

"I'm all right," Will said.

Graves bent over his lunch pail and flipped an orange in Will's direction. Reaching to his right, Will one-handed it, nodding to Graves.

"Did you see that catch? What an outfielder!" yelled the plumber. "Knucklehead that I am, I had him play first base on my Little League team." Will approached him to shake his hand. "Now you see I'm not the great Casey Stengel you guys all thought I was. I'm just a plumber."

"We'd be in deep shit without you," Will said.

The electrician stepped forward, "How are you, son?"

"Hey," Will said. "Thanks for all the good scout trips together. How's your son doing, sir?"

"He's doing great, Will. I'll tell him you asked. He's just been accepted to UCLA med school, so tell your old man to keep building these houses, cause I'll have to keep wiring them." The group pulled apart a stack of empty spackle buckets and spotted them around in a circle as seats. Apprentices and two summer workers joined them.

Graves was the last seated, kicking his lunch pail along the floor to his place, as he finished his chicken and wiped his hands on his jeans. "Forgive me, gentlemen, for not waiting until tea was served, but I had a hole in my belly," he said.

"Hey, Will," one of the summer helpers called out, "we hear you're shacking up with some little blonde with her own apartment up on College Hill."

"Big ears can screw you up almost as bad as a big mouth," Will said.

"Don't know anything about a strawberry blonde in a yellow two-family with an Austin-Healy Sprite?" the other summer worker joined in.

"Why don't we all just mind our own business?" Will asked.

"Didn't you go out with Sarah Legato, Will?" asked Johnny. "She had some crush on you."

"Hey! Now we're getting somewhere. Hot pants, huh?" called out one of the summer workers.

"Miss Leg!" called out the other.

"Hey, what is this, The Many Loves of Will Stone?" Graves called out.

"Down, boy, down," Johnny leaned forward to speak directly to one of the helpers.

"You're doing quite a job here," the plumber said softly, elbowing Will. "Josh taught you well. He's a good man."

"Thought you might want to know, Will, that Sarah's taking off next week to study in France all next year," Johnny added.

Will nodded. "I know," he said quietly.

"Then I guess you also know her roommate, Sharon Spencer, is headed for the Deep South. Some civil rights stuff," Johnny said.

Graves pivoted on his bucket to face Will directly. The others followed his lead.

"The jungle tom-toms are calling," one of the apprentices said aloud to the other.

"It's a literacy program," Will said. "Part of the voter-registration drive."

"She's going down to get balled by the niggers," another apprentice spoke out deliberately.

"What am I hearing?" Graves said, laughing and cupping his ear with his hand.

"She's going down to teach people to read and write well enough to pass the literacy tests so they can vote," Will said.

"Ha!" said one of the apprentices. "That's what they say."

"But what it's really about," the other continued for him, "is animal instinct, interracial sex."

"Get off it!" said Will.

"Only they call it 'Free Love'," continued the first apprentice.

"Does it make any difference whether it's in the South or in Paris?" the second asked.

"She's going down there to help people," Will said. "You don't even know her, for crissake."

"Don't take the Lord's name in vain," said Graves, grinning.

"I don't need to know her," the second apprentice said. "I know the type. Only the natural rhythms of the Dark Continent can satisfy the urgency of this primitive craving."

"You're crazy," Will said, turning his head away.

"You know, Will," the other helper interjected, "he's right, at least to the extent that they all sleep around when they get down there. They're just like us. It's the most freedom they've ever experienced. Once that expectation of satisfaction is created, it's very difficult to resist. These kids are moving around a lot. They're practically anonymous. They can't fall back on their parents' rules because, well, aren't they there to assert their independence? The young Negro men are predators on guilt-ridden white youths."

"Like you, Will," one of the apprentices said.

"They inject the racial issue into personal relations," the helper continued. "They imply any girl's unwillingness results, in part at least, from latent prejudice. To prove they're not bigots, white girls must perform, and white boys must let them.

"Couple that with the fact that this type of girl has probably slept it all over campus for the past couple of years anyway, and that she's ready for something new, maybe better, like the supernatural black organ she's heard so much about—"

"She's going with her fiancé," interrupted Will, rising to confront the helper. "So stick it in your supernatural ear."

"Hey, Graves," the plumber spoke up, "don't you think this is getting a little—"

"What do I think? I'll tell you what I think," Graves said, jumping to his feet and smashing down a long-handled shovel against the plywood floor deck so hard it bounced up and hit him in the shoulder. "Niggers are like cockroaches and rats. You gotta tolerate them, that's all."

The apprentices and summer helpers scrambled to make room for Graves, regrouping at the far corner of the floor deck and snickering among themselves. The plumber rose up and stepped away from the group, peering to the side by the lumber pile. The electrician and Will lifted their hands to ward off Graves's shovel in case it came their way and then rose slowly.

"What in hell is going on here?" Harry said, bursting from nowhere into the group and grabbing Will's shoulder to spin him around. Instinctively Will slipped his grip and dropped back a few paces. "What is Josh doing here?"

"Josh?" Will said. "What? Where?"

Harry turned and faced the lumber pile. There stood Josh, silently surveying the group on the floor deck, ignoring the little wave the plumber offered him. Josh looked from one face to another, slowly nodding his recognition of each. When he completed the circuit, he glanced back at Will and then to the ground away from them, shaking his head. Tall and lean, he bore the rugged lines of one who worked outdoors his full fifty years, but he appeared tired now, tired of it all. He kept his hands stuffed in his jeans until he jerked his head to glare at Will. His fists, now out in the open, were clenched. A trace of a grin crossed his face, and he reached up with his right hand, ran his fingers twice through his near-gray, nappy hair and scratched the back of his neck. Again he shook his head and looked away, biting hard on his lips.

In a moment, he strode crosswise in front of the main section of the foundation, forty-four feet. He never looked down as he crossed the rough and rocky grade, but rather stared up at Will. His stride was sure and deliberate. Any appearance of fatigue was gone, and his energized body seemed younger. When he reached the corner where the foundation stepped back, he paused for a last look at the group, turned away, shook his head again and spit on the ground. With his back to the others, he thrust his chin in the air and stepped to the road with the same purposeful stride. To a man, the group on the platform stood in silence until he reached the road.

He's stone cold sober, thought Will. "What time is it?" said Will.

"Where'd he park?" said the electrician.

"It's three o'clock."

"He parked down the road somewhere," the plumber said. "What difference does it make?"

"He wasn't supposed to be here until four," said Will.

"For what?" Harry shouted.

"So we could talk," Will said. "I told him to come by so you and he could talk."

"You know, I thought I saw something dark moving a couple of times by the lumber pile, but I didn't think nothing of it," said Graves.

"He could've heard the whole thing from there," the plumber said. "Too bad. Josh is one of the good ones, one of the best. "

"Will, I didn't schedule any meeting with him," Harry said. "Why didn't you tell me?"

"I did. I tried to tell you this morning," Will said. "I've got to go after him."

"Whoa! Hold on there, young buck," Harry said. "You can't leave now. What are you talking about? I need this backfill done today."

"Who knows what he's going to do?" Will said. "I've got to catch him."

"Will," Harry said, throwing his arm around Will's shoulder to steer him away from the rest of the group, "listen to me, please. Are you listening?"

"I'm listening, but I gotta go."

"Will, listen to me. You can't go. Do you hear me? You can't go. I need you here on that machine. My partners are coming first thing tomorrow morning."

"I'll come back."

"Listen to me, Will. You can't go, dammit. They advanced me money last week on my word that this foundation was already backfilled. You have got to finish the backfill for me. You can't leave. Do you understand me?" Harry said, letting go of Will and heading for the plumber and the electrician.

"I hear you, but then you gotta catch Josh," Will called after him.

"I will in just a moment," Harry called back, as he signaled for the plumber and the electrician. "Now, will you please get back up on that machine?"

"Harry," Will said.

"What?" Harry yelled, stalking back to Will. Harry again slung his arm around Will's shoulder and turned him away from the others. He spoke right into Will's ear. "Do you see me as a liar? Or a thief?"

"No! I never said that."

"Then get up on that machine, because if you don't, everyone's going to call me both."

Will looked around at the others, glanced at the machine, and nodded. The plumber and the electrician stood by, having sent their crews back to the other job. Graves grabbed Johnny around the neck, rubbed his unshaven chin against Johnny's ear, and propelled him toward his half of the shield. Laughing, Graves gestured toward Will like he was next. Will dragged his feet as he moved to the machine.

Satisfied things were back on track, Harry was fast in conversation with the plumber and the electrician, who said, "The other young guys got on him cause he was speaking up for those civil rights agitators down south. That's all. It was nothing."

"All right," Harry said, "this is just one of those things."

"Harry, are you going or not?" Will called from his side of the foundation dig. "We don't know what Josh is going to do."

Harry wheeled around. "Goddammit, Will, you're supposed be up on that machine running it. Daylight's burning—"

"You're not gonna go, are you?" Will said.

"I'm going. I told you I was going, didn't I?" Harry said.

"When?" Will said. "You gotta go now."

"When? I'll tell you when. Maybe when I can leave you on a job for more than a half a day without you turning everything upside down, that's when. Now get on that machine. You said you were going to backfill it for me, and you know I need it."

"I'll get on the machine, Harry," Will said with a cold stare and a steady voice, "but there's something I want you to know first. I never went on that March on Washington in '63, but I will be going on next week's Freedom Ride to the South."

"No!" Harry roared, lunging toward Will. Graves intercepted Harry, afraid he might leap off the foundation where it still needed backfill. "You bastard!"

The drone of Will's machine made further words pointless. "I'm OK," Harry said to Graves, shrugging himself loose of his grip. "Let's sit down. I want to know exactly what happened here."

By the time the plumber and the electrician reprised the whole incident for Harry, he was less severe in his judgment of Will. Harry was just as determined, though, to prevent Will from heading south. They agreed upon laying in wait for him to complete the backfill and then appealing to his better judgment, relying on their strength in numbers. "Graves should sit in on this, Harry," the plumber said. "He was one of the culprits, but Will respects him. He respects each one of us in a different way. He might not listen to any one of us, but to all of us? It's your best bet."

Graves let Johnny go just after 5:00 p.m., once the shield was no longer needed. He remained alone to help Will with the work too close to the foundation for the machine to do. He also had his instruction to see that Will would be on hand when Harry and the plumber and electrician returned from dinner. About 6:30 p.m., when the other three returned, Will slowed the machine to an idle to cool the engine. The backfill was complete. The rough grade may have been more rough than graded, but the backfill was done. Will looked over the machine before shutting it down. No sooner did he head for the street than Graves called out, "Hey, kid! You know we ain't waiting up here for our health."

Will approached the group, looking from one to the next. No one made eye contact with him. "Sit down for a minute with us, please, Will," Harry said. "We won't be long."

Will sat next to Harry and asked, "Did you ever go after Josh?"

"No, Will, you know I didn't," Harry said. "I wouldn't know where to look for him."

"I'll look for him after I get cleaned up," Will said softly.

"Will, we know this incident was upsetting to you this afternoon," Harry said. "We want to talk about it quietly. No shouting. Just so we all understand a little better."

"We want you to rethink this going to the South," the electrician said.

"Look, my problem is not with you," Will said. "The problem isn't what happened up here on this mountain this afternoon. It's in the South." The others stared at him.

"Maybe you do have a problem with us, Will," the electrician said.

Will hesitated. "Maybe I do," he said. "Here, there, maybe it's all the same."

"We're thinking of you, Will," the plumber said, "of your safety."

"Some things are more important," Will said.

The others exchanged glances. Will lowered his gaze.

Harry took over. "You are not going down South, mister!"

"I'm committed," Will said.

"Will, how can you do this? This isn't the way you were raised," the electrician said. "You know it isn't right, your going into a strange town and causing trouble for the people there. What your dad is trying to say—"

"Is that I'm an outside agitator?" asked Will. "Don't you see, your outside agitators aren't subversive agents. They're people like me."

"Not subversive agents," Graves said, "subversive assholes."

"Right," the plumber said, "people like you who don't know their ass from a hole in the ground about what's really going on down there, but that doesn't stop them from going anyway to subvert the way of life there."

"I don't see it that way," Will said. "I'm going there to help people to read so they can vote. It's pretty simple."

"By doing that you're going to be causing a lot of people trouble," the electrician said.

"By forcing them to change, because they'll no longer be able to keep the downtrodden down?" asked Will.

The electrician held up the palms of his hands toward Will, "Will, a whole social structure is based on—"

"Injustice," Will said.

"You can't force people to change what's in their hearts, Will," Harry said.

"Their public acts are unjust, and they won't change them until they are forced," answered Will. "As for what's in their hearts, well, I'm not saying they have to like it."

"Why you?" the electrician said.

"Why not me?" Will said.

"I'll tell you why," bellowed Harry, "because I didn't raise you to be any commie dupe, that's why."

"Who, then?" Will replied.

"Will," the plumber said, "we want to help people, but not this way. You can't force people to change. The change has to be gradual, willing. The church—"

"Well," Will said, looking at each of them before settling on Graves, "if we're talking how to bring about change, then have we agreed that change is necessary?"

The sound of crickets pervaded the silence as everyone awaited Graves's answer. He grinned.

"To help who? The niggers? Fuck 'em," he said, leaning his head in toward Will. "Fuck 'em."

"For crissake, Graves!" Harry said.

"Then Jim Crow must go," Will said getting to his feet.

"Will, for the last time," said Harry, jumping up at the same time, "you are not going down South. I worked like a slave to scratch out what I have, and I'll be damned if I'll see any of it go to someone I can't respect."

"I gotta go," said Will.

"Think it over, wise guy," said Harry, walking away before quickly turning back to Will. "Everything I ever dreamed of can be yours, if you'll just work with me."

"There is nothing here I want," Will answered.

Harry took a step closer to Will and leaned to his ear, whispering, "You're not going, Will."

One Says "No" To the Army

"I told you," Zack suddenly said, "I'm here to be with you because one day someone finally said 'No' to the Army. And all this 'Right Way, Wrong Way, and the Army Way' crap just sailed right out the window. In all my years, no one ever just said 'No,' but you did it, Stone. That morning started off like any other, then 'Wham'!"

One morning, Will was on a sandbag detail with eight other troopers from Headquarters Platoon, which every day had been furnishing far more than its share of men for the daily detail. The resentment of the others began to boil over. Will was the ranking man from the platoon, so he took it upon himself to take a stand. He put his shovel down.

Confined to quarters, Will thought fast. He knew the Army would not care about what he thought was fair. He concluded the only way he could defend his refusal was to make a case that he refused for the good of the Army. Will wrote a statement patterned after Martin Luther King, Jr.'s "Letter from a Birmingham Jail." In it, he stated his long hours on both guard duty and sand-bagging were depriving him of sleep necessary to his reliable performance of assigned guard duties, which could threaten the safety of his unit. He dummied up some records of the hours he worked on guard and sandbagging and the hours he slept the past thirty days.

When the first sergeant threatened him with an Article 15 and loss of pay-grade, Will countered he would not sign it, which would force a court martial. Captain Harkness, the Battery Commander, wanted no part of the embarrassment of any court martial, least of all one involving a defense of this sort.

The captain also took into account Zack's glowing account of Will's work record. In the end, the captain concluded Will was right and, starting that very day, called daily sandbagging formations for everyone not then on guard duty. This included officers, NCOs and all enlisted men, including cooks. The captain sent word to Will that if he did not want to sandbag, he should hangout on the perimeter while these details took place. Will sent word back to the captain to save him a shovel the next day. These daily details lasted only a couple of weeks, but Headquarters Platoon was fairly treated thereafter with regard to sandbag details.

When Zack brought up the incident on the listening post, it was the first time anyone had mentioned it to Will since that day. Will had been ambivalent about what happened. *Campbell and the others on the detail probably figure I knuckled under when I showed up for the formation the following day. The rest probably figure I caused them a hell of a lot of trouble.*

"That fuckin' light is getting brighter, Stone," Zack whispered. "You watching it?"

"Got an eye on it, Sarge."

"You see it getting brighter?" Zack questioned.

"Yep."

"Well?"

"We'll keep an eye on her," Will said.

Zack looked hard at Will, who stared straight ahead though his mind was elsewhere. Recalling the sandbag incident had unloosed forgotten feelings. *The whole thing wasn't worth everyone's time. If I had some credibility to arm me in such a confrontation, it shouldn't have been squandered on that! What about the last night of our last mission? Were they roughing up those detainees? I don't know.* He recalled the night they were camped adjacent to National Highway 2, three miles south of the new base camp.

O

When the cavalry regiment increased its use of the highway, the Viet Cong stepped up land mining. As a countermeasure, L Troop, which camped with How Battery that night, was patrolling the highway between where they camped to the north and a rubber plantation further south. At first a single ACAV was dispatched every ten to twenty minutes from dusk to dawn. When the Viet Cong blew it up with a recoilless rifle, a second ACAV was added to the replacement patrol element, so each could provide security for the other. But again, the VC took aim, this time disabling the trailing ACAV. A response team from Will's encampment returned within an hour of the attack with three detainees in custody. Rumor had it they were picked up while walking alongside the road.

Later that night cries pierced the darkness, startling Will from slumber. "What the hell's going on over there?" he shouted in the direction of the interrogation point.

"Nothing," said Sergeant Artsy, resting next to Will. "Don't let it get to you, Stone."

Will realized Artsy knew no more about the situation than he did. Neither could make out what was going on. Will was never nearer than a hundred yards from where the cries came, and it was wooded and dark all about.

"It's not getting to me," Will answered, "and that's the problem. I don't feel anything. My mind tells me I should."

"Of course the goddamned line troopers are pissed at them," Sergeant Artsy said. "Them goddamned gooks just killed two of them—two of us."

"How do we know it was them, exactly?" Will asked.

"I said don't let it get to you."

Will had put that night out of his mind until now, when Zack brought up the sandbag incident. *Much better to have used up the same chits making sure those prisoners were not abused. But where's the line between abuse and properly thorough interrogation that could very well save some of our own lives?* Will glanced at Zack, who was still locked in on the approaching light.

"That gig with the sandbags could have turned out differently," Will whispered. "I was fortunate Captain Harkness was fair and reasonable."

"More to follow on that," Zack whispered back, as he peered ahead. "Is that light moving? Is it getting higher? Did goddamned Charlie climb up a tree with that goddamned light?"

"It is higher."

"What'll we do?" Zack asked. "We have to do something now. This guy's forced our hand."

"Yeah," Will whispered, "but let's just sit tight for another couple of minutes."

"What the fuck are we waiting for?"

"Our mission is to observe, not engage," Will said. "Something's not right here, but we're not necessarily threatened. Not directly."

"Jesus, Stone," Zack went on, "I say you'd wait till the cows come home. Let's wake Whiteman and see what he says."

"Sit tight, Sarge."

"OK, but only for a few more minutes."

"What about Harkness?"

"Later," Zack whispered, squinting ahead at the light.

"The goddamned light will still be there, and we'll still be able to see it if you tell me about Harkness," Will said. "C'mon. Help me stay awake."

Zack stared at Will. "He's still climbing and don't push me."

Will looked at Zack. "You've never once taken your eye off that light since you spotted it, have you?" Will asked.

"You're goddamned right. It's a good thing one of us—"

"That's it, right there, isn't it?" Will interrupted, pointing with his M-16.

"Yes, you know it is, goddamn it. Now if you're ready to fire, first we gotta get Whiteman up."

"That's OK," Will responded. "I just wanted to make sure we would both be firing on the same star."

"What?"

"Wait a half hour, Sargie," Will said, holding out two fingers at arm's length, "and that light will be a good inch above the tree line."

"What?"

"Now, unless you think the Cong are coming for us in balloons—"

"Shut the fuck up, Stone," Zack ordered. "Are you sure?"

"Tell me about Harkness," Will said.

"You're telling me that's a star?"

"Well, it could be Venus, the Morning Star, but tell me about Harkness, and by the time you're done, you'll see it for yourself."

"Jesus," Zack said.

"Harkness."

"Harkness played it reasonable, like you said," Zack began, "but at a price to himself. Not every one in the orderly room thought the same way. You fomented a crisis. Fortunately, the Exec backed Harkness even though he thought he was wrong. The other officers were up in arms about having to sandbag themselves, you know, and, of course, Top and Grovel egged them on.

"You see, Stone," Zack said, looking back to the light. "You fuckin' smart ass, I think it is a star. Goddamn, for crissake. Jesus." Zack rolled on his side and unzipped his flak jacket. "Getting hot out here. Now, if you think this sandbag thing is long since over, you're wrong. This has been the bone of contention between Harkness and the other officers since then. They didn't like having to fill sandbags when you were lying on your bunk pulling their strings.

"Anyway, Stone, it all came to a head this afternoon. I'm not privy to all the particulars, but the long and the short of it is that the other officers are transferred out of here, except for the exec. It is a fuckin' star, you son of a bitch!"

"What?"

"You heard me. They're gone, finito, kaput. Oh, it wasn't just you. Infusion played its part. The captain had to transfer officers so they all wouldn't rotate at the same time, but he let them all go without getting replacements first in order to make it a clean sweep."

"So where does that leave us?" Will asked.

"For one thing, it leaves the battery without any forward observers," said Zack. "And it sure puts two people on the spot—the captain and you."

"What?"

"The captain says if you were smart enough to get him into this mess, then you're smart enough to help him out of it."

"What the hell does that mean?" Will asked, as he gestured toward Zack's star in the sky above the tree line.

"I know. I can see it," Zack grumbled. "I thought I was going to feel bad telling you this, but you're making me enjoy it."

"What?"

"You're the new FO," Zack answered, "and, unless I'm awful wide of the mark, you're going to be doing double duty. You're going to be filling in for not one but maybe three lieutenants, because the captain's under heavy pressure to get observers in the air and on the ground at the same time."

"Why me?"

"I told you."

"I don't know the first thing about FO'ing," Will confessed.

"Didn't they teach you in survey school?"

"Had KP that day," Will said. "So this is why you're out here?"

Zack nodded, barely able to conceal a smirk. "In the morning you better grab one of the guys from the FO section—Campbell, I suppose—to go over the adjustment of fires with you. You're scheduled to go up in the bubble with Big Three at 1000 hours."

"They don't want to use the guys already in the FO section?"

"The captain said you're more cut from the same cloth."

"Son of a bitch," Will said. "Is this a punishment?"

"The guy needs you," Zack said, "and you proved you got what it takes."

Will's head was buzzing. He did not want to talk anymore. He wanted to sort some of this out for himself. "You ready to catch some *zzzz's*?" he asked Zack.

"Not yet. I'm wired."

Will shook Whiteman's leg. "White Man," Will whispered, "it's time to spell me."

Whiteman sat up as if he had never been asleep. "Uh-huh," he said. Will switched spots with him, reclining where Whiteman had been.

With his legs up out of the foxhole and his head running up the side, Will felt like he was in a hammock. He relaxed as the blood drained from his feet back toward his head. *Son of a bitch, me an FO? Wonder why Zack suggested I speak with Campbell, and not Franco. Everybody respects Franco and he's a corporal, but no NCO ever said a good word about Campbell.*

Will overheard Whiteman address Zack, "Sarge, how come we betrayed the purpose of this morning's MEDCAP?"

"Franco's dead because yesterday the Cong attacked I Troop's MEDCAP in a different village."

Will tried to swallow, but his throat was too dry. *Am I some fucking kind of asshole, or what?* He tried to ignore his sudden thirst, but it choked him. *Can't cough.* He reached carefully for his canteen to avoid any accidental noise and tried to swig water but could not get it down. He kept it in his mouth and passed the open canteen to Whiteman. Will lifted his head from its reclined position and trickled water down the back of his throat. He thought about Franco as Whiteman passed the canteen to Zack. That's when they heard something.

Somethin's Comin'

Alarm shot through the three like lightning. No one moved or spoke. Each glanced at the others to be sure they heard it, too. Zack and Whiteman were totally focused to their left, intent on apprehending any sight or sound. Whiteman's right thumb wrapped around the handle grip of his M-16 and butted up against the safety lever, ready to swing it into full automatic.

Still on his back and unable to see beyond the foxhole, Will concentrated all his attention on the sounds around them. Silence, waiting, waiting, breeze rustling grass in front of them, not the same sound, more silence. Zack turned his head to Whiteman. There it is! Whiteman tensed. Zack's head snapped back to the left. Will jerked his head from the rim of the foxhole. *We all heard it. Something's in the gully.*

Whiteman's knee bounced up and down just enough for Will to notice. *Whiteman's alive.* Then they heard it again: a sound like someone moving through the grasses. Will grabbed the handset of the field radio. He squeezed the black activator bar three times and listened to the handset, which was jammed as hard as possible to his ear.

"Lima Peter One, this is Niner-eight, is that you, over?" Will heard.

Will squeezed the black bar twice.

"If you can speak, do so," Niner-eight ordered. "If not, break squelch three times, over."

Will squeezed the black bar three times and heard it interrupt the reception of the radio with static each time.

"This is Niner-eight. If you have confirmed enemy contact, break squelch twice. If not sure but possible, break squelch three times, over."

Will squeezed the black bar three times.

"This is Niner-eight. If we should alert the perimeter, break squelch twice. If not, break squelch three times, over."

Will looked up at Zack and Whiteman. Zack's face looked like it was fused in steel to the barrel of his rifle. Whiteman slowly rotated his head around from left to right and looked at Will. The moon lit his face enough for Will to see that he lifted an eyebrow and a smirk began to emerge. *There it is again. Shit.* Will tensed. Whiteman snapped his neck to face left.

Will squeezed the black bar on his handset twice. Moments later engines started on the ACAVs guarding the perimeter nearest them. *Fuck, if I only had gotten those trip flares in place. Could be an animal, could be Charlie. We would have known.*

He looked around and saw four trip flares stacked on the right edge of the foxhole within his reach. *I could pull the pin and throw one like a grenade.* While he debated this with himself, the noise came from the gully again. *Christ, it's coming right up here.*

Will picked up a flare in his right hand and gauged its weight. He tapped Whiteman's leg with his left hand, showing him how he could throw the flare with his right. Whiteman tapped Zack, so Will could repeat the demonstration. Zack nodded and smiled.

Will picked up the handset and whispered, "Niner-eight, this is Lima Peter One, over."

"This is Niner-eight. Go ahead, over."

"This is Lima Peter One. Am going to throw a flare in direction of noise. Stand by to fire on any movement you see in area."

"This is Niner-eight. Roger that. Wait one." Twenty seconds later, the voice resumed, "This is Niner-eight. We're ready. Proceed."

When Will saw Zack and Whiteman were watching, he signaled he was ready to let it rip. He pulled the pin and reached his arm out at full extension, squeezing the handle tight to the body of the flare. Will wanted not just a good throw, but a great one. He wanted that flare as far away from them as possible so they remained in the shadows. He wanted it on the other side of the gully to backlight anyone in it.

Will's every muscle strained as he powered the flare upward with his arm, but the wrist strap on his sleeve caught on a root in the side bank of the foxhole. As he threw, he ripped the strap free, but at the cost of most of the thrust of his upper arm. Will had figured on completing the whole throw on his back. Now, near panic, he made a split-second decision to prolong the upward movement of his arm by rolling on his side. It helped, but it also changed the timing and angle of the throw. The flare made it over the fallen tree to their left, but it bounced off a branch, fell to the ground and ignited a dozen feet from the foxhole.

As soon as Will began the throw, Zack and Whiteman had gotten down and stayed down. It was bright as day around them. They tried to look into the gully, but it was like looking into the sun. The intensity of the flare robbed them of any night vision for several moments after they looked away from it. They could not hear any movement because the burning flare made so much noise. They had no clue what, if anything, was taking place to their left.

The three stayed snuggled close to the ground. If seen, they would make an easy target for a grenade attack. Fire support from the perimeter would be their only hope if anything moved toward them. Will felt like puking. *Jesus, maybe call the perimeter and tell them not to fire right of the flare. If they open fire at us, well, shit, I wish this hole were deeper. At this range, those rounds may start dropping. Better eat dirt.*

Head down, Zack was frozen on his side, still facing the gully. All Will could see of Zack's head was his helmet. Whiteman was on his back in what he had thought was going to be a momentary position while he leaned back on his heels to stay clear of Will's throw. When he saw Will glance his way, he whispered, "Don't bother trying out for pitcher next spring."

"Sorry 'bout that," Will answered.

Whiteman smiled. He picked up one of Zack's beer bottles and poked him with it. Zack shook his head. "I pissed my pants," he said.

They waited for the flare to burn itself out. After several minutes, there was only a bright glow from the other side of the log.

Suddenly, a voice came from the radio handset. Will put it to his ear. "Lima Peter One, come in, come in, over."

Will broke squelch twice by squeezing the black bar.

"This is Niner-eight. Are you all right, over?"

Will broke squelch twice.

"This is Niner-eight. If you are all right, break squelch twice. If you want us out there, break squelch three times, over."

"This is Lima Peter," Will whispered back into the handset. "Wait one."

"This is Niner-eight. Standing by."

It was quiet and dark again. Slowly Zack lifted himself to a position from which he could look into the dark gully. Whiteman followed suit, slowly leaning forward to look straight ahead. Will considered crawling into the gully, as an act of redemption. *If it moves, we'll hear it. If I go down there, they'll never know what's me and what's not. Now's the time to play it smart. If it moves, we'll hear it. Just can't let our guard down.* Will slithered to where he could watch, too.

The three held their positions, motionless. Every sense, every thought, every feeling was focused on what was beyond—what they knew, what could be, what they did not know. So attuned were they to everything about them, they could hear their own breathing and take comfort in it. That was how they would make it to dawn. One blessed breath at a time.

Part Three:
Heroes Or Something

Chapter 6

The View From Above

A Crash Course On Hot Potatoes

Will ignored the sounds of approaching helicopters, focusing instead on the crib sheet Campbell had made for him. Already he had been fooled twice since positioning himself for pickup by Big Three's bubble. Once by a Huey gunship armed with two banks of rockets, 20mm cannon, and a M-60 machine gun at each side door. Then again by three slicks, transport Hueys armed only with the M-60 door guns.

He continued to rehearse the script for calling in a fire mission. *I don't know much about being a forward observer, so what I do know, I better know cold. Campbell gave me enough basics to work with. I can't worry about what I don't know. No one ever knows it all about anything.*

When a glint from the shiny glass bubble front of the light observation helicopter caught his eye, Will rose from his kneeling position to be seen from above. The chopper approached, descending on a slope to a point twelve feet above the landing zone. As it lowered from a hover, the turbulence from the rotors spewed a backwash of dust and debris. Will shielded his face and spit out pieces of dried grass before he looked to Captain Harkness and Lieutenant Brown, his executive officer, at the perimeter.

They waved him on when the ship lowered to two feet off the ground. Will scrunched down and made it for the ship. The pilot waved him in. The ship had no doors so Will could slide his radio along the floor, climb in, and buckle his shoulder harness. He waved in Harkness's direction, just as the pilot lifted the ship and banked it away.

Will had been expecting to join the squadron operations officer, Major Finn. Will had never met the major, but he had listened to him directing field operations over the radio net. At times, Will had felt the ground troops were pawns in a grand chess game played by Major Finn. Will found comfort, though, in confirming someone had an idea of the purpose of their moves and efforts. He looked forward to seeing things from the major's vantage point.

The pilot turned to Will. "We have to go back to base camp to fuel up first," he shouted. "Big Three will meet us there."

Will nodded and ran through a mental inventory. Radio, M-16, map case, crib sheet. The pilot passed Will a flight helmet. As soon as Will put it on, the pilot plugged it into his control panel, and Will could hear him speak. "Niner-one, I presume?"

"Affirmative," Will answered.

"Figured as much," the pilot continued, "but you can understand me checking. It wouldn't do to show up with the wrong passenger."

Will smiled.

"What frequency is your arty net on?" the pilot asked. "You can tune in here. Better do a commo check with your support base. You receive with your right ear, and there's a lever built into your helmet there. Push the handle all the way forward to transmit; when you let go, it defaults back to the receive position."

Will tried the lever, breaking squelch each time. "Bandit Niner-five, this is Niner-one. Commo check. Over."

"This is Niner-five. Read you Lima Charlie, Niner-one. Are you in progress now? Over."

"This is Niner-one. Negative. Just putting in at the stable for some oats. Picking up the big package there. Over."

"This is Niner-five. Roger. Let us know when you are operational. Over."

"This is Niner-one. Wilco. Anything else? Over."

"This is Five. That's it. Good luck. Out."

In a few minutes they approached the regimental base camp. As soon as Will glimpsed the camp, he marveled at the changes since he last saw it from above. That was several months ago when he flew in with Survey Section to lay it out.

That day Survey Section arrived to a dense jungle surrounded by a swath of clearing a hundred feet wide. Tanks and ACAVs manned the perimeter at the sparsest of intervals, the equivalent of a football field between positions. Now the camp was a model of military order with row after row of parallel barracks tents along company streets, neatly arranged to the plan Will unfolded when he first arrived.

Laying Out the Base Camp

As soon as the seven surveyors off-loaded their equipment that first day, the slick that had transported them took off like a freed bird. Will remembered his orders: "Start on the layout as soon as you get there. You can't wait till you set up a camp because we have earthmovers on the way, and they're depending on you for advance layout."

As soon as the surveyors hit the ground, they set out to find a survey monument on the adjacent national highway pinpointed on their maps.

All the distances they measured in laying out the base camp, whether horizontal or vertical, were related back to that known point. It was nothing sophisticated, just hot, sweaty work. The men took turns cutting lines of sight through the foliage with machetes when not working with the tools of their trade.

Will wiped his brow with his shirtsleeve every time he squinted into the survey instrument to line up the rod and tape men in the proper directions. Mounted on a collapsible tripod, the instrument, a Wild T-16 Theodolite, looked like a typical builder's transit but was far more accurate. As they staked out the centerlines of the rectangular roadway pattern, a recorder wrote down the actual angles turned by the instrument and the distances measured by the tape men, and then fed the numbers to the computers.

The computers were two men, seated side by side, cross-legged on top of their books of log tables. When they started, they already were sweating profusely from their stint with the machetes. When they finished, they were sweating from hours of converting angles and distances back and forth to logarithms, and from adding and subtracting long columns of seven-digit figures with pencil and paper alone. The six different artillery and mortar fire bases had to be precisely located.

The computers each input their calculations into the same blank forms. Independently, they had to arrive at the same result. Only then could they prove their accuracy whenever they crossed back on one of their own prior survey points. Fatigue and one-hundred-fifteen degree heat added to the challenge.

The first day the crew forged ahead until 6:30 p.m. to get a jump on the land-clearing equipment due in. They were exhausted by the time they ate their C rations. Their only respite from the heat had been an afternoon monsoon, but even that had sent them scurrying around to protect the equipment. After eating, they turned to setting up their camp. Without a vehicle, they could not afford to be selective about where they pitched their tents. The main thing was to be more or less behind one of the M-48A tanks manning the perimeter.

Night was fast approaching as they set up the last of the four tents. There was no time for sandbags, drainage ditches, or mosquito nets before total darkness fell. They only had time to slop water around the inside of their steel helmets to cool their brows and wash the sweat from their bodies. Finally, they sat in a half circle facing the perimeter. No one spoke. Will got up, took a few steps into a shadow, and looked back at the others. *They're probably wondering how secure this perimeter is going to be tonight. Good question.* In a few minutes, they all turned in to sleep.

An hour later, at 10:30 p.m., automatic weapons fired along the perimeter nearest to them. Clutching their M-16's, the seven surveyors hit the red clay dust in front of their tents in flak jackets and olive drab underpants. Tracers from the tank in front of them and the ACAV to its right converged on a point halfway between their positions. "A sapper," someone speculated.

"If he's coming through there, we can be his only target," Will said. "We'd better post a guard." No one complained as they worked it out.

Faced to the perimeter, Will sat on a case of C rations for the first watch. At first, he systematically moved his eyes from left to right, on both sides of the nearby tank, scrutinizing every foot of perimeter for signs of sappers. After several minutes, he found this discipline exhausting, and he caught his mind wandering. *I was a jerk for not posting a guard in the first place. How did I miss that?* He relaxed into a pattern of glancing back and forth from one side of the tank to the other, relying on his natural instincts to spot anything out of the ordinary. It was quiet through the rest of his shift.

"Your turn, White Man," Will said, waking Whiteman about one o'clock in the morning. Will waited for Whiteman to get to his feet before heading back to his sleeping bag. A half hour later, he awoke with sudden and severe pain all over his body. At precisely the same moment, the other three in the tent screamed out. It was the same for everyone, as if many needles had been jabbed into different parts of their bodies. Only Whiteman, who hustled in from his guard position, was exempt. The three surveyors in the next tent quickly lined up behind Whiteman for a look in Will's tent.

"Army ants!" Whiteman said. He flashed a beam of light at a collective mass of ants, tens of thousands of them hanging onto one another and moving as a single unit, three and a half feet wide. They seemed to vibrate across the ground. The men gaped as the mass slipped under the back of the tent like a wave of rusty water ebbing away. Whiteman shifted the light to where the men had fought off the attackers by blindly slapping at their wounds. Hundreds of quarter-inch insect carcasses littered the area. Those in the tent brushed them away from their sleeping bags while those outside saw that the rusty ants actually were a combination of reds and yellows and browns.

"You can't get in their way," Whiteman went on. "They never change their course. They're blind, navigate by scent and gravity somehow. They bite on a signal. All at once."

"How the hell do you know all this, White Man?" someone asked.

"I'm a farmer, for crissake," Whiteman said.

"Better get that light out before you're a dead farmer," Will said.

"Now what do we do?" someone asked.

"We'll dope that out in the morning," Will answered. "For now, set up your mosquito gear."

"There's the storage tents," someone else said.

"The storage tents are filled up," Whiteman said. "You'll be OK here. They won't be back. You may even find this swath of ground to be the most insect-free part of all of Vietnam right now."

So it went for twenty-one days. From dawn to dusk they slashed through untamed jungle. After the first week, they felt more secure because the land-clearing equipment arrived and started work behind them. Only Day Thirteen provided any respite. The sun was blistering and humidity staggering by the time they had worked their way back to the perimeter around 3:00 p.m. A Huey slick roared down and hovered just above them.

"You guys want ice cream?" the door gunner called down.

The surveyors looked at one another. "Yes," Will shouted.

"How many are you?" the gunner called.

"Seven," Will called back.

The Door gunner dropped fourteen half-gallon containers of vanilla ice milk one at a time. The soldiers played outfield for those few moments. "Happy Thanksgiving!" the gunner called out before the ship dipped its nose and headed to the nearest vehicle on the perimeter for its next delivery.

"Happy Thanksgiving, men," Will said. "Take ten."

◯

Will began to extricate himself from the past while his pilot approached what was now a serviceable military airstrip capable of supporting not only helicopter operations, but fixed-wing, supply craft as well.

"I'm Mr. Watters," the pilot said to Will, as soon as they touched down.

"Will Stone," Will replied, extending his hand. As a warrant officer, Watters had been appointed directly by the Army on the basis of his special occupational skill—flying helicopters. Will was accustomed to dealing with commissioned officers, who were nominated by the Army but commissioned by the United States Congress. It was the first time Will was face-to-face with a warrant officer.

"Good to have you aboard, sir, " Watters resumed. "I'll let the major know we'll be ready in ten minutes.

Will watched Watters step toward flight headquarters. *He thinks I'm an officer. They told him he was picking up a forward observer, so he assumed I'm a second looey. Shit. Gotta straighten that out.* Will climbed out of the helicopter for a stretch. Sitting on a sandbag wall, he resumed studying his crib sheet for adjusting artillery fires. A half hour later, he was sure he knew the crib sheet cold, though he wondered what the sheet might not have covered. Events would soon answer that question, but not before Watters returned with Major Finn.

While he waited, Will tried clearing his mind, but thoughts of the past intruded. He remembered meeting Harry in the street just before Josh's shooting.

Ultimatum At Midnight

After his impasse with Will on the construction site, Harry raced to his weekly card game with his partners at the Pittston barbershop. Only Harry's outspoken denunciation of Will saved him from embarrassment when he explained his lateness. His partner who owned the local lumberyard jumped up, paced, stared at Harry and said, "How'd your boy get such gall? If it weren't happening all over the place, I'd say you did a pretty lousy job of running your family, Harry."

"I haven't forgot seeing that bastard son of yours standing across the street causing trouble for me," said the barber, a town councilman. "He wants to tell me how to run my shop. I been doing it thirty years, Harry, thirty years. How was I to know that kid they brought here was some African diplomat's kid? He looked like an ordinary nigger to me. Who knows what my customers'd say had I cut his hair. Hell, I don't even got the right equipment."

Harry's other partner, a politically connected lawyer, kept still until asked. "I came here to play cards, not to psyche your kid, Harry," he said. "And, gentlemen, if we may, let's leave the young man's parentage out of this. We mustn't forget his natural father fell in the line of duty for this country, and it's to Harry's credit that he's taken the boy in. But, well, it looks like in order to play cards, we're first going to have to deal with this. All right, let's see. You've no longer got any leverage with this kid, right, Harry? I mean he doesn't sleep at home, take your money or your advice. You got to have a lever to control him."

The lumberman and barber grunted their assent. The lawyer fussed around selecting and lighting up a cigar until he smirked. "I'm on the Selective Service board," he said. "I can call one of the secretaries and tell her to notify the bas— excuse me, the young man, to report for a physical.”

The lumberman and barber applauded. Harry shied back. “Now wait a second.”

“Relax, Harry. I didn’t say call him up. I just said call him for a physical. It’s just a verification of his classification. These days, it precedes induction by seventy-five days. Every flatfoot who gets that notice, though, thinks he’s being inducted. If the US were threatened Will would rise to the call of arms, but under current conditions, he’ll see it as a waste of his time. He isn’t dumb. You can’t explain his nigger-loving that way. Unless I miss my mark, he’ll be quick to beat on your door, Harry, to regain his student deferment.”

“He better be,” the barber muttered.

“That’s right,” said the lumberman.

Harry authorized the lawyer to proceed, but not without misgivings. “I understand their point,” he mumbled as he waited at a traffic signal on his way home. “But this is no good. I gotta do something.”

Will tooled slowly through the Pittston business district, keeping an eye out for Josh. As he approached the Plaza intersection, he missed Harry’s black Cadillac waiting at the traffic light.

“Dammit, there’s gotta be some way out of this thing,” Harry said out loud, as Will idled past him. As soon as Harry saw Will, he leaned on his horn. He startled and embarrassed himself with the disturbance, and he pulled straight through the intersection against the red light to where Will had stopped. Will walked back to Harry’s open window.

“Will, I’m asking you not to go. I’m begging you,” said Harry, “but I’m also telling you, you can’t go.”

A police officer on foot patrol rounded the corner to investigate. Harry’s hopes sank as he saw the blue uniform approach in his rearview mirror. “Let me handle this guy. I know him,” said Will, moving behind Harry’s car.

“Yeah, it’s me,” said Will to the officer, “and this is my old man. Everything’s OK, just a little family disagreement, but it might be just as well if you ran us both off so we pick it up at a decent hour.”

The policeman scrutinized Will and yawned. He led Will back to Harry’s window and asked both for their driver’s licenses. Then he told them to be on their way and walked back toward the corner. Harry and Will searched each other for signs of retreat.

As Will turned, Harry called to him, “You better quit this. I can have you drafted.” When Will spun and met Harry’s glare, Harry pointed and shouted, “I’m telling you to give it up. I can do it. I’ll have you drafted!”

He lowered his voice. "Will, my lawyer can do it, and he will unless you give me your word—"

"Get moving!" the policeman yelled from the corner.

"You can call it off by getting to me by eight in the morning," Harry shouted at Will.

Will got in his car and rolled the two blocks down the street to his rooming house in hopes of finding Josh there. When he arrived, Josh was there, but things were not as Will had hoped.

O

"Niner-one?" a voice addressed him from behind.

Will spun around and snapped to attention when he saw Major Finn. "Let's go," the major said, nodding to the helicopter pad where Mr. Watters now waited. He was ready to take off.

"Yes, sir," Will said.

The major had spotted Will's right arm jerk momentarily at his side and knew Will had suppressed a salute. A telltale sign of importance at the wrong time and place could mean a sniper's bullet.

Will hustled to the airship. *Don't want to be the one to hold anything up. Shit, I wonder if Finn knows I'm just a Specialist Fourth Class.* He already was buckled in and helmeted down by the time Major Finn climbed in on the other side of the pilot. Watters fumbled with his control panel before putting on his helmet and grabbing his map case. The major elbowed him and pointed to a location on the map.

Will watched as the two took turns running their fingers in different patterns on the map, but he could not make out anything without hearing the conversation. He pulled off his helmet just as the other two laughed and put on theirs. *Gotta know where we're going. If they tell me to call in fire support, I'm gonna have to know where the hell we are.*

As the whoosh of the helicopter rotors picked up speed, Will focused on his own map case, determined to chart every movement of the ship. The chopper lurched upward, then forward. "You OK, Niner-one?" Major Finn asked over the intercom system built into their helmets.

"Roger, sir."

Baptism Of Fire

The chopper set out over territory familiar to all three. They flew above Highway 2 past the first hamlet to the South and then changed course to cut across the Swiss-owned Courtenay rubber plantation. For the first time from above, Will looked over this area. He knew well what it looked like from the ground. His heart jumped when, to the east of the plantation, he spotted a recent clearing in the jungle. Fresh paths jutted from the old logging trail. It was obvious the clearing and trails were made from armored vehicles riding roughshod over the jungle understory. Will could not help remembering what had taken place down there.

Two months earlier Survey had been searching these same logging trails. The mounted patrol, a platoon of ACAVs headed up by a dozer-bladed M-48A tank, moved slowly along the trail, widening it as they went along. Foot patrols of ten men each explored various spur areas on either side of the trail at what seemed propitious intervals.

Suddenly, there was havoc—an explosion to the north, followed by the bark of small arms fire and squawking over the radio. Track vehicles raced to the continuous small arms fire. The periodic roar of beehive rounds from the lead tank added to the deafening din of machine gun fire unleashed by each vehicle as it joined the fray.

Will manned an M-60 machine gun in the back of an ACAV racing to the call of battle. He and O'Rourke on the M-60 across from him exchanged glances. *What the fuck is going on?* Will steadied his footing by grabbing onto his gun shield with one hand and his M-60 with the other in order to compensate for the lurching ride. The roar of the gunfire left no doubt they would fast be upon the battleground.

Will lowered his head and frame behind his gun shield when he caught his first glimpse of the smoke and fire. He readied to aim when all at once his legs went limp. Still mindful of O'Rourke standing tall next to him, Will commanded his body to resist such weakness as soon as he realized what was happening. His body was coming to the rescue of his mind.

Get down, fool! his body ordered.

You can't do that, his mind countered.

Get down, fool! Don't expose yourself.

Stiffen up, you fucking bastard.

Down.

Shut the fuck up.

You're gonna be killed, you're gonna be killed, you're gonna be killed, you're gonna be killed! This is it, the end of life, there is no more. Get down. Get down now.

I'm going down. I can't believe it. I'm going down. Me! I'm going down. I'm saving my ass.

Yes, we're gonna live. Yahoo! We're gonna live.

No!

Yes! It's the only way to save your life. Don't you want to live?

Fuck it. Fuck it. Fuck it. With that, Will found strength to tighten his grip on the stock of the M-60 with his left hand up around the barrel and his right around the trigger guard. He lowered his shoulder to the butt end just enough to sight through the slot in the gun shield in proper firing position. *Fuck it. Fuck it. Fuck it!*

Fuck it? Are you crazy? What does that mean, FUCK IT? *Do you think you can say '*FUCK YOU*' to Death? It doesn't work that way, and you know better. Get your ass down.*

Fuck it. Fuck it. Fuck it. Fuck it. Fuck it.

Is that all you can say? Don't you want to live?

Fuck it. Fuck it. Fuck it. Fuck it. Fuck life.

What? Doesn't life matter?

Fuck it. The only thing that matters now is standing here.

The bursts of his own machine gun fire punctuated the continuing repetition of his invective.

Looking back on the scene from the chopper made Will go pale. *I thought courage would be defying death, not devaluing life. I weighed honor over life only because I gave life no weight. But life is precious, I know that now for sure. I wanted to live. I wanted the air. I wanted shelter. Still, honor took precedence, as it should have. Why did I have to desecrate life in order to stand in place? Why does honor have to include death?*

"Niner-one, Niner-one," Will heard the ship's intercom system through the left ear of his helmet, "you with us?"

Will twisted to Major Finn, who leaned forward to see past Watters. Will shook his head to escape his reverie. "Yes, sir," he said.

"Not getting airsick?" the major asked.

"No, sir."

"You know where we are?" the major continued.

"Yes, sir."

The major nodded and cracked a slight smile.

Will jerked his head to look out the right side door opening. *Where the hell are we?* He shivered when he saw.

The Point Man

Below were a series of trails Will had walked only weeks ago. No one was more surprised than he that day, five weeks after his baptism of fire, when he was picked to go with the line troops on foot patrol. He had been assigned as a side gunner to fill out a FO's ACAV crew. Each track crew was levied one man for patrol duty, and Will got the nod from Lieutenant Riggs, the FO at the time. On one level, Will was glad for the challenge. It came about so unexpectedly, however, it caught him off guard.

Ranksaw, a twenty-four-year-old, ramrod West Pointer, was thrilled with his promotion earlier that morning. A month earlier he had been given acting command of the troop. Now his command was official, and it would be his springboard to career success. Hesitant at first as he ran his fingers through his flattop haircut, Ranksaw went ahead and pinned his shiny new captain's bars on the canvas camouflage cover of his helmet. "I'd rather a subdued insignia," he said to the platoon leader with him. "But I earned these bars, and these little bastards aren't going to cheat me out of wearing them. Not today they're not."

First, they ran out the trails to the west, the direction of the plantation. The patrol moved at a much faster pace and for a much longer time than Will would have guessed. Ranksaw was with them, and he constantly belittled whoever walked point for not moving faster still. The point man led the way by at least twenty feet, even in the thickest of jungle understory. Ordinarily stealth and vigilance were considered more a part of the job description than speed. Caution came naturally to a point man, as he was the most vulnerable to ambush.

Will was not long afoot before he tapped the bottom of his canteen. It was empty. *Damn, how could you of all people fuck up like this? I don't care why your canteen is empty, whether someone else helped himself to your water or what. You should have checked.*

When they came upon a clearing, they squatted down to rest at its edge for five minutes. "Go ahead and drink," said the line trooper next to him. He held out his own full canteen. "It's OK, go ahead."

Will recognized him as the latest man walking point on the patrol that morning and scrutinized him from his matted hairline to his sweat-soaked trouser blousers, the garters that cuffed his pant legs. Will saw his benefactor had yet to take water for himself. "I'm really not thirsty," Will said.

"Go ahead," the trooper said. "You're gonna need it."

"Thanks." Will took a measured swallow.

"Take more," the trooper said. "It's OK."

Will did, glancing at the nametag of his benefactor. *Perez. Thank God for this guy. I can't believe I didn't check my water. I would have resented someone horning in on my water after I had to hump it around all day. Ah, fuck it.*

After lunch Ranksaw announced they would run two patrols that afternoon, one along each path headed east in hope of linking up with one another at some Viet Cong facility. The official hope always was they would find the elusive COSVN, the communist headquarters for all of South Vietnam. This would have been akin to the British capturing George Washington during the American Revolution. The likelihood of such a discovery was more modest. If anything were found, most likely it would be a military outpost, infirmary, re-education camp, or perhaps an arsenal or supply depot. Chances also were that whatever they found would have been deserted, not defended, which was all right with most troops. Unless cornered by surprise, the Viet Cong engaged American forces solely at their own time and place of choosing. If a patrol found as much as a rice store, weapon cache, enemy map or document, the patrol was deemed successful.

This time when they headed out on foot patrol in the afternoon, Will had a full canteen. It was a good thing. Ranksaw drove his group at the same pace in the afternoon heat as he had in the morning. Perez was back on point. It did not surprise Will that Ranksaw went out on foot patrols when he was still a first lieutenant, even if he was acting troop commander. But he was a captain now, and it seemed unusual to Will that Ranksaw would be walking behind him on patrol. *It'd be better, should either of these patrols make contact, if there was a captain coordinating the support and relief.*

As in the morning, Ranksaw yelled that Perez was moving too slowly to overtake any Viet Cong pulling back. It was obvious to everyone else they were moving too quickly to detect any Viet Cong staying put. Nonetheless, Ranksaw was out front with the men taking his chances, so most felt obliged to give the captain the benefit of any doubt.

"Look," Ranksaw suddenly called out, pointing to the man in the No. 2 position, "you take over on point. Let's get this thing moving."

Will glanced back at the clench-jawed Ranksaw and saw him gesture to Perez to fall back behind him and allow the next guy to take over the point. As the line squeezed its way past Perez, he scowled and glared at Ranksaw. Point was not a job for which anyone volunteered. It was not an assignment lightly taken. Most troopers performed it with as much care and pride as Perez had shown, and any of them would have resented being relieved.

The same could not be said about Perez's replacement, who moved slower than Perez and without his stealth and attentiveness. The heat had weakened him to such an extent he seemed out for a stroll in the woods. Five minutes later, Ranksaw signaled for the next in line to replace him.

Will knew that before long he would be on point. As he observed and maintained the relative distance between the point and him, his mind was so clouded with thought and emotion that he could apprehend little else. *No way I'm going to give him an excuse to relieve me.* In his mind's eye, Will already was racing ahead of the others left struggling to keep up. A shove from behind interrupted his musings. Ranksaw hand-signaled him to stride ahead to the point.

Will bound to the front, fueled by anxiety from the captain breathing down his neck. He settled into a lengthy, forceful stride that set a pace just slower than jogging. Any faster and Will would have had to give up even the smallest pretense of stealth and watchfulness that he forced himself to maintain. Each time Will ducked to miss branches overhanging the trail, he would lurch ahead so as not to break his stride.

Ten minutes passed at this pace. Sweat flowed from Will's every pore. He knew it was difficult for the taller men to keep up because of the low branches. When he stole a few glances back, he saw a gap developing now and then between Ranksaw, who was hot on his tail, and the others, who rushed to catch up whenever they could.

Already, Will's mouth was pasty from thirst. His eyes stung with sweat dripping from his brow. Fatigue had set in and he knew it. The adrenaline flowing from that knowledge returned bounce to his stride and refocused his search for anything out of the ordinary. His eyes scanned the trail with high-beam intensity.

At the same time Will spied a fork in the trail twenty-five feet ahead, he realized his right hand had let go of the stock of his M-16 long enough to pat the bottom of his canteen. *He must have seen it. He knows I'm tiring, that I'm thirsty. Shit.* Will pushed ahead even harder to the fork. He was sure he should go right. It was the general direction they wanted to follow to close with the other patrol. He had every intention of rushing around the bend to the right but, just as he came to the fork, instinct told him to hold up. *Gotta check each way for any sign of recent enemy activity. Gotta really check.*

Will glanced left, with Ranksaw's hot breath on his neck, and was about to rush right, when again he held up. *Gotta check.* Will dipped his left knee and peered in that direction for just a moment. In that moment, Ranksaw rushed past Will headlong up the trail to the right. Will sprang after him. *Jesus!* A carbine shot rang out and Ranksaw flew backward into

Will's arms, the back of his head and neck a bloody pulp. As they hit the ground, Will saw the bullet had entered Ranksaw's head at the bridge of his nose, two inches below its likely target, the shiny new silver captain's bars on his helmet.

Will scrambled to return fire with the captain's M-16. His own rifle had dropped when he caught Ranksaw, whose body now covered the weapon. Perez was the first to reach Will in support with the field radio. The two called for an air strike to suppress the heavy small arms fire pinning them down.

"Throw smoke," Will shouted, repeating the command received over the radio. Perez pitched a canister grenade just in front of them to mark their location.

The response came back from the fighter pilot, "I see Red."

"Affirmative," Will screamed into the handset.

Before he heard the jet's roar, Will felt his eyebrows singe with the heat of napalm flashing before his eyes like a waterfall of fire poured from the heavens to hell beneath. He dared not look up. A second burst of heat signaled a second plane's expansion of the inferno further away from them.

The two jets returned in their wide elliptical pattern to strafe the attack area with 20mm cannon before they broke off their counterattack and flew homeward. Will looked on with amazement and relief as this portion of the jungle yielded to the firestorm.

"Get a dust-off on the logging trail," Will shouted into the radio.

The Phantasmal Face

Will became increasingly conscious of the whoosh of the rotor of the chopper. *Everyone's always saying dust-offs are a great thing. Get you to the field hospital real quick. Yeah, yeah, yeah. That's fine. So long as they don't mean it's OK for us all to get shot to shit because we can always be rushed to a field hospital.*

Will could not get the last skirmish out of his head. *Ranksaw. How much of this is about honor, and how much is about a headlong rush to oblivion in the name of glory? And the Cong? What made them do it? Charlie had to know that if he hung tight in order to pin us down, we'd call for napalm. He had to know.*

As Will searched his own experiences for an answer, an image came into focus. It was the face of a Viet man that came to him over and over again, and it was always the same. The same now as it had been two months ago in the Iron Triangle when Will rushed from his perimeter post as soon as the shooting stopped. He had been in a bunker they dug into the ground and half-covered with earth-filled, artillery-shell crates. Suddenly, the shooting started. It seemed like it was coming from behind them, which they could not understand because the perimeter was so large and reinforced so well. They were on a multi-divisional operation and had armor and artillery pieces making up their half of the perimeter. The crack troopers of the 173rd Airborne manned the other half. There was no way any portion of this temporary base could have been overrun with the small arms fire they heard.

Will looked about. Tracer bullets laced the air behind him. There was no fire or movement to his front. When the firing to the rear increased, Will told Whiteman and Deddson to get down and cover the side entries. He would cover the front and back. He could see nothing except that the firing was getting closer. He wanted to get down, too. *Why get hit by a stray?* Just then a shot lodged itself in the M-60 ammunition can barely six inches to the right of his neck. *Wanna get down. Can't get down. Someone could run right in here from any direction without warning. Could frag us. Gotta stay up. Fuck it!*

Will heard M-60 gunfire from the ACAV nearest them and saw O'Rourke had spun his M-60 machine gun and was firing back inside the perimeter. *Jesus!* The firing stopped, followed by shouting. "It's all right. It's all over. Cease fire! Cease fire!"

"Take over, White Man," Will said, and he ran to where a small crowd was gathering a hundred feet behind their post. Whiteman, who had been lying next to Will faced to one side, went to work digging out the bullet in the ammo can.

"M-16 slug," Whiteman said. He passed the bullet to Deddson, who looked it over carefully. Deddson dropped the slug in his chest pocket and met Whiteman's stare.

Will jostled his way to the center of the crowd and caught his first glimpse of the face that had haunted him ever since. The man was bareback and barefoot in black silk pants. He lay facedown toward Will's section of the perimeter, suggesting he was cut down from behind rather than by O'Rourke's M-60. The man's eyes and mouth were open. His back and legs were riddled with gunshots.

In search of some sign, Will studied the man's face, its smooth skin stretched over high cheekbones. What first seemed yet alive paled to a greenish hue. Yet somehow the dead man's stare locked onto Will's like a laser beam. So engrossed was Will he barely heard an intelligence interrogator blurt out, "We call it the Bell Telephone Hour. You know, wire a field phone to his nuts and shock him till we get some answers. Little bastard sprung up and slugged me with my own carbine. Ripped it right out of my hands. He was like a spooked animal or something. Probably Cong. Must've been Cong. He was Cong. Bet the farm on it."

Just as he had then, but this time closing his eyes, Will looked to this phantasmal face for some sign. Now, as always, at the very moment Will seemed about to catch a glimmer of insight, the report of an M-16 rang out, the face exploded, and blood splattered him and everyone else.

"What'd you do that for?" someone yelled at Rogers, who dropped his rifle after firing it into the back of the interrogee's head.

Will vented some unformed thought of outrage as he reflexively spit and cast loose a minute skull fragment that had lodged itself in his upper lip. He wiped his splattered sleeve against his torn lip, smearing as much blood on his lip as he wiped off.

Rogers was stumbling backward, trying to distance himself from his act. "It's my birthday," he cried, before falling on the ground and vomiting.

"He's nineteen today," someone added. "Said he was gonna get a Cong for his birthday."

Up in the chopper now, Will swiped his hand across his mouth as he recalled watching Rogers crawl away on all fours.

A Shot To Remember

"Bandit Niner-one, this is Bandit Niner-five. Come in, please," the voice on the radio whispered until Will became aware he was receiving a transmission. Immediately he twisted the volume control and then heard loud and clear, "This is Niner-five. Come in, Niner-one. Over."

"Niner-five, this is Niner-one, over."

"Thought we lost you, Niner-one," the fire direction officer said. "You having equipment trouble? Over."

"This is Niner-one. Uh, affirmative that," Will responded. "Think we got it straightened out now, though. Over."

"This is Five. None too soon! We need you patched into Fire Support Base Juliette. We've been monitoring the big net. You'll be out of our range, but well within Juliette's. Add two five-five to our signal. Call for Rambler Five! Over."

"This is Niner-one," Will said, "Roger all. Over."

"Bandit Niner-five, this is Bandit Niner-eight," a voice broke in, "Fire mission, contact. Over."

"This is Niner-five. Niner-one, clear the air and good luck! Out. Break. Niner-eight, send your mission! Over."

Will desperately wanted to listen to the mission being called in, but he dared not. *Why the fuck are they patching me into Juliette? Where the hell is that? Where the hell are we racing to across these treetops? Jesus, I don't know where the hell we are.*

Will added two hundred fifty-five kilocycles to the frequency of his battery net. "Rambler Five, this is Bandit Niner-one. Over," Will said.

"This is Rambler Niner-five. Come in, Niner-one. Over."

"This is Niner-one," Will said. "Commo check. Over."

"This is Rambler Five. Read you Lima Charlie, Niner-one. Over."

"This is Niner-one. Am approaching within your range shortly. Briefing by my five cut off by press of business. Over."

"This is Rambler Five. Affirmative. You are headed into light contact situation within seven klics of our fire base in order to spot for us. We have an FO on the ground with a grunt unit pinned down by small arms fire. Over."

"This is Niner-one. Didn't get there yet. How good was the location your observer gave you? Over."

"This is Rambler Five. That's the problem. They've been humping the boonies all day. Hard to tell for sure. Over."

"This is Niner-one. Roger that. Over."

"This is Rambler Five. That's where you come in, Niner-one. Our observer on the ground can adjust fires, once you zero him in. Understand your Big Three wants to be somewhere else. Appreciate your help. Over."

"This is Niner-one. Roger. Where are you?"

"This is Five. From checkpoint Sierra, right three point three, down two."

Should have just given me his coordinates. By now Charlie knows where those guns are, and now he knows where our checkpoint is if he was listening and works it backwards from the gun location.

Will studied his map, which was superimposed with fine black grid lines eight-tenths of an inch apart, horizontally and vertically. The lines connected Universal Transverse Mercator (UTM) coordinate points plotted to scale every one thousand meters up and down and across the map. Checkpoints were pre-selected grid intersection points that were given temporary names from the military phonetic alphabet, so that they could be referred to by other than their actual grid coordinates. In theory, the temporary names were rotated often enough that no one would know where, say, checkpoint Sierra was, unless he had been given the current list of names for the selected grid intersections. By giving a location over the radio relative to a checkpoint, Will could say where he was or where he was headed without tipping off the enemy and perhaps bringing a rain of mortar rounds down upon himself.

"Rambler Five, this is Niner-one," Will spoke into the mouthpiece built into his air helmet. "Where's your observer party relative to your own position?"

"This Five, Niner-one. Try the northwest quadrant. Direction 5-800, range 6-600. Over."

"This is Niner-one," said Will. "Wilco. Out."

Will's eyes darted back and forth from his map to the treetops racing beneath him. He was looking for some clue—a road, a church, a stream, a hamlet, any landmark that showed up somewhere on his map. He saw nothing but a rush of jungle.

"Rambler Niner-seven, this is Rambler Five," Will heard Juliette call over their net.

"This is Seven," came the reply from Rambler's forward observer, who was with a ground patrol lost in the jungle and under attack. "I monitored, Five. Over." Seven hoped that an aerial observer—Will—could find his location and drop a registration round near his target from which he could adjust to bombard the ridge with the Viet Cong pinning them down.

"This is Five. Good," said Rambler's Fire Direction Center. "Stand by. Out."

Will took account of the situation. *That had to be their observer on the ground. I could ask him to advise when he spots us. Could ask him to throw smoke. No. Big Three must have already worked that out with whoever's in charge there. Could do a commo check. Fuck it. He just told his five he monitored our conversation.* Will looked down again at the jungle canopy racing below. *Gotta know where we are. Why hasn't Big Three tipped me off over the intercom?*

Will looked toward Major Finn, who was intensely conversing with his own air helmet while making frantic reference to his maps, unfolding and refolding them. Will leaned toward the pilot and was able to read the major's radio frequency. *He's on the squadron net. He's wrapped up in wherever Niner-eight's in contact. Could switch to his net, but it won't do me any good. It's got nothing to do with where we're headed. Shit, he's relying on me to spot this location for them.*

Will scanned the panorama before him. *Give me a railroad, a logging trail, a mountain, for crissake. If we weren't flying so damn low, I'd be able to see some landmark.* The thought made Will more aware that the pilot was flying in a straight line. Will looked up at the ship's compass. *Watters must have a pretty good idea where we're going.*

There was still nothing recognizable on the ground. Will rested his map on his left knee next to the pilot. He nudged Watters and pointed to his best guess of where they were headed on the map. Watters glanced down at Will's map, but quickly refocused on his flying. It seemed like a lifetime to Will before Watters reached down, almost without looking, and pointed to a grid square three thousand meters north of where Will had guessed and then moved his finger in an arc of some fifteen hundred meters. When his finger stopped, it tapped the spot on the map three times. As soon as Watters removed his finger, Will circled the grid with his grease pencil. Watters began his turn, following the arc he had depicted for Will.

"Rambler Niner-seven, this is Bandit Niner-one. Commo check. Over."

"This is Niner-seven. Read you Lima Charlie, Niner one."

Will glanced at Finn and saw he was still on the Bandit radio net. "This is Niner-one. We should close in on you in about thirty seconds. Throw smoke."

"This is Niner-seven. Wilco, Niner-one, over."

When he looked up, Will realized Watters was climbing rapidly as they flew toward gun flashes. *Small arms fire from the ridge. Enough to keep our guys pinned down at the toe of the slope.*

"Niner-seven, this is Niner-one. I see yellow."

"This is Seven. Affirmative. Over."

Watters pulled back some as tracers from a machine gun located on the ridge headed their way. Will looked to Finn and saw he was still on the squadron net. As Watters backed off, Finn glanced up and saw the tracers coming their way. He grimaced at Will and pointed at the ridge, demonstratively waving his hand up and down. Will nodded back.

"Take them out, Niner-one," Finn said to Will over the intercom. "Take them out."

Will nodded to Finn. "Rambler Niner-seven, this is Bandit Niner-one. Over."

"This is Seven, Niner-one. Over."

"This is Niner-one. Please confirm none of your party is on that ridge?" Will said.

"This is Seven. Affirmative. We're behind the yellow."

"This is Niner-one. Roger, Seven. Thank you. Out. Break. Rambler Five, this is Bandit Niner-one. Fire mission. Contact. Over."

"This is Rambler Five," Juliette answered. "Send your mission, Niner-one. Over."

"This is Niner-one," Will said, before pausing. He still was not sure of his location or that of his target. Watters had gotten them there, but he had flown to a grid location furnished him by the troops on the ground, and they already had confessed they were unsure of their whereabouts. Both could have been slightly off about their positions. In the end, after all, Watters had flown to the gun flashes and smoke, rather than adhering to the flight plan he traced across the map with his finger for Will.

"This is Niner-one. Grid 6-1-3 0-3-4, direction 900, VC ambush party hidden in triple canopy above clear ridge, shell Willy Peter, fifty meters height of burst, fire when ready, will adjust. Over."

Will looked over at Finn, who gave a quick glance in his direction after checking the ridge for more fire directed at them. "This is Five," came the confirmation. "Grid 6-1-3 0-3-4, direction 900, one round shell Willy Peter, fifty meters height of burst, fire when ready, adjust fires. Over."

"This is Niner-one. Roger that. Give me time of flight. Over."

Will had ordered that a single white phosphorus round—in effect, a fire bomb—be exploded in the air by a timed fuse because he was still unsure of the location of the target. He was more apt to see this shell explode in the air, and it was less apt to harm friendlies than if it exploded on the ground.

The small helicopter flew in a tight circle just south of the friendly position and just out of range of the hostile machine-gun fire. Will elbowed Watters, who looked at him and signaled for him to speak over the intercom. "You gotta hover," Will said. "We could miss this, and I gotta maintain sorta this line of sight, an azimuth of nine hundred mils."

Watters nodded as the radio barked its message.

"Niner-one, this is Five. On the way; splash in forty-five seconds. Over."

Will glanced at his Timex. "This is Niner-one. Roger, Five. Stand by."

Glancing once more at his watch, Will noticed Finn observing him intently. Watters, too, stole furtive glances at Will, who pointed to the two o'clock position on his watch. "Twenty seconds," Will said.

They nodded and followed Will's example of staring patiently at the sky above the targeted ridge. Will kept his wrist alongside his line of sight, as his eye flitted back and forth between his watch and the ridge. The second hand neared the big two. Will swallowed hard.

"Splash," Rambler Five advised.

Will braced himself for a few seconds and then sagged. *Nothing? Bad fuse, maybe?* Watters elbowed Will and pointed sideways past him to a wisp of smoke far away, just dissipating. *No, can't be. Gotta be. Gotta adjust before it's gone. It's probably a thousand meters to our right. I'll be moving it mostly our way. Better cut it in half, just to play it safe.*

Will remembered hearing a "pop," like a wine bottle opening, at the time of the explosion. Finn looked on silently.

"Five, Niner-one. Adjust left five hundred; add two hundred. Repeat fires. Over."

"This is Five. Understand adjust left five hundred; add two hundred. Shell Willy Peter, fifty meters height of burst. Over."

"This is Niner-one. Affirmative, Five," Will said. "Fire when ready and advise. Over."

Will looked about him. Finn caught his eye. "You make an adjustment?" the major asked over the intercom.

Before Will could answer came Juliette's call, "This is Five. Shot. Splash in forty-seven seconds. Over."

Will glanced at his watch, and then replied to Finn on the intercom, "On the way. About thirty seconds, sir."

The three of them—the major, the pilot, and Will—returned their attention to the sky above the ridge. Will kept one eye on his watch as the time drew near.

As Juliette shouted, "Splash," a thunderbolt exploded just to their right, sending them rocking and skipping to the left on a wake of blinding, sizzling sky. Will grabbed the frame of his seat as Watters fought to regain control of the ship. Instantaneously, Will knew, now or never, he had to get it right. They were turned from his nine-hundred-mil line of direction, but he knew where the next round had to go. He knew that he could allow for being spun about somewhat and that he had to make the adjustment before Finn lost confidence in him.

By the time Watters and Finn caught hold of themselves enough to turn his way, Will sat looking straight at the ridge with his chin up as if things had gone exactly the way he had planned. Watters and Finn followed suit, unsure of what they should have expected and unwilling to give in to doubt and panic.

"Rambler Five, this Niner-one. Left one-fifty, add four hundred. Shell Willy Peter on the deck. Fire when ready and advise. Will adjust. Over."

"This is Rambler Five. Adjust left one-fifty; add four hundred. Shell Willy Peter on the deck. Fire when ready. Over."

"Niner-one," Finn broke in over the ship's intercom.

"This is Niner-one. Affirmative. Over," Will transmitted on the radio, holding the intercom lever so that Finn would figure that he was busy, although he had nothing more to say. *Get it in the air, you bastards, before he tells me to shut it down and jump out the doorway.*

"Niner-one," Finn called over the intercom again.

Shit. Will's upper body twitched before he answered, "Sir?"

"Uh, Niner-one, we really have to bug out of here. We've got big problems to the north."

"Niner-one, this is Five. On the way. Over."

"This is Niner-one. Roger. Over." Then Will asked Finn, "Did you monitor, sir?"

"Affirmative," Finn answered. "OK, we'll see this out. Tell me, will I need my flak jacket?"

The roar of the M-110 8" howitzer round passed by, followed by an explosion. The white phosphorus round smeared the ridge dead center.

"Niner-one, this is Rambler Niner-seven. Over."

"This is Niner-one. Over," Will responded.

"This is Seven. Nice shot. I can take it from here. Thank you. Over."

"This is Niner-one. Roger, Seven. Love to Juliette. Out."

"I monitored, Niner-one," Finn broke in over the intercom. "Watters, move it out straight up to Route One, just west of Soui Cat again."

Will glanced at Finn and saw he was back on the squadron net. Will left his radio tuned to Fire Base Juliette's frequency.

"Five, this is Seven," Will heard. "Fire mission, contact. Over."

"This is Five. Send your mission. Over."

"This is Seven," the ground observer resumed. "Fire for effect, two volleys, Shell H-E, repeat fires. Fire when ready. Will adjust. Over."

"This is Five. Fire for effect, Shell H-E, two volleys, on last round fired. Adjust fires. Over."

"This is Seven. Affirmative. Over."

Watters swung the helicopter around in order to give the target area a wide berth and then continued past it to the north. For a moment, Will had an impulse to look back and see the entire ridge aflame. *Don't have to.*

As he left, Will took satisfaction in a job well done. He gave no further thought to the necessary relief of his comrades-in-arms. Nor did it much concern him that he had just taken human life. He had proven up to the job. The Army had him ready.

When the three finally arrived just to the west of Soui Cat along Highway One, they found it was the Americans who had been plastered, and the damage was already done. A supply convoy had been ambushed—the second one in that spot in a month. By the time they evacuated the dead and wounded, Finn already had resolved what to do about the attacks. "We're going to have to establish an escort service for these convoys," he said. "The ARVN will have to help."

Finn, Watters, and Will flew back to the base camp in mournful silence. It would be dark by the time they touched down. Will's heart was full, but his mind was empty. *I got no explanation for all this, but I gotta find one, the right one, soon. We can't keep doing this without a damn good reason.*

Eavesdropping

Once on the ground, Will acquainted Watters with his own lowly station in the military scheme of things. Watters offered to bootleg some dinner from the officers' mess so they could eat together while a ground crew checked out his ship. Afterward, Watters would fly Will back to his unit perimeter for the night and return for him in the morning. While Watters updated his flight log, he noticed Finn's map case under the seat next to him.

"You might want to walk this up to Major Finn's CP," he said to Will, who wasted no time following Watter's directions. His command post was a military version of an oversized mountaineer tent, stretched over a 2 x 4 frame. Divided into three compartments by interior canvas partitions, the tent afforded ample work area in the front for the major, his aide and his orderly, and still reserved room in the rear for a private office that also gave access to the major's sleeping quarters. Like the troop barracks, the CP had no windows, but the olive drab canvas sidewalls might be rolled up, weather permitting, during daylight hours. At this early hour of the evening, though, such exposure would be a breach of sound and light discipline.

So Will was left to peek into the front section of the tent to be sure the major was there. It was dark in the front office section, except for the light that leaked under the partition and through the doorway that separated the major's private office. Will took it upon himself to walk in, entering far enough to hear scuffling and grunting from the major's private office. Someone was in there pacing about, most likely on the field telephone. He heard the major say, "You asked for it, sir, so I'll let you have it straight. I'm sick of the whole thing. I'm tired of writing letters to young officers' widows, and I'm tired of seeing their men loaded onto dust-offs in pieces. And to what end? What have we gained by these losses?

"You see, sir," Finn continued, "I happen to agree with our illustrious former Marine Commandant David Shoup, when he said he didn't think all of Southeast Asia was worth the loss of one American life. At least, I think it was General Shoup who said it, but he's not the only one. Ike wouldn't come in here in '54. Didn't MacArthur himself caution against a land war on the Asian mainland? And when he disregarded his own injunction, General Ridgeway was given his command to redeem our position in Korea. And he, Matt Ridgeway, that is, and Jim Gavin, too,

Lieutenant General Gavin, sir, both have stated publicly that this policy is ill-advised.

"So, when I say this, sir, in specific response to your inquiry, there is certainly ample room for a difference of opinion as far as our current strategic policy is concerned, at least within our own officer corps."

Finn fell silent, except for more grunting and pacing about. Will was uncomfortable eavesdropping and readied himself to back out of the tent, but he could not tear himself away. *I have to hear this.*

"It comes down to this, sir," Finn resumed. "The United States is an air, land, and sea power. The terrain here and the political nature of the struggle are compromising our effectiveness on the ground. There is nothing here particularly vital to our own national defense. It makes sense, therefore, to hold the line where we will be most effective, namely at the sea. There our overwhelming air and sea power logically can be expected to destroy any credible threat mounted by this enemy, or some combination of enemies from this theater, against any part of the United States or against any of its Pacific bases or allies. Of course, sir, we would do so far more economically than what we are now expending for dubious results."

Finn fell silent for a moment, but then seemingly interrupted his listener to say, "No, that's right, sir. It doesn't leave much of a role for the Army. But that's not the point—" Will was sure Finn was interrupted and waited anxiously for him to resume, which he did in a moment. "I think my statement allowed for that, sir. Even if I concede your *domino theory*, and there are a lot of reasons why I don't, but even if I did, the effective line of defense, of containment, is at the sea for the reasons already stated."

Finn again paused to allow for response before resuming, "Sir, first of all, let me say there is a history here that we are both, no doubt, familiar with that belies the simple assertion that this is all Moscow's doing or Peking's doing. What happens in Vietnam may be influenced from Moscow—or Washington, for that matter—but ultimately it will be determined by what most Viets choose from the options available to them. Will most Viets opt to support or resist a nationalist revolution that happens to be communist-led? And what is the upshot of that question? That it is by no means automatic that Vietnam will fall because China did, nor that Thailand will if Cambodia does. Largely it will depend on the politics internal to each of those countries and who mobilizes the most internal support.

"Here in Vietnam, sir," Finn went on, "our Viets are doing a pretty lousy job. Why? Ultimately, power is concentrated in a handful of families—mostly Catholics in a country where Buddhists are the majority—with ties to the old French colonial regime. It is only natural that they should seek to preserve their privileges, and they need make few concessions to the populace in order to garner support as long as we prop them up. They have, therefore, forfeited any valid claim to the nationalist banner our enemy waves so successfully, and they offer little hope of the type of change for a better life that could possibly rally the support of the majority.

"Sir, we picked the wrong horse. Call it what you will, it's a bag of worms. We can spill our guts trying to control things, or we can pull back and defend the high seas. You know my choice."

Again, Finn was quiet. This time he seemed not to pace about. "If we pulled back to the sea line, perhaps the Russians or the Chinese would come in the way we have, and my bet is that they would run into the same problems. The goddamned Viet Cong would probably be calling us for help against them. Let them have it and defend the seas, I say. These area management problems will bleed them dry, the same way they are us." *Area management problems? I should have looked at it that way.*

Major Finn reached from his desk chair and pulled aside the canvas door to the front office. "Perhaps, if you wish, sir, we should continue this discussion some other time," he said into his telephone. "It seems I have someone waiting in my front office." In a moment, he concluded, "Good-bye, sir."

"Niner-one," he resumed immediately, "how long have you been here?"

"I just got here, sir," said Will, extending his arm, map case in hand to the major.

"What did you think about what I was saying, Niner-one?" the major asked, looking at Will askance.

"I'm sorry, sir," Will responded. "I didn't hear what you were saying."

Major Finn studied Will before continuing. "Come in here, Niner-one," he said, motioning for Will to join him in the private office. Will shuffled his way forward. "Be seated," the major went on, gesturing to the chair alongside his desk. "How about a drink with me, Niner-one?"

"Actually," Will responded, still standing, "Mr. Watters is waiting for me so we can eat together."

"Sit, sit, sit, Niner-one," Finn said. "Mr. Watters is used to waiting for us." Will slipped into the chair.

"Why don't you join me in a drink before dinner?"

"I'm on the wagon, sir."

The major jerked his head away from pouring his bourbon to scrutinize Will. Patiently he waited for Will to elaborate. Will tried to wait him out, but realized the futility of it before long.

"I took a vow," he said.

"Well?"

"Well," Will continued, "I've seen the hardships the bottle can bring families, and I don't want to be any part of it."

"Where did you do your OCS, Stone? Sill, I presume."

Will hesitated. "I'm an EM, sir. A US." He squirmed while the major looked him up and down. Finally, a controlled smile emerged on Finn's face as he rose from his desk seat.

"Well, I know you want to find some dinner, and it's not right for you to be keeping Mr. Watters waiting," he said, "so you best be on your way. I'll expect to see you around the same time tomorrow morning.

"Tomorrow," he continued, relaxing to a more genuine smile, "let's both hope the need for your services will be more routine."

"Yes, sir," Will said, having risen. Their eyes met as Will turned to leave.

"Niner-one," Major Finn called as Will was about to exit the private office.

"Sir?" Will turned.

"Understand this," Finn responded. "I am a professional military officer for what I believe to be the greatest country in history. I believe in our country's need to command an army to do its bidding. That need has to override any doubts any of us may have at any time about any particular bidding. Do you understand that?"

"Yes, sir," Will answered. "I respect that."

"Good. Then, good night," the major said. "Good job today, but cut us a little more slack next time with those adjustments."

Will nodded before saluting. The major waved him off.

Will was puzzled as he walked back to catch up with Watters. *Area management problems? I can see how you could tie this whole ball of wax into a neat package by labeling it like that. I gotta think about this hard, though, because what it doesn't take into account is that we're here to help these people, not manage them. Aren't we?*

Chapter 7

Ambush At Soui Cat

At the Rock Quarry

Over the next several weeks, Will had plenty of time to think about Major Finn's conversation on war policy, much of it in the observation helicopter escorting supply convoys. Watters flew overhead in tight little circles in order to keep the slow-moving vehicles in view. The repetitive pattern bored Will and made him dizzy, so he did not mind thinking about other things.

Long ago Harry Stone had ingrained in his sons the acquired skill of cutting down problems to bite-sized pieces. Will found he could digest some pieces of what Finn said more readily than others. He recognized, for example, he had little way of verifying the nationalist nature of the struggle. Was this a case of a foreign-backed puppet—our guys—resisting government of the Viets, by the Viets, for the Viets?

Finn suggested the USA had virtually stepped into French shoes on the wrong side of a colonial struggle. Will was haunted by the specter of the lanky medic shaking his finger in his face at the ship's rail and demanding, "Don't people have a right to be free?" *Of course they do. That seems like the simple truth of the matter, until you consider that their side is led by a communist government dedicated to totalitarian control at the expense of all the personal liberties generally rallied 'round the flag of freedom. Like it or not, there's truth on all sides here, but it's hardly simple. It's a matter of which is the greatest truth.*

What struck Will most about the major's remarks was his advocacy of shoreline defense. The logic seemed undeniable. *If they're coming for Frisco, blow them out of the sky and water. Don't wait until they land. Don't fight on the enemy's terms in monsoon mud or jungle nights. This air and sea versus land battle thing gets down to our basic purpose for being here. They've been mixing all these policy justifications in one big pot, but when you keep them separate, you come up with different conclusions.*

On the one hand, if you say we gotta fight the commies and they gotta fight the commies, therefore it's the same battle because we got the same enemy, our war policy makes pretty good sense, especially if we're going for an all-out defeat of communism everywhere. What the hell? We've got an ally.

On the other hand, if you're thinking like Finn that this is a limited effort to contain the commies, you say it's going to cost us this much blood and coin to fight the commies at the shoreline, but it's going to cost us that much and more to fight alongside our Viet friends in these difficult conditions. Therefore the only reason we're spilling this extra blood is for them, not us. That seems obvious now, but it's been getting lost in the shuffle. We say a couple hundred Americans are getting killed every week because we gotta stop communism. But it's not because we're trying to stop commies. It's because of where and how we're trying to stop them.

And that opens up a different way of looking at the whole thing. If you're scared shitless about the commies coming for your own ass in the States, and someone says "fight," you fight. But when you know the commies can be stopped anyway without this ground fight, who wants it?

No American can know what's happening here until he first understands that his survival is not at stake. As long as he thinks it is at stake, he'll make any excuse, accept any mistake, buy any reason, in support of this policy. But just show him what I've seen, give him a glimmer of Finn's insight and he'll turn so fast.

"What the hell are they waiting for? Will asked Watters after the helicopter revolved around itself several times while hovering above a road intersection.

"I don't think they know which way to go," he answered, smiling.

Will's head throbbed. He clutched his seat and plunged back into his thoughts. *Finn says there's no vital interest here. What could it be? Rubber? Oil? Tin? Do we need any of that so bad we would hemorrhage our nation's youth here? No. The only vital interest here we should die for would have to be strategic. There would have to be some military value to holding this particular piece of real estate. But like Finn said, it wasn't important enough for us to back up the French all the way in 1954. No, I don't buy it. He's right about this shoreline-defense thing. That's the way to contain the commies from strictly a selfish point of view. But is that how we should be looking at this thing—selfishly?*

Whenever Watters and Will touched down, Will had a headache. Before long he was ordered back on the ground as K Troop's FO, and he did not mind a bit. He looked upon his new assignment as a way to check out just whom he was fighting to save and whether they were worth it.

Will resolved not to bring up this subject when he joined his crew at the rock quarry seven kilometers northeast of Soui Cat, a village where three bloody convoy ambushes had taken place in the last several months. The ARVN maintained an outpost at the quarry not just to secure the quarry itself, but also because it was a water station for the steam-driven national railroad. *I still got more questions than answers. Sometimes I wonder if it's any good, having all these questions. They don't help get the job done.*

When Watters dropped off Will, the ACAV crew waiting for him already had brought his duffel from base camp. Will was glad to see

Whiteman would be his track driver and figured that was Zack's doing. He looked to see who else rounded out the crew. *Campbell, Shard, and Swindell—The Three Musketeers. No doubt they'll think I requested them.*

"Gentlemen," Will addressed them matter-of-factly.

Couched in the back of the track vehicle with the rear panel down, they looked up from their blackjack game with mock embarrassment. Months before, they might have chosen to ignore Will, but the sandbag incident had garnered him a grudging respect—certainly more than the miniature black sergeant's chevrons he now sported on his collar would have commanded by themselves. Everyone knew the story of Will's promotion several weeks before.

A Buck Sergeant

Will had come into base camp after more than a month of flying days and camping out nights as an observer for various line troops. Compared to the rest of How Battery, he was spending far more than his fair share of time at risk.

Will came back only because, with the return of L Troop, all three squadron line troops were in camp. When L Troop rumbled its dusty way into the camp, almost all hands were asleep. If Will had not stopped in the battery orderly room to report his arrival, his return would have gone unnoticed.

The following morning his name appeared on the KP list. So, awakened at 4:00 a.m. with three hours of sleep under his belt, Will considered his options. *There's a certain poetic beauty here,* he chuckled on his way to the mess tent.

"Will," Rick Franklin called out, "what the hell are you doing here?"

Will sized up the situation. *No cooks yet. They have Franklin opening up. That's good. They trust him.*

"Came in with L Troop late last night," Will answered, slapping Franklin on the arm. "You're looking good."

"Start opening those juice cans and emptying them into that vat," Franklin called to a couple of Firing Battery troopers. "I'll be with ya in a sec."

"Yeah, I'm glad to see ya," Franklin said, returning his attention to Will. "Glad to see ya still alive. But what're ya doing on KP?"

"They woke me up and said it was my lucky day." Will laughed. "I get to work alongside my good buddy, Rick."

"You're mocking me," Franklin murmured.

"No, Rick," Will said, "I respect you and all the others that get the job done here every day."

"Yeah, right," Franklin countered, "you're blowing smoke up my ass. You're out there doing it, and you tell me you respect me for being back here?"

"Let me ask you a question, Rick," Will said. "You know I spent quite a few nights with my ass in the grass, right?"

Franklin nodded.

"The nights when they fly hot meals into our perimeter, do you think we take that for granted?" Will said. "You think we just as soon eat C's? You think we forgot somebody put it together and got it to us through hell or high water?" Taken aback, Franklin said nothing. "There's not a man out there that hasn't had KP," Will went on, "so every last swinging dick knows what it takes to put it together, whether it's this mess or another. So I'm here 'cause I respect this job and the men that do it."

Choked up, Franklin stepped toward the serving line before circling back to confront Will. "Thank you," Franklin said, "but you're not getting no extra fuckin' hash browns."

Will smiled and shook his head.

"Look, I don't want to piss you off, Will," Franklin said, "but it really isn't right your being here. The job you're doing is a looey's job, and you shouldn't be pullin' no KP."

"Yeah, well, I'm a Specialist Fourth Class, not a looey," Will said. "So here I is."

"I can let you off," Franklin said.

"Yeah," Will said, "and then the CQ would drag some other sorry ass out of his sack."

"Not an FO, who just got in at 1:00 a.m. from the field."

"But maybe some other Specialist Fourth Class who's got his own story," Will said. "Let it go, will ya, Rick? Allow me the pleasure of your company."

"Jesus," Franklin said, looking at Will cockeyed before walking away.

Will had an abbreviated version of the same conversation when Sergeant Zack passed through the serving line in the morning. "This isn't right," Zack said. "You don't have to—"

"I'm here," Will said. "So be it. How many more times can this happen?"

Zack bit his tongue. So went the day. The change of pace and faces energized Will. It was good to be without his flak jacket and good to set aside his M-16 in the pantry. It was good to be out of the jungle, out of the sun, out of harm's way. Certain officers and NCOs seemed to find satisfaction in Will's assignment there, as if he needed to be taken down a notch lest he pretend to their privileges. At lunch, Sergeant First Class Grovel bellowed, "Stone!" three times from his table to call for refills of iced tea. Will did not let them spoil his day.

That evening Major Finn decided to take advantage of a long-standing invitation to dine at How Battery. "Mashed potatoes, sir?" Will asked, after Finn cut in the serving line. From the moment Will's serving spoon clanged potatoes onto the major's metal compartmentalized tray, Captain Harkness received more than he bargained for when he invited the major to dinner. From the first, the major had ambivalent feelings toward Will. He had a nagging suspicion Will had overheard him on the field phone. Clearly the major did not want such conversation repeated among the troops. In his worst moments, the major might have wished that Will fall victim to an ambush, but never would he have wished on him the indignity of KP.

Any such demeaning of an apparent part of the major's staff could be seen as an insult to the major himself. So no excuse would do, as far as Finn was concerned. Certainly not when Captain Harkness lamely repeated the first sergeant's explanation, "He's a Specialist Fourth Class."

"Then make him a sergeant, goddammit!" the major snapped.

The Fuel Depot

Back at the rock quarry Shard beckoned Will to the track vehicle. "What's that," he asked, fingering the dark metal sergeant's chevrons pinned on Will's collar. "A chaplain's insignia?"

"That's good, Shard," Campbell said. "Yes, there is something messianic about this lad's behavi—"

"Skip the bullshit, gents," Will interrupted. "White Man, let me see the maintenance logs on this tub, please." While Whiteman retrieved the logs from the driver's compartment, Will added, "Awfully hot today. Be a shame to have to get that involved in working this baby over. Right, Campbell? But we'll have to see what these logs show."

"OK, OK," Campbell said as Whiteman returned and passed the logs to Will. "You made your point, Sergeant."

"How much fuel ya got, White Man?" Will asked, handing the logs back without looking at them.

"Less than half a tank."

"When did you guys get here?" Will asked.

"Yesterday afternoon," Swindell said.

"That a fuel dump over there?" Will asked, pointing at a group of trucks behind him next to a grove of trees.

"That's what we hear," Swindell responded.

"We better top off," Will said, glancing at his watch. "Then we'll have some C's."

"If we eat first, we might not have to wait as long in line over there," Swindell said.

"What net are you monitoring?" Will asked, looking at Swindell.

"AFVN," Swindell said, referring to Armed Forces Vietnam Network, a military-sponsored music and news station.

"We gotta have one radio on the K Troop net and the other on either our battery net or the squadron net, depending on what's going on."

Shard, nearest to the radio banks, tuned one to the K Troop frequency. Will waved his pointing finger upward in a circle to signal to Whiteman to fire up the track vehicle. When Whiteman started the engine, the others scrambled to secure odds and ends before the vehicle moved. "I'll say this," Campbell said to Will, "it didn't take you long to make the adjustment."

"I hope you guys can," Will said, smiling.

"We're still better off with you," Campbell mumbled, "than with some lifer."

When they arrived at the fuel dump, they took up the third position in line. While the fueling took place, the crews from the three vehicles swapped yarns with one another and the fuel crew. Will noticed Campbell had stayed in the back of the vehicle to read.

"Maybe I am a lifer now," Will interrupted, "and you just don't know it."

Campbell lifted his head to gaze on Will. "No, Stone."

"Listen, Campbell," Will said, "I've been thinking about our discussions and the situation here, and I've reached some conclusions. At least one."

"You reached a conclusion?" Campbell said. "I thought you just sort of regurgitated these matters. Like a cow."

"What about a cow?" Whiteman interrupted, as he came around the rear corner of the track. "I know something about cows, at least as far as dairy farms go."

Will was caught off guard. *Campbell's one thing. He's already so jaundiced. Ah, what the hell?*

"Listen, Campbell," Will said out loud, "it took me a while to figure this out, but there is no doubt the US can best defend itself on the high seas, not in some foreign jungle. When we put our asses on the line here, therefore, it is for the sake of the native people, not for ourselves. I hope they're worth it."

"Wrong," Campbell said quickly, "That's an interesting question, whether they're worth it. But that's not it, not why we are fighting this war. We are not dying for them. That's the cover story. The real reason is to protect the political careers of those at home who voted for this policy and refuse to admit their mistaken knee-jerk reaction."

"Ya lost me," Whiteman said, sliding into the back of the ACAV.

Campbell looked for direction from Will, who remained standing, propped against the rear corner of the vehicle. Will nodded for Campbell to proceed.

"Who lost China?" Campbell said to the blank-faced Whiteman. "Do you know who McCarthy was?"

"He's the senator from my state—from Minnesota."

"Not bad, Whiteman," Campbell resumed, "but wrong McCarthy, wrong state. The one I mean was Senator Joe McCarthy from Wisconsin. He and his protégé Richard Nixon, a first-term congressman from California at the time, terrorized the Democratic Party with that question, 'Who lost China?'

"Not that it was ever ours to lose, mind you, but that didn't stop them," Campbell continued. "They purged the Foreign Service and red-baited the Truman Administration, fixing blame on any Democrat that they could for the loss of China to the communists, as if it were ever in our power to control events there.

"Now, let me say I am sure you could point to select instances where McCarthy's witch-hunt did root out certain subversive elements planted in the nation's power structure," Campbell allowed. "And, to be sure, they also embarrassed numerous people for having, in the 1930s, flirted with or been associated with various left-wing groups in which they may have mistakenly placed their hopes for a much-needed better world, but which history has subsequently revealed as unwitting tools of the Stalinist terror.

"But the point is, without doubt, these red-baiters went too far," Campbell continued. "They injured the reputations of many loyal Americans. More germane to our discussion, however, is that they struck fear in the hearts of all who influence or control the nation's foreign policy. They had a chilling effect on discussions about how to handle situations such as this one in Vietnam. It is plain to all who foray into this arena that there will be hell to pay if we lose Vietnam. Maybe we won't have Richard Nixon to kick around anymore, as he himself put it, but there will be other young men in a hurry willing to gain political advantage at the expense of truth and fairness, and sound policy.

"You see," said Campbell, shifting his gaze from Whiteman to Will, "the real problem is that this punitive aversion to losing precludes even any discussion of what winning means and what it costs. Having left both our ends and means unexamined, we hardly should expect them to remain in proportion to one another."

"What are you saying?" Whiteman interrupted. "I don't know what you mean."

"No member of our government dares allow himself to be labeled as soft on communism," resumed Campbell. "Hesitate, ask the wrong question—that is, the right question—and you'll be called a pinko. You'll be smeared with guilt for all the communist misdeeds. You'll be driven from office in apparent shame. Do you get it now, Whiteman?"

Campbell and Whiteman stared at one another. After a moment, Whiteman answered, "I got this much. Somebody's been covering their ass with our blood and guts. I don't know about the right and wrong parts, but I did get it that, even if they thought we were wrong, they'd keep us going full bore to cover their own asses."

Will cleared his throat and was about to speak when he glimpsed a moving shadow. He glanced up as the fuel tender jumped from atop the ACAV next to theirs. The nozzle was pointed at him. He had enough time to turn his face from the flow of diesel fuel and close his eyes before he was doused.

"Stop it!" The fuel tender yelled to the pump man, who controlled the flow from a remote switch at the storage tank.

Will dropped to his knees. "Water," he called out. "Get me water." While he waited, he thought of a time years before when the straps on a fuel tank broke away from a pickup while Josh worked underneath. Gasoline burnt Josh's eyes until Will came running with a hose to flush them out. *No running water here. At least it's not gas.*

"Here, take it," Whiteman said, passing him his helmet full of water and swinging in place a five-gallon jerrican of water for refills. After repeated saturations of his head, Will could no longer taste diesel fuel, but he was drenched. He swabbed his left ear with toilet paper from a package of C rations. "Point me in the direction of the shower, will ya?" he said to Whiteman, who quickly obliged. "Where I met you, is that our permanent station?" Will asked.

"Yeah, they told us to set up there," Campbell answered.

"I'll meet you back there," Will said. "Whiteman, you'll log in this refueling? Of course you will. Let me grab a change of clothes and get out of here. When you guys are back in position, go ahead and chow down. Don't wait for me."

"Now there's a smart sergeant," Campbell said. "He doesn't give orders he knows he can't enforce."

Will snapped his wet towel at Campbell. Once in the shower, Will thought of Josh washing off with a garden hose without soap the time he was doused. Shampooing his hair, Will closed his eyes and saw Josh face down bleeding on the street and then the intern in the hospital telling him he could not visit Josh. Finally, in his mind's eye he traced his movements back to Pittston after he left the hospital that night.

Seduction At Gina's Pad

Will was in no rush on his way back to Pittston, because he had no place to go for the night. He put in at a deserted farm he often haunted on such occasions, keeping company with the frogs as he brooded upon his reflection in the pond. Things were different this time, though, given what had just happened to Josh. In the water he saw Harry pointing and shouting at him, "I'll have you drafted, Will Stone! I'm telling you to give it up. I can do it. I'll have you drafted!"

Will shivered. *What good are you? What kind of life are you making? And now, what about Josh? Could you have stopped the deputy? Could you have stopped Josh? Could you have headed all this off at the construction site that day?*

Will touched his reflection with his right hand. It smiled at him as he pinched its cheek. The water was warmer than the night air. The image was peaceful, free of strife. Will bent further forward and lowered his face. The touch of water on his skin startled him. He jumped to his feet and stumbled backward several paces, even as a part of him remained captivated by the pond. He swiped his face with his sleeve and ran to his car. Grasping the steering wheel with both hands, he shook himself against it until, finally, he rested his head on it. "OK," he whispered. "OK, Will, cool it. It'll come soon enough." *No need to rush it. Might as well enjoy the story as it unfolds, even if you can't write it.* He made it back to town just before dawn as Stanley was readying his luncheonette for the day's business.

Stanley let Will in for hot tea and an omelet. Will told about Josh being shot and Harry's ultimatum. Stanley had served his two years after being drafted and was no friend of the Army. "Why don't you marry MaryAnn?" he said. "It'll exempt you."

Will smiled but said nothing, picking up yesterday's newspaper instead. While he finished his toast, a headline caught his eye: "Screamin' Eagles Land in Vietnam." Will read on:

CAMRAHN BAY, RVN July 29 - A brigade-sized unit of the 101st Airborne Division landed yesterday in South Vietnam. Fifty thousand more American soldiers will soon receive orders to join them. Until now, the fighting strength of American combat arms in Vietnam has been made up of the 173rd Airborne and the 3rd Marine Divisions.

Will had not paid much attention to events in Vietnam, having read only occasional stories about Special Forces in remote outposts and accounts of enemy sapper attacks on American installations in Pleiku and Bien Hoa.

"Why don't you sit in that corner booth, Will?" said Stanley on his way to unlock the front door for business. "Have another tea."

"Thanks," Will said, but his mind was on the other side of the earth. *Di-en-bi-en-phu! Di-en-bi-en-phu!* The name rang out in his mind as he tried to relive the daily newscasts of the fall of the French stronghold in 1954. All he could remember was the mystery evoked by the constant repetition of the catchy name, and his mother Margaret finally putting his mind at ease by explaining, "They're trying to stop the communists from taking Indochina."

Now President Johnson said much the same thing: "We are there, first, because a friendly nation has asked us for help against communist aggression. To ignore aggression would only increase the danger of a larger war. What is at stake is the cause of freedom." *Maybe this is a cause worth dying for. How much more noble to make the ultimate sacrifice in the cause of freedom than to founder in a farm pond? How senseless to waste a life like that.*

The counter was busy with customers, so Will grabbed his cup and, standing, finished his cold tea. He pushed the newspaper across the table, left five dollars, and nodded to Stanley, who was at the grill.

Stanley snapped to attention and saluted him, spatula still in hand. Will affected a look of disgust and shook his head. *Only got fifteen bucks. Gotta get some money, maybe see Harry for that day's work. Down to a hundred bucks in the bank.*

"Don't volunteer for anything!" Stanley called after him.

Will headed over the hill toward the dawn, following the winding road until he turned left down a dusky lane. He sniffed as he backed the roadster into an empty parking spot aside a yellow two-family. *Damn, definitely exhaust fumes.* His roadster was more in keeping with the age-worn dwelling than the colorful sports cars on either side of him. Will sat behind the wheel for several minutes, resisting the notion of disturbing anyone so early. The cold soon prompted him to action.

At the sound of the bell a bearded man Will's age scurried down the stairs from the upper flat to open the door. Will closed the outside door behind him and followed his friend Gary upstairs. "Gotta put on some pants," laughed Gary, taking them from a svelte arm outstretched from a bedroom.

Gary motioned for Will to take a seat at the kitchen table as he put a kettle on the stove.

"Josh is in the hospital, shot in the back and maybe paralyzed for life," Will began, and I'm being drafted."

Sheila, wrapped in a robe, appeared from the bedroom and slid into the straight chair next to Will. Both Gary and she gaped. "You heard me right," Will said.

"Josh shot?" said Gary. "What happened?"

Will told them everything. When he was done, they sat silently. Finally, Sheila rose and said, "I'll fix tea. Coffee for you, Gar?"

Gary nodded her way and then frowned at Will. "Let me get this straight," he said. "The sheriff started a witch-hunt to make Josh out as forcing himself on Mrs. Lyons? She's not so bad that it's out of the question."

"For crissake, Josh didn't force himself on anyone," Will said.

"So it was consensual," Gary said. "You're sure?"

"If anything took place between them," Will answered, "it couldn't have been much and it was consensual."

"Did it?" Gary asked.

"That's not the point," Will said.

"It shouldn't be," Gary said. "No, it should come down to the question of her consent. But you just saw that it won't. More than a question of her consent, it is a question of society's consent. And I'm afraid we're a long way from that."

"You'd think we were in the Deep South," Will said.

"Legally speaking, the test will be the use of force," Gary said, "but society will express its outrage by twisting, shading and understanding every morsel of evidence toward a finding of force."

They fell quiet again until Sheila asked, "How is he?" Will told what he knew.

Finally, Gary asked, "What do you mean you're being drafted? You've got a 2S. Shit, it's not like there's a war."

"That's what we always said, isn't it?," Will said, his eyes brightening. "Well, Gary boy, ya know something? It looks like there just might be a war." Will went on to tell them of Harry's ultimatum at midnight.

Gary stroked his beard until Will finished, "I might be able to put on enough weight to be rejected," he said, "but you never will."

"Why don't you just go back to school?" asked Sheila, as she flipped her long blonde hair over the back of her chair.

"I can't do that."

"Cause of this thing with your father?" she asked.

"I'd really have to swallow hard to knuckle under to Harry on this, no doubt, but it's more than that," said Will. "Ya know, there are a lot of people who'd never have the chance to hide behind a student deferment. Maybe a lot of them even wish they had the chance to go to school just for the education."

"You want an education," she said.

"This game's for keeps, Will," Gary broke in.

"Exactly," said Will. "These are the same people we've always been saying deserve a fair shake. Now I can pull my fair share of the load or I can let them—someone like Josh—pull it for me. It really says what I'm all about, doesn't it?"

"We're talking pretty high stakes, Will," said Gary. "You won't do anyone any good by dying in a rice paddy in Vietnam."

"Not sure I'm doing anyone much good right now, anyway," Will said.

"But is it worth it?" Gary asked.

Will reflected on President Johnson's statement. "It would not have been in vain," he said.

"Don't you care whether you die?" Sheila asked.

"Let's say I care a great deal about the way I live," Will answered.

The other bedroom door opened and a young man several years older and several inches taller than Will approached the table.

"Come on, honey," he called back to the bedroom. Another young blonde joined them. "What's going on here? Did I hear something about the draft?"

"Will, meet Don John, a.k.a. the preacher," Gary said. "He's a grad assistant in the Religion Department at the college. He teaches one of my classes."

"Hey, Will. Say hello to my pal Gina," the graduate assistant said.

"Gina," Will said, looking to the young lady propped against Sheila's chair from behind. Then he turned back to the graduate assistant, "Nice to meet you, *Perfessor* John."

"Hello, Will," Gina said, smirking. "Just call him Don."

Sheila and Gary smiled. "We gotta get ready, Will," Gary said. "We gotta be outta here by 7:00 a.m. Make yourself at home."

Don and Gina slipped into the vacated chairs. "So now, who's getting drafted here? I know it's not Gary, so you must be it, Will. Fill me in."

Will gave him a thumbnail sketch of his circumstances. When he finished, the graduate assistant said, "You're thinking of actually letting this happen to you, of going in the military? Why on earth do you want to go in the Army, for crissake? None of us here is from the peasant class, you know."

Will said nothing and Don continued. "I was six months on active duty as a ROTC officer, and I can tell you wouldn't like being treated the way enlisted men are treated. They have to treat them that way. It's the classes. Lots of coloreds. Rednecks, too. Will, you don't know what it's like. They smell, they booze, they steal and fight with one another. If they're not on duty, they're either drunk or doped up or debauching some whore."

"Hold it!" interrupted Will. "Even if what you say is true, I'm prepared for worse. And what if there are lots of coloreds? What's that got to do with it?"

"You're missing the point," Don said. "The NCOs—the sergeants and the like—come from among these classes. The only way they know to deal with them is by being better at their tricks. They're trained to be meaner and tougher and dirtier and more underhanded, and they are. Will, they're not going to take to your strange ideas. They're going to grind you into the dust. They don't need Will Stone as their champion. They're going to tell you not just what to wear but how to wear it, when to wear it, and whether it looks good on you. They're going to tell you whether to stand in it, sit in it, or sleep in it. They're going to tell you whether it needs sewing, ironing, or cleaning. These bastards are going to stick their noses into every last little detail of your life."

"Hey, man, I'm going into this thing ready to face communist guerrillas out to kill me in the jungles of Vietnam. Nothing that you've described sounds more scary."

"These are going to be the guys you depend on," said Don.

"Why, Will?" asked Sheila, returning to the discussion with Gary. "Do you want to be a hero?"

"It's just my turn," he answered. An image of Josh bleeding on the concrete walk shot through his mind.

"If Harry could get you into this mess, he can get you out of it," said Gary. "You can get out of this, goddammit."

"I don't want to get out of it," broke in Will. "Sure, he could get me off, but it would still be my turn. I'm not going to leave it to one of the 'peasant class' to take my place."

"Why not?" shouted Don.

"Will," Gary said, "it was never your turn. It can all be called off. They're only going to call you for a physical, anyway. Let's talk about getting you back to school. You still have your student deferment."

"That's questionable," said Will. "But now it is my turn and I've got to take it."

"Why, you fool?" demanded Don. Will glowered at him. Don softened his tone. "Will, I don't feel and Gary doesn't feel, no one feels, that we should risk dying in Vietnam. Fighting isn't what we do best. I'm going to be a minister. He's going to be an attorney. Society needs our skills, our brains. Surely you can find some higher purpose to serve our society and leave this fighting to those who can't."

"He's right," Gary added. "That's the process. It's like natural selection. Society keeps alive those whose skills it most values. The whole aim of life is to keep yourself out of these situations. Please recognize that, Will."

Will looked to Sheila and Gina, who managed a smile. She nodded. Sheila did, too. Will considered the argument. *Might as well shoot Josh in the back again myself.*

While Will paused, Don no longer could restrain himself. "Who do we even know who's gone to Vietnam? No one. They're all professionals," he said. "They're mercenaries really. There are so few men there compared with the size of our country. No one just goes there. You have to be looking for trouble."

Will calmly held up his hand for Don to stop. The others fell quiet. "When it comes to bleeding and dying for our country, you cannot say one will do it better than the next, nor that any could have found a higher purpose," he said. "So, please, just say you don't want to go, that it's not for you. Don't try to dress it up, not this way or any way. You insult every man who ever wore a uniform. OK? Please. It's not that any of us is too good to serve. In fact, it's more likely the opposite."

"Our country needs more than warriors," Don shot back, jumping to his feet. "I'm telling it like it is."

"Don't tell me about the needs of the state, then, 'cause that's not like it is," Will said. "Our system's not based on the needs of the state. That's the Soviet perversion. Our system is based on the rights of the individual, and with those equal rights come equal duties, like it or not. I don't like it, but I will take my turn."

All eyes were upon Will when he stopped speaking. He managed a weak smile and nod to each, before directing his final remark to Gary. "With your permission, I'm going to grab a couple of hours shut-eye on your couch and then take a shave. After, I'll go to the draft board and see just what all this means to me, then back to the hospital to see if there's further word."

Two hours later Will stirred from his fitful sleep on the couch. Gina stood, prodding him with a stockinged foot. "What are you doing here on my couch?" she laughed, jumping back when Will grasped for her outstretched leg.

"I went to sleep dreaming of you," he said, looking around to see if the others were gone and then propping himself up on one arm.

"You never come up here anymore, not to see me, anyway."

"Can you stay, maybe take the day off?" Will asked. She shook her head, her long blonde braid bouncing across her back. "Please," he added, his once-over gliding up her silken leg to the slit in her mandarin dress. Sitting up as she approached, Will drew her to him and embraced her waist. "Please."

" I have to assist with a presentation for work. My boss is depending on me."

Will let his left arm slide down along her dress until he could slip his hand through the slit and around her thigh. He was about to ask again but realized her resolve. "I hope they deserve you today," he said. "You look great."

"Thanks," she said and pushed away from him after a quick kiss. "I'm sorry about Josh, Will," she said. He followed her movements out the door with saddened eyes and a more complete knowledge of her than he had gained in several intimate nights. He lay back and reflected. *She told me no, not because she rejected me, but out of a sense of responsibility. I hadn't taken the trouble to know Gina at all, not this Gina, anyway. We don't know one another. Something might have clicked, but we'll never know. We're out of time. I can't just weasel out of this draft thing. It's my turn.* He rose, shaved, and headed off to the draft board to see how much time he had.

Ambush Reaction Force Moves Out

Will had just finished cleaning himself of diesel fuel and dressed when he had to race five hundred yards back from the shower hooch to his crew. "What's going on?" he shouted as he approached the ACAV. The crew was enjoying a leisurely lunch. "Everyone's fired up and forming a line to move out!"

Campbell nodded to Shard, who turned and manipulated the radio dials. Will realized they had missed an order because his crew had tuned in AFVN, rather than monitoring the K Troop net. Twenty-five to thirty ACAVs led by an M-48A tank headed their way. The first two vehicles passed. The third skidded to a halt.

"Aren't you ready?" the K Troop commander shouted. "What's the matter?"

"Radio was down, sir," Will answered. "We'll be cranked up in a minute."

"We don't have time," Captain Ashe called back, looking at the tarp re-slung from the side of Will's track only ten minutes before. "Grab your radio. Come in here with us. Let's go."

Will ran twenty feet to the back of his own track vehicle. Whiteman pitched Will his flak jacket and then his M-16. Swindell passed him the field radio and his ammo belt. Will patted his chest and, sure the flak jacket pockets still contained all four magazines, rushed back to the troop commander's track. He passed the radio and rifle up to a side gunner and scrambled up the side. It was the hardest way up, but the quickest. Immediately the column roared ahead, anxious to close the gap between them and the two lead vehicles.

As he shouted for his radio, Will sized up the crew in the back—two side gunners and an ammo handler. Each gunner leaned forward so his line of sight fell just above his gun shield. Each searched his side of the road, ready to respond. At their feet was the ammo handler, on hands and knees, positioning ammunition ready to hand up to the gunners.

"What the hell's going on?" Will asked.

"Ambush, sir," answered the right side gunner.

Will fingered his collar and realized he had not yet switched his rank insignia to his fresh uniform. *Shit!*

"Just east of Soui Cat, Niner-one, a truck convoy, ambushed," Captain Ashe said, grabbing Will's arm. "We've got to relieve them. Will we be in range of a fire support base?"

The relief column raced down the hardpan road from the quarry to Highway 1 at breakneck speed, spewing a trail of dust more than a mile long. By the time they reached the national highway, the command track had caught up to the two lead vehicles. Once they turned right onto the asphalt, two-lane Highway 1—the main highway connecting North and South Vietnam—they had only two miles to go before passing through Soui Cat, which could be trouble. Moving the ambush to surprise the relief column was not beyond the Viet Cong, especially if the village afforded protective cover.

Will propped himself against a corner of the rear top hatch opening. He secured his radio to the top deck with a firm grip and called in on the battery net. "Can't help you with artillery, Niner-one," the fire direction officer told Will. "Fire Base Juliette's mortar platoon usually covers Soui Cat for us, but they're on the move. I'm trying to get you an air strike right now. We'll be back in touch if we need you to coordinate it from the ground. Over."

"This is Niner-one. Roger, Five," Will answered. Heavy automatic weapons fired in the distant east. "What about that 1-7-5 outfit to the east of me? Over."

"This is Five. Cochise is available, but you will be right at their maximum range capability. Over."

"This is Niner-one," Will responded. "Roger, Five. We'll know in a couple of minutes what is required. Put me on to them for now. Over."

"This is Five. Roger, Niner-one. Add eight-seven-six! Over."

"This is Niner-one," Will confirmed, "understand add eight-seven-six. Over."

The radio crackled, "This is Five. Affirmative. Good luck, over."

"This is Niner-one," Will said, "Roger. Out."

Will scanned both sides of the road as they sped through the village. Scrunching themselves behind their gun shields, the side gunners looked across their sights through the slit where the gun barrel penetrated the shield. The highway, usually flanked by street vendors, urchins, pedestrians, and civil traffic, was deserted. Unabated machine-gun fire continued ahead.

Will cranked his radio to the other fire base's frequency. *Be there any second. Fuck it.*

"Cochise Five, this is Bandit Niner-one," Will spoke into his mouthpiece, "commo check, over."

"This is Cochise," the radio spit back. "We hardly read you. Over."

"This is Niner-one." Will raised his voice as they crossed the bridge at the eastern edge of the village, and he caught his first glimpse of gun flashes. "Roger, out."

"We've got support," Will said to Captain Ashe. "They're at their range limit, so we can't be sure how accurate they'll be, but we have artillery support, and my Five's lining up fighter support."

"I know about the jets," the captain said. "They should be here soon."

Securing the Ambush Site

Once the battleground came into view, Captain Ashe held up the relief column to survey the situation. As they ground to a halt, each vehicle cocked itself at a forty-five degree cant to the side opposite the vehicle in front of it, forming a herringbone pattern. Before their own dust trail caught up with them, the captain made out three significant concentrations of gun flashes on the battlefield, which proved to be the retreat routes of the ambush party.

The besieged convoy vehicles had run off both sides of the highway to avoid being overrun. On the north side, to the right of the relief force were the smoldering remains of five ACAVs interspersed among ten trucks. To the south were an additional five charred ACAVs mixed with twenty burnt-out trucks. All gunfire appeared to be incoming, as if the convoy had ceased defending itself.

Even if he saw the ambush party was baiting him into a further trap, Captain Ashe was going in. But the odds were the withdrawing ambush party would want no part of the relief force. The sporadic fire came from a cover force scattered behind to slow up pursuit of the withdrawal. The captain immediately dispatched one of his three platoons to each of the enemy retreat routes in pursuit.

"Niner-one," Captain Ashe called to Will, "we'll do the mopping up ourselves. Can you block their avenues of retreat while we move all around?"

Will signaled his response with a nod before uttering, "Yes, sir." Will had been out with the troop on several occasions, so the captain took Will at his word.

Immediately Will proceeded to call for fire support from Firebase Cochise, one target at a time. The grid coordinates were easy to pinpoint, given their nearness to the well-mapped highway, village and stream. Still, Will was careful to identify his target coordinates deep enough into the jungle to allow for greater range dispersion, so that a short or long round would not impact any friendlies.

The blocking fires were intended to contain the fleeing ambush party near the clearing so the air support could plaster a more limited area when it arrived. That is the way it worked out. Before long, the jet bombers arrived and dumped their ordnance in each of the three areas Will had been saturating. As soon as the jets arrived, Will discontinued his fire missions to keep the skies safe for them.

Dust-Off Of the Wounded

For the first time in ten minutes, Will turned his head from his maps, radio, and regular inspections of the surrounding jungle to survey the battlefield. The command vehicle had moved in and among the burnt-out hulls of the supply convoy. Now and then, they were still fired on with automatic weapons, and, in one instance, with an RPG, or rocket-propelled grenade. Though RPGs accounted for disabling most of the

ACAVs escorting the supply convoy, land mines, hand grenades, and thrown satchel charges blew up others.

Each time an ACAV was fired on, at least two of the three machine guns mounted to it would respond with suppressive fire. Will had been so focused on adjusting fires, he had been oblivious to the ear-shattering din of their own weapons. Now he was fully aware of a M-60 machine gun bursting forth with the first return fire, followed by the slower and more powerful, deep-throated counterfire issued from Ma Deuce, the .50-caliber, heavy machine gun mounted in the turret. The suppressive fire sometimes was directed at hostile fire from the edge of the jungle, other times at nearby well-disguised foxholes, and, when necessary, at the burnt-out remains of convoy vehicles sheltering hostile snipers.

Will could taste the gunpowder in the air and waved his hand futilely to waft it away. Their vehicle was halted. The ammo handler was in the turret. The man door built into the rear retractable ramp was open. *Where the hell's the captain?*

The guns fell silent. Will spotted Captain Ashe scurrying over to another ACAV of the relief column. Drake, the right side gunner watched the captain, too. The captain shouted some instruction to the vehicle and then became involved in a verbal exchange. Will looked toward the radios, wondering if they were malfunctioning but saw nothing out of the ordinary. When he looked back, Captain Ashe was scurrying across open field, unarmed.

"Where the hell's he going?" Will said to Drake.

"I don't know," Drake shouted back over a sudden burst of fire from the left side gun.

"I'm going after him," Will yelled, as he grabbed his M-16. "You have this vehicle follow that captain like a dog at heel. Got it?"

"Yes, sir," the gunner replied.

"I'm a sergeant," Will shouted, before he ducked down to scramble out the man door, "a buck sergeant and a US, like you, no doubt."

Will hit the open field at full stride. Tracer rounds sizzled around him. He overtook Captain Ashe just as he braced himself to rush into a burning vehicle to rescue any wounded. Still at top speed, Will caught him with an arm on the shoulder. "It's too late, sir. No point," Will yelled. "It could blow."

Startled, Captain Ashe stared at Will, then nodded.

"I'll run around the other side and see if anyone's been thrown clear," Will said. He circled to the left at full tilt, dropping to his knees to survey the nearby area. Captain Ashe came racing to him, having circled the vehicle from the other side. He, too, fell to his knees when tracers passed too near.

"Nothing on the other side," Captain Ashe said.

"Nothing here," Will reported. "Here comes your track."

Will felt uneasy about having stopped Captain Ashe so hastily. He glanced back at the flaming ACAV as the two of them ran toward their own vehicle. *Gotta be sure no one's left.* He spun around and scrambled up the rear ramp of the wreck. The gunners were charred on the floor where they had stood by their guns. Will picked a path in and confirmed the driver was dead. He rushed back out, swatting at a flame on his pant leg.

Captain Ashe rushed to Will. "We must check all these vehicles," he ordered. "We cannot assume any are dead. We have to aid the wounded as soon as possible."

"Yes, sir," Will said.

"I have to get it organized," the captain said, ticking off a list of what needed to be done. "Dust-offs, involve more crews, maintain security, follow-up on the platoons in pursuit. You check in this direction, Stone. I'll get someone going in the other direction. We'll follow you with the ramp down. God help us, and we'll find some wounded in time."

Before responding, Will looked to make eye contact with Captain Ashe, who stared into the back of the flaming ACAV at the charred bodies. Will backed away three steps. "Yes, sir," he said, turning and running the forty yards to the next vehicle—a truck, rolled on its side and burnt out. Whoever was in it had been thrown out. Will spotted two bodies about twenty feet apart. He dashed to the nearest, sliding next to it. *Dead,* he concluded as he rolled over a corporal, who had been dismembered by grenade attack.

Ducking from tracer rounds passing overhead, Will broke for the next body, again sliding to a halt next to it. As soon as he went to turn it over, Will realized the charred man was still alive. *Must have been engulfed in flames before he escaped the cab. Hit with gunfire on the way out or on the ground. Gotta be in shock.*

"He's alive." Will stood, waving his arms and calling, "Over here!" When the ACAV headed his way and the crew acknowledged their understanding with waves, Will headed for the next vehicle. On his way, he was more alert this time to whom might have been thrown clear.

So it continued, Will running ahead to locate the wounded, and the command track following, with the ramp lowered level, to pick them up. By the time they made it back to the highway, conditions had changed. Hostile fire stopped. The platoons discontinued their pursuit in order to set up perimeter security and broaden the search for wounded south of the highway. Traffic re-emerged on Highway 1, and the command track hooked up with Zippo Man, who just completed the search for wounded north of the highway in the other direction. He was the TC, the track commander, for the ACAV with a M10-8 flamethrower attached.

"Set up a skirmish line," Will overheard Captain Ashe say over the troop net. "Walk it from the highway to the limit of disturbance, first to the north, then south. Look for any wounded we might have missed, but keep your eyes peeled for VC in the grass."

Captain Ashe noticed Will standing by at a respectful distance for further orders. He eased his way over. "Thanks for your help," he said. "As soon as the dust-off picks up these guys, we'll cross the highway and check on the situation there. Should be just a minute or two. From what I've heard on the horn, it's going to be more of the same over there. Christ, between both sides of the highway, the first count seems to be about forty dead and just these eight that we picked up wounded. Be a miracle, too, if any of them make it."

Will nodded as he assessed what had just been said. A convoy moving toward them from the west interrupted his reflection. With his binoculars Will made it out as an ARVN armored column because of its yellow and red South Vietnamese flag. Otherwise, he might have mistaken it for an American armored cavalry unit.

"It's ARVN," he announced.

All eyes turned toward the approaching column of dust. The armored personnel carriers lacked the gun shields of the ACAV, but in other respects, notably firepower, they were much the same as K Troop's. *Hope they help us. The hell with that. Want to do this ourselves. Can't let them see us like this. This is private.*

The side gunner next to Will on the near side of the highway gripped his M-60 and lowered himself behind his gun shield. The same thing happened on K Troop's other vehicles on both sides of the highway.

Will felt himself slip down an inch or two. *Someday, this will be a North Vietnamese force coming to confront us this way. But not today.*

"Look," someone shouted, as the ARVN began passing through the relief column positioned on both sides of the highway. "The gooks are laughing about this. These bastards are laughing at us spilling our guts here."

Will scrutinized the Vietnamese soldiers. *Bastards do look like they're laughing at us. Can't tell for sure, though. Are they laughing or just nervous to the point of hysterical? They're shouting something.*

An American soldier darted between vehicles across the highway to the command vehicle. Will overheard him say to the captain, "One of the wounded we picked up, sir, swore that an ARVN armored column had just passed them headed in the other direction, not more than two minutes before the ambush. The ARVN had to hear the firing, sir, but wouldn't come back to help."

Several Americans heard this remark and glared back and forth between one another and the ARVN column. Will looked back at the ARVN force. *They do look like they're enjoying our suffering. Bastards.*

A Father's Daughter

After the ARVN passed through, the evacuation helicopter appeared in the sky against a backdrop of smoke funnels rising from where the jets had dumped their ordnance.

"Stone, hold up traffic and bring him in right on the highway," Captain Ashe ordered. "It'll keep the dust down, and we'll back right up to him to off-load."

Will bumped Drake and pointed to the west before heading for the highway. He pitched a green smoke canister in the center of the road. Then he made his way down the road to the east, as Drake had done to the west. They stood in the center of the highway and held up their rifles with one hand overhead until traffic halted from both directions.

The evacuation helicopter touched down. At once the command vehicle backed up to it and began to transfer the wounded. Will looked on from his post, keeping one eye on the traffic lined up behind him. The devastation of the convoy was so complete. Any wounded who survived would be maimed for life. *I don't know what, but something's going to come of all this.*

An ox cart rumbled its way up the highway in the empty eastbound lane toward Will, passing the other oncoming traffic waiting for Will's signal to proceed. A leathery-skinned, white-haired old man drove the cart. A toddler sat next to him. The man stoically looked ahead. The boy wept.

When they reached the lead vehicle of the waiting traffic, Will stepped in front of the cart to hold it up. The old man was slow to react, but brought the ox under control. Will approached them. "No tricks," he said in English, while signaling with his rifle that he was ready to react, if necessary.

The old man looked straight ahead, the boy to the ground. Will half-faced them as he backed alongside the cart for a look in the rear. There, on a bed of straw, lay a beautiful, peasant women in black silk pants and loose-fitting, short-sleeved top, the kind commonly seen in rice paddies. Next to her head rested the conical straw hat that no doubt protected her smooth-skinned face from the sun.

Will studied the woman for several moments while keeping an eye on the old man and the boy. *Is she sick or just sleeping?* His eye was drawn to a small hole in her blouse right at the midsection. It was ringed with dark, dried blood. The old man craned his neck to gaze at his daughter. The little boy turned to the rear, repressing tears for a clearer look. Will's eyes met theirs as the fingers of his right hand reached under the woman's blouse and lifted it at the waist just enough for him to see a blood-ringed hole where her navel should have been. Will looked up for a second, but, even as he viewed the old man, his mind continued to inspect the bullet hole. It had penetrated the skin and continued on. *She's dead.*

Suddenly the old man came into focus, and Will sensed both his heartache and fatalistic acceptance. Will searched the old man's eyes for contempt or anger, but found only hurt and sorrow.

Focusing his mind on the bullet in the woman's belly, Will wondered, *What caliber was it? Was it one of ours? Was she a part of the attack party? Was it a stray that hit her? Did the Viet Cong do it as some sort of reprisal?* He saw none of that mattered to the old man. It mattered only that her time had come and gone.

Reaching his hand into the back of the cart, Will checked the straw around the woman for contraband. He knelt and checked under the cart. Then he walked forward to the old man, who resumed his stare forward. Will looked at the toddler, who hid his face under the old man's arm.

"Xin loi," Will said. "Sorry, sorry."

The old man showed no acknowledgment. *There's nothing to be said. What can words mean? I was being polite.* Will made eye contact with the driver of the lead motor vehicle still waiting, and signaled for him to remain in place. Then he signaled the old man to start his ox and steered them a wide berth around the helicopter on the ground. He left them only after they were well clear of the landing zone. "Xin loi," Will said again to the motherless child, before returning to his post in the east.

Soldiers carefully passed the wounded into the helicopter. After a time the rotary wings of the dust-off ship picked up speed. The dust-off lifted slowly, dipped its nose, and headed west. With it went the hopes of all those left behind for the survival of the few just evacuated. Will watched it get smaller and smaller as it flew above the highway until finally it passed over the wooden-wheeled ox cart, which carried no hope at all, no hope at all.

A *Final Salute*

Will waved on the waiting traffic and headed back to the command track with Drake. Captain Ashe was there wolfing down a can of cold chicken noodle soup. "You eat anything yet, Stone?" the captain asked.

Before Will could answer, the captain flipped him a can of bread from the C rations he had just invaded. While Will hacked his way through the top of the can with his P38, the tiny can opener he carried on his dog tag chain, the captain tossed Drake a canned pecan roll. Will pulled the doughy bread roll from its can and stuffed half of it in his mouth in one gulp.

"It's just past fifteen hundred hours," Captain Ashe said. "You men know what we have to do now. We'll pick up the dead and bring them back here by the road for the return ride home and at the same time check one more time for wounded. We have to pick up the dead in time to search Soui Cat before dark."

Will swilled water from his canteen before passing it to Drake. When they were done, Captain Ashe ordered, "OK, let's get started."

The driver fired up the engine. Looking back to the captain for a nod, the driver inched ahead with the rear hatch down level with the ground. They pulled across the highway to the first group of wrecked vehicles.

Will and Drake hit the ground running, each headed for a different truck. Each came back with a body. Will carried his in his arms like a bridegroom. Drake used the fireman's carry. They placed the bodies on ponchos covering the open rear hatch until the next dust-off brought them body bags.

After two more trips, Will concluded there were no more dead or wounded near these two burnt-out trucks. He and Drake forged ahead to the next vehicle, a smoldering ACAV, where the smell of burnt flesh was heavy. Will shouldered a side gunner whose left leg was burnt off. Most likely, he had died by the time that happened. Drake scooped up the remains of his counterpart, charred beyond recognition.

Will was heartened when first he saw two soldiers, one as tall and thin as the other was squat, together in the field behind the track. They appeared to be resting after the ordeal. The taller soldier seemed to be seated, leaning against a stump. The other lay on his side, facing the taller one. With Drake in tow, Will approached the pair. Only as Will drew near did he realize the two most likely were dead. He grabbed the taller soldier under the arms and pulled him to his feet. Will stood face-to-face with the body and wrapped it in his arms. He prepared to dip his knee to shoulder the load, but before he could, the soldier slowly slipped down through his grasp. Will pulled the body tighter against him. *Hands warm and sticky. Guy's melting through my fingers.* Will leaned back to catch the body as it slid, which helped, but he still felt the soldier could fall.

Will stepped forward, using his body to push the limp soldier ahead. *Gotta just waltz him to the track.* The herky-jerky movements of the soldier's lanky frame tested Will's grip with each step. As if in some primitive dance ceremony, Will struggled with the body to make headway to the command track.

Each sensation of slipping caused Will to tighten his grip on the soldier's back. The more he did, the more wet and warm his hands felt. Will fluttered his fingers, seeking something firm to latch onto as he strengthened the pressure of his palms against the body. When twenty paces from the command track, he realized his hands were not around the soldier's back but in it, and there was nothing there to keep them out. *Can't let this guy fall to the ground.* Again Will tightened his grip and leaned further back, pulling the soldier even more on top of him in a limbo dance with death. A side gunner from 1st Platoon passed between them and the command track. "Who's your honey?" he remarked, laughing.

"You think this is funny?" shouted Drake, who was behind Will with the other soldier on his shoulder. "These are our people."

Will made it to the vehicle where outstretched ponchos waited on the rear hatch cover. Still holding the lanky soldier dear to his chest, he dropped to one knee and leaned over a poncho. He let the soldier's legs and bottom sink to the poncho first. Then, straddling the soldier on his knees, Will withdrew his lower hand from inside the soldier's body and used it to cradle the neck and skull. He held the body tightly as he leaned forward all the way to the poncho, relaxing his arms so the body came to rest. Slowly he extricated his bloody hands and straightened himself, still kneeling astride the soldier. Eyes burning with sweat, he could barely see. As soon as his arms were free, he involuntarily jerked back his neck and swiped his brow and eyes several times. Each swipe left a swath of blood across his crown, which quickly mixed with the perspiration flowing down his cheeks. It looked as if he wore tribal war paint.

When he could see again, Will looked down at the soldier he had struggled so to bring to rest in dignity. His gaze passed from top to chest when suddenly his arms dropped to the hatch cover, elbows locked to catch himself from falling. Will remained motionless for several long moments before trying to look at the face. Again he turned away. Finally, he mustered the resolve for one last look at the face, the rank insignia on the collar, and the nametag on the soldier's chest. "Captain Mike," he said aloud.

Drake had stood by after depositing the squat soldier to make sure Will would not need help. "Captain Mike?" Drake asked.

Will winced and twisted away. *Leave me alone. This is between Captain Mike and me. This man, this prince of a man, this one, the only one who would accord us the respect due all, the one who came to us in our hour of need, who led by example and inspired by deed. This was a man too great to be proud, too considerate to be petty. Here was a man for whose life I would trade all the world's riches. Oh, Lord, why him and not me?*

In some outer reach of Will's consciousness, he heard Drake punctuate his reverie by firing a single gunshot to the heavens, and he saw everyone jump and scan the battleground to find who had fired. There was Drake waving his M-16 overhead and bellowing, "Captain Mike! Captain Mike is dead!" Those who could not hear him called to those nearer to relay his words. All the while, Drake looked back at them, searching from face to face for some sign of the meaning of all this. No one knew what to say.

Then, Will spotted a single soldier kneeling to tend the wounded in the farthest ring of troopers. Slowly the soldier drew himself up to the position of attention and saluted where Captain Michaels lay. A second soldier, on the other side of the command vehicle did the same. One by one, to a man, all followed suit. Captain Ashe did, too, though he first waited for the others so his action would not be seen as a command. Still kneeling astride the fallen leader, Will swung his head first to the left and then to the right, looking everywhere for some holdout. There was none. There was only Will, shaken from the shock.

Will knew he must rise to return their salute on behalf of the fallen captain. He shifted his weight to his right knee and raised his left, ready to push off that knee with both hands. Before Will could muster the strength, he leaned forward and rested his forehead on his clasped hands, as if in prayer. On his knee, Will anticipated to the minutest detail the events next to unfold. Finally he would rise to a position of attention, having grasped Drake's rifle to his side. He would raise the M-16 to present arms, before striding forward and shouldering it to the standing firing position. His rifle angled halfway to heaven, Will would fire off three rounds in slow succession. After the last shot, he would hold his aim for half a minute and then return his rifle to present arms.

"Call it, Drake," Will would barely gasp.

"Order - Arms," Drake would boom, and, as Will sped the M-16 alongside him to the ground, so would a hundred arms drop their heartfelt salute as one.

He was everybody's hero, Will would reflect, as he stepped down from the back of the ACAV.

That was what Will foresaw and sensed as he remained on one knee. But, in fact, Will did not thrust upwards to snap to attention, rifle alongside. He did not shoulder the M-16 and fire a three-round gun salute. A hundred arms did not drop their salute upon command, because there were no salutes and no soldiers standing at attention. All that was how it should have been in Will's mind, before he began to see things for what they were.

There was Drake standing by. The others continued to retrieve the dead and wounded, search for snipers and maintain perimeter security. Theirs was the business of survival. If Drake stood by, he was there for Will alone, no matter what Drake may have thought of Captain Michaels. Will had weakened, but he was alive. Captain Michaels was dead, and that made all the difference. The dead no longer counted with the living.

Will lifted his forehead from his hands and slowly rose. As he looked about, he licked his parched lips. Sticky drying blood covered his hands and forearms and face.

"You want to wash?" a trooper asked, holding out his canteen to Will.

"Thanks," Will answered. But before he took the canteen and instead drank from it, he wiped his arms on his fatigue jacket and his hands on his trousers, unwilling to let more of their blood spill in the sand. "Thanks," he said, gurgling down the water.

Will faced the next overturned truck. *How can I keep doing this?* Then he thought of Captain Michaels. *Just do it.* And he did. He did it because it needed to be done. He did it because it was his duty. Most of all, though, he did it because he knew Captain Mike would have been the first to do likewise, so to do so was to honor his memory, to count him. *We carry his spirit. And, just as he touched us, so can we touch others.*

Will forged ahead, but not without first looking back to the command track. Ponchos wrapping other bodies now lay on both sides of the captain. Two soldiers stacked another body wrapped in a poncho crosswise on top of him. Will strained to shoulder a body from the next burnt-out hull.

The Black Dot

By the time the command track had made three trips to the dust-off landing zone, Captain Ashe felt he had recovered as many dead as possible. Besides his command track, he had monitored by radio the efforts of three others performing the same function in different sectors. When Major Finn called on the radio from his helicopter, Captain Ashe said,

"This is Two-six. I think we got them all, except for one, over."

"This is Three. We need them all, over."

"This is Two-six," Captain Ashe resumed. "I agree, but I have not seen the situation for myself, so I have to respect the problem until I do. Over."

"This is Three. Either you get him, or someone just like you will do it for you. Over."

"This is Two-six," Captain Ashe said, "Roger, out."

"Niner-one," the captain called to Will.

"Sir?" Will responded.

"Take my vehicle and go up the northern edge of the battlefield," Captain Ashe ordered. "There's a toasted ACAV up there with the driver still in his seat. I don't know why. The other crews up there got the rest but not that driver. He has as much right to fly out of here as any of us. Can you handle it for me? I have to meet with my lieutenants and dope out the search of the village next."

"Yes, sir," Will responded. The crew and he set forth and approached the burnt-out ACAV in a counterclockwise movement five minutes later. That left Drake on his right side gun to cover the northern perimeter along with the ammo loader on the .50 caliber in the turret. Will tapped the left side gunner and gave him the nod to follow. The track was burnt badly, but no worse than several others that day. The driver was in plain view.

Will and the left gunner bent over and headed into the open rear hatch. Sandwiched alongside the engine area, the driver's compartment accessed the personnel area by an opening just wide enough for one man to slip through. Just the same, the two of them squeezed together to get a view of the driver. All skin and uniform above his chest were burnt beyond recognition. Below his chest, there was nothing but a charred skeleton partially supported by the backrest of his seat.

"You get up on top to lift him out through his hatch," Will said to the side gunner. "I'll stand him up from behind here, so you can get him under the arms."

The side gunner complied. Once Will attempted lifting the torso, he immediately recognized the problem. The lower end of the driver, together with his seat, had melted and fused to the aluminum alloy floor deck. The driver's spinal cord attached the remains of his torso to the floor where he had been seated.

"Hold him here a second, will ya?" Will said.

The side gunner was able to do that by lying facedown on top of the vehicle and reaching down through the driver's hatch opening. Will ripped the back of the driver's seat out of the way, enabling him a closer inspection of the situation. "His spinal cord goes right into what looks like it could have been a molten mass of flesh and metal. Must have been Willie Peter or some other type of thermal grenade," Will said. "Hang on to him. I'm gonna get something to free him."

Quickly Will returned from the command track with a shovel. "Still got him?" Will called. "Keep hanging on."

While the side gunner supported the driver, Will figured to free the spinal cord by sliding the shovel into a seam between the congealed mass and the floor itself. But there was no seam.

"Pull some more," Will called, as he examined where the spinal cord fused with the floor.

The side gunner lifted hard enough to put the spinal cord in tension but not enough to help the situation below. Each time Will called for him to try again, the side gunner lifted a little more until he was to the point of overstretching the spinal cord. Finally, it snapped.

"Let me have him," Will said. He had a clear path from the driver's compartment to the rear hatch. They eased the driver to daylight and a waiting poncho.

In his mind, Will again saw the driver's wiry spinal cord stretching and snapping at the black dot where it entered the floor.

"Why the shovel?" Drake yelled as Will entered the command vehicle with the remains wrapped in the poncho. "What's wrong with your hands?"

Will understood Drake's question had to do with the respect due the dead, but he did not feel like talking about it. "Too hot," Will said. "Still too hot." Drake said nothing more but turned his back to Will.

"Did you know him, Drake?" Will asked. "I hardly know any of you guys. This'll be my third extended mission with K. You weren't in the command track before, and neither was the rest of this crew."

"They just moved us in here," Drake said. "The captain wanted those longest with the unit to be in the command track with him. There's only ten of us boat people left in K. The rest, well, all killed or sent outta here badly mangled. We got hit pretty bad a couple of times before, and this didn't help."

"Him?" Will said, pointing to the poncho he had left on the rear hatch.

"Blair. That would have been Blair, I guess," Drake said. "He was the regular driver for that track."

"We just got his top half," Will said. "There was nothing left below his chest except his spinal cord, which got fused to the fuckin' floor. We used the shovel to try and get more, but no way. There was just a little black dot where it went into the floor. I'll show you if you want."

Drake looked down and shook his head. "Good kid, no more than nineteen," he said. "Back in the world, didn't hang with nobody when we'd go out at night—not with us, not with the brothers. Sent 'bout all his paycheck home to his mother to help raise his younger brother and sister. From Detroit. Went to college at night before we got orders for Nam. Had to finish a remedial program before they'd give him any credits. The Army paid for it. Good kid."

"Thanks," Will said. He sat on the level rear hatch next to Blair's body. "Have the driver head to the highway, will ya, Drake?"

Will leaned back, yielding to his fatigue for a moment. He rested his hand on Blair's remains. *I didn't know you, kid, but I'm not gonna forget you.*

As they rode along, Will tried to re-create Blair in his mind from the bits and pieces Drake told him. *"Didn't hang with nobody…not with us, not with the brothers." Colored? There was no color. There was no skin.*

"This is Six. All right, what's the count, then? Over," Captain Ashe said over the K Troop radio as soon as Will returned with the command vehicle.

"Uh, this is One-six. We have eight. Over," the First Platoon leader answered.

"This is Six. Roger on eight. Put four on the rear hatches of each of the first two tracks," Captain Ashe ordered. "Move out now. Just the way we went over it. Use four ACAVs. The last two should sit just across the bridge to cover the first two. The first two should speed into the edge of the village, push off the goddamned Viet Cong bodies and speed back out. When we go in to search the village in a few minutes, we'll find out who was so goddamned interested in those fucking bodies. Over."

"This is One-six. Wilco, out."

Captain Ashe's lips curled into a wry smile when he saw Will was listening. "I should have told them to piss on the VC dead before they kick them off," he snarled. "Now it's our turn."

Chapter 8

Under Attack By Night

Talk Of War Crimes

Will sat on the floor of the ACAV and scanned *Stars and Stripes*.

"It's not in there," Campbell said as he approached. Will looked up. "You really expect to read about Soui Cat in the official newspaper of the US Armed Forces?" Campbell went on. "It's not in there 'cause it didn't happen."

Campbell paced behind the track vehicle, stopping now and then to kick at the ground as he glanced inside at Will. "You don't have to worry," he continued. "Your folks won't read about it in their local paper or see it on TV. As far as anyone else is concerned, it never happened. It's not the type of news they'd print. And if they did, they'd have said we won because the relief column chased the attackers already withdrawing."

Every chance he had for the past twenty days, Will had rifled through *Stars and Stripes* and listened to AFVN radio for some word that might clarify the significance of the event or at least confirm it happened.

"It's not in there," Campbell continued. "Captain Mike didn't spill his guts in your arms, and fifty other guys we hardly knew never bought it that afternoon. They must be on Temporary Duty elsewhere—TDY. They didn't die." Campbell slid onto the bench seat across from Will, turned around and rummaged through the wall bin for fragmentation grenades.

Will lifted his gaze from the newspaper to Campbell. "I'm sorry, I went too far, but it's like it never happened, and it pisses me off," Campbell said, turning to face Will. "We deserve better than that. The guys that got it deserve better than that. Their folks, our folks, everybody deserves better than that. Makes you sort of wonder what the hell else has been happening here they aren't telling anybody."

Will said nothing. He resented Campbell's negativity, though it expressed his own worst fears. *Something different about Campbell today.*

"Look at the bright side," Campbell said. "At least they're not reporting we're committing war crimes. They could be reporting how we've torched about twenty villages since the ambush and relocated their populations at gunpoint."

"What the fuck are you talking about, Campbell, you sonofabitch?" Will said. "No one's running around here collecting enemy ears as trophies. You seen any rapes while you're on duty? Has any one of us shot any prisoners? What do you want from us, Campbell? We're trying to stay alive. We're fighting back the only way we can."

Even as he spoke, Will shuddered at the recollection of the track vehicle right behind his when they moved in column formation through the last several villages they visited. Zippo, the armored flamethrower, had spewed out its hundred-foot napalm blowtorch at anything combustible. Villagers scrambled after chickens and shrieked in protest when forced onto Chinook transport helicopters for resettlement in the Mekong Delta. Their children ran wild-eyed with terror. The older people huddled by their ancestral burial plots.

One old man had thrown his arms around a water buffalo and would not budge. "Get Grandpa in the Chinook, Shark," Will had ordered.

"Better let me do it, Stone," Whiteman said. "I need the stretch anyway. Let Shark drive for a while." Will nodded and remained in place as the rest of the crew watched with interest.

Covered with little more than a loincloth, the leathery man remained stooped over the carabao, hugging the beast around the neck as Whiteman approached. Whiteman spoke to the old man with little effect, but nonetheless went on speaking.

Finally, Whiteman reached across the beast, took the man's wrists in his hands and gently pulled them away from the ox. Powerless, the old man straightened up and looked at Whiteman, who smiled and nodded toward the Chinook. Alarmed, the old man tried to free himself to grab the carabao again. Whiteman held him tight until he relented, then let him go, waving his forefinger in front of the old man's face. Whiteman put one arm around the carabao and pointed with his other to the helicopter. He kept nodding in that direction until, with a quick hand movement, he spurred the ox to move ahead. The old man hurried to keep abreast. Whiteman kept reassuring the old man as the two walked the creature all the way to the helicopter.

"Shard, ease this tub closer to the Chinook," Will said through the intercom built into his TC helmet.

"Where the hell does Paul Bunyon think he's going with Blue?" Shard replied. "He can't be thinking of talking the pilot into taking a fucking ox along, can he?"

The pilot—a captain—stuck his upper body out a doorway and called to Whiteman, "You, come here and bring the old guy with you." The peasant dove for his animal, but Whiteman grabbed him before he could latch on again. Whiteman tried to soothe the old man as he drew him toward the helicopter pilot.

"This way," the pilot called. When they stood safely in front of him, the pilot called to his door gunner, "Dust'im!"

The door gunner let rip a burst of M-60 gunfire until the water buffalo fell to the ground and bled profusely. The old man shrieked and flailed his arms, trying to free himself from Whiteman's grip.

"Now get him on the ship," the pilot ordered. The old man continued his struggle but was no match for Whiteman and the flight crew. On his way back to the track, Whiteman stopped to look at the carcass. Flies were settling on it even as the many bullet holes still spurted blood.

"What'd he have to kill the animal for?" Whiteman said when he made it back to the crew.

"Tell him," Will said, looking at Campbell.

"You're the expert, White Man," Campbell said. "How many nights would a water buffalo feed a company of VC?"

Campbell cleared his throat, bringing Will's attention back to the rock quarry. "We are doing this to civilians," Campbell said, "these forced relocations."

"Look what the other side does to them," Will said.

"I would have expected more from you, Stone," Campbell said. "That's how the Army would want you to look at it. As we both learned at our mothers' knees, two wrongs a right don't make. We don't judge ourselves by our enemies' code of conduct. If we are defending anything here, it is our differences with them on this sort of thing."

"We can't just let them smear us and run away," Will said. "We gotta do something."

"It's difficult," Campbell said, "but that's why the rules of war were developed—in anticipation of all types of difficult situations. And those rules are clear: Civilian populations shall not be forcibly relocated in a wholesale manner."

"Yeah," Will said, "well, that was before Chairman Mao trained partisan guerrillas to swim as fish in a sea of local peasants. Our job is to dry up that sea, relocating it, if necessary, but, one way or the other, to deprive the fish of its nurture and protective cover."

"There's nothing like it, is there?" Campbell said. "I mean the rush we get from the God almighty power these rifles give us when we point them at unarmed old men, women and children."

"Maybe the rush is from never knowing when one of them is going to drop a dime on us," Will said, "or from half expecting each time we enter a hooch that a carbine will blast hot lead in our faces. Or maybe we just saw one too many of us medevacked with half a leg blown to hell after stepping on a land mine that these villagers somehow happen to miss every day."

"You didn't hear what I said, Stone," Campbell said. "There are rules about these things. Everyone always claims extenuating circumstances.

Don't think it's totally impossible that these events might someday be brought before some bar of justice."

"Saint Peter's Gate?" Will said. "Listen, we're doing our job. We're doing what we're told. Following orders."

"But we have consciences. Dante had something to say about this. 'I wept not, so to stone within I grew.' I'm forewarning you, that's all."

Will looked at Campbell resentfully but nodded. *I'm losing Campbell. I don't want to lose him. Something's wrong here. He's still got a lot to tell me.*

"Wait, Campbell," Will said. "When you said we were fighting for a political cover story, and not to save the Vietnamese or our own skins, weren't you saying our whole involvement is a big sham?"

"Why do we fight here?" Campbell said. "Stone, Will, if I may, that is, Sergeant—"

"Skip the bullshit."

"Don't be reductionistic, Stone. Reducing anything complex to a single cause denies reality. One cause may be dominant, but there are others that still influence the result. It's like when people insist you must choose between two extremes, denying there is a middle ground between them. It's called excluding the middle. You can't make a wise choice if you deny some of the possibilities available to you.

"We both know," he continued, "that human motivation is complex. People do things for more than one reason. We are simultaneously aware of several goals toward which we can gain or lose ground whenever we make a significant choice or decision. So each choice is a mixture of purposes. As for supporting the war policy, our Congress needs to believe (a) there will be hell to pay if they don't, (b) we're saving our own asses, and (c) we're saving the gooks—our gooks, that is."

"Excluding the middle?" Will said.

"Same thing, basically," said Campbell. "For example, I say that I don't want to die in Vietnam so I'm labeled a coward or a communist. The middle ground between where we're fighting today and our national surrender has been excluded from consideration. No matter, as you point out, that the most effective defense we might muster would be on the high seas, averting any surrender and saving our soldiers' lives."

"Why, though?" Will asked. "Why can't we see we've limited ourselves to extremes?"

"Ha, when people do that to me—call me pink, you know," Campbell resumed, "I say 'Well, then, let's attack Moscow or Peking! Let's hit communism at its heart.' They never accept that risk. Now we have really excluded the middle by extending their thinking to its logical conclusion, by making it into an all-or-nothing nuclear firestorm. Then I say to them, 'You see, it's not about whether I want to fight the commies—I'll bomb Moscow and you won't—it's about where and how best to defend ourselves.'"

"But why?" Will said. "If saving our national ass is a necessary belief, or ingredient, in this mix, how can they not see that it can best be done on the seas away from the jungle?"

"Emotions, I guess," Campbell muttered. "Fear, anger, self-righteousness. Ask yourself, Stone. After all, you've just announced your happy conclusions in the last several weeks, after mulling it over for how long? And, by the way, I respect you for that.

"They say that this is the first television war," Campbell said, raising his voice. "Maybe that's it. The American people have been watching too much boob tube. 'Why?' you ask. That is as good a reason as any I can think of. Americans have gone soft in the head, not soft on communism. It's muddled thinking as much as anything else that has gotten us into this trouble."

"It was so clear the way Finn laid it out." Will said.

"What?"

"The way I said it to you about the shoreline defense and everything," Will said. "That's what I meant."

"I don't think that many Americans have broken down the logic of this policy as carefully as you have, so the truth of each of the various components can be weighed and offset," Campbell said. "I doubt very many of them have said, as you did, that the cost over and above that of a shoreline defense must be attributed solely to our trying to save the Vietnamese from the Red tide.

"Hell, that's it," Campbell said, his eyes twinkling. "What we need, Stone, is an accountant for President—someone who can account for why we spill our blood."

Whiteman stirred from his nap on the floor of the ACAV next to where Will was seated. "You guys are back at it again?" he asked, pulling a towel over his head.

"Then there is this political dynamic, of course," Campbell went on. "Political self-defense has become an indispensable ingredient to the mix. In his heart, your Congressman may know better, but yielding to the majority view is going to make it easier for him to capture votes."

Campbell stopped talking and grabbed his ammo belt. "I have to fill up my canteen," he said, heading off for the water trailer.

Whiteman sat up. "What's this about Finn?" he asked, when Campbell was out of earshot.

"Nothing," Will countered. "Now what's with Campbell? Did he seem uptight to you?"

"K Troop's First Platoon leader—" Whiteman said.

"Lieutenant Morales," Will broke in.

"Right. He came over here while you were passing your malaria pill in the bush," Whiteman continued. "He fingered Campbell as the ranking man and told him to name a volunteer from our track for tonight's ambush party. Campbell glanced at Swindell and Shard and wanted no part of naming either of them. Then he looked at me and figured that he couldn't name me if he wouldn't name his buddies, and he knew he couldn't name you. So he said that he would go himself. Been a little jittery since."

"I guess old Campbell isn't so very different from you or me, when you look at him carefully," Will said. "If the CO had busted him for that AWOL gig, then you would have been ranking man and would be getting ready for that ambush patrol right now."

Whiteman stared at Will and smiled. "Nah, I would have named you to the patrol," he said. After a moment or two he added, "Rick was around, too."

"We know that feeling before you go on a patrol," Will said. "So when push came to shove, for all his bluster, the great slacker wouldn't send another man where he hadn't himself gone first. It'd almost be funny, wouldn't it, White Man, if the stakes weren't so high?"

"What the hell was he talking about?" Whiteman asked. "He sure seemed like he had to get it out. He acted like it was so important that he say this stuff to you, whatever the hell it was about."

"Our Rick was around?" Will asked.

"Franklin, yeah," Whiteman answered. "He left you a letter."

"What was Campbell so hell-bent on telling me?" Will asked. "He wanted to make me understand how men deceive themselves with the gravest of consequences, not the least of which is that Campbell and fifteen others like him are about to cross our perimeter wire to seek out a death struggle with strange men under similar misguided duress."

"Yeah, well, anyway, Rick got a letter from his wife," Whiteman said. "He wanted to talk to you about it. Seemed happy enough. He's in one of How Battery's ACAVs on the eastern perimeter."

"What's he doing out here?"

"Flew in with the hot meal," Whiteman explained. "Talked Royce into letting him stay out for the night after he served it. Going to fly back with the breakfast chopper. Just wanted to be out here with us."

"Letter for me?" Will asked. Whiteman passed it to him without comment. When Will glanced at the return address, his heart jumped. *Jenny.* He looked at Whiteman, who was still attentive to him.

"So Rick seemed all right?" Will asked. "Listen, White Man, we're gonna have to change the guard rotation with Campbell on patrol. Where the hell are Swindell and Shard now?"

"My guess," Whiteman answered, "is that they are sitting it out in one of the other tracks until Campbell leaves, just in case he changes his mind."

"Well, it's up to me now," Will said, "so please sniff them out and tell them to get back here before I do change Campbell's mind."

"One question," Whiteman said. "Does Campbell know what he's talking about, or is all that just a lot of mumbo jumbo?"

"I hope he makes it back OK," Will said. "He will. Of course he will."

As Will started preparations for his shower, he thought about Campbell's having to put behind him his entire past in order to serve. Will thought, too, about his own past—the part Harry's ultimatum played in his induction and how, in retrospect, it really would have made little difference had he known sooner that Harry had relented. He remembered going to dinner to announce his induction to the family.

Telling the Family

Will stopped home and spoke privately with Harry while Margaret readied dinner. Harry had already heard the official version of Josh's shooting. He listened carefully to Will's account. When Will told him about volunteering for the draft, Harry let out a loud sigh and bit his tongue.

After they finished eating, Harry announced Will's decision to Margaret and Will's two brothers, home from college. In making mention of Josh's shooting, he announced his intention to look into Josh's situation. When he finished, no one spoke.

Finally, Margaret turned to Harry and said, "Help me upstairs, please." The two of them rose. Margaret looked at Will. He tried to smile. She kissed him on the cheek as she passed, and Harry squeezed Will's shoulder before continuing to the stairway. Will rose from the table, looked to his two brothers, shrugged his shoulders, and headed for the front door.

Harry called after him from the stairs, "Where are you going, Will? I mean, to spend the night."

"Grandpa's."

Harry nodded.

Before Will closed the front door, his oldest brother called after him, "Will, for your own sake, don't play the sap. Dad can get this handled."

Harry stopped in his tracks. He turned Margaret around and sat her in place halfway up the stairs. Visibly shaken, he leaned over the banister and called toward the dining room, "I gotta tell you boys something." When they reached the foot of the stairs, Harry said, "You didn't know your Uncle Sam, but how I wish you had. There was none finer, take my word for it. He was anything but a sap, and yet I'm alive tonight probably because he died in my place during the war. We had our doubts at times, but tonight we were never more certain that he was Will's natural father. Will's a lot like him. Will's no sap."

Margaret began sobbing, and Harry helped her the rest of the way up the stairs. He supported her with one arm and, while passing her his handkerchief, wiped his eyes with the other. At the top of the stairs he turned a moment and said, "Good night, boys. We love you all. Lock the doors before you turn in, please."

As Harry helped Margaret to the bedroom, he said, "Will probably won't be sent to Vietnam, Mag. So let's not draw any conclusions. I'm so sorry about Josh. This whole thing just got away on me. That's all."

Night Laager Under Attack

In order for Will to rig a shower for himself, first he spun the track commander's turret a full quarter turn, pointing the barrel of the .50-caliber machine gun down and fully to the right. Next, he climbed out of the turret to prop the gun barrel up almost level using an ammo can perched at the edge of the top deck of the vehicle. Then, he climbed down the front of the vehicle and walked alongside it back to where he had placed a pail of water beneath the gun barrel, which overhung the side by fifteen inches. He stretched to loop the strap handle of the canvas pail over the gun barrel so it caught on the flare at the end. Then he pointed the showerhead built into the bottom of the pail away from the vehicle to where he would stand. *Grassy. No mud.*

Will went behind the ACAV and laid out a change of clothes from his duffel. He stripped, grabbed his gold Dial soap and green Prell shampoo, and headed for his improvised shower.

It was 9:30 p.m. The others were asleep, having gladly conceded the first guard watch to Will because they knew he would take it till well past midnight. They had turned in an hour earlier as the jungle darkened, figuring they each might have to waken for a two-hour shift. Inside the perimeter, guard duty was lax and Will, using a concealed light, had puzzled over the letter from Jen.

Dear Will,

I'm coming of age. The world is an exciting place and I'm full of questions. I miss you, hon, and I need you. And I don' mean as a big brother. I'm proud of you. I got lots of boys here after me, but I want you as my old man. What the hell!

Love,

Jen

Will pulled at his trousers in the crotch before he unlaced his boots to undress for his shower. *More of the same.*

As he stepped to the shower, he visualized Jen beset by high school suitors. He saw her as she had been almost two years earlier—pretty and pert, her eyes glowing with wonder and underscored by that unabashed grin. He recalled several summer evenings when, supposedly on her way to bed, she slipped out onto the front porch in her Baby Dolls and he had said, "Jesus, you better put some clothes on."

Will reached up to open the showerhead. *Blossoming then. Must be a knockout now.* He shut the showerhead as soon as he wet his hair, lathering it with Prell. *Good kid.*

Then, even though it never had happened quite that way, he pictured himself putting his hands on her bare shoulders to turn her away from him, and gently shoving her back toward the screen door. She playacted like he had pushed her with much more force, and when she glanced back she caught him inspecting the fit of her Baby Dolls. Looking over her shoulder, she shook her finger and wagged her tail the rest of the way to the door.

Her image dominated his mind. He bent over for the Dial and soaped up the rest of his body. *Needs someone to watch over her. Shit, everyone else is counting the days, and I don't have a clue how long ago I got left here. Fuck it. I'll die here, where I belong. There's no love for me. For some, there is, for others, there's only this. What month is this? Forget it. I'm a dead man walking. I'm just waiting for my number to come up.*

Nearby gunfire pierced the jungle night. Will turned his head in its direction. His pulse quickened after the second burst. *Not the perimeter, but close. Who's nearby? Where's the mortar platoon and L Troop?*

Will flipped the bar soap away from underfoot and twisted the showerhead on. He rinsed his head and body, rushing as much from fear of running out of water as from alarm. When the bucket ran dry, he looked in the direction of the mounting din of battle. He pulled the empty pail off the end of the gun barrel and let it fall to the ground. *The ambush patrol!*

Will darted around the back of the ACAV, grabbed his clothes off the back ramp, and scurried inside.

"Wake up! We're under attack," he said, shaking Whiteman, Swindell and Shard. "White Man," Will shouted as he pulled on his underpants, "fire'er up and get this rear ramp buttoned up. The ambush patrol is under heavy attack." As he spoke, light automatic weapons fire broke out on the northern portion of the perimeter. "You hear it. Snap to."

"I don't want to fuckin' die," Shard cried out.

Will jammed his legs into his trousers and watched Shard. *Entire perimeter is firing.*

"Why couldn't they just leave me the fuck alone?" Shard said, cowering in a rear corner of the track vehicle. "

Will slipped his bare feet into his jungle boots. "Just stay down for now. We're not on the perimeter—yet." *Swindell seems to have his wits about him.*

"What's going on, White Man?" Will asked, buttoning his fatigue jacket.

"We are taking heavy incoming," Whiteman answered as he peered through the periscope fitted into the driver's compartment.

"You guys just lie low here for now," Will said as he scrambled beneath the turret. "It's just 'cause it's your first time. When it's our turn, I'll signal and you'll stand up and answer the bell like everyone else. You're gonna do fine."

"Cease fire! Cease fire!" a voice squawked over the K Troop net.

Will was heartened by the words as he squirmed his way up the track commander's turret. It meant the perimeter was overreacting and firing at nothing in particular, just saturating the area with bullets. *Recon by fire,* Will thought before his head emerged and he could see.

"Cease fire!" the radio crackled again.

It's Captain Ashe, Will realized as he looked over the perimeter and its various fields of fire. *He's downhill. I wonder how much he can see from there.* Will had chosen his location for its excellent views. He needed those views to call in mortar support, if necessary. Earlier that evening he had fired in def cons, or defensive concentrations, at various points around the perimeter to pre-register target locations. Will called for a single mortar round and then adjusted the fires until the point of impact matched each of the locations he selected. The mortar platoon recorded the settings on the mortar tubes and the charges they used to hit those locations, so that on Will's order they could strike the targets again without the delay of adjustments.

"Cease fire! Hold your fire," the captain's voice repeated.

"Six, this is Niner-one, over," Will called over the K Troop radio net.

"This is Six. Go ahead, Niner-one," Captain Ashe answered.

"This is Niner-one. Have excellent visibility here, particularly of the northern and northeastern portions of the perimeter. We are still receiving heavy incoming fire from crew-served weapons there. Suppressive fire is well targeted on those points and seems warranted."

"This is Six," the radio replied. "Roger, Niner-one. Out. Break. Two-seven, come in, over."

"This is Two-seven, over," came the response.

"This is Six. Mount your platoon up. We're going out to bring in that ambush patrol. Line up on me," Captain Ashe ordered. "Out." He went on. "Break. Two-eight, this is Six, over."

"This is Two-eight, over," the second platoon leader answered.

"This is Six," the Captain ordered. "Have four of your vehicles line up with Two-seven behind me, over."

"This is Two-eight. Roger, over."

"This is Six. Roger. Out. Break. Five, this is Six. Over," the captain continued.

"This is Five. Over," the K Troop executive officer answered.

"This is Six. Fill in the perimeter formation where we pull out. Use Headquarters Platoon and if you have to commandeer some elements from Niner-six, for crissake, do so. Every track we pull off-line should be replaced. This includes making sure you have reserve elements to reinforce any breach of our perimeter. Don't forget that Big Three is our houseguest tonight. Then figure out how to mount a relief force without compromising the perimeter, in case I need you to reinforce me. Over."

"This is Five. Wilco. Maybe you should let Two-seven lead the charge. Over," the Exec said.

"This is Six," the captain said. "I'm taking them out, and I'm bringing them back. This could get pretty dicey. Out."

Let There Be Light

By this time, gun flashes and, at times, rocket-propelled grenades appeared up and down the whole perimeter, except for the western leg, which overlooked a wide, open field sloping away from the formation. The heaviest concentrations of incoming automatic weapons fire still came from outside the northern and northeastern portions of the perimeter. *RPGs. Could be worse. We can handle this. We 're returning three times what they're sending our way.*

Will glanced down at Shard and Swindell through the top hatch as he called over the radio, "Six. This is Niner-one. Over."

"This is Six. Over," Captain Ashe answered.

"This is Niner-one. Want us out there with you?"

"This is Six. No. You stay here in case the perimeter needs fire support," the captain answered. "Over,"

"This is Niner-one. Wilco," Will answered. "Do you want illumination out there? Over."

The captain deliberated a moment. "Affirmative, Niner-one."

"This is Niner-one," Will said. "Roger. Out."

"Hey, we're ready when you are, man," Swindell called to him, clapping Shard on the back, "but how come you offered us up?"

Will turned in the turret and faced them. "I guess you forgot Campbell's out there," he said.

Will turned back to the northern perimeter where incoming fire was intensifying. *Could be a regimental attack. Our ambush patrol screwed up their timing. Their larger elements could just be getting in position. Hope the captain's taking enough force.* He could not make out the exact location of the ambush patrol, although he saw a separate concentration of gunfire beyond the perimeter at a bearing slightly east of due north. He wanted to spot the illumination rounds, giant flares suspended from parachutes, directly over the patrol, so that Captain Ashe's relief force had a star to guide them.

Will grabbed the hand grips inside the turret to support himself long enough to draw his legs up and wedge his feet on the two-inch ledge where the turret overlapped the top deck. He stood for a better view of the ambush patrol, then quickly squatted back down inside the turret. "All right, we're on deck, men," Will said. "There's a burning ACAV on the northeastern section. Zippo just relieved them. The next time a track's hit, we're up. Check your weapons."

Will readied himself to climb atop the turret for the best possible view of things, though he knew that was neither necessary nor expected. Illumination did not have to be that precise. *Anyone on Charlie's side spots me will know I'm not up there for fun. I'll see the tracers before they zero in on me. It's the stray round I gotta sweat.* Will took the chance because he was ashamed his crew was not ready from the start. He sprang up and balanced himself on the very top edge of the turret, where he struggled to orient his map and compass. *They can kill me, but they can't make me cower.*

"Niner-five. This is Niner-one. Fire mission. Contact. Over," Will called over the howitzer battery radio net.

"Niner-one. This is Five. Send your mission. Over," the Fire Direction Center answered.

"This is Niner-one," Will responded. "Grid, 4-3-2 8-6-3, Direction, 0700. Shell, illumination. One round. Fire when ready! Will adjust. Over," Will responded.

"This is Five. Understand Grid, 4-3-2 8-6-3. Direction, 0700 mils. Shell illumination. One round. Fire when ready. Adjust fires. Over," the Fire Direction Center read back.

"This is Niner-one. Roger. Over."

Will readied himself for the blast. He was not used to being with the battery when he called for support, and he knew they would fire right over his head, though at the steepest of angles.

"This is Five. Five seconds, Niner-one," the Fire Direction Center said.

The noise and concussion rocked Will on his perch. He fought for his balance and composure, thrusting his arms out spread-eagle as he waited for the flare to ignite high in the sky above its target. Will looked to the popping sound, where the sky brightened first. As the flare fully ignited, the entire sky was aglow. At first it blinded Will, but then he could make out the dark parachute up above the flare itself, tossed by the wind, slowly making its way down. *That's as good as it gets. So far as I can tell, it's right over them.*

"Five, this is Niner-one. Over," Will spoke into the radio handset.

"This is Five. Go ahead. Over."

"This is Niner-one," Will said. "Nice shot. Maintain continuous illumination until further word. Over."

"This is Five. Wilco, Niner-one. Over," the Fire Direction Center acknowledged, indicating they would keep firing replacement parachute flares before each preceding flare burnt out.

"This is Niner-one. Roger. Out."

Will made a point to smile down at Swindell and Shard before he squatted and lowered himself into the turret. *One thing gone right anyway.*

"Switch me to the K Troop net, will you, please?" he called to Shard. Then Will added, "Where's Captain Ashe's column, do you know?"

"They formed up down by our big guns. I think they crossed the western perimeter down there and then ran north alongside it. I guess they continued straight when the perimeter curved."

"I didn't see them," Will said. "I was looking to target the illumination."

"We were watching you," Swindell said.

"Six, this is Niner-one. Over," Will called on the K Troop net. There was no response. "Six, this is Niner-one. Over." Again he waited. "Six, this is Niner-one. Come in, please. Over," he resumed. "Shard, switch us to first platoon's freq."

"I don't think we've ever done that," Shard answered. "Do you know what it is?"

Will shook his head. "Six, this is Niner-one. Over." No response. "Switch us to the squadron net, Shard."

Shard quickly complied.

"Bandit Two-six, this is Niner-one. Over."

Will looked around the perimeter and gauged that the threat on the northern and eastern perimeters continued to mount. The perimeter defense continued to outgun the attackers, but the attackers continued to mount in numbers.

"Switch me to the battery net, Shard," Will said.

"You got it on the other radio," Shard said.

"Niner-six, this is Niner-one. Over," Will called for the How Battery commander.

"This is Six. Go ahead, Niner-one. Over," Captain Harkness answered.

"This is Niner-one," Will said. "From what I can see, the attack continues to strengthen against the northern and eastern perimeters. So far, we outgun them, but as new attackers arrive, our superiority lessens. If they take out one or more of our positions with RPGs, we will be vulnerable to probe attempts.

"I've tried to reach Bandit Two-six to determine if he wants their staging areas for attack softened up with mortar fires. I haven't been able to reach him—"

"This is Six. I monitored that on the squadron net, Niner-one," Captain Harkness broke in. "Stand by, Niner-one. I'll be back in one."

Will exchanged glances with his crew. "If something happens to me," Will said, "Shard, you call Bandit Two-five. Suggest that some additional reactive elements be stationed up here to reinforce the perimeter, as necessary. If he's got them."

"Niner-one, this is Six. Over," Captain Harkness said.

"Gotcha, Stone," Shard said.

"This is Niner-one. Over," Will answered over the radio.

"This is Six, Niner-one," Captain Harkness resumed. "Big Three said for you to go ahead and walk fire support down the eastern perimeter. Now listen, Niner-one, Three's already got a Huey gunship due in here in about one minute. That Huey will saturate the northern perimeter with cannon fire. Coordinate your fires to keep the skies safe for him. Over."

"This is Niner-one. Wilco. Out. Break. Niner-four. This is Niner-one. Fire mission. Contact. Over." Will continued working the How Battery net, leaning back in the turret, taking a deep breath after each transmission and slowly letting it out while receiving.

"This is Niner-four. Send your mission. Over," answered the Fire Direction Center for How Battery's mortar platoon.

"This is Niner-one. Grid, Def Con One. Direction, 6-400. Shell, H-E. One volley. Will adjust. At my command. Give me a time of flight. Over," Will said, just as the helicopter gunship entered its flight pattern to start its first run over the northern perimeter.

"This is Four. Def Con One. Azimuth 6-400. Shell H-E. One volley. At your command. Adjust fires. Computing time of flight. Wait one. Over."

Will clocked the time as the gunship passed over the location of Def Con One. The helicopter poured 20mm cannon fire directly below its path of flight over the northern perimeter. At twenty percent tracer rounds, there were enough tracers to make it seem like the gunship was pouring actual fire from above. Will waited for the helicopter to complete its loop back past Def Con One in order to note the elapsed time. *What a break to have this guy on our side so early in the battle.*

"Niner-one, this is Four," the mortar platoon advised. "Anticipate time of flight at twenty-five seconds. Ready to fire. Over."

"Niner-one, fire, over, " said Will, satisfied that the assault helicopter would be clear of the target area before the mortars arrived. The gunship approached the target for its second pass just after Will gave the command to fire. *A minute and twenty seconds, round trip.* The gunship began its second approach with a rocket attack, followed by more 20mm cannon as it passed over the target. As it looped back for its next pass, incoming mortars screeched through the sky and exploded on ground contact.

"Damn. Jesus Christ," Will said over the battery net, "that was way off. This is Niner-one. That was way off."

Will climbed back on top of his turret in hope of a better view of the actual point of impact.

"This is Niner-four. What do you mean way off? Over."

"Well, uh, the impact was nowhere near Def Con One," Will answered, glancing at Whiteman, then at Shard and Swindell, finally toward the How Battery command post. He swiped his hand across his mouth twice before continuing. "This is Niner-one, can you confirm that you fired Def Con One?"

"This is Niner-four. Affirmative. Over," the radio squawked.

"This is Niner-one. It was way off. It was nowhere near Def Con One." *Could try Def Con Two. If it's no better than Def Con One, who knows where the hell it'll land? Could blast us to hell. Could start from scratch with a new grid and zero it in again.*

"This is Six," the How Battery commander interrupted from his command post within the perimeter. "We have to proceed deliberately."

"This is Niner-one. Well, who's going to call in these fires?"

"This is Six. How is your visibility, Niner-one? Over," Captain Harkness asked.

What's the matter with me? I've a lot better chance of pulling it off than anyone else. "This is Niner-one. I have excellent visibility of the target area. Over."

"This is Six," Captain Harkness resumed. "Niner-one, then you adjust fires. Can you make an adjustment of the last fires? Over."

Will immediately focused. He had not seen exactly where the mortar round impacted, but he could recall the sound of the explosion with precision. That gave him a sense of direction and range to the point of impact.

"This is Niner-one. Affirmative. Over," Will answered Captain Harkness, though he realized he still could not say where the prior rounds had impacted.

"This is Six. Then proceed with your fire mission, Niner-one." Captain Harkness directed.

"This is Niner-one. Wilco. Out," Will said. He took a deep breath and blew it out. *Gotta go right. Add range, keep it away from us till I can make a real adjustment.*

"Break. Niner-four, this is Niner-one. Over," Will called.

"This is Four. Go ahead with your adjustment, Niner-one. Over," the mortar platoon Fire Direction Center responded.

"This is Niner-one. Adjust right three hundred; add three hundred. One round, shell H-E. Over."

"This is Four. Right three hundred; add three hundred. One round, shell H-E," the Fire Direction Center confirmed. "Stand by, Niner-one. Over."

"This is Niner-one. Roger. Over." Will glanced back at Shard and Swindell, who looked away from him to one another.

"This is Four. Ready, Niner-one. Over," the Fire Direction Center advised.

"This is Niner-one. Stand by, Niner-four."

"Four. Roger. Over," came the reply.

Will waited until the helicopter gunship was almost in position to start another pass at its target. Then he gave the order. "This is Niner-one. Fire, Niner-four. Fire," Will directed. "Over."

"This is Niner-four. Shot. Two-five seconds till splash. Over."

Will waited on top of the track commander's turret. *Better be good. Just don't hit someone on the perimeter and not me.*

"This is Four. Splash in ten," the mortar platoon advised. Will braced himself, ready to meet his maker. Seconds later the mortar roared through the sky to an explosive meeting with the earth. *There's the impact. We fuckin' made it.*

"This is Niner-one," Will called over the radio. "Left fifty, drop one-fifty. Over."

"This is Four," the Fire Direction Center answered. "Left fifty, drop one-fifty. Repeat fires. Over."

"Niner-one. Roger. Over," Will said.

"This is Four. Ready, Niner-one."

"This is Niner-one. Stand by," Will directed, searching the sky for the re-approaching gunship. "Fire. Over."

One more adjustment and Will fired a full volley for effect right where he had earlier zeroed in Def Con One, which was as close to the north-eastern corner of the perimeter as he dared bring the mortar fires. Will continued to adjust fires after each volley, moving the support fires generally south along the perimeter in fifty-meter increments. He was mindful the Viet Cong likely would attempt to escape the incoming mortar rounds by moving closer to the perimeter, rather than running away from it. He already had determined that the mortar fire base was practically due north of his own position, which afforded him an advantage when adjusting fires closer to the eastern perimeter. Big guns are better at left-to-right adjustments than range adjustments, or distance changes. *I want it close, just not too close. Our guys will duck when they hear the incoming and the armor will protect them from shrapnel. Just gotta keep it off their heads.*

"Niner-one. This is Six," Captain Harkness said. "Big Three says you're too close. Cut us some slack. Over."

"This is Niner-one," Will responded. "Wilco. Out. Break."

"Four, this is Niner-one," Will called, as he formulated his next adjustment. Now that they had passed the midpoint of the circular perimeter, the rounds, coming from the north, would start falling further from the eastern perimeter, just as before the midpoint they moved closer. He wanted desperately to keep the mortars close to the perimeter. In part, he wanted to protect the perimeter from grenade attack by sappers moving closer to avoid the mortars. Mostly, though, he just did not like the idea that the Viet Cong might beat him by moving closer. *Don't have to shift it right, but if I don't and something somehow does go wrong, my ass is grass.*

"This is Niner-one," Will said over the radio. "Right forty; drop fifty. Over."

"This is Niner-four. Right forty; drop fifty. Repeat fires. On your command. Over," Fire Direction said.

"This is Niner-one. Roger. Over."

"This is Niner-four," the Fire Direction Center called back. "Ready. Over."

"This is Niner-one. Fire. Over," Will directed after checking the gunship's location.

"This is Four. Shot. Over," the mortar platoon advised. Will waited. "This is Niner-four, Niner-one. Five seconds to splash."

Will strained to see the explosion from atop the turret, but he could barely make it out. The adjustment away from the perimeter had pushed the fires into a patch of jungle. *Maybe the adjustment tricked the bastards.*

Will continued the adjustments so the volleys continued to land due south of one another, fifty meters apart. Just as he reached the southern-most point on the eastern perimeter with the mortar fires, he readied himself to repeat walking the fires down from north to south using the previous sequence of adjustments.

"Niner-one, this is Six," Captain Harkness called over the battery net.

"This is Niner-one, Six. Over."

"This is Six. Nice work," the captain went on. "Discontinue your mission. Puff the Magic Dragon is about to enter our air space to provide us with close-range air support."

Puff was a C-47 outfitted with 20mm electric miniguns patterned after the Gatling gun, each capable of firing 6,000 rounds per minute. Puff appeared within a minute of Captain Harkness's order to break off the fire mission. As soon as it came alongside the line of the perimeter, its miniguns poured tremendous 20mm cannon fire below it. It fired further from the perimeter than his mortars had, which surprised Will. With each pass, it seemed to move still further from the perimeter, as if it was interdicting the avenues of retreat left to the attackers.

Will surveyed the battlefield and noted that incoming fire was now sporadic and from individual small arms, rather than from the crew-served automatic weapons fired at them earlier. *They've just about broken off the attack, unless it's a trick.*

Whenever it was fired on, the perimeter continued to react with overwhelming suppressive fire. Will let his mind go blank and watched. *They're pulling back. That's it! These occasional fires are a delay tactic to cover their retreat, just like the ambush at Soui Cat.*

The Pain Of Good-bye

The repetitive movements of the gunships had a hypnotic effect on Will's crew. Shard, Swindell, and Will leaned against their gun positions and gazed at the sky to the east. Whiteman sat with his seat cranked up so his head could rest on his crossed arms on the front of the driver's compartment, but he, too, was transfixed by what took place in the eastern sky. When the airships fired their miniguns, it was as if the heavens were raining hot lead.

The four remained silent in their positions for more than a half hour. Shard knelt to grab his canteen. "Puff's gotta be a good half mile from us," Will said. "I hope that Huey gunship is looking out for Captain Ashe's force and the ambush patrol."

What Will really had been thinking made him uncomfortable, and he set out that decoy for fear Shard might suspect those thoughts. *My God! What must it be like down below there? Fire and brimstone right out of hell itself. It isn't fair.*

"It doesn't seem fair, does it?" Shard said.

"When the Cong hid in the tall grass by the road at Soui Cat and hurled grenades and satchel charges into our ACAVs, it didn't seem so fair either, Shark."

"OK," Shard said, "but there is a difference, isn't there?"

"What do you mean?" Will asked.

"There's a difference," Swindell chimed in. "For certain."

Will listened. *Campbell's influence. I should have figured. I hoped that he'd figure this subject off-limits for them. I guess they've as much right to try to figure all this out as I do. So long as they answer the bell.*

"And the difference?" Shard asked.

"I'm not sure I can say it, but the difference is real, for sure," Swindell continued. "It's a struggle between our technology and their commitment to personal sacrifice. You know what I mean?"

"I think so," Shard answered.

Will nodded. *I could kill that Campbell.*

"Look," Swindell said, "back in the world, life goes on as normal. People may pay a few dollars more in taxes or maybe they don't. Either way, they pay for all our super-weapons without blinking an eye. Back here, some guy is rousted from his cot, where he may have been watching some retread television show in air-conditioning, and he's told to come to our rescue. So he shows up maybe a half hour later, who knows, maybe still in an air-conditioned cockpit, and he heaps down on our enemy below the most astonishing volume of light firepower the mind can imagine. And all the while, he's thinking what he'll do when he completes his mission. Will he sleep? Will his post barroom be open? Will there be an easy lay around somewhere? This guy virtually takes it for granted that he'll be back there before long, and that's because the odds are very much in his favor. It's the machine that makes the difference. It's mechanistic. The man hardly gives it a second thought. He doesn't have to."

"Uh-huh," Will grunted when Swindell paused and looked at him.

"On the other hand, for them to kick our ass at Soui Cat was very personal for them," Swindell went on. "For them to frag us, the way you were saying, Stone, they gotta know going in that they got less than an even chance of making it back in one piece. But still they do it. Why?"

"Fear? Drugs? Discipline? Or commitment? We're talking about not just one pilot confident of his return, but about fifty to a hundred-and-fifty grunts certain that more than half of them will be carried away feet first. And still they come. We say that they are not the people's choice, but they are people, and all too many choose to follow headlong into these fatalistic actions. What would it take for one of us to plunge ahead against such desperate odds to carry out this type mission? Stone, what about you? Do you really believe our cause here is so worthwhile that, given the chance to walk away with no one the wiser, you would still dare the odds?"

"What's the point?" Whiteman asked, turning around in his seat.

"That's so hypothetical, I don't expect ever to have to answer it," Will countered Swindell.

"The point, White Man, is that we don't give much of a shit about any of this," Swindell said. "We'll fight for our lives, but that's about it. You gotta back me into a corner before I'll take a chance and then only to save my ass. These gooks, on the other hand, believe in all this. They believe enough to lay down their lives. This is their Holy Grail. I don't know why, but it is."

"Yeah, so?" probed Whiteman.

"Who do you think is going to tire of all this first?" Swindell asked.

"You say they're the ones doing the dying," Whiteman said.

"So are we," Swindell said.

"The difference is they are doing it willingly to accomplish a purpose. To them, it is an honor, to us, a tragedy. We do it only because we're trapped by the system."

"Maybe they're trapped by a different system," Whiteman said.

"Can you imagine any system being able to send us on their types of missions, time and again, if we weren't willing?" Swindell said. "Even super-soldier Sergeant 'Stand-on-Top-of-the-Turret' Stone here, when asked if our mission was worth his volunteering when there's a fifty/fifty chance of his returning, answers that it is 'too hypothetical' to consider. Ultimately, it comes down to the worth of the cause, and that ain't hypothetical. It's an easy call. I rest my case."

Will felt like swinging his fists. *What does the choice say about the man? Ask your fucking buddy Campbell.* "Maybe we better knock off, guys," he said. "At the crack of dawn, they'll have us beating the bush all goddamned day."

"Can anyone here sleep now?" Shard asked.

No one spoke.

"No takers, huh?" Will asked. "OK, Shark, how about scurrying around and seeing what you can find out. What do you say?"

"Roger," Shard replied.

"Shark," Will said. "You hear three blasts on the horn, it means get your ass back here. We're on the move."

"Rog," Shard acknowledged, as he exited through the man door built into the rear hatch.

"OK, Swindell," Whiteman called. "How can you say Stone's not committed? You just saw him risk his neck up on the turret."

"That wasn't commitment," Swindell answered. "I don't know what it was, but it wasn't commitment. It was a death wish maybe, but it wasn't commitment to a cause."

"Stone!" Whiteman called. "Something's going on at the northwest corner of the perimeter. They may be regrouping. Wait, it's our vehicles. Got to be Captain Ashe with the ambush patrol."

Will barely heard him. *I ought to ream that Campbell a new asshole.*

"It is the rescue column," Swindell said.

"What did Campbell tell you about his and my conversations?" Will asked Swindell in a hushed tone.

"He said you thought we were trying to save the gooks," Swindell answered slowly. "He laughed when I asked, 'Save them from what? From themselves?'"

That sonofabitch, Campbell. Will's thought was interrupted by a radio transmission.

"Niner-one, this is Six. Over," Captain Ashe called over the radio.

"This is Niner-one. Over," Will answered.

"This is Six, Niner-one," Captain Ashe continued more evenly now. "Did you send a man named Campbell on the ambush patrol? Over."

"This is Niner-one," Will answered, glancing with alarm first at Swindell and then Whiteman. "Affirmative. Over."

"This is Six. Better come to the dust-off LZ," the captain said. "We need you to ID him. Over."

"This is Niner-one," Will said. "Roger. Out."

A minute passed before they could look at one another. Finally, Will lowered himself through the turret into the cabin below. Swindell and Whiteman watched as Will grabbed his M-16. After he climbed through the man door, Will stuck his head back in and said, "When Shard comes back, please have him wait. All of you should wait here. We have to be ready in case we get an order to move out. Now, about that last transmission, we don't really know what it meant. I better go down to the LZ and find out. Thank you both for your help in all this. Shard, too, of course.

"When I do get back," Will continued, "it sounds like I'll be calling Captain Harkness for a replacement for Campbell, at least temporarily, so if any of you want off my crew, now's the time for us to handle it."

Will had not been gone two minutes before Shard returned. He stuck his head in the rear man door and called, "Rick Franklin is down. I'm going over the LZ. Maybe I can see him."

"Stone's on his way over there now," Swindell said. "Sounds like Campbell got whacked, too. Don't know anything more than that. Better try to hook up with Stone at the LZ. He wants us all to be together so we can react if we have to."

"How'd it happen?" Whiteman asked. "To Franklin? Get any details?"

"He was spending the night with O'Rourke and Deddson. Their track's on the eastern perimeter, just north of the *squadron* CP. The shooting started. Rick jumped up to man an M-60 side gun, but he stepped in front of a bullet before he got there. Never fired a shot. The slug hit him in the side of his neck and knocked him right to the floor again. O'Rourke said Rick kept calling to them, 'Don't worry about me, I'm all right.' So they did what they had to without paying Rick much heed, until Charlie broke off the engagement.

"Then they rushed him over to the LZ, where the medics were sorting them out. Rick kept calling out, 'I'm OK, take these other guys first.' So they've been evacuating everybody else first, at least up until when O'Rourke left the LZ. I guess Rick can't be all that bad."

"No, I guess not," Whiteman said.

"Let's hope not," Swindell said.

"On the way," Shard said, pulling his head back out the door opening and making his way toward the LZ.

"Swindell," Whiteman asked, "did Franklin tell you what was in that letter he got today?"

"Rick was upbeat," he answered, shaking his head. "He felt it was all going to work out between him and his wife because she wrote she was breaking off with some guy she'd been shacking up with."

"Oh," Whiteman said.

Upon approaching the LZ, Will slowed up to make sense of the surreal confusion. A dust-off chopper taking off spewed a backwash of dirt and debris across the landing zone. The chopper's down-directed spotlights blinded Will from getting much of a look at it. Fifteen body bags were lined up to Will's left—occupied. A row of troopers lay to his right. Once the chopper flew away their moans and groans were audible. The smells of medicines and blood and death were everywhere. Captain Ashe broke from his conversation with the medics when he saw Will.

"Niner-one!" the captain called.

"Sir."

"We were too late," the captain said, "as you can see."

"The ambush patrol? All of them?" Will asked.

"Yup," the captain said. "One badly wounded. Not yours."

Will paused, realizing he had his answer about Campbell. "And these?" he asked, gesturing toward his right.

"Some dead, some wounded. The dead have the body bags underneath them, pending ID. Your guy's down the end. That dust-off was loaded with wounded, too."

Will nodded. "The relief column?" he asked.

"Some, maybe five, wounded. They pulled back when we went in there in force. But we had an LP out beyond the northern perimeter that didn't make it, and maybe a dozen killed or wounded on the perimeter. Their losses, of course, were much, much higher," the captain said. "The blood trails—"

After backing away a few steps, Will turned to head for Campbell. *Who gives a shit about their losses? What does it matter? Maybe Campbell's still there, somehow. Gotta get to him.*

"You never did get to call in your artillery, did you, Stone?" the captain shouted after him.

Will paused. *He's gone. What am I thinking? The captain said he's dead.* "Three authorized me to walk it down the eastern perimeter." As he answered, he already was heading toward Campbell.

"Oh," the captain said.

Will made his way slowly in front of the row to his right, not wanting to appear unsympathetic to the wounded he was passing by. He also was readying himself. Near the end of the row, Will knelt and faced Campbell. He felt like crying. Though he recognized Campbell, he read his nametag. He studied where a bullet had penetrated Campbell's trachea and where another had shattered his jaw. Then he sat back on his heels. *Campbell saw all this as dumb. He never could have died thinking he made some noble sacrifice. Just, he was wasted.*

The wounded man to the right of Campbell propped himself up on one elbow. "We was OK until the illumination came," he rasped.

Will bristled. *Did I hear that right? Why'd he say that to me?*

"We was all right in the dark," the survivor went on. "They couldn't see where we was. I already been hit in both legs. The others are pulling back. But this guy next to me, your buddy, he don't leave me. Then somebody turns on the lights and they sees where we was. Too many of 'em. Your buddy gets hit and falls on top of me. Saves my ass. Gooks pass me by for dead. If only there wasn't no lights."

"Yeah," Will said. "What'd he say at the end? When the lights went on, I mean."

"They was right on top of us by then, all over us," the man answered. "He's just trying to protect me. But when the sky lights up, we see them all around us, and we know they can see us, too. 'Stone,' he says. Then he laughs and goes down."

"The guy behind you knows him, too," the survivor said. "They put him down the end 'cause he keeps calling out, 'Take the others out first.'"

Will turned to see, but did not recognize the wounded soldier behind him.

"Not one of us," the survivor went on. "Must be from the perimeter How Battery was guarding. They bring him in and he sees he's next to your buddy. He rolls over and grabs him and holds your buddy's head to his own heart and sobs his eyes out. Then he strains himself to let your buddy down easy before collapsing himself. Last we hear from him."

Will turned and this time looked more carefully. *Don't know him.*

No sooner did Will turn forward than he felt a hand clasp his wrist. Will twisted back toward the man behind him. His eyes fell on the name patch: Franklin. Will's eyes scanned up and down the body from tip to toe. *Can't be. Rick was gaunt and pasty. This guy is all puffy and pink.*

Will pried himself free from the grip around his wrist so he could turn all the way around for a better look. He grabbed the soldier's hand and leaned over his face. "Rick?" There was no sign of life in the soldier's eyes or face, only the wheezing sound of his labored breathing, until a tear ran down his right cheek.

"Rick," Will whispered again. Still no sign of recognition, but Will felt his hand squeezed. He was sure of it. *Christ, he's paralyzed.*

"Doc! Doc!" Will shouted for a medical corpsman. Will leaned over Franklin and spoke directly in his ear, "Listen, Rick, you're gonna make it. You're gonna make it through this. We're gonna do it together." Will pulled back from Franklin a moment. *Careful, don't make promises you're not going to keep. You might have to live closer to wherever they send him and give up a good part of your life to keep this promise. And it all depends on your making it back to the world. You really ready for this? Don't ask the man to live for a lie.*

"Listen, Rick, you hear me, right?"

Franklin squeezed Will's hand weakly.

"I'll stick with you and do this with you. I won't quit on you, but you can't quit on yourself. You hear me, Rick?"

Will waited for a squeeze. He felt a tremor.

"You hear me, Rick?" No response. "Medic!" Will called out. "Medic! Don't quit, Rick. I'm with you. We're gonna do this together."

A corpsman slid into place on the other side of Franklin. "We losing him?" Will asked. "We can't lose him. Don't lose him. Don't quit, Rick."

The grip on Will's hand loosened. The corpsman withdrew his stethoscope from Franklin's chest and shook his head.

"I'm sorry," the corpsman said. "He never had much of a chance. He practically doubled in size before our very eyes. The wound triggered some sort of reaction. He told us to dust-off the others first. We would have done that anyway. We didn't figure him for much of a chance."

Will looked at Franklin's body. *He just wanted to get it together with his wife.*

Shard approached from behind and placed a hand on Will's shoulder. "You OK, Stone? Campbell, huh? Jesus."

"He saved my ass," the survivor said.

"We better get out of here," Will said to Shard.

"I'm looking for Franklin."

"Squat here a second," Will said, patting the other side of Franklin's legs.

"Oh, my God," Shard said.

"You just missed him," Will said.

"C'mon, don't hang out here," the medic told them.

"Let's go, Shark," Will said. "He's got stuff to do."

"He saved my ass," the survivor said, clawing his way partly over Campbell.

Will and Shard rose and slowly made their way clear of the dust-off area. Will told Shard what he understood of Franklin's condition and his last few minutes. Silently, absorbed in their thoughts, they shuffled back to their post.

Over and over Will reviewed the decision to call for continuous illumination. *I just asked. The captain decided. Go ahead, blame him, Will, like he had time to consider it. Would have taken three times as long for the rescue column to reach them in the dark. The rescue force would have been like ducks on a pond. Moving through the bush with their headlights on at night, fragging them with grenades would have been easy. We could have lost the ambush patrol and the relief force both. But it had to be right above the patrol. If I could have gotten it behind them enough so they could see Charlie but he couldn't see them. I didn't even know where the hell they were. It's done. Fuck it. Don't mean a thing. Fuck it. Jeez. Campbell was out there. He's gone. For what? He was a fucking pain in the ass, anyway.*

In his mind Will visualized the last few seconds for Campbell: the others pulling back, Campbell protecting the survivor, the illumination, the moment of recognition that he could be seen and was vastly outnumbered with moments to live, the realization Will had contributed to his end by calling in the illumination. *He laughed and accepted it as the nature of the situation. He didn't curse me. He forgave me.*

Hampton Comes Around

Shard and Will made it back to their ACAV. They climbed through the open man door in the rear hatch and left it that way. Whiteman and Swindell were seated on the floor in quiet conversation with Hampton, whom Will had not seen since the night Montana popped Bandle in the nose to avert a racial confrontation.

"I'm to report to you, Sergeant Stone," Hampton slurred. "Sergeant Grovel sent me over, per the captain's orders. I'm your replacement side gunner."

Will looked at the whites of Hampton's eyes in the dark and remembered the last time they met. Hampton had flashed his white mother's picture to make a point. "How does that sit with you, Hampton?" Will asked.

"Orders is orders," Hampton answered. "Be just as glad not to hump any more of those 1 - 5 - 5 shells."

Will tried to size up how willing a member of the crew Hampton would be. "You look like you're the only one of us who could fill out Campbell's fatigues," Will said. "You need any? He won't be needing them anymore."

Hampton shrugged.

"What happened, for crissake?" Swindell asked.

At first Will paused, but after Shard deferred to him, he related Campbell's story. When he finished, no one said anything until Whiteman asked, "What about Rick?"

Shard hung his head and Will recounted how it had been with Franklin. When he was finished, it was quiet again.

"Fuck this fuckin' war," Swindell said.

"Fuck the Army!" Shard said.

"Why?" Whiteman demanded, turning to Will. "Why? They were both just fucking wasted. Can you tell me why?"

Will glanced at Hampton, who held his peace. Nonetheless, Will sensed Hampton was pleased by the others' reaction. *If it were anybody but Whiteman, maybe I could duck this, but I owe him more than that.*

"Look," Will said, tapping his hand on his heart, "Campbell and Franklin each had a special place here. You know there was a connection between them and me, just like I know you guys had your own connections to them. Neither would have bought the idea he was wasted. Both chose to risk death, rather than to live by laying off that risk on someone else. Neither would make one of us stick out our necks in his place. For them, living that way gave life a worthy purpose. Life is a journey, not a destination. So it's how you live, not where you end up, that determines whether you wasted the trip. Their deaths were the price they risked to avoid a wasted life."

Whiteman nodded. Swindell and Shard leaned back against the side-walls of the ACAV and shrugged their shoulders. Will looked to Hampton, who looked askance at Will, as though debating whether to speak. A wry smile crossed Hampton's face. Noisily he snorted through his nose and cleared his throat. He took one last look at Will before turning his head toward the left side of the ACAV. He spit a mighty gob up through the top hatch above them, over the left side gun shield, and into the darkness beyond. All eyes could not help but follow the trajectory until the projectile was lost in the night. When their eyes naturally returned to the point of origin, Hampton held a sullen stare in a direction slightly left of where Will sat cross-legged.

Rage mounted within Will. He swallowed hard. He did not know whether to give it free rein or choke it back, whether it would help or hinder him in dealing with this situation. *What the hell?*

He glanced at the others studying him. Then, gazing up at the trajectory of Hampton's missile, Will said in measured tones, "You know, Hampton, any other time I might not even say anything about that, but somehow at this particular moment that seems very much inappropriate."

Hampton slurred his words selectively. "I could say that was a pussy way of calling me out—"

In his mind, Will all but had the hunting knife on his belt drawn and to Hampton's throat before he suppressed himself. *You can't run this crew by violence. How they perform can't be based on who gets a knife to the other's throat first. But he's challenging for control, and it can't go unchecked.*

"But I won't," Hampton went on. "You showed caring and respect in what you said, Stone, but there's a problem with it. And it makes for a problem between us. Sorry to say it, buddy, but you're a little bent—just enough to be misleading, just enough to be dangerous, just enough to get me and maybe all of us killed."

Again Will felt his hand about to go for the knife. Again he checked it. *This isn't about control for its own sake. This is more serious. This is about life and death, at least as far as he's concerned.* Will looked at the others. Their attention was riveted on Hampton and Will. *It's not Hampton that's dangerous. It's his ideas. Just gotta flush them out. Hopefully, he'll be as honest as I will in recognizing truth when we expose it. My bet's that the others will, at least.*

Will met Hampton's stare. "How now, brown cow?"

A grin flashed across Hampton's face, and there were twinkles in his eyes. "See, you couldn't leave that shit out it, could you?" he laughed. "But that don't change that you bent. Ya got it wrong, see. What you really mean is the old 'Death Before Dishonor,' no?"

Will nodded. *Why didn't I just say that? Of course, that's what it amounts to.*

"I'll take that for a *Yes*," Hampton resumed, "but it's not the same, see. For us, death is the lesser evil, that's all. But for you, Stone, *Death* creates some kinda worth that makes up for a worthless life. My man, you selling glory."

Hampton pressed ahead. "I mean, really, what did White Man ask you when he asked, 'Why they wasted?' He didn't need to hear 'bout some commonplace bullshit 'bout his duty to the rest of us once he's here and in this motherfuckin' situation. He asked why the hell we all gotta be in this racist motherfucker in the first place. And you, Stone, playing with your fancy words like you do, is just covering over things, so we don't see da shit till we step in it."

"Everything's racist to you, Hamp," Swindell immediately threw out.

"How can you say this war is racist?" Shard asked.

"OK, I'll tell you why this motherfucker is racist," Hampton said, "but when I'm done, then we're gonna hear from the sergeant on this other thing. No other questions."

The other three nodded their agreement. Will bit his lip.

"This is a *racist* mother," Hampton emphasized, "in three ways. Number three, it's being fought by far more brothers than it ought to, especially when you get to the line troops. I mean, look around you. Boo!

"Number two, we using weapons and tactics on a wholesale basis against the gooks that the US of A would never use against a white people. Not today, not in this day and age. You can bet on it.

"Number one, and most fundamentally, we waging this war to impose Western—that is, white—values and culture on these gooks, because we can never accept that the gooks can have a valid culture and value system of their own. There's no place for gook culture in a white world."

Will looked to the others. They remained silent. He realized they expected him to respond in his own defense. Shard and Swindell almost seemed to be gloating. Whiteman seemed genuinely interested in just sorting out the issues. Hampton seemed more interested in what Will's response would reveal about him as a person, than in any light it might shed on the subject.

"Thank you, Hampton," Will said. "I needed to hear that, and now I guess I need to think about what you said on both scores. You're probably right about a lot of it. I got going in that direction because I just thought both Campbell and Franklin were great, and I thought this somehow proved it. Don't forget each of them chose to put the survival of others ahead of his chances at the moment of truth, and that's above and beyond the call of 'avoiding self-contempt.'

"I'm not saying it's death that confers worth to life, but rather how you live life, and in The Nam, this can mean whether you live it without cowering before death by serving up someone else. I wasn't trying to gloss over anything, though I can see how it could have that effect and piss you off." Tears welled up in his eyes as he tried to go on. "I just, these fuckin' guys, man..." Will sobbed.

Hampton moved to Will and threw his arms around him. "It's all right, man," Hampton said. "You OK."

"It was the fuckin' illumination, goddammit. Our flares killed Campbell and the ambush patrol," Will said. "My fuckin' illumination. Now do you understand? Campbell can't have died in vain."

"You were right about them guys," Hampton said, patting Will softly on the back. "We're saying the same thing really."

A voice came from where a red-beamed flashlight shone through the man door. "What are you men doing, goddammit? Don't you guys have to observe sound and light discipline? Why don't you have a man up on the fifty? It's 0400. You gotta be up in an hour, 'cause we're beating the bush when the sun rises. It may be the last hour's sleep you get in a long time. Don't waste it! You ought to know better, Sergeant Stone."

Will recognized Zack's voice. "Sorry, Sarge," Will said. "We were hit pretty hard by Campbell and Franklin gettin' zapped. We were just talking about them, that's all."

"Yeah, too bad about them," Zack said, "but get with the program. It's not like they were heroes or something."

Walking Tall

"You guys get some sleep," Will said as he crawled beneath the TC turret. "I'll man the fifty."

Will stood for a while leaning back against the turret. Then he sat on the inside lip where the turret fastened to the top deck of the vehicle, drawing his feet upon the support bar. *It's not just Campbell and Franklin that got wasted. It's everyone on that ambush patrol and the perimeter. Jeez! We feel for Campbell and Franklin 'cause we know them—knew them. The others from How Battery may forget the guys from K Troop, and vice versa. If I had directed those aerial flares differently, they all might be alive, so I got my private reasons for caring for them all. But we all should care about all of them the same, because they were all the same in one important way. They all showed up. They answered the bell. They were there for one another. Didn't Campbell die saving the wounded survivor? Tell me these guys are not my brothers. Not just the dead, not just the wounded, tell me these guys that showed up aren't my brothers. Tell me that an' you don't know shit.*

Will looked around and tried to calm himself. His mind went to the row of wounded soldiers waiting for dust-off at the LZ, then to the row of dead and dying. He could see Campbell dead and feel Franklin's last squeeze of his hand and Josh lying facedown with blood oozing from beneath him. *Josh?*

Josh said a man is what he does. And what these men have done is show up. Maybe they don't like it, maybe they don't think it's smart, maybe they didn't volunteer, but when it's their turn, they take it.

The rest of what Josh said was you don't take your turn and you become something less. You can compromise your principles only to the point where it would change who you are. You do what's right and you can walk tall.

I know a lot more now about Vietnam and everything wrapped up in it than I ever did when I volunteered to come here. Most of it I don't like. But if I had the choice again, if even just one of these guys had to serve a tour of duty here, I'd serve it with him. I gotta walk tall.

Part Four:
Brothers

Chapter 9

In Pursuit Of the Attackers

Comfort To the Enemy

Captain Harkness summoned his officers and senior NCOs to his command post before dawn. The first to arrive caught a shadowy glimpse of Major Finn concluding his own visit with the captain and slowly making his way out of the tent and back to the squadron operations center.

When the others arrived, Captain Harkness spoke to his cadre. "Big Three has had enough," he said. "He's convinced we can't move our armor through the jungle fast enough to overcome the early warning its noise gives Charlie. We can't be satisfied with just repelling these attacks, he says. We must overtake and punish them in their retreat.

"Three's coordinated with an ARVN leg unit to pursue these aggressors," the captain went on. "Our mission is to furnish them fire support. Every day we'll move to stay within firing range of the ARVN element, but not close enough to spook Charlie. Each night we'll laager with one or more of our line troops, which we'll hold in reserve until needed as a reactive force. If the ARVN engage the Cong in a fixed battle, our line troops will respond to smash them with cross-firing pincer movements. If, on the other hand, the Cong attempt to slip away, our close air support will drive them into our line troops positioned as a blocking force. Either way, our 155mm cannons will keep the ARVN in the game until reactive forces are in position to help them.

"To be effective, we need our best observer team with the ARVN. We can't depend on direct communication with them."

"We'd never make them out over the radio," Lieutenant Brown added.

"I'm glad you appreciate the need, Brown, because you've got the job," the captain said. "I'll run the Fire Direction Center. The ARVN big brass insisted on a commissioned officer as their forward observer, which, we know, an FO should be. Who do you want to back you up, Brown?"

"If we're going by the book, I get a recon sergeant and also a radio operator—an RTO?" Brown asked.

The captain nodded. "I'll give you a second RTO with a spare radio and Binh as your interpreter."

"Maybe you ought to ask us who we got available first, sir," Sergeant First Class Grovel said.

"Fair enough, " the captain said. "Who's available?"

"No one, sir," Grovel answered. "You better get them from Zack."

"Sir, you asked who I wanted," Lieutenant Brown said. "It makes sense to give me Stone. If something happens to me, and this mission is as decisive as you're making it sound, Stone's our best shot to finish the job. When it comes to adjusting fires in a contact situation, he's the most experienced in our battery. My time's been on the other end controlling fire direction."

"Sir," Zack said, "I'd ask you to take into account that Sergeant Stone is getting short. I'm not sure how short. Sir, we also have to bear in mind he's been covering as FO for two of the three line troops and as Big Three's aerial observer when he's not out on the ground. We're still gonna need him to cover those bases. And maybe, sir, he's earned the right to miss this one."

"Stone's got fifteen days till his ETS," First Sergeant Manor said. "We got a right to make the most of them. Montana just arrived back from the States. His old man finally kicked after six months. It's time we broke Montana's ass in right so we don't put up with any more of his pushy shit. Could use him to cover the line troops or to go with Brown. I don't care which, but get him away from the battery. The man's like poison ivy in your ass. I told them an hour ago in base camp to ship his ass out here with the next slick, so he could be here already."

"Send somebody to fetch him if he's already here," Captain Harkness ordered Manor.

The first sergeant eyeballed Zack, who retreated from the command tent.

"Another thing, sir," Manor resumed. "The others may not be aware we got three fresh Gooey-Looeys on orders here due in any day. They can take Stone's place with the line troops. Should anyway, being officers."

Zack returned. "Montana came in with the breakfast slick, and Martino's gone to get him," he said.

Captain Harkness turned the discussion to other areas of the mission until Montana sauntered in and asked, "So how is everybody?"

"We're glad to have you back," the captain said. "We're sorry about your dad."

"We're shorthanded and we're losing men left and right," Manor said. "You saw the bags when you landed, I figure."

Montana's face flushed. "You made Stone a buck sergeant, I hear," he said, turning to the captain. "Don't you think it's about time I was made Staff Sergeant E6, sir? You know goddam well I been running the Survey Section and even the entire Headquarters Platoon off and on for near two years. You can't let Stone outrank me. I taught him everything he knows. You can't trust him, either. You forget about his refusing to fill sandbags? I'm a career soldier, sir. I should be an E6, but until I am, you gotta at least give me three stripes."

"We've got a major mission, Montana," Captain Harkness responded. "Lieutenant Brown's to lead an FO team accompanying an elite ARVN infantry company in pursuit of these attackers. Big Three's trying to fix their location long enough for us to pile on. We've been talking about you going with Lieutenant Brown."

"ARVN, huh?" Montana said. He zeroed in on Zack. "Why don't you send your boy, Stone?"

"Ho hum," First Sergeant Manor yawned, standing up and scratching his backside. "Ya can't scratch it wit'out gettin' your hands dirty."

"Stone's spent a lot of time in the field while you were back in the States," Zack answered, ignoring Manor's distraction.

"I hope his father dies so he can go back and enjoy it, too," Montana said.

Captain Harkness winced. "What do you think, Top?"

"Send them both out!" Manor said. "And you just might be interested in knowing, Montana, that I got a letter right here saying Sergeant Stone's grandfather, his nearest blood relative, is dying right now."

"Brown?" the captain asked.

Lieutenant Brown nodded.

"OK, Montana," the captain said, "you better get ready. You'll be Lieutenant Brown's RTO. Sergeant Stone will be recon sergeant and second-in-command. Any questions?"

"What about what I said," Montana asked, slow to add the obligatory, "sir?"

"We'll look at Lieutenant Brown's report when he comes back," the captain said, "and we'll talk with Sergeant Stone as well. That's all, Montana. Hear those airships, Brown? That's the air cav ferrying in the ARVN. You'll shove off as soon as they're ready. Good luck to you both.

"Sergeant Zack," the captain continued, "you better run down Stone and get him ready. I'll get Bandit Two-six on the horn and tell him to expect you to replace Stone as K Troop's FO until one of these new lieutenants we got due in arrives. Find out the status of the ARVN arrival, and how soon they can move out. Report back."

"Yes, sir," Zack said. "About K Troop, sir, I'm getting kind of short myself—"

"Then maybe you should go out with Stone on this mission, 'stead of Montana," First Sergeant Manor said.

"I'm on my way, sir," Zack said, exiting. "No thanks, Top."

After Montana followed Zack from the command post, Captain Harkness asked, "What the hell did Stone do to piss off Montana so?"

"He got promoted, sir," First Sergeant Manor replied.

Lieutenant Brown laughed. "Interesting," he said. "My money says Stone'll hold his ground with Montana."

"If I didn't think so, I wouldn't have made him a sergeant," the captain said.

"Just the same, sir, I'll lend Corporal Woodman to Lieutenant Brown, as the second RTO," Sergeant First Class Grovel said, "so he'll have someone he can depend on in case things go bad between Stone and Montana."

First Sergeant Manor nodded his assent. "Thank you," said the captain. "You better get him ready."

"Thank you, Sergeant Grovel," Lieutenant Brown said, "and Top."

○

As soon as Zack spotted Will's ACAV, he pointed to it so Thich, the ARVN sergeant walking with him, would know where they were headed. Thich had said nothing since they hooked up, despite Zack's constant prodding. Finally, Zack had clammed up. Thich seemed not to understand him, although Captain Harkness had said Thich spoke "The King's English."

As the two moved closer, Zack made out Will headed on foot to where Whiteman was pointing from his driver's seat. Since first light, Will's crew had been part of a detail scouring the perimeter for remains of last night's attack. Zack and Thich saw a Viet Cong soldier seated in the tall grass in front of Will. Zack muttered, "Kill him and check for booby traps. That guy can pitch a grenade at him or the track."

Will worried about the same thing. "You guys stay back and cover me with your sixteens," he ordered, "but don't be too quick with them."

The Viet Cong soldier stared at Will with dull eyes. His black pajama top made it easy to figure he was VC. His khaki shorts made it plain his right leg had been sheared off halfway up his shin during the night's battle. Nonetheless, Will looked twice to be sure he was seeing right. The soldier's lower leg lay at a right angle to the rest of his leg, his foot still in its boot. Both ends of the severed leg had stopped bleeding. They were brown and dried.

"Finish him," Zack muttered again. Thich barely glanced at Zack, so intent was he on Will's next move.

Will's eyes scanned the situation for some clue to the intent of the wounded soldier, who licked his parched lips while awaiting his fate. *Is he sitting on a grenade, so when we move him, he takes us with him? What if there is no grenade and I kill him? Then it won't be war. It'll be murder.*

"Water," Will shouted to his crew. "Pitch a canteen."

Shard took his canteen out of the case attached to his web belt. He underhanded it to Will, who caught it with both hands. Will took a long look at the wounded man and tried to imagine how he felt—the pain, the loss, the fear, the uncertainty, the hopes he must let go. Will eased toward the man and felt his forehead. He was on fire. Will opened the canteen and passed it to him.

Slowly, the man raised it with both hands to his lips. There was no gulping or spilt water running down his neck to the ground. After seven swallows he passed the canteen back to Will. He showed no emotion.

"Shark," Will called, "open a can of bread, please."

Shard underhanded Will a ball of doughy bread from a C ration can. Will held it before the man's face. The man waved his hand to refuse it.

"You speak English?" Will asked.

The man made no response.

"Vous parlez Francais?" Will asked.

No response.

"Phap?" Will asked him, remembering the Vietnamese word for *French.*

The man tilted his head and looked at Will curiously.

"Somebody want to give me a hand getting this guy up?" Will called. It took a few seconds, but Hampton started over to them. Will was glad that Whiteman did not have to get out of the driver's compartment. Will also was glad Hampton did not keep him waiting until he had to pick someone, the way Campbell often had.

As Hampton drew closer, Will knelt next to the wounded man's good leg. Will lifted slightly under the man's arm, pantomiming how they would lift him to his good leg.

Suddenly, the man lurched forward, reaching by his bad leg. Will shot his hand in the air for the others to hold their fire, though he stayed ready to reverse the signal in an instant. The man stretched to grip his foot in both hands.

"It's not all the ways cut off," Hampton said. "It's hanging on there by about a half-inch of gristle or something."

Will lowered his hand slowly, as he leaned over the man's thighs to see what Hampton meant. *The man's trying to save his leg.*

Will waved to Whiteman to back the ACAV to where they were. "Keep him 'bout ten feet away," Will told Hampton.

Should we cut off that foot right here and now? Will wondered.

"Let him carry it, Sergeant, just like he's got it," said Zack, rushing around Hampton with Thich trailing by several paces. "It'll keep his hands busy. Rough break, huh?"

"Yeah," Will answered, still staring at the man's leg.

"You should have made him roll over so you could tell if he was wired?" Zack said.

"Yeah, well, I don't know." Will looked to Zack and saw Thich alongside. Will assumed he was an interpreter. "Hey, tell this guy we're gonna pick him up from under the legs and behind his back, like a chair," Will shouted and pantomimed. "Tell him to hang on to his leg. Hampton, you ready?"

Thich began jabbering to the VC. At the same time Zack said to Will, "Not sure how much English he understands, Stone. Listen, the captain's got new orders for you."

"Sargie," Will responded, "can it wait till I get this guy on the back of the ACAV?" Will turned to Thich, who continued talking to the VC soldier far longer than it would have taken to translate Will's simple message. He thought he heard the VC soldier say, "Phap."

Thich lifted his face deliberately to study Will. For a moment, they looked into one another's eyes until Thich uttered something like, "Ready," and signaled with his hands to go ahead and move the wounded man.

Will looked to Zack, who shrugged and nodded for him to carry the man to the waiting ACAV. Hampton and Will gripped one another's forearms to make a sling that supported the wounded man under his arms and knees. The man held on to his leg until they set him down on the ramp. As they released the man, Will looked at him a last time. *Don't think he's on drugs. Yet it's like he's been able to tune out his pain.*

Before rising from his kneeling position, Will looked around. Hampton was already on his feet, rocking his head back and forth, apparently awaiting further orders. Zack was gesturing with his hands for Will to get on with it. Thich stared at Will, as engrossed with him as Will had been with the wounded man.

Will stood. "Take him over to the landing zone," he said to Hampton. He looked to Zack and smiled.

Once Hampton jumped on the departing ACAV, Zack said, "Sergeant Stone, this is Sergeant Thich from the Army of the Republic of Vietnam."

Will stuck out his hand. "How are you, Sergeant?"

Sergeant Thich offered Will his best limp-fish grip, but said nothing. He looked away from Will.

"What did that guy have to say?" Will asked.

Thich ignored the question. Will was not sure he understood it. Zack smirked.

"Hey, you're going to be credited with two confirmed kills from last night," Zack said, pointing south. "We found some bodies over there so chewed up everyone agrees the mortar fires you called in did it."

Will noted Sergeant Thich's dour face. "Let's go, Sargie," he said softly to Zack.

FO's Go With ARVN

It was the close of the third day for the joint pursuit party, which moved on foot through the jungle at a slow, steady pace. Will kept watch for operational differences between the ARVN and American line troops he had supported. He was too far back to judge what degree of stealth they employed, but he saw enough to know they were much more relaxed in the jungle than the Americans were.

For one thing, the ARVN were much less careful about maintaining sound and light discipline. It also seemed they did not drive as hard, although they took fewer and shorter breaks. The ARVN officers also had more direct contact with their men, rather than delegating through their noncommissioned officers, at least as far as Sergeant Thich was concerned. All too often, Thich spoke to an officer who then made an announcement or gave an order. At times Thich interacted with the men, particularly when they were on the move. Often he would fall back, then overtake and pass a part of the line of troops. Along the way, he would jabber with them, and tease and joke with them. Will drew no conclusions from any of this, not knowing what they said.

Thich did not tire easily and seldom perspired. His hair always seemed combed, even when he removed his steel helmet. He held a steady course and his walking pace was always strong. He took water in small, measured quantities and at regular intervals. In no way did he seem anxious about reporting to anyone.

By the end of each day Will was dragging, but no worse than the others. They traversed forests, triple-canopied jungles, rice paddies and swamps, and they marched along logging trails, railroads and streams. For the most part, they skirted around villages and hamlets, although they came close enough to see and be seen.

Will was pondering the pattern of the last three days as he slipped off his gear, when Montana approached him from behind. "You're carrying this fuckin' radio tomorrow," Montana said.

"Hot, huh?" Will responded.

"You bet I'm hot."

"I mean the weather," Will said. "Gotta be 115."

"Yeah."

"Tramping around all day, this heat can play tricks," Will said.

"What?"

"With a man's mind," Will said.

"I'm getting my C-rats," Montana said, slipping his gear.

"I'll take care of this baby for tonight," Will called after him, patting the twenty-three-pound PRC-25 field radio. "I told Woodman I'd carry his for a while in the morning. I'll spell you when I can."

"What?" Montana said, rushing back to confront Will. "What are you talking about, Stone? Woodman's an E-4; I'm an E-5. He's from Firing Battery; I'm from Survey. And he's— he's not one of us."

"I told you, Montana, I'm humping his radio in the morning," Will said. "I'll spell you when I can."

"What?" Montana arched his back in order to lower himself right in Will's face. "Listen, you little sonofabitch—"

"Sergeant," Will interrupted. "I'm a sergeant in the US Army, and don't forget it."

"I don't have to take this shit from you," Montana said.

"Then take it upstairs," Will said. "Now buzz off."

Montana turned on his heel and headed to get his rations, but not without audibly muttering, "This won't be the end of this, you little sonofabitch."

A few minutes earlier, an American helicopter had passed over the half-acre clearing they occupied. It dropped several cases of C rations and jerricans of water. Will watched the ARVN bunch around the ration point. *The ARVN obviously feel they're traveling first class for a change.*

For Will, the forced march had been a lesson in just how good the living conditions had been for him during his entire tour, even if the dying conditions remained much the same. *With the armor, we travel like fat cats with enough food, water, clothing, and shelter—all the basic essentials. But we make fat targets, too.*

Will looked around the clearing to get a sense of where they would spend the night. A skeletal perimeter guard was setting up machine gun emplacements at strategic points. Will noted that Sergeant Thich for the first time seemed to be involved at that level of detail with his men. Will also spotted Layton's old friend Binh, the interpreter, laying out his bedroll near the eastern perimeter. Binh was expected to take a turn on guard duty, but the Americans were not. The ARVN officers told Lieutenant

Brown there was too much chance of miscommunication. *Could've had us set up one guard post anyway and plopped Binh in with us.*

Will was frustrated by his limited access to Binh since the mission started. Lieutenant Brown had commandeered the interpreter the first night in order to speak with the ARVN officers. Along with Woodman and Montana, Will sat in on most of this conversation, which so far had degenerated into a two-night floating poker game. Will did not join the others in the card game. This joint mission was, perhaps, his first and last chance at finding out what was really happening in the war. He was not going to miss the opportunity, and he was counting on Binh for help.

Will looked about. Brown and Woodman already had left their gear near where Montana left his. *This figures to be where they'll play cards.* Not wanting any more of Montana than necessary, Will grabbed his own gear with one arm and Montana's radio with the other, and headed toward Binh.

"Ah, you nee' help clean shithouse, Sergean' Stone?" Binh said.

Will maintained his smile while he shook his head. "I am forever indebted to your family, Binh, and it seems you will forever remind me."

Binh gestured with his arm for Will to put down his gear. "Binh house your house," he said.

"You figure they need you to keep their card game going tonight?" Will asked.

"Once start, t'ey OK," Binh responded. "What want you?"

"Ready to get your grub?" Will asked.

"Huh?" Binh asked.

"Let's get our C rations," Will said.

"C's, OK." Binh smiled, picking up his M-16 and heading out.

Binh's M-16 turned many a head in the unit, which typically equipped its line personnel with hand-me-down carbines from French colonial days. Will sensed many of these soldiers saw Binh as too close to the Americans, as a tool rather than a patriotic soldier. *That's unfair, cause I see Binh as the opposite. No doubt he's a man with a mission. We just happen to share that mission.*

"Binh," Will asked, "what makes you tick?"

"Stone play game wit' Binh," he responded. "What want you say?"

"What about the VC?" Will asked. "How do you see them?"

"No hide how Binh feel 'bout VC," Binh answered, accepting a box of C rations from an ARVN soldier. "VC kill Binh' brot'er, kill fat'er, cause no want fight, want only farm. So now Binh soldier, but hunt VC, no join VC. VC want maybe good t'ings, but how get no good. How get vewy bad, mean."

Will held up his finger for Binh to give him a minute, and then he stepped over to Woodman, who was seated on a stack of C rations, eating his meal. Will whispered over Woodman's shoulder, "Be humping your radio tomorrow morning. Give you a break. Montana may not like it that I'm carryin' yours and not his."

"Why ain't ya carryin' his?" Woodman looked back over his shoulder and asked with a grin.

"Didn't like the way he asked," Will answered. He patted Woodman lightly on the back, before getting back to Binh.

"Tonight I want to speak with some of these ARVN soldiers and you about the VC and what's going on here, the war, you know? I'm just trying to find out more about all this," Will said to Binh. "Will you help me?"

"Better t'an clean shitters, Binh t'ink," he answered. "Binh must get done wit' card game first, t'en help, OK?"

"You are a good friend, Binh," said Will. "Thanks."

"You American' here cause you know how be numbah one good friend, Binh t'ink."

ARVN Speak About VC

Will sat cross-legged in a circle with a dozen ARVN soldiers, who squatted on their haunches. He was tired of small talk but would not chance his real purpose until Binh arrived, in case direct communication broke down. Besides, Binh had promised to speak up if he felt these ARVN were misleading Will.

When Binh arrived, Will had just noticed that squatting next to the only ARVN corporal in the circle was a woman dressed as a soldier. Her loose-fitting uniform made it difficult to discern her figure. Nonetheless, the color of her cheeks and gleam in her eye sent a signal of youth and beauty that stirred Will's interest.

"Where did she come from?" Will said. "She wasn't with us before."

"It all right, Sergeant," the only ARVN sergeant among them spoke up. "T'at Corporal Hahn' wife. Lib by here. She visit. It OK."

Will was at a loss for words. Corporal Hahn broke the uncomfortable silence. "You want?" he asked, looking at Will while gesturing toward the woman next to him.

Will knew he was on the spot and could ill afford the luxury of confused indecision. Instantly he balanced the pros and cons. He felt the natural urges of any young male, and he was alert enough to be sensitive to offending the corporal by rejecting his wife. On the other hand, Will knew better. Aside from other considerations, he was sure the security of their perimeter and entire mission had been breached. Perhaps nothing would come of this breach, but no way would he be part of it.

Will looked to Binh, who offered no clue. "Thank you, but no," Will said to the ARVN corporal. "You are both very generous and good friends." Will paused and looked directly at each member of the circle, before glancing back at Binh, who nodded that he was now ready.

"Who are the VC?" Will asked in a hushed but forceful way.

The ARVN soldiers, realizing the new direction of the conversation, looked at one another tentatively.

"VC here, ebbywhere. All around here VC," the ARVN sergeant responded. "T'is VC land."

Binh nodded. "But our governments say their soldiers came from North Vietnam," Will said, "that the North invaded the South."

This time, the sergeant first spoke quickly in Vietnamese to the others, before responding, "Most Viet lib 'round here VC. T'ey help VC. VC soldats come part from here and from ot'er province in Sout' and part from Nort' Vietnam, too. But most from Nort' really from Sout', beaucoup from 'round here."

Puzzled, Will turned to Binh, who explained, "When patriotic army fight French, beaucoup soldier come from here. Beaucoup fight for Viet independence in t'ese zones. When ceasefire in 1954, most Viet Minh army go nort' of DMZ and all colonial armies group sout' of DMZ."

Will knew the rest of the story. If anything surprised him, it was how accurately these ARVN soldiers could recite their own written history. Their testimony gave an authority to Will's reading that until now he had not acknowledged. For Will, what till now were only ideas in print became the essential facts of this conflict and perhaps the determinants of his fate.

Binh paused so the ARVN sergeant could resume his narration. "Division Vietnam at DMZ supposed be temporary only, meant keep warring armies separate till free election in 1956 show which side rule all Vietnam."

"Geneva Accord say all t'is," Corporal Hahn added.

"But no election held," the ARVN sergeant resumed. "Supposed be election, but still no election see who side rule all Vietnam."

"So soldats from Sout' in patriotic army trapped in Nort' away from family and honored ancestor," Corporal Hahn said, "till start come back when see be no election."

"Sergeant Thich libbed by here," an ARVN soldier said. "Thich' fat'er fight with patriotic army and go nort'. Nebber heard from him. T'at why

Thich no be officer, 'cause fat'er. Officers wit' us now grow up wit' Thich. Thich always leader when boy, but army no want Thich be officer. Officers listen OK to Thich still anyway."

"Why not?" Will asked. "Why weren't the nationwide elections held?"

"Two sides point at one anot'er," the ARVN sergeant said.

"But ebbyone know," the ARVN corporal interjected, "side gonna lose election be side gonna block election."

"But how can we be sure who would have won an election that never took place?" Will asked.

The group guffawed. "It sure Viet people pick Ho Chi Minh, not colonial puppet," the ARVN corporal said.

Will knew from his reading that this assessment was widely shared. Yet he could not help but marvel at hearing these views from the very ally that asked he accompany them against this same leader. "What about Ho Chi Minh?" Will asked. "What do you think of him?"

"Ho Chi Minh?" the entire circle seemed to rush to offer their reverence. "He vewy great man. Ho Chi Minh vewy great man. He vewy great man!"

Will tried to absorb what they said. *Whoa! Ho Chi Minh's the goddamned George Washington of his country.* Will looked at the others. They all seemed to hang on his very next word. It was as if Will had tapped into some fundamental wellspring of energy able to animate all Vietnamese as a single people. *These are our allies responding this way to the leader of our sworn enemy.*

"If Ho is so great, how come people left the north in droves when he took control there?" Will asked. "Weren't they afraid of blood baths?"

"Yes, many work wit' French company," an ARVN soldier said, "and most were Cat'olic."

"Cat'olic priests told Viet to move sout'," the ARVN corporal said. "T'ey say ebbyone, *Christ has gone to the sout'*. Whole villages move as one."

"Many Cat'olics in Vietnam, t'anks to French," the ARVN sergeant continued, "but still small part of all Vietnam. Yet t'anks to French, t'ese Cat'olic families control beaucoup land, government, ebbything. If not born right family, no chance for better future Sout'. T'at way Saigon government is, too."

"What about the VC?" Will asked, not knowing what to expect.

"VC bad. VC very bad people," the group seemed to echo. "VC do bad t'ings to people."

"Family no so important to VC," Corporal Hahn continued, "so anyone can rise in VC rank', but VC bad."

Will tried to discern how sincerely they answered this last question. *It's what I would have expected, what I would have hoped, but it does seem to contradict what they've been saying. Or does it? This is a bloody civil war. It's north against south just like the US Civil War, but here the south is not of a single mind. Here, some of the south is with us, some against us, and those against us are part for the VC and part for the north. Maybe the largest group of all, though, the devout Buddhists, wants nothing to do with any of this, but all Viets stand in tribute to the northern leader who led them to independence. This is clearly more a civil war than our own. It's not just north against south, it's south against south. And where it's north against south, these bastards coming from the north are as often as not southerners prevented from coming home sooner by any other way. They haven't been able to come home because of the breach of a treaty by the south—with our support, I'm sure.*

What a can of worms. A civil war! I knew this. I read it, but I wouldn't accept it. I denied it. Why wouldn't I admit this to myself? Was it because I was so sure our nation's security was at stake that I'd say 'To hell with Vietnam's right to self-determination'? Was it because I was so sure that the commies had already violated this time-honored right, so our involvement was really just balancing the scales? Or was it really because I didn't have the guts to face the truth and stand up and speak it the way Campbell did? Because I knew if I did I'd be treated the way he was and be called a traitor and a coward and a commie and a dupe. Was it just easier to park my ass in the grass here and say 'To Hell with Life'? Or was it that it didn't matter what I thought because it still was my turn? Maybe the real question is who makes that call?

Will did not get to answer that last question, because Sergeant Thich emerged from a shadow behind the group. He growled some command to the three ARVN soldiers who had been speaking, and momentarily feigned conviviality by squatting next to Binh. He went on speaking to the group in sharp tones in Vietnamese, but when he was almost finished he reached his arm around Binh's shoulder and confronted Binh face-to-face until he concluded with a sardonic laugh and clapped Binh on the back several times.

Even in the dark, Will saw Binh's face flush. Will looked gravely at Sergeant Thich as the others arose. Thich stared back at Will.

"Let go, Sergeant Stone," Binh said. "Time we go."

Will nodded at Thich before rising. Thich did likewise.

"What'd he say?" Will asked once he was sure they were out of Thich's earshot.

"Thich, he say, 'Situation here so complicated, it difficult enough for Viets who lib' t'rough all to understand,'" Binh said. "'So hopeless for outsider try and understand.' Maybe he right, Stone."

"Is that all Thich said, Binh?" Will asked. "I mean at the end when he was in your face?"

"Binh never like Thich," Binh answered.

"What'd he say?"

"He say something like, 'Talk be futile. Binh shaped more by past than hope for future,'" Binh responded. "Make Binh feel like he know 'bout my family been killed. Like t'at only reason for Binh hunt VC. Make Binh vewy angry, 'cept Binh know that Thich, he may be right in t'is, too. Binh still angry, no like Sergeant Thich. He mean."

"Was that corporal really offering me his wife?" Will asked Binh.

"Why ask Binh?" the interpreter answered. "Corporal said English."

With Uncle Ho

After he bedded down next to Binh on the perimeter, Will's mind raced on. *Who makes the call? Yeah, that's the question, but what's the answer? What call? What's the right question? Whether it's a civil war? Whether it's a necessary war? Whether it's a just war? Whether it's a cause worth dying for? Whether Americans or Asians should do the dying? Whether it's my turn? And if it's my turn, whether there still comes a time when I make my own call?*

Will looked up at Binh, who was rubbing the safety on his M-16 with his thumb as he peered into the jungle. Binh had pulled out of the foxhole about twenty-five meters to his right when Will said that he would bed down with him. Binh had made sure the guard posts on either side of them knew that Will and he were between their positions, but he did not pinpoint the spot for them. He was just as glad to be with Will. He felt safer with Americans. He trusted them.

It's a goddamned civil war, Will said to himself, fighting off his hard-earned sleep. *But we didn't understand that at first. This guy Ho is practically worshipped by all the Viets. Doesn't he see this is all a big misunderstanding and we really are trying to help his people? Doesn't he see his people are the losers in all this?* Will tried to shake the drowsiness from his head to be alert enough to finish his thought, but sleep was overcoming him. *Doesn't Ho see he's running with the wrong pack?*

Will tossed and turned in his sleep. Binh glanced down at Will, worried he might make enough noise to give away their position.

Will's subconscious picked up where his conscious mind had checked out. *Gotta get to Ho Chi Minh. There's been enough dying on both sides. This is a mistake. I just gotta explain it to him.*

When Will arose in his dream and slipped away with his rifle into the jungle, it was as if he were watching himself from outside his own body.

Gotta find Ho, he said to himself over and over as he pushed ahead blindly. Will stumbled upon an isolated hamlet. "Take me to VC," he asked an old man squatted in a squalid alley off the beaten path.

A word from the old man, and three young men in black pajamas hustled Will into the back of a small truck and rushed him to a jungle enclave. VC cadre there attempted to question Will, but quickly fell under the sway of his invocation of Ho Chi Minh's name. With Will in tow, two VC set off on foot, headed north into the night jungle. Will's spirit was buoyed. *Didn't know if they'd just waste me right off the bat. Gotta make this work. It's all a big fuckin' mistake. Ho will see it, and then so will LBJ.*

Will rolled over into the watchful Binh. For Binh, it was a gentle reminder of Will's unsettled presence. For Will, it was a slip and fall as he struggled to keep up with his VC escorts through the jungle. No matter how far or fast they scrambled, Will saw burning villages, always to his right. As soon as one passed, another appeared. Upon approach, each village seemed familiar, but Will could not make out why. Smoke and sweat blurred his view of the animals and small children straying about, but he could hear clearly the wailing of young mothers and old men trying to maintain control of what was left of their lives as they were herded toward transport helicopters. Every so often, a long stream of fire would appear over a village. *Zippo*, Will thought, visualizing the napalm-spewing armored vehicle. Finally, as Will marched past the last village, he saw an old man sobbing next to a dead water buffalo. Two American soldiers walked away from him. *Me and White Man.*

The two VC and Will reached a murky roadway. They could not make out whether it was a highway or logging trail, but something on it was coming toward them. They gathered alongside the road until an old man driving an ox cart reached them. The scene was familiar to Will, but he could not make out what was missing.

The VC escorts halted the old man and moved to the rear of his wagon to check his cargo. They gestured for Will to pull back the tarp. Will first uncovered a young mother, who could have appeared asleep on her back except for the dried blood around her navel, where a bullet had entered her stomach. Continuing to remove the tarp, Will uncovered a young boy with dried tears on his cheeks. There was no mistaking him for asleep because his chest, stomach and legs were torn with lacerations from bomb or artillery fragments. Will resisted recollecting the mother and boy from the ambush at Soui Cat.

Quick to avert his gaze, Will suddenly saw the phantasmal face that tormented him day and night. Once more, he was captivated as the Viet interrogee's high cheekbones came into focus. As always, Will searched the face for some clue, some meaning, and just when he honed in on those haunted eyes for a glimmer of insight, the face again exploded. This time, however, out of the turbulent debris coalesced another face, no less clear and no less haunting—a long-necked, old man with mustache and long wispy goatee and thinning gray hair pulled straight back.

"Vous êtes Ho Chi Minh!" Will gasped, as he took in the numerous guards positioned about the compound. Ho seemed to have been working with his general staff examining maps. The general officers appeared more surprised than curious about Will's arrival. Ho, however, seemed to have expected him.

"No French, not here," Ho said. "One foreign devil at a time."

Despite having come so far for this purpose, Will's mind whirled with what to say. He swiped his brow and rubbed his jaw.

"I speak English," Ho said. "Of course I do. I studied in New York, long before you were born. Tell me, soldier, is Harlem ready yet to explode? It almost was when I lived there. Why can't your country enter the twentieth century when it comes to racial matters?"

"Sir—" Will began.

"You mean Mr. President," an officer interrupted. "You will accord our leader proper respect."

"Mr. President, sir," Will addressed Ho Chi Minh, "might we speak more privately?"

"Soldier," Ho responded, "state your business or be gone."

"Mr. President," Will began, "I've seen how you are loved by your people. I've seen the death and suffering of so many Vietnamese. Let me help you resolve this terrible, unnecessary conflict."

Ho stared hard at Will a moment, stroking his goatee before glancing at his generals with a quizzical smile. "Soldier, you are either an instrument of heaven or a flaming asshole. Around here, we place our faith not in your heaven, but in the barrel of an AK-47. If you were in my army, I would have you shot. Now, one more time, what do you want?"

What a fucking nightmare. Will's conscious mind began to stir, but he slid back into the dream.

"Mr. President," Will said, "you wrote your country's constitution based upon my country's. If we respect the same principles, we can put our differences aside. The American people don't want war with your country. Most of them don't even know where it is—"

"That's the problem," Ho said, lifting both arms in exasperation that a dogface soldier would presume such a role for himself. By the same token, Ho did not ignore the risks and hardships Will had undertaken in evident good faith.

Will wondered how Ho might view him. *He must be thinking how he could use me. He can't be sure how much I know.*

"We trusted your country before," Ho continued, staring coldly at Will, "only to be betrayed. The US promised it would keep the French from returning to power here after World War II if we helped drive out the Japanese. We were the backbone of your commando operations here. Come the end of the war, America lifted not one finger to prevent the colonial regime from resuming its exploitation of our country. Instead, your people helped the French in their war against us. We have learned not to trust in the words of others, but rather to take our destiny in our own hands."

Will waited until he was sure Ho had finished. "When Stalin rode the Red Army roughshod over eastern—"

"This is not Europe," Ho interrupted. "Spare us the dominos, soldier. Here our people's revolution was our own doing. For seven long years, soldier. Do not dishonor our sacrifices by crediting others for our victories."

Ho walked to Will until he stood right before him, until Will could feel the old man's breath and the fire in his eyes. "Did the French control you when you sought French aid in your own struggle for independence from British colonialism?"

Will's jaw dropped. He bit his lip.

Ho raised his voice. "Our struggle today is still about ridding Vietnam of the last vestiges of colonialism," he said. "We fight for the future of Vietnam against the privileged classes of its past. We have struggled a thousand years to maintain our independence, and we will be here a thousand years after the last American finally has skulked away and the Russians have been sent packing back to Moscow.

"The Russians, damn them, forced us to give up at the '54 Geneva Convention what we already had won on the battlefield. They were so worried that a communist victory here would upset the chances for a communist electoral win in France itself."

"The Chinese, too—" Will started to say.

Ho cut him off. "The Chinese are our historic enemies. You worry the Chinese and the Russians will march together. We worry the Chinese and the Russians will try to destroy one another, and in so doing destroy us.

"Now, do you understand, soldier, that the Vietnamese, not the Russians, not the Chinese, control events here? We decide when and how far we travel down each road based on what's good for the Vietnamese people."

Asleep or not, Will was slow to concede to the enemy the basic tenet of American foreign policy—the containment of an expansive, monolithic communism. He searched his mind for some crack through which peace might be found. *It's there. I can feel it. Gotta buy time, just a second, and I'll spot it.*

"But, Mr. President," Will said, "if the Russians could make you give up at the conference table what you had already won on the battlefield, are they not then controlling you?"

"You have not heard a word I said!" Ho shouted. "You Americans don't care who *controls* Vietnam. You only care who *owns* Vietnam. Why did I waste everyone's time with you?"

Then Ho shouted a command in Vietnamese for Will's guards to fall upon him. A hand clasped an iron grip across Will's mouth to silence his protests. Will tried to fight free, sure his only chance was in being heard, but the guards threw him to the ground. A hand gripped his throat, and a knee crashed down on his shoulder, ending Will's struggle to free himself and causing such intense pain that he awoke in desperate fright. Will stared up in disbelief at a Vietnamese figure kneeling on his chest and holding his mouth and throat. *This is real*, Will thought. *This nightmare's for real.*

Chapter 10

A Soldier's Code

Betrayal

Binh stared down at Will with terror in his eyes. Only when Will was fully awake did Binh chance withdrawing his hand from Will's mouth. He signaled for silence and pointed before sliding off Will's body. Will lifted his head and scanned the campsite. His heart pounded. *What in hell?*

Everywhere shadows of soldiers skulked. Three M-60 machine guns positioned along the northern perimeter opened fire, their tracer rounds intersecting in the sky above the center of the encampment.

Binh shook Will's shoulder and gestured for him to roll into the jungle. At first Will was captivated by what was going on until Binh's well-placed knee to the ribs engaged his better judgment.

Once Binh and he were concealed by the edge of the jungle, Will whispered, "What the hell's goin' on?"

"Shh, you look!" Binh answered. He pointed to the southern portion of the encampment. "VC inside perimeter. You look. Must come in from nort'. Now control M-60. See, many ARVN soldats now try run 'way sout', but VC catchin'. Some ARVN, a few maybe, join up with VC. Most ARVN no know what do. Wake up now too late."

Will stared at the open field in shock, but then he remembered Corporal Hahn's presumed wife, shyly beguiling him. *She came through the perimeter. Was she Cong? Were they all?*

"You look, look!" Binh said, pointing.

"Oh, Jesus Christ," Will said, "they've got the lieutenant and Montana and Woodman."

The sight of VC soldiers pointing carbines at the three Americans and escorting them to the knoll at the northern end of the clearing galvanized Will's attention. Binh elbowed Will a second time to divert his focus to a VC party of six headed their way.

"We go," Binh said, tugging on Will's arm.

"They fuckin' changed sides," Will said.

"Must go," Binh said.

"The others?"

"We come back," Binh said. "We go now, t'en come back."

"They fuckin' changed sides."

"Most ARVN not bad, Stone. Let go now."

Will and Binh rushed through the dark another fifty feet before stopping to see if any of the six VC entered the jungle in pursuit. Satisfied no

one had followed, they inched halfway back to the clearing. They heard
the pursuit party combing the edge of the clearing and adjacent jungle
near where they had abandoned their perimeter guard post.

"They could jump into the jungle at any time, as soon as they find
where we were camped," Will whispered.

Binh nodded, but signaled Will to follow him back toward the perimeter line. After ten more feet, Binh squatted and reached behind a tree
until he caught hold of an olive drab canvas laundry bag. As he dragged
it toward them Will saw, even in the moonlight, that it contained three
Claymore mines and about a dozen hand grenades.

"Good, huh?" Binh asked. "I put way out here just 'fore dark, just in
case."

"Did you get the radio?"

Binh glanced at him and averted his eyes. "No radio," he said.

Will and Binh could sense the pursuit party was giving up looking for
them. Will waved his hand for Binh to follow him closer to the clearing.
They stopped just short of it, but close enough to see Brown, Montana
and Woodman sitting back to back at the crest of the knoll. They were
bound together.

"How we gonna get them?" Will asked.

Will turned and realized Binh was gone. He spotted a shadow moving slowly toward him from where Binh and he had camped earlier.
Immediately Will focused on the moving shadow. He clicked off the
safety of his M-16 and lowered its sights to just above the emerging,
uniformed figure. Binh. Will slacked his forearms, letting the gun barrel
point to the ground.

"No radio," Binh said when he was back next to Will. "Sorry."

"You sure?" Will asked.

"Binh no take chance for nothin'."

"Of course," Will said, realizing Binh probably had saved his life in the
last several minutes. He looked back to the rise where the VC held the
captured Americans and then at Binh, who was shaking as he jammed
hand grenades in his web belt.

The First Rescue

"What? What is it?" Will asked.

"Binh no want VC take him 'live, ebber," he answered. "You promise."

"What do you mean?" Will asked.

"You promise," Binh said.

"OK, OK," Will said, "but what do you mean?"

"You make promise to Binh, Stone. You good friend. Binh good friend. Here Binh knife. Beaucoup sharp, vewy sharp," Binh said, handing Will his hunting knife, still in its sheath. "Fix, fix, put on belt, Stone."

Binh trembled. *He's a man against himself. He's telling himself to do something and his body is rebelling. His body knows better than his mind what's good for him.*

"See shadow where ground go up?" Binh pointed to direct Will's attention. "You make way in t'ere. Hide, hide. Binh be on ot'er side of camp twenty minute from now. Binh t'row four grenade, fire Binh own M-16. Stone, Binh proud have M-16. VC run at Binh. You jump up, cut GI loose. VC chase Binh. You get away. OK? Binh piss now."

When Binh had finished, Will asked, "Where will we meet you?"

"Maybe hebben, Stone," Binh said, "maybe base camp. We try t'is. Last highway we cross, maybe two klick sout' here. Stream cross highway, just east of hamlet where kid all call boom-boom to us. You know where Binh say?"

Will nodded, "Boom-boom, short time, yeah."

"If you no be chase', walk ober bridge, t'en hide where you can see if Binh walk ober bridge alone," Binh continued. "Binh do same t'ing if get t'ere first. Come out when see ot'er cross bridge alone. OK, OK?"

"OK," Will said, "but first sundown forget about bridge. Too late, OK?"

"If you get radio, blast whole camp to hell. No worwy 'bout Binh, Stone," Binh said. "Send chopper for me at bridge just 'fore sunset if you no can come."

"OK," Will said. "Good luck, Binh."

"Good luck you, Stone."

In a moment Binh vanished in the dark jungle. Will trembled as he peered at the shadow along the base of the knoll. *Gotta piss, too.*

No sooner did he commence relieving himself than Binh's head appeared through the foliage. "Stone no forget promise to Binh," he said.

He'd been gone only a few seconds, but Will was glad to see him alive, even if he was intruding. "Binh good friend. Stone good friend," Will said.

"Good," Binh said, before he again disappeared into the night.

Will moved toward the clearing and dropped to one knee to check his watch. *Can this work? Should we just have beat it out of here and tried to get help? Should we have saved ourselves? Should two be risked to try and save three? It's too late now. Binh's on his way.* Will worked his way along the jungle's edge until he reached the point nearest to the dark swale he would traverse. His thoughts turned to the VC sappers that first night when he was laying out the base camp. *If they can do it, so can I.* He checked his watch. *Ten minutes if Binh's on time.*

Will looked for his return route of escape. He moved several paces north to where moonlight shone on two barkless trees and rigged trip wire between them and two Claymore mines from Binh's sack. Then he edged his way back south to where the jungle met the dark swale. Again, he checked his watch. *Five minutes. Can I get in position in time? Don't be early, Binh. Don't be early.*

Methodically, Will crawled from the edge of the jungle inward along the toe of the slope. Every now and then he looked around, but no one seemed to notice him. He checked his PX Timex. *Three minutes. Should come out just about right.* By the time he was as near the detainment area as he dared go, he was soaked with sweat. The area held just the three Americans, but there were five VC with them. He strapped his M-16 on his back, figuring to use Binh's knife. *Binh's diversion has gotta attract at least three of them, or we're fucked. If I gotta use the rifle, they'll be on us like bees.*

The concussion of Binh's first grenade rocked the encampment. Will held himself in check until the second grenade exploded. Sticking his head up, he saw three of the prisoners' guards rush in the direction of the explosions. Will sprang to his feet and lunged up the hill twenty feet to the nearest guard, who was focused on the commotion. He never knew what hit him when Will's knife blade ripped across his throat.

Will darted for the remaining guard, who swung his rifle but not before Will's shoulder caught him full force just above the waist, knocking the carbine loose. The guard fell backwards down the knoll with Will riding his waist all the way. He was dead before he hit the ground. Will pulled Binh's knife from the guard's trachea and swiped it on the dead man's uniform. He took a quick look around. *So far; so good.* Will sprang to his feet and slid to his knees next to Lieutenant Brown.

"Follow me out of here," Will said as he cut the three loose. "When I jump through two barkless trees, make sure you jump, too, or you'll trip a wire. Let's go!"

Will never looked back as he bolted for the jungle. *If they're not with me, it's on them.* The others were hot on his heels. There was no reaction within the camp until the four Americans were two-thirds of the way to cover. Then carbine shots rang out. The four kept legging it. When they reached the two barkless trees, Will jumped. The others followed suit. They rushed headlong through the jungle until they heard the two Claymore mines explode. Only then did they stop to look back and catch their breath.

Lieutenant Brown panted and clapped Will on the back. "Thank God for you, Stone," he said. "We thought you must have already been dead when they didn't bring you with us."

"Binh saved my ass," Will said. "What the hell happened back there?"

"The fuckin' ARVN officers must've gone over to the other side," Montana answered. "The whole thing was rigged."

"That's right," the lieutenant said. "How the hell did you pull off that diversion?"

"All the officers?" Will asked, before answering Brown. "Binh threw the grenades."

"How do we know if it was all their fuckin' officers?" Montana said. "It only takes a few. Now let's get the fuck out of here."

"I think they got him," Woodman said.

"C'mon, Lieutenant," Montana said, "let's get this show on the road."

"Right," the lieutenant said, straightening up, but still panting.

"Who?" Will asked.

"Let's go!" Montana said.

"Who'd they get?" Will asked, grabbing Woodman's arm.

"Binh."

"Lieutenant, let's go!" Montana said.

"You sure?" Will asked Woodman, releasing his arm.

"I think they did," Woodman said. "I didn't know it was Binh, but it had to be whoever pitched those grenades. The firing stopped when they got him."

"Goddammit, c'mon, Lieutenant," Montana said.

"They dragged him in from where the explosions were," Woodman said. "I stopped to grab these carbines."

"Montana is right, let's go, men," the lieutenant said.

"That somebody they got just saved all our asses," Will said.

"C'mon, you heard the lieutenant, Stone," Montana said. He shoved Will down the path. "You got the point. Woodman, you cover our ass."

"Wait a second," Will said, spinning around and bracing himself to confront the others. "Binh just saved our lives."

"There's nothing we can do, Stone," Lieutenant Brown said. "It'll never work another time. They'll keep too many men on him. It's hopeless. We'll lose more men trying to save one. I'm sorry, but it's hopeless."

"Binh and I could have looked at it that way, sir," Will said, "but we didn't."

"I'm the lieutenant here, and I gave you an order, Stone."

"He's our fuckin' ally, sir."

"Well, think of him as just another fuckin' dead gook," Montana said. "You just saw none of them are any good." He shoved Will again.

"Move it out, Sergeant Stone," Lieutenant Brown said. "You got the point."

Will scrambled down the path until they ran out of trail. They had to pick their way through vines, over rocks and under branches. "If it was me who was caught, would you run out on me, too?" Will called behind him.

Will was able to determine that Lieutenant Brown was directly behind him when he heard Montana answer him from further back. "The best gook is still just a gook, Stone. Pick up the pace."

"I never thought that—" Will said.

"Never mind, Stone," Lieutenant Brown cut him off. "Don't say it."

"—that Americans would desert their ally," Will said even louder, as he forged ahead.

"We try to help, Stone," Lieutenant Brown said, gasping for breath, "but when it comes to them or us, it's an easy call. It's their country, not ours. It's their fight."

"Pick up the goddamned pace," Montana shouted.

Will did, especially when he reached jungle growth that was easier for him to traverse than for the taller lieutenant. He rushed ahead until he was sure the lieutenant would not see him jump off to the right. Will secreted himself alongside their line of travel, as the other three passed by him. *They're having enough trouble just moving through the jungle without trying to baby-sit me.*

Will watched until their fleeting movements disappeared into the dark. *Now what the fuck do I do? Why the fuck didn't I just stay with them? I was given a direct order.* Will recalled Binh trembling when he left to create the diversion. *Get a grip on yourself. You can't walk away from Binh. You know what's right. You could never face yourself otherwise. You gave Binh your word. You're gonna do it.*

The Second Rescue

Ten minutes after he left the others, Will heard AK-47 fire. The gunfire was short-lived, and Will figured it involved the rest of his party. As soon as he heard it, he shifted directions to help the others. When it quickly fell quiet, though, he figured the fight was over and he was too late. Will thought of Woodman grabbing the dead guards' carbines before he bolted from the clearing. *I had the only decent weapon in the group. Fuck it. If it was them, they were so outgunned that my one M-16 wouldn't have made much difference. Whoever they ran into didn't come from the camp. They were already out there in force.*

It was still an hour before sunup when Will made it back to the edge of the clearing. He had moved with stealth on his way back, assuming VC were in the jungle looking for him in all directions. *Seems quiet again in most of the camp. There, up on the knoll, the same fuckin' spot, there's a group of them, bigger than ever. What the hell are they doing? Christ, they got somebody on the ground. What the hell are they doing to him? It's gotta be Binh.*

Will continued to study the situation. *You already know this isn't going to work and you're about to die. So, fuck it, this is about how you're gonna give it the best shot. What are your assets, Will? Marginal surprise? Possible diversion, if you can figure out how the hell to create one? C'mon, Will, it's gonna get light soon. You gotta go in the same way you went in before. Just fuckin' tough it out. They may be waiting for you at the edge of the jungle there, but you're going in.*

Still got three grenades. Could crawl in and try to frag all the guards, but you'd just as likely kill Binh. Worse, you might only wound him. That would be unforgivable. Could use the grenades to cover your retreat theoretically. Jesus. Come on, Will. The goddamned sun's gonna come up. Get in there. Gotta get in there now, if there's to be any chance. OK! You're gonna go do it. Are you ready? Take a minute. Steady. There's no halfway once you start.

Are you gonna do this or not?

Yes.

Are you sure?

Yes.

The only reason you're alive now is 'cause you left the lieutenant, right?

Right!

And you left them to do this, right?

Right!

So you gotta do it, right?

Right.

If you don't do it, you're a piece of shit, right?

Right.

Are you sure?

I'm sure.

How do you feel about it?

Don't want to live if I don't do this.

You're gonna die, right?

Right!

I mean now, right?

Right.

How do you feel about dying now?

Fuck it.

The final curtain, lights out, the end of suckin' air, how do you feel about it?

Fuck it!

You're young yet, you haven't lived your life. No wife, no kids. Your folks'll be left without your help. No test of life's challenges. All robbed from you, just lights out, you're bein' cheated, how do you like it?

My test is keeping my promise.

Good. Then, you're gonna do it, right?

Right!

Do it!

Will edged along the perimeter of the clearing, just inside the jungle foliage. *Fifty/fifty they're watching where the swale joins the jungle.* He stopped at the edge to observe the camp, focusing on the point in the swale from which he had sprung into action before. *What are you going to do when you get there? Figure that out then. Gotta go in now. Gonna be light soon. There's nobody left who would remember that's where I attacked from last time, anyway.*

That little insight encouraged Will to continue inspecting the encampment. Maybe there were other possibilities he had ignored. He watched soldiers on the other side of the camp occasionally walking to the perimeter with their carbines on their shoulders and then returning. Their movement gave Will an idea. He backed out of the foliage into the clearing and passed water again, continuing to face the jungle. Then slowly he turned to face the encampment. Will casually pulled a book of C-ration matches from his pocket and struck one, bringing the flame to his face before quickly extinguishing it. He started walking to what appeared to be a makeshift headquarters positioned in the center of the encampment. Will walked deliberately with his rifle slung upright on his shoulder. Now and then, he brought his hand to his mouth momentarily, as if he were being careful not to be seen smoking. He appeared to have nothing more to hide than that. *Good thing I'm not bigger, after all.*

Two VC soldiers were moving in his direction from the headquarters. Will unsnapped the sheath of Binh's hunting knife. When they closed to within fifty feet of him, a scream from the detention area stopped all three of them in their tracks. Will watched the two VC rivet their attention toward the scream.

Without hesitation, Will turned on his heel and marched toward the scream. After several paces he glanced back to see if the two would try to intercept him. He saw enough to feel confident that the one VC had continued ahead in their original direction, and the other had returned to the headquarters.

A dark cloud was just about to pass in front of the three-quarter moon. As the sky darkened, Will altered his course to intersect with the dark swale one hundred feet from the detainment area to avoid approaching it head-on. Once he reached the swale, he squatted as if tying his bootlace. *More than halfway up the swale. Still don't know if they're back there at the jungle waiting for me.*

Will paused to brood about the promise he had made Binh. From the movement of the cloud in front of the moon, he realized there would be more moonlight in a moment. He slipped down to the night crawl position with his M-16 set on full automatic. Every three or four crawl strokes, he stopped to look around until he made his way within fifty feet of where he figured Binh was held. *Gotta get close enough to see for sure what the hell's goin' on. So damned hard 'cause they're mostly down on the ground.*

At that moment, the VC sprang to their feet in unison. There were at least fifteen. *Christ, I thought there were only seven. Yeah, only seven, asshole, like seven's not enough.*

There was a groan when the VC propped up their prisoner. They had spread-eagled his arms to a bamboo stick. There was a VC on each end but too many around the prisoner for Will to see who it was. Those in front of the prisoner were poking at him with hand-held bayonets or knives. Will crawled closer. *Seven I could've maybe sprayed with a single magazine and had a prayer of disarming.*

Binh! Will's eyes widened.

The VC in front knelt to watch. Will grabbed a grenade from his web belt. He tugged on the pin just enough so that it would come free at the slightest yank. He placed the grenade uphill from him on the ground to his right. *Something's gonna happen.*

There was a glint of steel in the moonlight. Binh shrieked and writhed. The two VC who held the stick struggled to contain him as the VC in front laughed and cheered. Binh's tormentor came from behind and held up for all to see a bloody knife in one hand and something small and bloodier in the other. *Binh's pinkie! The dirty motherfucker whittled off Binh's pinkie!*

The tormentor lifted Binh's chin with his bloody knife blade and shouted some demand. Will understood he demanded information. Then the interrogator stuck the finger in Binh's mouth, until Binh limply let it drop to the ground.

Will reached for the grenade he had pre-positioned to make sure it was at the ready. The interrogator yelled another demand at Binh, again lifting his head with the knife blade. Will gripped his M-16 to aim from the prone firing position. The interrogator let Binh's head drop and turned to his audience with some remark in jest. Will backed the safety switch on his rifle to the semi-automatic firing position, so he could fire one round at a time.

The interrogator walked behind Binh until he appeared again with his knife ready to cut off another finger. Will lowered his head to his gun sights. Once more the interrogator yelled his demand at Binh, offering him his chance for relief. Will raised the barrel of his rifle and inched it sideways, lining up the interrogator in his sights. The interrogator paused a moment to jibe with the crowd.

Will was close enough that ordinarily hitting the interrogator would have been a routine shot. The interrogator, though, stood where he was shielded by Binh, who twitched and jerked his head often enough to obscure the interrogator's face.

The tiny audience cheered as the interrogator took hold of Binh's wrist, lifted his knife high, and began lowering it slowly to Binh's hand. Will caught the interrogator in his sights. *Gotcha, you bastard. I'll see you in hell!*

For the last time the interrogator yelled for Binh to answer. Will sucked in the deep breath taught on the rifle range. The knife was halfway to Binh's hand. Will began the requisite exhalation. The tiny audience murmured with increasing enthusiasm. Will stopped breathing with his lungs half-empty, and in that breathless moment nosed a final sixteenth of an inch correction to the right with his front gun sight. *Sorry, Binh. You made me promise. These guys aren't gonna stop with the fingers. God bless, baby.*

Will's eyes never left their target after he squeezed off the single shot, despite the recoil. They saw Binh's face shatter and the interrogator's hand come up to wipe the splatter from his own eyes. Immediately Will pushed himself to his knees, grabbed the grenade, pulled the pin, and let it fly. He burst afoot, managing three full strides back to the jungle before he hit the deck, more fearful of being seen in the flash of the explosion than of its effect. When the noise and concussion jolted him senseless, and shrapnel and debris spewed past his prone figure, Will felt content as he never had before. *Finally, I made some difference.*

He wasted no time pushing himself off the ground and into a running position. Bent over, he strode away, staying within the shadow of the rise behind him. As he made his way, he grabbed his second grenade with his right hand and pulled its pin. He made it to the spot where the four of them were fired on when he rescued Brown, Montana and Woodman. As if on cue, automatic weapons fire again commenced, this time solely at him. They were not just carbines this time. One of the M-60s had opened fire on Will, too.

Still hugging the toe of the slope to avoid making himself a backlit target, Will burst into full speed. He had no thought. He was guided only by instinct. He was running for his life. Will's stride was strong and sure, even as tracer rounds skipped about his feet. His eyes still scanned ahead for trip holes and stumbling blocks, though his every step was packed with his full force and fury. Animal cunning checked Will from climbing the rise until the last possible second when he could still have a direct path to the two barkless trees at the edge of the clearing.

Will made it to within sixty feet of the two barkless trees before he let the grenade fly toward the path ahead of him. Without breaking stride, he flew ahead another two full seconds before hitting the deck headfirst slightly short of the jungle's edge and just before the flash of the exploding grenade. Instinct propelled Will toward the protective cover of the jungle. No sooner was he up again and charging the onrush of dust and debris from the explosion than an M-60 round spun him back to the ground.

He scrambled on all fours for the jungle before realizing he was still intact. That only drove him to move faster, until finally, he dove head-long into the bush. An M-60 round had lodged itself in the heel of his jungle boot.

Alert to possible gunfire in the immediate area, Will kept moving down the overgrown path into the jungle until he heard shouts behind him. He pulled the pin out of his last grenade and let it fly back up the path to where five or six VC were about to enter the jungle in pursuit. Will turned and broke full stride down the path, hesitating momentarily to look back when the explosion roared. *Fly, Will! There'll be more. They'll never stop till they get you. Gotta trick 'em somehow, evade them.*

Soon Will was ten minutes on the run at breakneck speed. As daylight broke, he followed the overgrown trail where in the darkness he had gone astray with the lieutenant behind him. Thorns tore his shirtsleeves and trousers. Sweat streamed down his face and soaked his fatigues. He was driven mostly by raw fear—of capture, of torture, of death—but pride played a part, too. If he were going to die, he wanted to be as formidable a foe as he had come to regard the VC. He wanted to make them pay the way he was paying. In the end, though, it was the survival instinct that demanded his legs stride on when they knotted in cramps, that urged him faster when he was already flying, that hoped for escape when capture was inevitable.

Will lowered his shoulder to burst through vines blocking the trail, but at the last moment he dove headfirst to slide beneath them instead. As he hit the dirt, carbine fire zinged over his head.

He scrambled ahead on all fours a few seconds before contorting backwards. An olive drab uniform hit the vines, and Will opened fire on it just in time. In another second, the VC were coming under the vines. Will fired on them, too, forcing them back. Their carbines shot wildly in the air.

Will bounced up and flew another twenty feet down the trail before dropping to the ground amid the whiz of bypassing carbine fire. Just as a VC pursuer lunged at him from behind, Will wheeled his rifle back up the trail and squeezed off a round. A second VC returned the fire. Will dropped him, too. *Gotta get off the trail. They gotta be moving along my flanks while I stay put.*

Will switched his M-16 to full automatic and emptied what was left of his magazine up the trail. Quickly, he changed magazines and threw the empty where it would be found farther down the trail. Dropping to a night crawl position, he clawed his way off the trail beneath the understory. Every so often, he turned, ready to cover his retreat with fire, but so far the VC were not on to him. There was shouting down the trail. The VC passed where he had slithered off. He listened for the crunch of footsteps and anticipated flanking movements along each side of the trail. *Gotta get farther from the trail than they do. Gotta be moving at a right angle to one of their flanking movements. Gotta beat them before they cross my line of travel 'cause any time, boy, they can turn and move toward the path, toward me, to create a skirmish line. Gotta cross their path before they cross mine. If I can make it, there's a prayer they'll only skirmish toward the path and not away from it. Move it, trooper!*

Will pushed himself up to his knees and, after a few short breaths, staggered to his feet. He tried to walk hunched over with stealth, but he stood more upright and bumbled forward. Still, he forced himself to cover ground as fast as he could. He knew what he had to do, and he was doing it—to a point.

Suddenly, Will's heart sank at the sound of movement through the bush to his left no more than fifty feet away. *What was that? It's them, the flanking movement. We're gonna cross paths at the same time.* Will had seconds to choose. *I can squat here and hope to hell these bastards keep right on going before they turn and skirmish. If they skirmish, they still could miss me. Or, hey, I can chance it and go for it. Can you beat it across their path without their knowing? Fuck! Let's go!*

The prudent choice was to squat. The only choice was to squat, but Will made no conscious choice. He chose with his feet. Still driven by instinct, he teetered ahead, determined to be the creator of circumstance rather than its victim. Adrenaline began to revitalize him. His step regained some bounce. He was more careful about making noise and leaving tracks. But his timing was off.

Peering through the foliage, Will had the advantage of surprise when he confronted the VC pointman ten feet away. Will cracked off a burst of four rounds at him and then thrust ahead. There was hysterical shouting and thrashing among the pursuers. Will pushed on, fighting his way through the undergrowth. *They're on to me. Maybe I didn't have to fire. He might'a blinked. No, I saw it in his eyes. He was on to me. I was dead meat from the moment he spotted me.*

Will pushed farther ahead. Carbine fire burst from behind. After another couple of lunges, he saw a clearing ahead. Without returning the fire at his back, he pushed on. *Need a defensible position. I slow up and they'll be all around me.*

The clear area was made up of a small stream and its sandy banks. It was only thirty feet between the jungle's edge on one side to the other. *If I go straight across, they'll follow my tracks in the sand. If I can run down the stream and make it around that bend just fifty feet away, maybe there'll be someplace I can jump in the bush without detection on one side or the other.*

Will made a hard right as soon as he hit the water and flew downstream. *Water good. Could be the last of it I'll feel.* He made it around the bend, but not undetected. At the last second an AK-47 fired hot lead after him. Around the bend, the clearing widened out an additional twenty feet on the right bank and maintained its width on the left as far as Will could see. *No way out!*

An idea took hold of him. *Don't want to go out this way. Don't want to be running in terror at my end. Gotta face it on my terms.*

Will lunged for the middle of the clearing on his right, attracted to two pikes stuck in the ground about six feet apart. *What the hell's this?* He slid to his knees between the two three-foot shafts and twisted himself around to a defensive firing position behind where the sand was mounded up. Only then did he notice heads impaled on top of the pikes.

"Brown and Montana," he cried aloud, and a chill ran through him. *Jesus Christ! This mound is their grave.*

The Unexpected Ally

Gunfire lit up the edge of the jungle he had just skirted. It tore up the sand mound in front of Will. He held his fire for a visible target. VC suddenly broke through that end of the jungle and opened fire. Will raised his M-16 to return the fire. At the same time, a long, husky yell permeated the clamor, "No!" A tattered hulk of a fighting man ran toward Will from the edge of the jungle with a carbine blazing suppressive fire at the VC. In the time it took return fire from the VC to cut him down, this newfound ally traversed fifteen feet. When he fell in the sand of multiple wounds, his head and shoulder crashed against Will's side.

"Woodman!" Will said, all bitterness and strength ebbing out of him. "Oh, why, man? Why didn't you just save yourself?"

At first Woodman's eyes were averted and distant, but then they made contact with Will's. A wry smile started to curl his lips and he said, "Bro—" A cough choked off his words and he spit up blood.

Will slackened his right arm and loosened his grip on the M-16. In these last few seconds, he cared only about comforting Woodman. He would use his M-16 only to avoid being taken alive. He placed his left arm over Woodman's shoulder and whispered, "We'll go out together, man."

There was shouting in Vietnamese by the edge of the jungle. The firing stopped. Will refused to let anything distract him from Woodman.

"Did ya free him?" Woodman coughed. "Binh, huh?"

"Freed him from these bastards," Will said.

The jungle fell quiet. So quiet that Will could hear a solitary set of footsteps in front of him. They were coming toward him. He was determined to pay them no heed, to share this last moment solely with Woodman. Still, he tightened his grip on his M-16. The footsteps stopped just ten feet away.

Will refused to dignify their presence by diverting his attention. He stroked Woodman's arm and patted his shoulder. He could hardly bear seeing Woodman this way. When Woodman's eyes drifted away again, Will thought, *Probably could be saved, given proper medical attention soon enough*.

Finally, Will yielded to the inevitable and raised his resentful eyes to the intrusive figure that patiently demanded confrontation. His gaze passed first across the sand and up the boots and uniformed trousers, before jumping to the face. "You!" he said from deep in his parched throat. "You bastard, I should have known. I should kill you! All along there was something about you. Just tell me why, Sergeant Thich, why?"

"My country, my choice, Stone. And you can see that the Peoples Army of Vietnam accords me a slightly higher station. It's Major Thich actually. Not that I don't value the contribution of any good soldier. That's why I saved you. I knew it had to be you."

Major Thich dropped his helmet in the sand and propped his AK-47 on it, before removing his canteen from its case to take a swallow. "I think we owe you this," he said, replacing the top. He underhanded the canteen so it landed in the sand in front of Will.

Will's grip tightened on his M-16. He glanced about him to see if he could unloosen the cap on the canteen without being rushed and overpowered. *Only Thich would have a chance, and I don't think that's what he has in mind.* Keeping one eye on Thich, Will drew himself up to his knees to pick up the canteen with his left hand. He let go of his M-16 with his right hand to unscrew the top. When Will had it open, he brought the canteen to Woodman's lips, parted them with his finger and removed some crusty matter from within. Glancing first at Thich, Will positioned Woodman's head and the canteen to pour water in his mouth. Woodman coughed it up.

"Whoa, now give me some," Woodman gasped. After two drags, he waved his hand for Will to stop and rested his head back against Will's knee.

Will looked at Thich again and took two long drags on the canteen, cutting the second one short because he sensed movement. Thich had unloosed his web belt with the canteen case attached and slung it to Will. "Put it on, Stone," he said. "You'll need it if you walk out of here."

"Thank you for the water, Major," Will responded, "but the only place we'll walk together is in hell."

"I don't blame you, Stone," Major Thich said in flawless English, "but a lot of my men feel the same way about you. You killed a lot of our people tonight."

"Listen, you sorry sonofabitch—" Will said, before Thich interrupted him.

"Get a grip on yourself," the major said, looking back at his troops. "Your trial is about to begin."

The Trial

"My what?" Will erupted. "Fuck you and your kangaroo court, too!"

Major Thich gazed at Will before asking, "Stone, why do you say 'kangaroo court'?"

"Because you're the judge, jury, and executioner, Major," Will answered.

"No, no, no, my friend," the major corrected, "not in your case. This is something special that I have chosen, in part because I have watched and respect you, but I have my own, more significant, reasons, too. No, in this case, it will be you who will be 'judge, jury, and executioner.'"

"Well, that's easy, then," Will said. "I'm acquitted, so I'm outta here."

"Yes, that's the point," the major said, "you can walk out of here if that's all you choose to do."

"What?" Will asked. "You guys just hunted me like a dog, and I just blew away maybe a half dozen of your guys, but now you're gonna let me walk out of here?"

"If that's what you choose, Stone," Major Thich said.

"Why should I believe you?" Will demanded.

"What do you have to lose?"

"The chance to kill you," Will muttered. The major made no response. "That's what you meant when you said that I was 'executioner,' too."

"Now you have cut to the heart of the matter," Major Thich said. "Your decision will determine not just your fate, but mine. True enough, I have given my men orders that you be immediately shot if you shoot me, as I now stand before you defenseless. That will happen, though, only if you choose to execute me. So, you see, there is a bond between us. We will live or die together, as you choose."

"So, then, aren't you saying that it is you who are on trial?" Will asked. "You who are the accused?"

"I suppose from your point of view that you might first look at it that way."

"So what then?" Will asked. "Why the hell did you put yourself in this position? I can only plug you because you walked into this. And, anyway, I'm not even sure I'd be able to pull it off before your men would cut me down."

"You'll agree that I have given you a fair chance to execute me," the major said. "The odds are better than fifty/fifty in your favor."

"I'm on full auto with a full mag," Will said.

"Let's not talk about such things."

"Why did you walk into this thing?" Will asked.

"Because it was the only way to have this trial."

"Do you think I'm gonna be your father confessor and forgive you for this?" Will shouted, pointing to the heads of Brown and Montana. "Or for paring off Binh's fingers?"

"Sometimes things get out of control."

"Bullshit out of control," Will said. "Your government or leaders, or whatever they are, make terrorism a matter of policy."

"I suppose, Stone, your government's free-fire zones, and napalm strikes, and carpet bombing and Agent Orange aren't terrifying to those of us who live and die here," the major said. "But that was someone else, wasn't it, Stone?

"So what about you?" he continued. "What about when *you* call in a contact fire mission to suppress a lone sniper's single bullet and then adjust artillery fires all around the area without any clearance as to who might be in the area you level? Is that terror? Or when *you* send sporadic H & I artillery shells to random targets through the night without regard to who might have some unforeseen need to be afoot in the area? Is that terror? And how many times did *you* stick your M-16 in some villager's face so you could uproot the people at the threat of death, and burn their hamlet and destroy all connection to their ancestors? Is that terror, Stone? How many hamlets did *you* destroy in just the last two months? Will you answer me that?

"Don't try to stand up in some lofty sanctuary and judge me, Stone," the major said. "If you're going to judge me, judge me fairly, and do it here and now."

"Why'd you mutilate Binh?"

"Binh was a fine soldier, but he picked the wrong side," the major said. "I was offended by what men in my command did to him. Now, do you really think that the man who ordered such an atrocity would come here willingly to submit himself to the judgment of the man who—"

"He made me promise," Will interrupted, glancing at Woodman. "He made me promise before we headed in for the prisoners."

"I understand," the major said.

Woodman sighed. "You want more water, bro?" Will asked.

Woodman opened his eyes and looked about. He swiped his upper lip with his tongue before he bit down hard on his lower lip and looked away from Will.

"Stone," the major said, "my men say you are bloodthirsty. You shot up at least twelve of my men tonight. Why?"

"It had to be," Will answered. "I'm sorry, but it had to be."

"You're not gleeful that you killed so many," the major asked, "eager for revenge?"

"Every man's death diminishes me."

"Well, if they so diminish you, explain to me, please, why you thought you had to blow away so many tonight."

"I killed to protect my own people," Will answered. "I killed to spare Binh. He made me promise. I killed to save my own ass."

"It was necessary, then. Is that your answer?" Major Thich went on. "Necessary for honor, for humanity, for survival?"

"Yes," Will said, nodding his head in resignation.

"Perhaps it would be a better world if men agreed that those are the only legitimate reasons for killing one another," the major said. "Do you agree, Stone?"

"It's not the world I would have created."

"So, what about us?" the major continued. "Can you and I at least agree on this one thing: Let us invoke the word *necessity* only when we mean any of those proper reasons?"

"OK," Will answered, "but you're not going to take me alive."

"That's not what this is about, Stone."

"So let me get this straight, Major. Either I die trying to kill you or I just walk out of here."

"Yes," Major Thich said, just loud enough for Will to hear. "Now, tell me Sergeant, why would you find it necessary to kill me if you can just walk out of here?"

Will looked to Woodman, who was concentrating on breathing. His eyes were a thousand miles away. Will patted him on the shoulder and avoided thinking about the choice foisted upon him.

"Let me make it easier for you, Stone," the major went on. "We've already ruled out revenge, but you hate me for betraying—"

"No!" Will called out. "That's it. I don't hate you. That's what's missing here. We're all victims. The truth is there's no one to hate. That's the one truth I've finally come to learn about this war. There's no one to hate."

"That's good, Stone." The major broke out in a smile and took a relaxed step toward Will, who whipped his left hand onto the barrel grip of his M-16.

"Don't move too quickly, Stone," the major said, "if you want to stay alive."

"That works both ways, Major."

"I thought we had this little problem solved," the major responded.

"It's not that simple."

"What then?"

"A soldier's duty," Will said.

"Shit," Woodman said, coughing as he spoke. "Ahm tired of this bullshit, Stone. The man's offering you a *Get Out of Jail Free*. Now you take it."

"Listen, bro—" Will said, but Woodman cut him off.

"Don't *bro* me. No bro of mine would have a hard time finding that trail what's open to you. Now get to it."

"Woodman, the man who masterminded this whole treachery is in my gun sights," Will said.

"And you're in his, little man," Woodman said.

"He could do it again," Will said.

"Or his brother will, or the guy next door." Woodman coughed.

"Stone, it comes down to this," the major said. "I'm offering you a choice, a chance to live. How many other men would have wanted that choice?"

Will said nothing. He gulped and rubbed Woodman's arm.

"Stone, it really comes down to whether killing me is worth your life," the major said. "Our deaths are not necessary."

"I save myself and I betray every guy that's fallen," Will said.

Woodman coughed and interrupted him. "I fallen, bro, an' I fallen cause of you. Not for any other reason but you. Not for Sam, or the flag, or momma's apple pie. No, sir, I did it for you. An' I sure might'a thought different 'bout it, if ah'd a known you was gonna flush it down the big zero. You shoot the motherfucker an' you betray me, that's who you fuckin' betray."

Will looked squarely at Thich. "I want to know why you're doing this."

"I will prove to my men that the best of the Americans who were with us would not willingly choose death for this misbegotten cause you champion" the major said. "Because you have no good reason. And from this, my people will take hope."

"You're taking quite a chance."

"No matter," the major said. "Unlike yours, mine *is* a cause worth dying for. If I am right, then I found hope for my people. Don't forget that I saw another side to you than the ferocious warrior—a sensible side. But if I am wrong, if Americans will not see that they should stop sending their sons here to die, then my life is not worth living because our cause is lost, though we will fight you till the last of us is dead anyway. You have the weapons, but we have the necessity."

Hope stirred within Will. *Can he be on the level? Can it be possible there's a way back from this hellhole, a ticket home?*

What started as a glimmer quickly surged as an unquenchable thirst for life. *I can walk out of this nightmare back to the world. No! Gotta nail this guy. He's too dangerous and I'm no traitor. Can't encourage the enemy! Can I get the shot off?*

Will looked quickly about the clearing. All was silence as he pondered, save for Woodman's labored breathing. *The President says we gotta stem the Red tide, but he's the one who said it was an Asian boy's fight, not ours, just as Lieutenant Brown said the same thing before he walked out on Binh. If we're gonna walk out on 'em, let's do it now, not after another twenty-five thousand of us are wasted.*

We're not defending freedom here. We're outsiders in a civil war. If we gotta hold the line against communism, an air/naval shoreline defense is the right way to do it. But the pols send America's sons to the meat-grinder rather than own up to these truths because they're afraid for their jobs and perks, and they don't trust the people with the truth, and all these guys, Rick Franklin, swollen up, all pink and puffy, and Campbell, lost, like his father before him, and Captain

Michaels, so warm and moist, warm and moist, sticky—Will glanced down at the fingers on his right hand, rubbing together involuntarily, before he went on. *All the others, all the others, too. Wasted. Wasted?*

Will stared at one VC soldier back at the tree line. *My mind playing tricks on me, or somethin', or somehow is that?* Will looked down at Woodman and threw his arm around his shoulder. Beginning to get faint and dizzy, Will let out a long sigh before lifting his head again to see the VC soldier he thought resembled someone from back home. Will kept trying to make him out, but the rising sun was behind the soldier. It blinded Will. Will tried to shield his eyes from the sun with his hand extended. *Gotta follow orders, orders, orders! What's the spirit of the bayonet? To kill, kill, kill! Gotta kill, kill, kill! Gotta kill someone! Everywhere it's the same, everywhere flames. Everywhere I look now, flames, flames, flames.*

Then out of the flames, faintly, came the phantasmal Vietnamese face that so haunted Will, that beset him day and night, asleep or awake. Once more it drew closer and, as always, it exploded, this time in fiery turbulence. Now, for the first time, Will could see the hellish backdrop was actually many burning villages, each with women and children scurrying to round up animals and possessions. Always, there were old men huddled in a corner and held at gunpoint. Always, the old men looked the same, familiar, especially one particular face. Glancing from village to village, Will tried and tried to make out the face but he could not.

While Will still scrutinized his face, that old man arose and gently pushed aside the American guard's M-16 as he hobbled to an ox cart. The old man lifted up a dusky little boy to the bench seat before climbing up himself. Finally, the old man cracked a switch over the water buffalo's back and it labored forward.

Patiently, Will waited as the small cart moved slowly closer to him. It was just a matter of moments, but to Will it seemed a lifetime before the cart finally came into clear view. He looked upon it with disbelieving eyes as it drew nigh. It was his grandfather driving the cart, and in an instant, Will knew that the boy next to the old man was the son he himself would never have if he made a wrong choice now.

Will remained kneeling, propping up Woodman, but in his mind he was on his feet and over to the cart. He called out to the old man and boy as he rushed to them, but they answered him only in Vietnamese. Will studied the old man carefully. There was no mistaking it. It was his grandfather, gone native.

Will looked to the boy, who was sobbing. Will could not help smiling for a moment in pride, but quickly he saw that the grandfather and boy were overwrought with grief. Slowly, Will moved to the back of the ox cart. He drew back the tarp that covered two bodies stretched out in the back. He shuddered as his eyes passed from top to bottom over the woman he recognized as the one with the blood-ringed bullet hole through her navel from the massacre at Soui Cat. Will glanced up at the boy, drying his eyes with a rag. The boy turned to watch Will.

Then Will's eyes passed back to an American soldier decked out in dress khakis lying lifelessly next to the woman. Will gasped as his eyes took in the familiar athletic legs, the lanky torso and well-chiseled face. Will marveled at the still jaunty countenance, framed between sunbeams reflecting off the silver captain's bars on his collar. *Captain Mike!*

This time, Will looked up at the grandfather and wanted to speak with him further. The grandfather looked back at Will a moment and then down at the two bodies, and shook his head. In that moment, Will realized all that could possibly be said between them already had been said in that single exchange with their eyes. Will accepted it was right and proper that the old man and boy were on their way to see that both dead were paid decent respect.

"Stone, Stone," Major Thich beckoned. He was but five feet in front of Will. Will shook his head as he returned to immediate awareness. Alarmed at the major's advance, he tightened his grip on his M-16. "Stone," the major resumed, "are you all right?"

Will nodded.

"I cannot let this go on any longer," the major said. "You must tell me now, is your cause worth your life to you? Does your country have reason enough to compel you to die?"

Will's Choice

Will realized he was out of time. If he gave any sign of intransigence, Thich would signal that he be shot. *Hard to miss you, you sonofabitch. It's now or never. Is killing you worth killing me?*

"It's now or never," Major Thich said. "Is killing me worth—"

"That's not the question," Will yelled out.

"What then?" the major demanded.

"Apart from whether I'll die for this cause," Will answered, "I can't kill you for it. Not just standing there. Not for these reasons. I can't hate you. There's no one to hate. I'll kill anyone who tries to take me alive. But I'll not kill anyone for just these fuckin' reasons, not so some self-serving bastard can get re-elected. We came here in good faith, you know, we soldiers who put our asses on the line, 'cause we thought we were doing the right thing. We risked our asses to help your people."

"Tragic," Thich responded. "The stuff the poets should beat their breasts about for generations to come. You and I may cry our hearts out together, but will the American people ever grasp what madness this is?"

"People always believe their own country is right," Will gasped. He let his head drop forward, and stroked Woodman's arm. It took all Will's strength and purpose to lift his eyes enough to make sure Thich's boots kept their distance.

"Stone," Thich said, "make no mistake, if you have no good reason to kill me, then you have no reason to kill yourself in some mindless sacrifice. We are not born to serve others. We are born to live for ourselves. We choose to serve others only for good and overriding reasons."

Will studied Thich before slowly reaching for the web belt. He drew it back to him and sighed. He strapped it around his waist, opened the canteen, gave Woodman two more drags, and took the same himself. Then he stuffed the canteen back in its case on the web belt. Finally, he stood up deliberately, making sure he did not jar Woodman.

"You must salute, Stone," the major ordered, looking away from him and biting a lip to conceal a smile. Will saluted, wondering if they would shoot him now that they had what they wanted.

"You are free to go," the major stated in a businesslike way. "Sling your weapon over your right shoulder. Follow the stream the way you were headed until it crosses the highway. It is only about two kilometers. You have our safe passage. There may be other units out there, which we do not know about. With them, you are on your own. Good luck. I hope not to see you again, at least not under these circumstances."

"Yes, sir," Will responded.

Major Thich smiled and then shouted some commands in a jovial way to his soldiers, who cheered.

Hope they're just celebrating their moral victory and not my cannibalization, Will thought.

As they took a last look at one another, Will smiled at the major before spinning around to kneel in front of Woodman. "Ready, big guy?" Will said, helping Woodman fight to one knee.

"What are you doing, Stone?" the major said in a hushed voice. "I didn't say anything about him. He stays. We made no deal about him."

Will craned his neck to look at the major and shook his head.

"We made no deal about him, just you," the major said. "I thought he was dead. It makes no difference to us, I know, but my men are not expecting this. I cannot lose face. We have to stick to the deal. I cannot guarantee what my men will do, Stone."

Will ignored the major and knelt as low as he could, still keeping one eye on Thich, until he got his right shoulder under Woodman's waist. He thrust his right arm between Woodman's legs and quickly passed his M-16 back to his right hand.

"Leave him be. I'm warning you, Stone," the major ordered.

Will grabbed Woodman's right arm with his own left hand and wrapped it around his neck. "This is it, baby," Will said to Woodman. "God bless you."

"Stone," the major called, "you're making a bad choice. Don't throw everything away. Don't make me give the order!"

Will pulled on Woodman's right arm as he leaned back. He took Woodman's weight on his shoulder and in the same motion strained his legs to lift the mammoth load. *Feel like an ant*, Will thought as he lifted himself almost to an upright posture. He quickly dipped his knees and jostled Woodman around until he felt he had him in a secure fireman's carry.

Still, the load was staggering, and Will buckled first at the knees and then the back. The sand offered no solid footing, and he careened toward the stream before he was able to steer himself more or less in the direction he wanted.

"Stone," the major called, "this is your last chance."

If I could pull that KP with the grease cans, I can carry old Woodman, Will thought.

"Did you hear me, Stone?" Major Thich called.

Will strained with each step. Every stride was a test. Every motion required a conscious order from Will's brain for his body to obey. *One step at a time, boy.*

As Will entered the stream corridor near the end of the clearing, Major Thich shouted a command in Vietnamese. There was crosstalk. The major repeated his command.

"Stone," he called out, "don't make me be your executioner."

Will stopped, but only to adjust Woodman's positioning. "What is your *necessity*, Major?" he called back, before he again strode ahead.

"Stone, comply!" the major ordered. "This is your last chance."

Will struggled forward.

The major shouted commands in Vietnamese.

"We're going out together, Woodman," Will said, as the bolts to several rifles slammed home. Will was uncertain whether Woodman heard him because his words were punctuated by gunfire, predominantly from carbines set on full automatic. The fire kept up for a full minute.

When the first round sounded, Will thought about falling to the ground in a last ditch play at possum. Instantly he rejected that idea, convinced once down, he would never be able to get Woodman up on his shoulder again. *They'll check and kill us anyway. I'll walk tall like Josh did.*

Fear took his breath away as fast as the clamor did his hearing. Time stood still for those endless seconds. Sulfur fumes wafted across the clearing. Finally, the barrage ended.

The laughter and jeers that followed the barrage had just about ended by the time Will regained his senses. He was shaken but still standing. He thought about turning for a look at his tormentors, but instead chose to keep going. He had strength only to struggle ahead. Will had no understanding of the din just made by the VC. For all he knew, they were calling for his death.

"Stone," Major Thich called, "didn't that convince you I'm serious? Leave him."

Will teetered before bouncing Woodman around on his shoulder to make sure he still held him securely. *Two klicks. I can make it, if I can just get started.* A thought flashed across Will's mind, as he strained to walk in the sand. *Maybe it's true that Thich gave the order for his men to fire around us but not hit us. But if any one of them had wanted to kill us, he could have done so, and no one would have known who did it.*

Will struggled to take another step. *I can make it. Now, how do you figure that no one popped us? Maybe because Thich told them about the captive with his leg in his hand? Was it because they know I went back for Binh, for one of them?* Will forced himself to take another step. *Can make it.*

"Good-bye, Stone," the major called out.

"We can make it, Woodman," Will whispered.

"Stone," Woodman gasped, "you shot Binh?"

Will's whole body went weak. Immediately his mind screamed in panic for his back to stiffen and his knees to hold. *Push off! Push now, goddammit. You can do it. Push!* After three awkward strides, Will felt he had it back under control.

"Woodman, bro," Will said, "did I tell you I'm short? My hitch is almost up. We can make it outta here together, back to the world."

"Leave me an' go for it, Stone," Woodman gurgled. "Ahm a goner."

"Like you left me, bro?" Will managed a laugh as he continued to struggle. "Don't know where or how, but we are goin' out together. We brothers, man. I feel it. Feels good. Jus' I mighta liked a brother who weigh' a hundred pound' less, y' know."

"What you got waiting for you?" Woodman asked, coughing a bloody spray. "Back in the world, I mean?"

Will grunted and forced his body forward. "My own little wars I gotta make peace about."

"Ahm ready for peace, bro. That for sure," Woodman said, "but you really think it possible?"

"I think so," Will said. "With love, it's possible."

Will strode ahead, his load lightened by the warm lift of this precious hope. Then a short burst of machine-gun fire blew away any hope. Will dropped to his knees, wracked with pain, as Woodman crashed to the ground, dead. Will burned and throbbed all over—hit in an arm, both legs, and his neck. His mind was afire. It was losing its tenuous grip on things, all the more with each pulsation of blood through his wounds.

Will peered at Woodman and a pain welled up in his chest. It was a pain apart from any physical wound, but as heart rending as if his very soul had been torn asunder.

He cast his eyes to the heavens and, though his body and soul screamed their torture in his mind, he marveled at the puffy white clouds set upon a field of pastel blue. For a moment, he glimpsed Josh in the clouds reaching out to Woodman, and there was Campbell with the Viet woman with the hole in her belly and Captain Mike with an arm around Franklin. Then Will saw his grandfather with Blair, the young track driver whose lower half remained fused to the wreckage at Soui Cat. That pleased Will, though he hadn't known his grandfather had passed on. All that pleased Will and eased him some, but then it was solely a marvelous sky again.

Wobbling on his knees, Will had a fleeting thought but could not quite make it out. He sensed its importance but could not bring it into focus. Still, he latched onto this germ of thought with every bit of strength he could muster, lest it escape forever. He opened his mind to it and drew it closer, though it would elude him as the pain ebbed and flowed. Finally, he captured what he was sensing and examined it enough so at the last possible moment he recalled Josh's parting words to him, "Kneel only to pray."

Once more Will cast his eyes aloft and teetered. Then he fell forward, mouth agape, and sunk his teeth hard into the bitter, blood-stained soil of Vietnam.

About the Author

Brad Kennedy served in Vietnam as an artillery surveyor, machine gunner, track commander and forward observer with the U.S. 11th Armored Cavalry Regiment from August 1966 through July 1967. Upon his return home, he played an active role in Vietnam Veterans Against the War. More recently, he has brought intergenerational perspective to the war in Iraq in his writings for Intervention magazine and other news outlets. He lives with his wife, Barbara, and their family in New Jersey, where he builds housing for people with disabilities. For further information, visit www.bradkennedy.net.

Acknowledgments

Thanks to the late Albert Gendebien, History Department Chairman Emeritus of Lafayette College, for the confidence he imparted to me. Thanks to high school class-mate Barbara Baraw, who unwittingly shamed me into actually starting to write this work by telling me of her son's own literary production. Thanks to Charles Bogusat for his encouragement and keen insights while reviewing early drafts of this work, and also to his son Craig Bogusat who made a valuable suggestion it took me years to appreciate and accept. Thanks to Ez Holley who gave the first complete draft a proper line edit and reminded me of many literary guidelines I had long forgotten.

Special thanks to Lorraine Ash, journalist and author *par excellence*, without whom this work would not exist in its present form; for her expert reexamination of what should be further cut, what should be restored and what should be rewritten; for her several line edits as various versions of the manuscript emerged; for leading me step-by-step through the literary maze, personally introducing me to endorsers and ultimately recommending I submit this final version of the manuscript to Plain View Press, the first and only publisher to have seen it; for enlisting the expertise of her wonderful husband Bill Ash in this project; but most of all for understanding from her first pass through the pages what I was saying and why I was duty-bound to say it.

Thanks to my other endorsers for their support, encouragement and belief in this work. Robert Bly is a superhero of a writer, thinker, and human being. All his life Jan Barry has walked the walk that others just talk. Joan Morrison learned firsthand the heartbreak of Vietnam and went on to chronicle those years indelibly for posterity. The late Pat Caruso was a hero to all for his service on Iwo Jima and had the scars to prove it; to me he was a hero for never glorifying war nor suggesting it should be lightly undertaken. And master story-teller John Del Vecchio, not only has written at least three authentic sagas indispensable to any Vietnam library, but he also deserves my special thanks for making two key suggestions that ultimately determined the structure and coherence of this story.

My thanks to Editor/Publisher Susan Bright at Plain View Press for taking on my work, for her sensitive treatment of it, and for its provocative title and cover design. I am especially grateful to be in the company of the many fine Plain View Press authors.

Always, to my wife and family, my heartfelt gratitude for relinquishing their prior claims on so much of my time so that I could write this book, because they knew—without me ever saying a single word about it even once—that this work was important.

Finally, there must be no doubt that, as sole author of this work, I alone bear responsibility for any shortcomings.

9 781891 386404